The History of the Siege of Lisbon

ALSO BY JOSÉ SARAMAGO

Baltasar and Blimunda

The Year of the Death of Ricardo Reis

The Gospel According to Jesus Christ

The Stone Raft

Blindness

JOSÉ SARAMAGO

The History of the Siege of Lisbon

Translated from the Portuguese by
Giovanni Pontiero

A HARVEST BOOK
HARCOURT BRACE & COMPANY
San Diego New York London

This is a translation of *História do Cerco de Lisboa*

Library of Congress Cataloging-in-Publication Data
Saramago, José.
[História do cerco de Lisboa. English]
The history of the siege of Lisbon/José Saramago; translated from the Portuguese by Giovanni Pontiero.—1st ed.
p. cm.
ISBN 0-15-100238-X
ISBN 0-15-600624-3 (pbk.)
1. Proofreading—Portugal—Fiction.
2. Lisbon (Portugal)—History—Fiction.
I. Pontiero, Giovanni. II. Title.
PQ9281.A66H5713 1997
869.3'42—dc21 96-46826

Printed in the United States of America
First Harvest edition 1998
C E D

FOR PILAR

Until you attain the truth,
you will not be able to amend it.
But if you do not amend it,
you will not attain it. Meanwhile,
do not resign yourself.

FROM *The Book of Exhortations*

The History of the Siege of Lisbon

THE PROOF-READER said, Yes, this symbol is called *deleatur*, we use it when we need to suppress and erase, the word speaks for itself, and serves both for separate letters and complete words, it reminds me of a snake that changes its mind just as it is about to bite its tail, Well observed, Sir, truly, for however much we may cling to life, even a snake would hesitate before eternity, Draw it for me here, but slowly, It's very easy, you only have to get the knack, anyone looking absent-mindedly will imagine my hand is about to trace the dreaded circle, but no, observe that I did not finish the movement here where it began, I skirted it on the inside, and now I'm going to continue below until I cut across the lower part of the curve, after all, it resembles a capital Q and nothing else, Such a pity, a drawing that was so promising, Let us content ourselves with the illusion of similarity, but in truth I tell you, Sir, if I may express myself in prophetic tones, the interesting thing about life has always been in the differences, What does this have to do with proof-reading, You authors live in the clouds, you do not waste your precious wisdom on trifles and non-essentials, letters that are broken, transposed and inverted, as we used to classify these flaws when texts were composed manually, for then difference and defect were one and the same thing, I must confess that my *deleaturs* are less rigorous, a squiggle is good enough for everything, I have every confidence in the judgment of the printers, that famous and close-related clan of apothecaries, so skilled in the solving of riddles that they are even capable of deciphering what has never been written, And then the proof-readers set about solving the problems, You are our guardian angels, in you we put our trust, you for example, remind me of my caring mother, who would comb the parting in my hair, over and over again, until it looked as if it had been made with a ruler, Thanks for the comparison, but if your dear mother is dead, it would be worth your while seeking perfection on your own account, the day always comes when it is necessary to correct things in greater depth, As for corrections, these I make, but the more serious problems I quickly resolve by writing one word over another, I've noticed, Don't say it in that tone of voice, I am doing my best without taking too many liberties, and who does his best, Yes, Sir, no more can be expected of you, especially in your case, where there is no desire to modify, no pleasure in making changes, no inclination to amend, We authors are for ever making changes, we are perpetually dissatisfied, Nor is there any other solution, because perfection only exists in the kingdom of heaven, but the amendments of authors are something else, more problematic, and quite different from the amendments we make, Are you trying to tell me that the proof-reading fraternity actually enjoys what it does, I wouldn't go so far, it depends on one's vocation and a born proof-reader is an unknown phenomenon, meanwhile, it seems certain that in our heart of hearts, we proof-readers are voluptuaries, I've never heard that before, Each day brings its sorrows and satisfactions, and also some profitable lessons, You speak from experience, Are you referring to the lessons, I'm referring to voluptuousness, Of course, I speak from my own experience, there has to be some experience in order to judge, but I've also benefited from observing the behaviour of others, which is no less edifying as a moral science, By this criterion certain authors from the past would fit this description, wonderful proof-readers, I can think of the proofs revised by Balzac, a dazzling exponent of corrections and addenda, The same is true of our own Eça de Queiroz, lest we fail to mention the example of a compatriot, It occurs to me that both Eça and Balzac would have felt the happiest of men in this modern age, confronted by a computer, interpolating, transposing, retracing lines, changing chapters around, And we, the readers, would never know by which paths they travelled and got lost before achieving a definitive form, if such a thing exists, Now, now, what counts is the result, there is nothing to be gained from knowing the calculations and waverings of Camoens and Dante, You, Sir, are a practical man, modern, already living in the twenty-second century, Tell me, do the other symbols also have Latin names as in the case of *deleatur*, If they do, or did, I'm not qualified to say, perhaps they were so difficult to pronounce that they were lost, In the dark ages, Forgive me for contradicting you, but I would not use that phrase, I suppose because it's a platitude, Not for that reason, platitudes, clichés, repetitions, affectations, maxims from some almanac, refrains and proverbs, all of these can sound new, it's merely a question of knowing how to handle properly the words that precede and follow them, Then why would you not say, in the dark ages, Because the age ceased to be dark when people began to write, or to amend, a task, I repeat, which calls for other refinements and a different form of transfiguration, I like the phrase, Me, too, mainly because it's the first time I've used it, the second time it will have less charm, It will have turned into a platitude, Or topic, which is the learned word, Do I detect a hint of sceptical bitterness in your words, I see it more as bitter scepticism, It comes to the same thing, But it does not have the same meaning, authors have always tended to have a good ear for these differences, Perhaps I'm getting hard of hearing, Forgive me, that is not what I was suggesting, I'm not touchy, carry on, tell me first why you feel so bitter, or sceptical, as you would have it, Consider, Sir, the daily life of proof-readers, think of the horror of having to read once, twice, three or four or five times books that, Probably would not even warrant a first reading, Take note that it was not I who spoke such grave words, I am all too aware of my place in literary circles, voluptuous certainly, I confess, but respectful, I fail to see what is so terrible, besides it struck me as being the obvious ending to your phrase, that eloquent suspension, even though the suspension marks are not apparent, If you want to know, consult the authors, provoke them with what I have half said and with what you have half said, and you will see how they respond with the famous anecdote of Apelles and the shoemaker, when the craftsman pointed out an error in the sandal worn by one of the figures and then, having verified that the artist had corrected the mistake, ventured to give his opinion about the anatomy of the knee, At that point Apelles, enraged at his insolence, told him, Cobbler, stick to your last, a historic phrase, Nobody likes people peering over the wall of his backyard, In this case Apelles was right, Perhaps, but only as long as some learned anatomist did not come along to examine the painting, You are definitely a sceptic, All authors are Apelles, but the shoemaker's temptation is the most common of all amongst humans, after all, only the proof-reader has learnt that the task of amending is the only one that will never end in this world, Many of the shoemaker's temptations make sense in the revision of my book, Age brings us one good thing which is bad, it calms us down, and quells our temptations, and even when they are overpowering, they become less urgent, In other words, he spots the mistake in the sandal, but remains silent, No, what I allow to pass is the mistake of the knee, Do you like the book, I like it, You don't sound very enthusiastic, Nor did I note any enthusiasm in your question, A question of tactics, the author, however much it may cost, must show some modesty, The proof-reader must always be modest, and, should he ever get it into his head to be immodest, this would oblige him, as a human figure, to be the height of perfection, He did not revise the phrase, the verb to be three times in the same sentence, unforgivable, wouldn't you agree, Forget the sandal, in speech everything is excused, Agreed, but I cannot forgive your low opinion, I must remind you that proof-readers are serious people, much experienced in literature and life, My book, don't forget, deals with history, That is indeed how it would be defined according to the traditional classification of genres, however, since I have no intention of pointing out other contradictions, in my modest opinion, Sir, everything that is not literature is life, History as well, Especially history, without wishing to give offence, And painting and music, Music has resisted since birth, it comes and goes, tries to free itself from the word, I suppose out of envy, only to submit in the end, And painting, Well now, painting is nothing more than literature achieved with paintbrushes, I trust you haven't forgotten that mankind began to paint long before it knew how to write, Are you familiar with the proverb, If you don't have a dog, go hunting with a cat, in other words, the man who cannot write, paints or draws, as if he were a child, What you are trying to say, in other words, is that literature already existed before it was born, Yes, Sir, just like man who, in a manner of speaking, existed before he came into being, What a novel idea, Don't you believe it, Sir, King Solomon, who lived such a long time ago, affirmed even then, that there is nothing new under the sun, so if they acknowledged as much in that remote age, what are we to say today, thirty centuries later, if I correctly recall what I read in the encyclopaedia, It's curious that even as a historian, I would never have remembered, if suddenly asked, that so many years have passed, That's time for you, it races past without our noticing, a person is taken up with his daily life when he suddenly comes to his senses and exclaims, dear God, how time flies, only a moment ago King Solomon was still alive and now three thousand years have passed, It strikes me that you've missed your vocation, you should have become a philosopher, or historian, you have the flair and temperament needed for these disciplines, I lack the necessary training, Sir, and what can a simple man achieve without training, I was more than fortunate to come into the world with my genes in order, but in a raw state as it were, and then no education beyond primary school, You could have presented yourself as being self-taught, the product of your own worthy efforts, there's nothing to be ashamed of, society in the past took pride in its autodidacts, No longer, progress has come along and put an end to all of that, now the self-taught are frowned upon, only those who write entertaining verses and stories are entitled to be and go on being autodidacts, lucky for them, but as for me, I must confess that I never had any talent for literary creation, Become a philosopher, man, You have a keen sense of humour, Sir, with a distinct flair for irony, and I ask myself how you ever came to devote yourself to history, serious and profound science as it is, I'm only ironic in real life, It has always struck me that history is not real life, literature, yes, and nothing else, But history was real life at the time when it could not yet be called history, Sir, are you sure, Truly, you are a walking interrogation and disbelief endowed with arms, That only leaves my head, Everything in its own good time, the brain was the last thing to be invented, Sir, you are a sage, Don't exaggerate, my friend, Would you like to see the final proofs, There's little point, the author has already made his corrections, all that remains now is the routine task of one final revision, and that is your responsibility, I appreciate your trust, Well deserved, So you believe, Sir, that history is real life, Of course, I do, I meant to say that history was real life, No doubt at all, What would become of us if the *deleatur* did not exist, sighed the proof-reader.

ONLY WHEN A VISION a thousand times sharper than nature can provide might be capable of perceiving in the eastern sky the initial difference that separates night from day, did the muezzin awake. He always woke at this hour, according to the sun, no matter whether summer or winter, and he needed no instrument to measure time, nothing other than the infinitesimal change in the darkness of the room, the first hint of light barely glimpsed on his forehead, like a gentle breath passing over his eyebrows, or that first and almost imponderable caress which, as far as is known or believed, is the exclusive and secret art never revealed to this day of those beautiful houris who attend the believers in Mohammed's paradise. Secret, and also prodigious, if not an impenetrable mystery, is their ability to regain their virginity the moment they lose it, this by all accounts supreme bliss in eternal life, thus proving beyond a shadow of a doubt that death does not bring an end to our labours or those of others, any more than to our undeserved sufferings. The muezzin did not open his eyes. He could go on resting there a little longer, while the sun, very slowly, began approaching from the earth's horizon, but still so far away that no cockerel in the city had raised its head to probe dawn's movements. It is true that a dog did bark, to no avail, for everyone else was asleep, perhaps dreaming that they were barking in their dreams. It is a dream, they thought, and went on sleeping, surrounded by a world filled with odours that were certainly stimulating, but none so potent as to rouse them with a start, the unmistakable smell of danger or fear, to give only these basic examples. The muezzin got up and fumbled in the dark until he found his clothes, and dressed before leaving the room. The mosque was silent, nothing but hesitant footsteps that echoed under the arches, a shuffling of cautious feet, as if he were afraid of being swallowed up by the ground. At no other time of day or night had he ever experienced this torment of the invisible, only at this early hour when he was about to climb the stairs of the minaret in order to summon the faithful to morning prayers. A superstitious scruple made him feel quite guilty that the inhabitants should still be sleeping when the sun was already over the river, and awakening with a start, dazzled by the light of day, would ask aloud, where was the muezzin who failed to summon them at the appropriate hour, someone more charitable might say, Perhaps the poor man is ill, and it was not true, he had disappeared, yes, carried off into the bowels of the earth by some evil genie from the darkest depths. The winding staircase was difficult to climb, especially since this muezzin was already quite old, fortunately he did not need to have his eyes blindfolded like the mules who drive the water wheels blindfolded to prevent them from becoming dizzy. When he got to the top he could feel the cool morning breeze on his face and the vibrations of the dawning light, as yet without any colour, for there is no colour to that pure clarity which precedes the day and comes to graze one's skin with the merest suggestion of a shiver, as if touched by invisible fingers, a simple impression which makes you wonder whether the discredited divine creation might not, after all, in order to chasten the sceptics and atheists, be an ironic fact of history. The muezzin slowly ran his hand along the circular parapet until he found engraved in the stone the sign pointing in the direction of Mecca, the holy city. He was ready. A few more seconds to give time for the sun to cast its first rays on the earth's balconies and for him to clear his throat, because a muezzin's declamatory powers must be loud and clear from the very first cry, and that is when he must show his mettle, not when his throat has softened with the effort of speech and the consolation of food. At the muezzin's feet lies a city, further down, a river, everything is still asleep, but restless. Dawn begins to spread over the houses, the surface of the water mirrors the sky, and then the muezzin takes a deep breath and calls out in piercing tones, *Allahu akbar*, proclaiming the greatness of Almighty God to the heavens, and he repeats these words, just as he will utter and repeat the following phrases, in an ecstatic outburst, calling upon the world to witness that there is no other God than Allah, and that Mohammed is the messenger of Allah, and having affirmed these essential truths he summons the faithful to prayer, Come to recite the *azalá*, but man being indolent by nature, although a believer in Him who never sleeps, the muezzin charitably reproaches those whose eyes are still closed, Prayer is better than sleep, *As-salatu jayrun min an-nawn*, for those who understand this language, and he ended by declaring that Allah is the only God, *La ilaha illa llah*, but once only this time, for that is enough when pronouncing definitive truths. The city murmurs its prayers, the sun has come out, lighting up the roof-terraces, and soon the inhabitants will start to appear in their patios. The minaret is bathed in full light. The muezzin is blind.

In his book the historian gave no such description. Simply that the muezzin climbed the minaret and from there summoned the faithful to prayer in the mosque, without specifying whether it was morning or noon, or sunset, for certainly in his opinion, such minute details would be of no historical interest and all the reader needed to know was that the author knew enough about the life of that time to be able to give them due mention. And for this we are indebted to him, for since his theme is that of battle and siege, and he is writing about the most virile of deeds, he could happily dispense with the raptures of prayer, which is the most submissive of situations, for he who prays, surrenders without a struggle and is for ever vanquished. Although, rather than ignore and fail to consider anything that might challenge these contradictions between prayer and warfare, we might here record, being so recent in time, and because of all the famous witnesses who are still alive, we might here record, we repeat, that much celebrated miracle at

Ourique, when Christ appeared to the Portuguese king, and the latter called out to Him, while the army, prostrate on the ground, began to pray, Appear before the infidels, Oh Lord, before the infidels, and not before me who believes in your powers, But Christ had no desire to appear before the Moors, and the more the pity, otherwise instead of that most vicious battle, we might today be able to record in these annals the glorious conversion of the hundred and fifty thousand barbarians who finally perished, a waste of souls who might have raised their voices to heaven. That's life, certain things cannot be avoided, we never cease to importune God with our wise exhortations, but destiny has its own intransigent laws, and so often with the most surprising and dramatic effects, as in the case of Camoens who was able to exploit that inflammatory battle cry, by casting it into two immortal verses. How true that in nature nothing is created and nothing lost, everything used to advantage.

Those were good times, when, in order to receive satisfaction, all we had to do was to ask with the appropriate words, even in difficult cases, already disillusioned, as it were, like a patient without hope of being cured. For example, this very same king, who, having been born with shrivelled, or atrophied, legs, as people say nowadays, was miraculously healed, without any doctor having laid a finger on him, and even if he had done so, it would have been to no avail. Nor are there any signs, no doubt because he was a person destined to rule, that he had to importune the heavenly powers, we refer to the Virgin and the Lord, not to the angels of the sixth hierarchy, in order to produce this edifying outcome, thanks to which, who knows, Portugal may owe her independence. It so happened that Dom Egas Moniz, the tutor of young Afonso, was asleep in his bed when Holy Mary appeared to him in a vision and said, Dom Egas Moniz, are you asleep, and he, not knowing whether he was awake or dreaming, asked, in order to be certain, My Lady, who are you, and she politely replied, I am the Virgin, and I command you to go to Carquere in the municipality of Resende, and if you dig there you will find a church which was once built in my name, and you will also find my statue, repair it for it is in a lamentable state after being so sadly neglected, and then you must keep vigil there, and you will lay the boy on the altar, whereupon I assure you he will be instantly cured and restored to health, and take good care of him thereafter, because I happen to know that my Son is thinking of entrusting him with the destruction of the enemies of the Faith, and obviously that is something he cannot do with stunted legs. Dom Egas Moniz awoke as happy as could be, convened his aides and, mounting his donkey, made his way to Carquere and ordered his men to dig at the spot pointed out by the Virgin, and lo and behold there was the church, but the surprise is ours rather than theirs, for in those blessed times warnings from on high were never gratuitous or misleading. It is true that Dom Egas did not carry out the Virgin's instructions to the letter, for when she told him to dig, it is our understanding that she meant with his own hands, and what did he do, he ordered others to dig, the serfs working the land most likely, for even at that time these social inequalities existed. Let us be grateful that the Virgin is not easily offended, otherwise she might have shrivelled up little Afonso's legs once more, because just as there are miracles that do good, some miracles have proved to be harmful, as those wretched pigs in Holy Scripture can testify, for they threw themselves over the precipice when Sweet Jesus put the demons that had been plaguing the possessed man into their bodies, whereby these innocent animals suffered martyrdom, and they alone, for much greater was the downfall of the rebellious angels who were immediately turned into devils when they rebelled, and as far as we know, not one of them died, which makes it difficult to pardon the improvidence of Our Lord God, who carelessly missed the opportunity of putting an end to this unfortunate race once and for all, wise is the proverb that cautions, he who spares his enemy, will perish at his hands, let us hope that God will not have cause to repent one day when it is much too late. Nevertheless, if at that fatal moment he should have time to remember his past life, let us hope His spirit will be enlightened and He will understand that He should have spared all of us, vulnerable pigs and humans, those vices, sins and feelings of discontent which are, as the saying goes, the work and mark of Satan. Between the hammer and the anvil we are a red-hot iron, which has been beaten so much that the heat is extinguished.

For the present, we have had enough of sacred history. We do want to know, however, who wrote the tale about the beautiful awakening of the muezzin at dawn in Lisbon, with so many factual details that it sounds like the testimony of some eyewitness here in our presence, or, at least, the ingenious use of some contemporary document, not necessarily relevant to Lisbon, because, for the purpose, one would only need a city, a river and a clear morning, the most banal of compositions, as we know. The reply, surprisingly enough, is that no one wrote it, and despite appearances, it is not written, the whole thing was nothing more than vague thoughts in the proof-reader's mind as he was reading and correcting what he had surreptitiously missed in the first and second proofs. The proof-reader has this remarkable flair for splitting his personality, he inserts a *deleatur* or introduces a comma where required, and at the same time, if you'll pardon the neologism, heteronomises himself, he is capable of pursuing the path suggested by an image, a simile, or metaphor, often the simple sound of a word repeated in a low voice leads him, by association, to organise polyphonic verbal edifices capable of transforming his tiny study into a space multiplied by itself, although it is difficult to explain in plain language what that means. Here it struck him that the historian had provided little information by mentioning the muezzin and the minaret, simply to introduce, if such rash judgments are permissible, a little local colour and historical atmosphere into the enemy camp, a semantic blunder we might as well correct at once, since this is the camp of the assailants, not of the besieged, for the latter, in the meantime, are installed with reasonable comfort in the city which except for the odd interval, has been theirs since the year seven hundred and fourteen, as counted on the beads of the Christians, for those on the rosary of the Moors are different, as everyone knows. This correction was made by the proof-reader himself, who has a more than adequate knowledge about calendars, and who knows that the Hegira began, according to the rules given in that indispensable reference book, *The Art of Verifying Dates*, on the sixteenth of July in the year six hundred and twenty-two after Christ, AD in abbreviated form, without forgetting, meanwhile, that since the Moslem year is governed by the moon and is, therefore, shorter than that of Christianity which is oriented by the sun, we must always discount three years for each century gone by. This meticulous fellow would make an excellent proof-reader, if he were to consider trimming the wings of a discourse given to inventions that are sometimes irresponsible, a case of someone who has sinned because it came so naturally, incurring obvious errors and dubious assertions, we suspect at least three, which if proved, would show conclusively that the historian had no reason whatsoever for flippantly suggesting that he should devote himself to history, As for philosophy, God help us.

The first dubious point, according to the inverse order of the narrative, is that fanciful idea that there existed on the parapets of the verandahs of minarets, marks in the stone which, probably in the form of arrows, pointed in the direction of Mecca. However advanced at that time the geographical and surveying skills of the Arabs and other Moors, it is most unlikely that they knew how to determine with the accuracy insinuated, the position of a Kaaba on the surface of the planet, where there is certainly no lack of stones, some more sacred than others. All these things, whether they be reverences, genuflections or upward and downward glances, are performed by way of approximation, upon sensing, if we may be allowed this expression, that what really matters is that God and Allah can read into hearts and do not take offence when, out of ignorance, we turn away, and when we speak of ignorance it can be as much ours as theirs, for they are not always to be found where they promised to be. The proof-reader belongs to that age when a man was taught to trust and firmly believe in road-signs, therefore, do not be surprised that he should have fallen into this anachronistic temptation, perhaps driven by sudden compassion, bearing in mind the muezzin's blindness. It is well known that, no matter the quality of the cloth, knots are inevitable, some even claim that the better the cloth the more knots there are likely to be, and that where there is one knot there are bound to be two, and there we have the second error, and this time much more serious, because it would lead the unsuspecting reader, had it been written, but fortunately it never was, to accept the description of the muezzin's actions after waking up, as being correct and in accordance with the Moslem way of life. This is wrong, we insist, inasmuch as the muezzin, the term preferred by the historian, did not carry out the ritual ablutions before summoning the faithful to prayer, consequently finding himself in a state of impurity, a most improbable situation if we consider how close we still are in time to the early origins of Islam, a little over four centuries, in the cradle, as it were. Later on there will be much laxness, no strict observation of fasting, spurious interpretations of the rules that seem reasonably clear, the problem being that there is nothing that tires people more than the strict observance of precepts, before the flesh submits the spirit has already weakened, but no one takes the spirit to task, it is the poor flesh they revile, insult and censure. Even in these days of total faith, the muezzin would be the lowest of men if he were to dare climb the minaret without having purified his soul and having first washed his hands, and so he is declared innocent of the crime attributed to him by the unpardonable flippancy of the proofreader. Despite the professional competence with which we hear him express himself during the conversation with the historian, it is time to introduce the first hint of doubt about the consequences of the trust invested in him by the author of *The History of the Siege of Lisbon*, perhaps in a moment of despondent weariness, or worried about a forthcoming journey, when he permitted that the final reading of the proofs should be the exclusive task of the expert in *deleaturs*, without any control. We shudder to think that the muezzin's description of dawn might abusively find a place in the author's scientific text, both the one and the other, the fruit of assiduous study, extensive research, detailed comparisons. It is doubtful, for example, although it is always wise to question one's own doubt, that the historian would mention dogs and the barking of dogs in his narrative, because he knows that the dog, for the Arabs, is an unclean animal, just like the pig, and therefore, it would be a display of crass ignorance to assume that the Moors of Lisbon, zealous as they are, would be living cheek by jowl with a pack of dogs. A pigsty by the door of the house and a dog-kennel or wicker basket for one's lap-dog are Christian inventions, it is not by accident that the Moslems refer to the warriors of the cross as dogs, and they might well have called them pigs, although there is no evidence to prove it. Clearly, if this is true, then it is a pity not to be able to count any more on a dog barking at the moon or scratching its ear infested by fleas, but the truth should we ever discover it, must be put above all other considerations, whether it be for or against, wherefore we should here and now take as unwritten the words that described the last tranquil dawn of Lisbon, were we not already aware that that spurious discourse, although coherent, and that is the greatest danger of all, never emerged from the proof-reader's mind and was nothing more than absurd and fanciful daydreaming.

It is proven, therefore, that the proof-reader was mistaken, that if he was not mistaken then he was confused, that if he was not confused then he was imagining things, but let him who has never erred, been confused or imagined things, throw the first stone. To err, as the wise man said, is only human, which means that, unless we are wrong to take things literally, anyone who never errs cannot be a real man. Nevertheless, this supreme maxim cannot be used as a universal pretext to absolve all of us from lame judgments and warped opinions. He who does not know should have the humility to ask, and the proof-reader should always be mindful of this simple precaution, especially since he does not even need to leave the house or abandon his study where he is now working, for here he has all the reference books he needs to clarify matters, assuming he has been wise and prudent enough not to believe blindly in what he thinks he knows, because this rather than ignorance is the cause of the greatest blunders. On these crammed bookshelves, thousands and thousands of pages await a spark of awakening curiosity or that direct light which is nothing other than doubt in search of its own clarification. Let us then give credit to the proof-reader for having collected throughout his life so many different sources of information, although a mere glance reveals that the inventory does not include a computer, but his finances, alas, do not cover everything, and this profession, it should be said, is one of the worst paid in the world. One day, but Allah is greater, every proof-reader of books will have a computer at his disposal which he will connect umbilically, night and day, to the central databank, so that all he, or we, need worry about is that amongst these comprehensive data, no tempting error has crept in, like the devil invading a convent.

In any case, until that day comes, the books are here, like a pulsating galaxy, and the words, inside them, form another cosmic dust hovering in anticipation of that glance which will impose some meaning or will search therein for some new meaning, for just as the explanations of the universe tend to vary, so does the statement that once seemed for ever immutable, suddenly offer another interpretation, the possibility of some latent contradiction, the evidence of his own error. Here, in this study, where the truth can be no more than a face superimposed on endless different masks, stand the usual dictionaries and vocabularies of the Portuguese language, Morais, Aurélio, Moreno and Torrinha, several grammars, the *Handbook of the Model Proof-reader*, the vade-mecum of the profession, but there are also histories of Art, of the World in general, of the Romans, Persians, Greeks, Chinese, Arabs, Slavs and Portuguese, in short, of almost everything that constitutes an individual race and nation, and the histories of Science, Literature, Music, Religions, Philosophy, Civilization, the pocket *Larousse*, the abridged *Quillet*, the concise *Robert*, the *Encyclopaedia of Politics*, the *Luso-Brazilian Encyclopaedia*, the *Encyclopaedia Britannica*, incomplete, the *Dictionary of History and Geography*, a World Atlas on these subjects, that of João Soares, ancient, the *Historical Yearbooks*, the

Dictionary of Contemporaries, the *Universal Biography*, the *Manual for Booksellers*, the *Dictionary of Fable*, the *Dictionary of Mythology*, the *Biblioteca Lusitana*, the *Dictionary of Comparative Geography, Ancient, Medieval and Modern*, the *Historical Atlas of Contemporary Studies*, the *General Dictionary of Literature, Fine Arts and Moral and Political Sciences*, and, to conclude, not the general inventory, but what is most in evidence, the *General Dictionary of Biography and History, Mythology, Ancient and Modern Geography, Antiquities and Greek, Roman, French and other Foreign Institutions*, without forgetting the *Dictionary of Rarities, Inverisimilitudes and Curiosities*, which, a surprising coincidence, fits in perfectly with this adventurous account and contains as an example of error the affirmation by the wise Aristotle that the common domestic fly has four legs, an arithmetical reduction that subsequent authors continued to repeat for centuries thereafter, when even children knew from their cruel experiments that the fly has six legs, for since the time of Aristotle, they have been pulling them off and voluptuously counting one, two, three, four, five, six, but these very same children, when they grew up and came to read the Greek sage, said amongst themselves, The fly has four legs, such is the influence of learned authority, to such an extent is truth undermined by certain lessons we are always being taught.

This unexpected incursion across the frontiers of entomology shows us, conclusively, that the errors ascribed to the proof-reader are not his after all, but of those books which have gone on repeating, unchallenged, much earlier works, and, this being so, we regret that he came to be the victim of his own good faith and of another's error. It is true that, by being so condescending, we might fall for that universal excuse we have already censured, but we shall not do so without one prior condition, namely, that for his own good, the proof-reader reflect on the extraordinary lesson about errors given by Bacon, another sage, in his book entitled *Novum organum*. He divides errors into four categories, as follows, *idola tribus*, or the errors of human nature, *idola specus*, or the errors of individuals, *idola fori*, or linguistic errors, and finally, *idola theatri*, or errors of systems.

In the first instance, these result from the imperfection of the senses, from the influence of preconceptions and passions, from our habit of judging everything according to inherited wisdom, from our insatiable curiosity notwithstanding the limitations imposed on our mind because of our tendency to find more analogies amongst things than actually exist. In the second instance, the source of errors comes from the difference between minds, some that lose themselves in details, others in vast generalisations, as well as from our preference for certain sciences to which we are inclined to reduce everything. As for the third category, that of linguistic errors, the problem is that words often no longer have any meaning, or that meaning is indeterminate, and, finally, in the fourth category, there are so many errors of systems that we should never finish if we were to start listing them here. So let the proof-reader avail himself of this catalogue and he will prosper, and let him also take advantage of that statement by Seneca, reticent as befits this day and age, *Onerat discentem turba, non instruit*, the perfect maxim which the proof-reader's mother, many years ago, without knowing any Latin and very little about her native language, translated with blatant scepticism, The more you read, the less you learn.

But if there is anything to be saved from this inquiry and debate, it is the confirmation that it was not wrong to write, for, after all, it is written, that the muezzin was blind. The historian, who only speaks of minaret and muezzin, is probably unaware that nearly all muezzins, at that time and for some time to come, were blind. And if he is aware of this fact, perhaps he imagines that the chanting of prayers is the special vocation of the disabled, or that the Moorish communities so decided, partly, as has always been and always will be the practice, to solve the problem of giving work to people without the precious organ of sight. An error on his part, this time, which invariably affects everyone. The historical truth, take note, is that the muezzins were chosen from amongst the blind, not because of any humanitarian policy of providing work or professional training they could cope with physically, but to prevent them from infringing upon the privacy of the courtyards and roof terraces from the dominant position at the top of the minaret. The proof-reader no longer remembers how he came by this information, he almost certainly must have read it in some book he trusted, and since nothing has changed, he can now insist that, yes, Sir, muezzins were blind. Almost all of them. Yet when he happens to think about this, he cannot help wondering whether they did not pierce the bright eyes of these men, as they once did and perhaps still do to nightingales, so that they might experience no other manifestation of light than the voice heard in the darkness, theirs, or perhaps the darkness of that Other who does nothing except repeat the words we are inventing, those words with which we try to say everything, blessing and malediction, even that which shall forever be nameless.

THE PROOF-READER has a name, he is called Raimundo. It is time that we should know the person about whom we have been talking indiscreetly, if name and surnames could ever add anything useful to the normal identifying features and other statistics, age, height, weight, morphological type, skin tone, colour of eyes, whether the hair is smooth, curly or wavy, or has simply disappeared, timbre of voice, clear or harsh, characteristic gestures, manner of walking, since experience of human relationships has shown that, once apprised of these details and sometimes many more, not even this information serves any purpose, nor are we capable of imagining what might be missing. Perhaps only a wrinkle, or the shape of the nails, or the thickness of the wrist, or the line of an eyebrow, or an old invisible scar, or simply the surname that has never been mentioned, the one that is most esteemed, in this case Silva, his complete name being Raimundo Silva, for that is how he introduces himself when necessary, omitting the Benvindo which he does not like. No one is satisfied with his lot in life, this is generally true, and Raimundo Silva, who above all else should appreciate being called Benvindo, which says precisely what it means, bem-vindo or welcome to life, my son, but no Sir, he does not like the name, and fortunately, says he, the tradition has been lost whereby one's godparents settled the delicate question of proper names, although he recognises that he is very pleased with Raimundo, a name which somehow conveys the solemnity of another age. Raimundo's parents expected that an inheritance from the woman who had accepted to be his godmother would provide for their son's future, and for this reason, since it was the custom only to give the godfather's name, they added that of the godmother in the masculine form. Destiny, as we well know, does not look after everything in quite the same manner, but in this case some concurrence has to be acknowledged between the possessions from which he was never to benefit and a name so resolutely disclaimed, although no one should suspect the existence of a relationship of cause and effect between his disappointment and disavowal. Raimundo Benvindo Silva's motives, which at no time in his life had been provoked by resentful frustration, nowadays are either merely aesthetic, for he does not like the sound of those two gerunds stuck together, or, in a manner of speaking, ethical and ontological, because according to his disillusioned way of thinking, only the darkest irony would expect anyone to believe that we are truly welcome in this world, without contradicting the evidence of those who find themselves nicely settled.

The river can be seen from the verandah, a narrow projection from another age beneath a porch which still has its coffered ceiling, and it is an immense sea which the eye can capture between one ray and the next, from the red line of the bridge to the flat marshlands of Pancas and Alcochete. A dank mist covers the horizon, brings it almost within reach, what can be seen of the city is reduced to this side, with the cathedral below, halfway down the slope, and staggered roof-tops, descending to the dark, murky water, where a fleeting backwash of white spume opens up as a boat quickly passes, others navigate with difficulty, sluggish, as if they were struggling against a current of mercury, this last comparison being more appropriate at night, rather than at this hour. Raimundo got up later than usual, he had worked into the early hours, a long, drawn-out stint, and when he opened the window in the morning, he was confronted by mist, thicker than the one we are seeing at this hour, noon, when the weather must decide whether it is going to get worse or clear up, as the saying goes.

Just then the cathedral towers were nothing other than a faint blur, of Lisbon there was nothing more than the sound of voices and indeterminate sounds, the window-frame, the first roof, a car travelling along the street. The blind muezzin had raised his cry to the heavens, the morning luminous, crimson, and then blue, the colour of the atmosphere between here on earth and the sky overhead, should we choose to believe in the blinkered eyes with which we see the world, but the proof-reader, on this day which is almost as blurred as his blindness, simply muttered, with the ill humour of someone who, after a restless night with troubled dreams about siege, broadswords, cutlasses and deadly slings, is annoyed upon awakening, to find that he cannot recall how these weapons of war were made, we are talking about the slings, and more could be said about the deep conversations of the person who was dreaming, but let us not fall into the temptation of anticipating the facts, for the moment we need only regret the lost opportunity of finally discovering what kind of weapon those so-called slings were, how they were loaded and fired, for it is not all that rare for great mysteries to be revealed in dreams, and amongst them we do not include the winning number in the lottery, the utmost banality and unworthy of any self-respecting dreamer. Still in bed, a puzzled Raimundo Silva was asking himself why he should be so concerned about deadly slings, or catapults as they were sometimes called, and just as effective. Known in Portuguese as *baleares*, the name has nothing to do with the Balearic Islands but comes from the Portuguese word *bala* meaning a pellet or shot, and these as we know are missiles, stones which were fired at walls or over the top of fortifications and aimed at houses and their terrified occupants, but the word *bala* was not in use at the time, words cannot be transported lightly here and there, back and forth, so watch out, otherwise someone will come along and say, I don't understand. He dozed off, remained like that for ten minutes, and on reawakening, now lucid, he dismissed any further thought of those weapons and rashly allowed the images of swords and scimitars to occupy his mind, he smiled in the shadows of the room, for he was well aware that these are obvious phallic symbols, almost certainly drawn into his dream by *The History of the Siege of Lisbon*, yet undoubtedly rooted in himself, for if sharp pointed weapons can be said to have roots, embedded as they are, you only had to look at the empty bed beside him in order to understand everything. Lying on his back, he crossed his arms over his eyes, and murmured prosaically, One more day, he had not heard the muezzin, how would a deaf Moor of that religious persuasion make sure that he did not miss prayers, especially morning prayers, he would surely ask a neighbour, In the name of Allah, knock loudly on my door and go on knocking until I come to open it. Virtue is not as easy as vice, but it can be aided.

No woman lives in this house. Twice weekly a woman comes from outside, but do not imagine that the empty side of the bed has anything to do with these visits, they meet other needs, and let it be said here and now, that in order to satisfy more pressing urges, the proof-reader goes down to the city, hires a woman, relieves himself and pays, he has always had to pay, no other solution, even when he did not get any satisfaction, for that word has more than one meaning contrary to popular belief. The woman who does not live in is what we might call a daily help, she does his washing, tidies up and does the essential chores, prepares a large pot of soup, always the same, white beans with greens, which will last for several days, not because the proof-reader does not like other food, but this was catered for by going to restaurants, which he frequents from time to time, without making a habit of it. So there is no woman in this house, nor has there ever been. The proof-reader Raimundo Benvindo Silva is a bachelor and has no intention of getting married, I'm in my fifties, he says, who is going to love me at my age, or who am I going to love, although, as everyone knows, it is easier to love than be loved, and this last comment, which sounds like the echo of some past sorrow, now transformed into a precept for the benefit of the presumptuous, this comment, as well as the preceding question, he addresses to himself, for he is much too reserved a man to go around pouring out his heart to those friends and acquaintances he is bound to have, although there will probably be no need to bring them into the story, judging from the way it is going. He has no brothers or sisters, his parents had died in due course, his relatives, if there are any left, have dispersed, and whenever he receives any news of them, it scarcely brings any reassurance, happiness has gone, there is little point in mourning, and the only thing really close to him are the proofs he is reading, for so long as they might last, the error he must ferret out, and also the odd problem that might arise, although best to let the authors cope since they are the ones who take all the credit, such as this nagging doubt about deadly slings which has come back to haunt him and refuses to go away. Raimundo Silva finally got up, searched for his babouches with his feet, Slippers, slippers, which is the proper term, and he moved into his study while pulling his dressing-gown over his pyjamas. From time to time, the charlady makes some solemn declaration about the need to remove the dust from his books, especially on the upper shelves, where he has placed the ones he rarely consults, the dust is more like an alluvial deposit that has accumulated throughout the centuries, a dust as black as ashes that has come from who knows where, it cannot have been caused by tobacco smoke, because the proof-reader gave up smoking ages ago, it is the dust of time, and there is nothing more to be said. Yet for some reason which remains unclear, the task is always being postponed, one suspects to the satisfaction of his charlady who, absolved in her own eyes by good intentions, never fails to remind him, You can't blame me.

Raimundo searches in the dictionaries and encyclopaedias, he consults *Weapons*, *The Middle Ages*, he consults *War Machines*, and finds the common terms for the primitive arms of the time, suffice it to say that in those days you could not kill the man you were aiming at if he were two hundred paces away, a serious loss, beyond comparison, and when it came to hunting, unless he possessed a bow or crossbow, the hunter had to grapple bare-handed with a bear or the antlers of a stag or the tusks of a wild boar, the only sport involving such dangerous risks nowadays is bullfighting and the toreadors are the last of those ancient warriors. No explanation is to be found anywhere in these weighty volumes, no drawing provides even the vaguest idea of what this deadly weapon looked like that so terrified the Moors, but this lack of information is nothing new for Raimundo Silva, what he now wants to know is why the sling was called *balear à funda*, and he goes from book to book, searches over and over again, loses his patience, until finally, the precious and inestimable Bouillet informs him that the inhabitants of the Balearic Islands were considered in ancient times to be the best archers in the world, that was the obvious explanation, and this is how these islands came to get their name, for the Greek word meaning to shoot is *ballô*, nothing could be clearer, any run-of-the-mill proof-reader is capable of spotting the direct etymological link between *ballô* and Balearic, the mistake in the Portuguese, Sir, having been to describe the sling as *balear* when *balearica* would have been more correct. But Raimundo Silva will not amend it, old habits die hard, usage sometimes becomes law, if not always, and the first of the ten commandments observed by a proof-reader aspiring to sanctity is that you must always try to avoid upsetting the author. He put the book back in its place, opened the window, and at that moment felt the mist on his face, thick, really dense, and if instead of the towers of the cathedral the minaret of the great mosque was still standing, he certainly would not be able to see it, the minaret was so slender, ethereal, almost immaterial, and then, if this were the hour, the muezzin's voice would come down from the white sky, directly from Allah, for once singing his own praises, something we cannot entirely censure him for, being who He is, He must surely know Himself.

It was mid-morning when the telephone rang. A call from the publisher who wanted to know how the proofs were coming along, the first to speak was Monica from the Production department, who, like everyone else working in this section, has a tendency to speak in the following high-faluting terms, Senhor Silva, she said, Production wishes to inquire, it is almost as if we were hearing, Your Royal Highness should know, and she repeats as court heralds used to repeat, Production wishes to inquire about the proofs, how soon do you expect to deliver them, but despite all the years they have known each other, Monica has not yet realised that Raimundo Silva hates being addressed simply as Silva, not because he finds the name as common as that of Santo or Sousa, but because he feels the absence of that Raimundo, therefore he replied curtly, unfairly offending Monica, sensitive creature that she is, Tell them the work will be ready tomorrow, I shall tell them, Senhor Silva, I shall tell them, and before she could say another word the telephone was snatched from her hand by someone else, Costa speaking, Raimundo Silva here, the proof-reader managed to reply, Yes, I know, the point is that I need the proofs today, my schedule is getting out of hand, and unless I get the book to the printers by tomorrow morning all hell will be let loose, and just because you're late with the proofs, Given the type of book, content, and number of pages, the proof-reading has taken no longer than you might expect, Don't you tell me what I should expect, I want the work finished, Costa had raised his voice, a sign that one of the bosses must be within hearing, a director, perhaps even the owner himself. Raimundo Silva took a deep breath and pointed out, Proofs corrected in a hurry invariably leads to mistakes, And books that come out late prejudice sales, clearly, the owner must be listening in on the conversation, but Costa goes on to say, Let me tell you that it's preferable to let a couple of misprints pass than to lose a day's business, no, the owner is not present, nor the director, nor the boss, otherwise Costa would not so readily have approved of misprints for the sake of getting the book out quickly. It's a question of criteria, replied Raimundo Silva, but the implacable Costa warned him, Don't talk to me about criteria, I know all too well what your criteria are, and as for mine, they are quite simple, I need those proofs without fail by tomorrow, so it's up to you, the ball is in your court, I've already explained to Monica that the work will be ready by tomorrow, It must be at the press by tomorrow, It'll be there, you can send someone to collect it at eight o'clock, That's much too early, at that hour the press is still closed, Then send for them whenever you like, I have no more time to waste, and he rang off.

Raimundo is accustomed to Costa's insolence which he does not take to heart, rudeness without malice in the case of poor Costa, who never stops talking about the Production, one has to keep to a strict schedule in Production, yes, Sir, says he, there may be authors, translators and proof-readers and jacket designers involved, but if it weren't for our little Production team, I'd like to see what all their skills would achieve, a publishing house is like a football team, some showy moves on the forward line up front, lots of passes, much dribbling, lots of headers, but if the goalkeeper turns out to be paralysed or rheumaticky, all is lost, farewell championship, and Costa sums it up, this time with algebraic precision, In publishing, the Production department is like the goalkeeper of a football team. Costa is right.

When it is time for lunch, Raimundo Silva will make an omelette with three eggs and chorizo, an indulgence his liver can still tolerate. With a plate of soup, an orange, a glass of wine, and a coffee to finish off, no one with his sedentary lifestyle could wish for more. He carefully washed up, using more water and detergent than necessary, he dried the dishes and put them back in the kitchen cupboard, he is a methodical man, a proof-reader in the absolute sense of the word, if any word can be said to exist and go on existing for ever with the same absolute meaning, since the absolute demands nothing less. Before getting back to his work, he went to look at the weather, the sky had cleared a little, the other side of the river is becoming visible, nothing but a dark line, an elongated blur, but it is still cold. On his desk there are four hundred and thirty-seven pages of proofs, two hundred and ninety-three of them have already been corrected and checked, the rest should not take too long, the proof-reader has the entire afternoon, and the evening, yes, the evening as well, because this meticulous professional always gives the proofs one last reading from start to finish as if he were an ordinary reader, finally there is the pleasure and satisfaction of understanding in a relaxed manner without looking out for mistakes, how right that author was who asked one day, What would Juliet's complexion have looked like if examined with the eyes of a hawk, now then, the proof-reader in his vigilant task, is just like the hawk, even when his eyes have started to tire, but when he comes to the final reading, he is that self-same Romeo gazing upon Juliet for the first time, innocent, and transfixed by love.

In the case of *The History of the Siege of Lisbon*, Romeo is fully aware that he will not find much cause for rapture, although Raimundo Silva, in the preliminary and somewhat labyrinthine conversation about the correction of errors and errors of correction, had told the author that he liked the book, and, in fact, he was not lying. But what does liking mean, we ask ourselves, between liking something a lot and not liking it at all, there is less and little, and it is not enough to write it in order to know how much yes, or no, or maybe, means in all of this, you would have to utter it aloud, hearing invariably captures the ultimate vibration, and when we are deceived or allow ourselves to be deceived it is only because we did not listen sufficiently to our hearing. It must be recognised, however, that there was no such deception in that dialogue, and it soon became clear that this was a vague or distracted kind of liking, as lukewarmly expressed by Raimundo Silva, I like it, and no sooner had he uttered these words than they turned cold. In those four hundred and thirty-seven pages he did not find a single new fact, controversial interpretation, unpublished document, even as much as a fresh reading. Nothing more than yet another regurgitation of those interminable, played-out accounts of the siege, the description of places, the speeches and deeds of the royal personage, the arrival of the crusaders at Oporto and their navigation until they entered the Tagus, the events that occurred on the feast of St Peter, the ultimatum given to the city, the efforts that went into the siege, the battles and assaults, the surrender, and finally the sacking of the city, *die vero quo omnium sanctorum celebratur ad laudem et honorem nominis Christi et sanctissimae ejus genitricis purificatum est templum*, words attributed to Osbern, who entered the pantheon of literature thanks to the siege and capture of Lisbon and what has been written about them, these Latin words, translated roughly by someone who knows the language, mean that on All Saints Day the corrupt mosque became the most holy Catholic church, and now the muezzin will definitely no longer be able to summon the faithful for prayers to Allah, he will be replaced by a bell or carillon after one god has been substituted for another, and what a pity they did not let him go. He is blind, poor man, but then just as blind with sanguinary wrath was the crusader Osbern, the same only in name, when, with sword in hand, he saw an elderly Moor who did not even have the strength to escape, floundering there on the ground, waving his arms and legs as if trying to bury himself under the earth, this fear being real while that other was imaginary, and he will have his wish, as sure as he is still alive, but not for much longer, say we, nor will he be able to bury himself because by then he will be dead, the proof-reader thought to himself, meanwhile the common graves are being dug. From time to time, the low bleating of a foghorn can be heard coming from the river, it has been doing this since morning, to warn ships, but only now has Raimundo Silva noticed, perhaps because of the great silence that has suddenly descended upon him.

It is January and darkness falls early. The atmosphere in the study is heavy and airless. The doors are closed. To protect himself from the cold, the proof-reader has a shawl over his knees, the heater right up against the desk almost scalding his ankles. Easy to see that the house is old and lacking in comfort, dating from more spartan and primitive times, when to go outdoors with the weather at its coldest was still the best solution for anyone who had nothing better than a freezing corridor where he could march up and down in an effort to keep warm. But on the very last page of *The History of the Siege of Lisbon* Raimundo Silva will discover the impassioned expression of a fervent patriotism, which he will have no difficulty in recognising unless a monotonous and humdrum existence has dampened his own patriotism, now he will shiver, that is true, but from that unmistakable breath that comes from the souls of heroes, note what the historian wrote, On the summit of the fortification, the Moslem moon made its final descent, and definitively and for evermore, alongside the cross which announced to the world the holy baptism of a new Christian city, slowly rising into the blue sky above, kissed by light, tossed by the breeze, the standard of Dom Afonso Henriques which bears the five shields of the Portuguese coat of arms is proudly unfurled in jubilant triumph, shit, and do not imagine that the proof-reader is insulting the national emblem, on the contrary this is the legitimate outburst of someone who, having been ironically reprimanded for inventing ingenuous errors, will have to allow the errors of others to pass, when what he is tempted to do, and rightly so, is to fill the margins of the page with a flurry of indignant *deleaturs*, however, we know he will do no such thing, because any such corrections would offend the author, Let the cobbler stick to his last, for that is all he is paid to do, said the impatient Apelles categorically. Now these errors are not as serious as those we found regarding the word sling or catapult, these are mere trifles hovering uncertainly between a possible yes or no, for in all truth, we do not give a damn nowadays whether these weapons are described as balearicas or as something else, but what is wholly unacceptable is this nonsense of referring to coats of arms in the time of Dom Afonso, the First, when it was only during the reign of his son Sancho that they appeared on the Portuguese flag, nor do we know how they were depicted, whether forming a cross in the centre, or each emblem in a separate corner, or filling up the entire space, this final hypothesis being the most likely according to the most reliable sources. A serious blot, but not the only one, which will forever stain the closing page of *The History of the Siege of Lisbon*, otherwise so richly orchestrated with resounding trumpets, with drums and rapturous outbursts, with the troops lined up on parade, and let us try to picture the scene, foot-soldiers and cavalrymen watching that abominable standard being lowered and the insignia of Christian Portugal being raised in its place, and calling out in one voice, Long live Portugal, and striking their shields vigorously with their swords in an outburst of military zeal, followed by a march past in the presence of the king, who is vindictively trampling underfoot, not only Moorish blood, but that Moslem crescent of the moon, a second error and totally absurd, for no such flag was ever raised above the walls of Lisbon and, as the historian ought to know, the crescent of the moon on a flag was an invention of the Ottoman empire, two or three centuries later. The tip of Raimundo Silva's biro was still poised over the shields in the coat of arms, but then he thought that if he were to remove them and the crescent, it would provoke an earthquake on the page, everything would come crashing down, an inconclusive history in keeping with the greatness of the moment, and this is an excellent way of teaching people the importance of something which, at first sight, appears to be nothing other than a piece of cloth in one or more colours, with designs also in different colours, such as castles or stars, lions, unicorns, eagles, suns, scythes or hammers, wounds, roses, sabres or machetes, compasses, wheels, cedars, elephants or oxen, birettas, hands, palm-trees, horses or candelabra, as I know all too well and, without a guide or catalogue, you could get lost in this museum, even more so if someone has remembered to embellish the flags with coats of arms, all belonging to the same family, for then it becomes an endless list of fleurs-de-lis, shells, buckles, leopards, bees, bells, trees, croziers, mitres, spikes, bears, salamanders, herons, rings, drakes, doves, wild boars, virgins, bridges, ravens, caravels, lances, books, yes, even books, the Bible, the Koran, *Das Kapital*, written by whom do you think, and so forth and so on, from which we may conclude that men are incapable of saying who they are unless they can claim to be something else, and this would be reason enough for leaving aside the episode of the flags, the one reviled, the other exalted, but bearing in mind that the whole thing is a lie, useful to some extent, the ultimate disgrace, simply because we did not have the courage to correct it or know how to replace it with the honest truth, the most ambitious but constant aspiration of all, and may Allah have mercy on us.

For the first time in all these years of painstaking labour, Raimundo Silva will not give the book one final reading from beginning to end. There are, as we explained, four hundred and thirty-seven heavily annotated pages, to read all of them would mean staying up all night or at least most of it, a torment he does not relish for he has positively come to dislike the book and its author, tomorrow the ingenuous readers will say and schoolchildren repeat that the fly has four legs, as affirmed by Aristotle, and on the next centenary of the conquest of Lisbon from the Moors, in the year two thousand and forty-seven, if Lisbon still exists and continues to be inhabited by the Portuguese, some president or other will evoke that sublime moment when the insignia of the proud victors triumphantly replaced the unholy crescent of the moon in the blue skies of our lovely city.

Nevertheless, his professional scruples demand that he should, at least, slowly go over the pages, his expert eyes scanning the words, in the hope that by thus varying the degree of concentration, he might discover some minor error of his own, like that shadow suddenly displaced by strong light, or that familiar sideways glance which at the last minute captures an image in flight. We do not need to know whether Raimundo Silva managed to tidy up those tiresome proofs, but what is interesting is to observe him as he re-reads the speech Dom Afonso Henriques made to the crusaders, according to the version attributed to Osbern, here translated from the Latin by the author of the *History* himself, who does not trust the lessons of others, especially when dealing with such an important subject, no less than the first speech of our founding king to be recorded, for there is no reliable evidence of any other. Raimundo Silva finds the entire speech absurd from start to finish, not because he is competent to question the accuracy of the translation, a command of Latin not being amongst the talents of this average proof-reader, but because no one in their right mind could possibly believe that this King Afonso, who had no gift for rhetoric, made such a convoluted speech, more like one of those pretentious sermons the friars would be giving six or seven centuries later than the limited phrases of a language which at that time was little more than childish prattle. There was the proof-reader smiling scornfully, when suddenly he felt his heart leap, if Egas Moniz really had been the excellent tutor described in the annals, if he was born not simply to accompany the little cripple to

Carquere or subsequently to go to Toledo with a noose round his neck, then surely he would have instilled a fair number of Christian precepts and political maxims into his pupil, and Latin being the perfect language in which to impart this knowledge, one might assume that the royal prince, in addition to a natural command of Galician, would have known *quantum satis* Latin in order to be able to make the aforementioned harangue at the right moment, to all those foreign and highly civilised crusaders, since at that time the only language they understood was the one they had learned in the cradle and a few words of the foreign language with the help of the friars who acted as interpreters. Dom Afonso Henriques, therefore, would have known Latin and not needed to send an emissary in his place to that famous assembly, perhaps he himself might even have been the author of those celebrated words, a wholly plausible hypothesis in the case of someone who in his own hand, and in Latin no less, had written *The History of the Conquest of Santarém*, as we are solemnly informed by Barbosa Machado in his *Biblioteca Lusitana* and who also states that the manuscript was preserved at the time in the Royal Convent of Alcobaça at the end of a book of about St Fulgentius. It has to be said that the proof-reader does not believe a single word of what he is reading, he is more than sceptical, he himself has already said so, but in order to be fair-minded, as well as to break the monotony of this obligatory reading, he consulted the primary source on which the modern histories are based, he searched and found, just as I suspected, the credulous Machado copied, without checking, what Fray Bernardo de Brito and Fray António Brandão had written, this is how historical misconceptions come about, So-and-So says that Beltrano said that Cicrano heard, and three such statements are enough to make a story, but what is beyond question is that *The Conquest of Santarém* was written by a member of the community of Santa Cruz in Coimbra, whose very name has not survived to take its rightful place in the library and remove that of the usurping king.

Raimundo Silva is on his feet, he has the shawl drawn over his shoulders but one corner trails on the ground whenever he moves, and he is reading aloud like a herald making a proclamation, that is to say, the speech our noble king made to the crusaders in the following words, We know, and can witness with our own eyes, that you are men of valour, fearless and well prepared, and, truly, your presence has not diminished in our eyes what we already knew of your prowess. We are not gathered here in order to know how much, men of such wealth, we need promise you, so that enriched with our gifts, you might join us in besieging this city. From the Moors, ever restless, we were never able to accumulate treasures, with which as sometimes happens one cannot live in safety. But since we want you to know what resources we have and what our intentions towards you are, we feel that this should not lead you to despise our promise, for we consider at your disposal everything that our land possesses. Of one thing, however, we are certain, and that is that your piety will incline you more to this enterprise and the desire to carry out such a mighty deed, than any promise of financial rewards. Now then, so that the clamour of your men does not disturb what I have to say to you, choose whomsoever you wish, so that once both sides have withdrawn, we may sit down quietly and discuss the reasons for this assurance and reach some mutual understanding about our proposals before making any statement in public, and so, with both sides in agreement and with the appropriate oaths and guarantees, may this be ratified for the greater glory of God.

No, this speech is not the work of some fledgling monarch without much experience in matters of diplomacy, here one detects the finger, hand and head of some senior ecclesiastic, perhaps the Bishop of Oporto himself, Dom Pedro Pitões, and almost certainly the Archbishop of Braga, Dom João Peculiar, who jointly and in connivance had managed to persuade the crusaders who were passing along the Douro to come to the Tagus and help with the conquest, saying to them amongst other things, At least, listen to the reasons why we think you should come to our assistance and see the evidence for yourselves. And the journey from Oporto to Lisbon having lasted three days, one does not need much imagination to assume that the two prelates, on the way, drew up their plans with the aim of advancing the enterprise, pondering the arguments, giving much advice, cautioning each other about possible dangers, with the most liberal assurances entangled in prudent mental reservations, not forgetting a little flattery, a beguiling strategy which rarely fails to bear fruit even if the ground is sterile and the sower somewhat inexperienced. Blushing, Raimundo Silva drops his shawl with a theatrical gesture, he smiles without happiness, This is not a speech one could ever believe in, more like some Shakespearian climax than the speech of provincial bishops, and he returns to his desk, sits down, shakes his head despondently, We're convinced we shall never know what Dom Afonso Henriques actually said to the crusaders, at least, good-day, and what else, what else, and the blinding clarity of this evidence, not to be able to know, suddenly strikes him as being most unfortunate, he would be capable of renouncing something, he does not ask himself what or how much, his soul, if he has one, his possessions, if he had any, in order to discover, preferably in this part of Lisbon where he lives and where the entire city was once located, some parchment, papyrus, sheet of paper, newspaper cutting, some entry, if possible, or stone engraving, as a record of what was really said, the original, as it were, perhaps less subtle in the art of discourse than this mannered version, which has none of the vigorous language worthy of such an occasion.

His dinner was a quick and simple affair, somewhat lighter than lunch, but Raimundo Silva drank two cups of coffee instead of one, in order to resist the drowsiness that would soon assail him, especially since he had slept so badly the night before. At a steady rhythm, the pages are turned over, scenes and episodes follow upon each other, the historian has now embellished his prose in order to deal with the serious disagreements which arose between the crusaders after the royal harangue, as they debated whether they should or should not help the Portuguese to capture Lisbon, whether they should remain here or travel on, as planned, to the Holy Land, where Our Lord Jesus Christ awaited them, fettered by the Turks. Those who liked the idea of staying on, argued that to expel these Moors from the city and convert them to Christianity would also render service to God, while those who opposed the suggestion replied that any such service would be inferior in the eyes of God and that knights as illustrious as those present prided themselves on being, had an obligation to assist where the struggle was most hazardous, rather than in this hell-hole, amongst peasants and the dregs of humanity, the former, no doubt, being the Moors and the latter the Portuguese, but the historian never found out for certain, perhaps because there was not much to choose between the two insults. The warriors yelled as if possessed, may God forgive me, violent in word and gesture, and those who supported the idea of continuing on their journey to the Holy Places declared that they would derive much greater profit and advantage from the extortion of money and merchandise from the ships at sea, whether from Spain or Africa, merchant ships in the twelfth century being an anachronism which only the historian could explain, than the capture of the city of Lisbon, with less danger of risking lives, because the walls are high and the Moors many. Dom Afonso Henriques could not have been more right when he predicted that any perusal of his proposals would end in turmoil, or, as the Portuguese would say, in *algazarra*, an Arabic word which serves equally well to describe the shouting and uproar of this mixed gathering of men from Cologne and Boulogne, of Flemings, Bretons, Scots and Normans. The opposing factions finally calmed down after a verbal dispute which lasted throughout the feast of St Peter, and tomorrow, which is the thirtieth of June, the representatives of the crusaders, now in agreement, will inform the king that they are prepared to help with the conquest of Lisbon, in exchange for the possessions of their enemies, who even now are watching them from the ramparts beyond, along with other concessions, whether direct or indirect.

For two minutes, Raimundo has been staring so hard that he looks distracted, at the page where these immutable facts of history are recorded, not because he suspects that some final error may be lurking there, some perfidious misprint skilfully concealed between the folds of this tortuous rhetoric, and now wilfully provoking him, safe from his tired eyesight and the drowsiness that is fast creeping in and making him feel numb. Although it would be more accurate to say, the drowsiness that *was* making him feel numb. Because for the last three minutes, Raimundo Silva is as wide awake as if he had taken one of the benzedrine pills left over from a prescription given by an idiot of a doctor and which he stores behind some books. As if fascinated, he reads over and over again, keeps going back to the same line, the one that emphatically asserts that the crusaders will help the Portuguese to capture Lisbon. As chance would have it, or perhaps it was fate, these unequivocal words occupied a single line and have all the impact of an inscription, a distich or some irrevocable maxim, but they are also provocative, as if saying ironically, Make me say something else, if you can. The tension became so great that Raimundo Silva suddenly could not bear it any longer, he got to his feet, pushed back his chair, and is now nervously pacing up and down within the confined space that the bookcases, sofa and desk leave free, saying over and over again, Such rubbish, such utter rubbish and, as if needing to confirm this radical opinion, he picked up the sheet of paper once more, thanks to which, we can now dismiss any earlier doubts and confirm that there is no such nonsense, for it is clearly stated there that the crusaders will help to capture Lisbon, and the proof that this actually happened, we shall find on subsequent pages, where there is a description of the siege, the assault on the ramparts, the fighting in the streets and inside the houses, the indiscriminate slaughter and the sacking of the city. So, Mr Proof-reader, show us where you found this blunder, this error that escapes us, true, we don't have your vast experience, we sometimes look without seeing, but we can read, we assure you, yes, you're absolutely right, we do not always understand everything, easy to see why, we lack the necessary training, Mr Proof-reader, the necessary training, and besides, we have to admit that we are often too lazy to verify the meaning of a word in the dictionary, with inevitable consequences. It is preposterous, insists Raimundo Silva as if he were giving us his answer, Never would I do such a thing, and why should I, a proof-reader takes his work seriously, he does not play games or tricks, he respects what has been established in grammars and reference books, he is guided by the rules and makes no attempt to modify them, he obeys an ethical code which is unwritten but sacrosanct, he must respect tradition, observe the conventions, and suppress his private inclinations, any doubts he may have, he keeps to himself and, as for putting a *not* where the author wrote *yes*, this proof-reader simply would not do it. The words just spoken by Mr Jekyll try to contradict others we could not hear, words spoken by Mr Hyde, nor do we need to mention these two names in order to see that in this antiquated building in the district of Castelo we are watching yet another titanic struggle between an angel and a demon, the two conflicting sides of human beings, without excepting proof-readers. But unfortunately it is Mr Hyde who will win this battle, as is clear from the smile on Raimundo Silva's face and a look of utter malevolence we would not have expected of him, all traces of Jekyll have gone from his face, he has obviously taken a decision, and such a bad one, he holds his biro with a steady hand and adds a word to the page, a word the historian never wrote, that for the sake of historical truth he could never have brought himself to write, the word *Not*, and what the book now says is that the crusaders will *Not* help the Portuguese to conquer Lisbon, thus it is written and has come to be accepted as true, although different, what we would call false has come to prevail over what we would call true, falsehood has replaced the truth, and someone would have to narrate the history anew, and how.

In all these years of dedication to his profession. Raimundo Silva would never have knowingly dared to infringe the afore-mentioned ethical code, unwritten but regulating the actions of proof-readers in relation to the ideas and opinions of authors. For the proof-reader who knows his place, the author, as such, is infallible. It is well known, for example, that Nietzsche's proof-reader, although a fervent believer, resisted the same temptation to insert the word *Not* on a certain page, thus amending the philosopher's phrase, God is dead, God is not dead. If proof-readers were given their freedom and did not have their hands and feet tied by a mass of prohibitions more binding than the penal code, they would soon transform the face of the world, establish the kingdom of universal happiness, giving drink to the thirsty, food to the famished, peace to those who live in turmoil, joy to the sorrowful, companionship to the solitary, hope to those who have lost it, not to mention the rapid disappearance of poverty and crime, for they would be able to do all these things simply by changing the words, and should anyone doubt these new demiurges, they need only remember that this is precisely how the world and man came to be made, with words, some rather than others, so that things might turn out just so, and in no other fashion, Let it be done, said God, and it was done immediately.

Raimundo Silva will read no more. He is exhausted, all his strength has gone into that *Not* with which he has just put at risk, not only his professional integrity, but also his peace of mind. As from today, he will live for that moment, sooner or later, but inevitable, when someone will ask him to account for his mistake, it might well be the outraged author, some witty and implacable critic, or an attentive reader who writes to the publisher, or even Costa himself when he turns up tomorrow morning to collect the proofs, for he is perfectly capable of appearing in person with that heroic and martyred expression on his face, I preferred to come myself, always better to take on more work, even if it is beyond the call of duty. And if Costa should decide to leaf through the proofs before putting them into his briefcase and he should happen to spot that page sullied by falsehood, if he should be surprised to find a new word in the proofs which are already in quarto, if he were to take the trouble to read the word and understand what has come to be written, the world, at that moment amended once more, he will have lived differently for one brief instant, Costa will say, still hesitating, Senhor Silva, there appears to be a mistake here, and he will pretend to look and be forced to concede, How foolish of me, I cannot imagine how it could have happened, probably because I was getting tired, It will not be necessary to put in a *deleatur* in order to eliminate that ominous word, he need simply delete it as any child would do, and the world will return to its former tranquil orbit, it will go on being what it was, and, from now on, Costa, although he may never refer again to this curious lapse, will have one more reason for proclaiming that everything depends on the Production team.

Raimundo Silva lay down. He is lying on his back with his hands clasped behind the nape of his neck, and he does not yet feel the cold. He has some difficulty in reflecting on what he has done and, worst of all, cannot acknowledge the seriousness of his action, he even feels surprised that the idea never occurred to him earlier to alter the sense of other texts he has revised. And just as he thinks he is about to examine his conscience, to become detached, he observes himself thinking, and feels somewhat alarmed. Then he shrugs his shoulders, postpones the anxiety that was beginning to invade his spirit, We shall see, tomorrow I shall decide whether the word stays there or whether I remove it. He was just about to turn on to his right side, turning his back on the empty side of the bed, when he noticed that the foghorn could no longer be heard and he wondered how long it had been silent. No, I heard it when I was reading the king's speech aloud, I can clearly remember, between one phrase and the next, that low bellow as if a bull were lost in the mist and lowing at the white sky, far from the herd, how strange that there are no marine creatures with voices capable of filling the vastness of the sea, or this wide river, I must take a look at the weather. He rose to his feet, wrapped himself in his thick dressing-gown which, in winter time, he always spreads over the bedcover, and went to open the window. The mist had disappeared, incredible that it should have concealed all those scintillations, lights all the way down the slope, more on the other side, yellow and white, projected on to the water like flickering flames. It is colder. Raimundo Silva thought to himself, in the manner of Fernando Pessoa, If I smoked, I should now light a cigarette, watching the river, thinking how vague and uncertain everything is, but, not smoking, I should simply think that everything is truly uncertain and vague, without a cigarette, even though the cigarette, were I to smoke it, would in itself express the uncertainty and vagueness of things, like smoke itself, were I to smoke. The proof-reader lingers at the window, no one will call out, Come inside or you'll catch cold, and he tries to imagine someone gently calling, but pauses for another minute in order to think, vague and uncertain, and finally, as if someone had called out once more, Come inside, I beg of you, he obeys, closes the window and goes back to bed, lying on his right side and waiting. For sleep.

IT WAS NOT YET EIGHT O'CLOCK when Costa rang the doorbell. The proof-reader, who had slept badly as one disturbing dream followed another, was at last sleeping heavily, at least this was what that part of him which had reached a level of consciousness that allowed him to think concluded, namely that this deep sleep finally prevailed, given the difficulty of awakening the other part, despite the insistent ringing of the doorbell, four times, five, now a prolonged ringing which went on and on, as if the mechanism of the button had jammed. Raimundo Silva realised, naturally, that he would have to get up, but he could not leave one half of himself in the bed, perhaps even more, what would Costa say, in all certainty it is Costa, now that the police no longer drag us out of bed in the middle of the night, yes, what will Costa have to say if he sees only half of Raimundo Silva appear, perhaps the Benvindo half, a man should always go in his entirety wherever he is called, he cannot allege, I've come with part of myself, the rest got delayed on the way. The bell went on ringing, Costa starts to get worried. Such silence in the house, finally the awakened part of the proof-reader manages to call out in a hoarse voice, I'm just coming, and only then does the part which is asleep begin to stir, but with reluctance. Now, precariously reunited, unsteady on legs which could belong to anyone, they cross the room, the door on the landing is at a right angle to this one, and both could almost be opened with a single gesture, it is Costa, clearly sorry to have disturbed him at this hour, Forgive me, then it dawns on him that he has not said good morning, Good morning, Senhor Silva, I do apologise for calling so early, but I've come to collect those little proofs, Costa genuinely wishes to be forgiven, the deprecating tone can imply nothing else, Yes, of course, says the proof-reader, go through to the study.

When Raimundo Silva reappears, tightening his belt and pulling up the collar of his dressing-gown, which is in shades of blue with a tartan design, Costa already has the bundle of proofs in his hand, he holds them as if he were weighing them, and even comments sympathetically, This really is enormous, but he does not actually leaf through the pages, simply asks somewhat nervously, Did you make many more corrections, and Raimundo Silva replies, No, while smiling to himself, fortunately no one can ask him why, Costa does not know that he is being deceived by that tiny word, *No*, which in a single utterance both masks and reveals, Costa had asked, Did you make many more corrections, and the proof-reader replied, No, with a smile, now on edge as he says, If you wish, take a look for yourself, Costa is surprised at such benevolence, a vague sentiment which soon dispersed, It isn't worth the bother, I'm going straight to the press from here, they promised me the book would go to press the moment the proofs arrived. If Costa were to leaf through the pages and spot the error, the proof-reader is convinced he would still be able to persuade him with two or three concocted phrases about context and denial, contradiction and appearance, nexus and indetermination, but Costa is now anxious to be off, they are waiting for him at the press, he is delighted because the Production team has achieved one more victory in the battle against time, Today is the first day of the rest of your life, he should, of course, be more severe, it is not acceptable that problems should always be solved at the last moment, we must work within wider and safer margins, but the proof-reader has such a helpless expression as he stands there in that pseudo-tartan dressing-gown, unshaven, his hair grotesquely dyed and in sad contrast with his pale complexion, that Costa, who is in his prime, despite belonging to a generation that has made a mockery of kindness, suppresses his justified complaints and almost with affection, removes from his briefcase the manuscript of a new book for revision. This one is short, little more than two hundred pages, and there is no real urgency. What he means by this gesture and these words is not lost on Raimundo Silva, he can decipher that semitone added or removed from a vowel, his hearing attuned to reading as clearly as his eyes, and this makes him almost remorseful that he should be deceiving the ingenuous Costa, envoy and messenger of an error for which he is not responsible, as happens to the majority of men, who live and die in all innocence, affirming and denying on account of others, yet settling accounts as if they were their own, but Allah is wise and the rest a figment of the imagination.

Costa departed, happy to have made such a good start to the day, and Raimundo Silva goes into the kitchen to prepare some coffee with milk and buttered toast. Toasted bread for this man of norms and principles is almost a vice and truly a manifestation of uncontrollable greed, wherein enter multiple sensations, both of vision and touch, as well as of smell and taste, beginning with that gleaming chrome-plated toaster, then the knife cutting slices of bread, the aroma of toasted bread, the butter melting, and finally that mouth-watering taste, so difficult to describe, in one's mouth, on one's palate, tongue and teeth, to which that ineffable dark pellicle sticks, browned yet soft, and once more that aroma, now deep down, the person who invented such a delicacy deserves to be in heaven. One day, Raimundo Silva spoke these very words aloud, at a fleeting moment when he had the impression that this perfect creation made from bread and fire was being transfused into his blood, because, frankly, even the butter was superfluous and he would happily have done without, although only a fool would refuse this final addition to the essential which only serves to increase one's appetite and enjoyment, as in the case of this buttered toast we were discussing, the same could be said of love, for example, if only the proof-reader were more experienced. Raimundo Silva finished eating, went into the bathroom to shave and do something about his appearance. Until his face is well covered in foam, he avoids looking at himself directly in the mirror, he now regrets having decided to dye his hair, he has become the prisoner of his own artifice, because, more than the displeasure caused by his own image, what he cannot bear is the idea that, by no longer dyeing his hair, the white hairs he knows to be there will suddenly come to light, all at once, a cruel incursion, instead of that naturally slow progression which out of foolish vanity he decided one day to interrupt. These are the petty misfortunes of the spirit which the body, although blameless, has to pay for.

Back in his study and curious about this new assignment, Raimundo Silva examines the manuscript Costa has left him, heaven forbid that it should turn out to be *A Comprehensive History of Portugal*, bringing further temptations as to whether it should be *Yes* or *No*, or that even more seductive temptation to add a speculative note with an infinite *Perhaps* which would leave no stone unturned or fact unchallenged. After all, this is simply another novel amongst so many, he need not concern himself with introducing what is already there, for such books, the fictions they narrate, are created, both books and fictions, with a constant element of doubt, with a reticent affirmation, above all the disquiet of knowing that nothing is true, and that it is necessary to pretend that it is, at least for a time, until we can no longer resist the indelible evidence of change, then we turn to the time that has passed, for it alone is truly time, and we try to reconstitute the moment we failed to recognise, the moment that passed while we were reconstituting some other time, and so on and so forth, from one moment to the next, every novel is like this, desperation, a frustrated attempt to save something of the past. Except that it still has not been established whether it is the novel that prevents man from forgetting himself or the impossibility of forgetfulness that makes him write novels.

Raimundo Silva has the salutary habit of allowing himself a free day whenever he finishes the revision of a manuscript. It gives him respite, or as he would say, relief, and so he goes out into the world, strolls through the streets, lingers before shop-windows, sits on a park bench, amuses himself for a couple of hours in a cinema, enters some museum on a sudden impulse to take another look at a favourite painting, in a word leads the life of someone who is paying a visit and will not be back all that soon. Sometimes, however, he does not fit all these things in. He often returns home in mid-afternoon, neither tired nor bored, simply because summoned by an inner voice with whom there is no point arguing, he has the manuscript of a book waiting for him, another one, because the publisher who values and esteems his work has never so far left him without work. Despite so many years of this monotonous existence, he is still curious to know what words might be waiting for him, what conflict, thesis, opinion, what simple plot, the same thing happened with *The History of the Siege of Lisbon*, nor is it surprising, for since his time at school neither chance nor inclination had aroused any further interest in such remote events.

This time, however, Raimundo Silva foresees that he will return home late, most likely he will even go to a midnight session at the cinema, and we do not need to be very perceptive in order to realise that he is anxious to keep out of the immediate reach of Costa, should the latter discover the deception, of which he is both author and accomplice, for as the author he erred and as the proof-reader he failed to correct the mistake. Besides, it is almost ten o'clock, at the press they must already be setting up the first frames, the printer, with slow and cautious movements which distinguish the specialist, will make any necessary adjustments after assembling the pages and locking them into the chase, any minute now the sheets of paper narrating the spurious *History of the Siege of Lisbon* will rapidly begin to appear, just as at any minute now the telephone might ring, strange that it should not have rung already, with Costa bellowing at the other end, An inexplicable error, Senhor Silva, fortunately I noticed it just in time, grab a taxi and get yourself here at once, this matter is your responsibility, I'm sorry but this is not something we can deal with over the telephone, I want you here in the presence of witnesses, Costa is so agitated that his voice sounds shrill, and Raimundo Silva, who is feeling just as nervous, or even more so, driven by these imaginings, gets dressed in haste, goes to the window to check the weather, it is cold but the sky is clear. On the other side, tall chimneys send up spirals of smoke which rise vertically at first, until broken by the wind and reduced to a slow cloud that heads southwards. Raimundo looks down at the roof-tops covering the ancient foundations of Lisbon. His hands are resting on the parapet of the verandah, he can feel the cold, rough ironwork, he is now tranquil, simply gazing, no longer thinking, feeling somewhat empty, when it suddenly occurs to him how he can spend his free day, something he has never done before, and those who complain of life's brevity only have themselves to blame if they have failed to take advantage of whatever life they have been given.

He left the verandah, looked amongst his papers for the first proofs of *The Siege*, still in his possession along with the second and third proofs, but not the original manuscript, that remains with the publishers once the first revision has been completed, he put them into a paper bag, and now the telephone starts ringing. Raimundo Silva shuddered, his left hand, raised out of habit, reached out, but stopped halfway and drew back, this black object is a time-bomb about to explode, a quivering rattlesnake ready to attack. Slowly, as if afraid that his footsteps might be heard where the call is coming from, the proof-reader moves away, muttering to himself, It's Costa, but he is wrong, and he will never find out who wanted to speak to him at this hour of the morning, who or for what reason, Costa will not say to him, within the next few days, I telephoned your home, but no one answered, not even some other person, but who, will repeat the statement, Such a pity, I had some good news to give you, the telephone rang and rang, and no one answered. It is true, the telephone is ringing and ringing, but Raimundo Silva will not reply, he is already in the passageway, ready to go out most likely, after so many doubts and worries, it must have been someone who dialled the wrong number, such things can happen, but this is something we shall never know, it is simply an assumption, although he would like to take advantage of this hypothesis, it would give the proof-reader greater peace of mind, which, all things considered, is a somewhat flippant way of putting it, given that any such peace of mind in the present circumstances, would be no better than the uncertain relief of a mere postponement, Let this cup pass from me, Jesus said, but to no avail, because the command would be repeated.

As he descends the steep, narrow stairway, Raimundo Silva is thinking that he might still be in time to avoid the evil hour awaiting him when his reckless behaviour is discovered, he need only take a taxi and rush to the press, where Costa is certain to be on hand, delighted at having proved once more that efficiency is his hallmark, Costa, who represents Production, loves coming to the press in order to give, as it were, the word to start printing, and he is just on the point of doing so when Raimundo Silva bursts through the door, shouting, Stop, hold on, as in that fictional episode about the breathless messenger who brings a royal pardon to a condemned man at the eleventh hour, such relief, but short-lived, for there is a vast difference between knowing that we shall die one day and having to confront the end of everything, the firing squad about to aim, and who knows it better than he who, having earlier made a miraculous escape, now finds himself in a hopeless predicament, Dostoevsky got away the first time, but not the second time. In the bright, cold light on the street, Raimundo appears to be still pondering what he will finally do, but this pondering is misleading, mere appearances, the proof-reader inwardly imagines a debate with a foregone conclusion, here prevailed that familiar saying of intransigent chess-players, once handled, a pawn has been played, my dear Alekhine, what I have written, I have written. Raimundo Silva gives a deep sigh, he looks at the two rows of buildings to the left and right, with a strange feeling of possession that embraces the very ground he treads, he who has no worldly goods under the sun nor any hope of ever acquiring them, having lost ages ago the illusory inheritance expected from his godmother Benvinda, God rest her soul, if she is being comforted by the prayers of her legitimate and rewarded heirs, no less or more grasping than nature generally ordains, and much the same everywhere. But it is true that the proof-reader, who has been living in this district close to the castle for more years than he cares to remember, and has all the reference he needs to find his way home, now experiences, along with the aforementioned pleasure of being the new owner, an open and liberating sense of pleasure which might even last beyond the next corner, when he turns into the Rua Bartolomeu de Gusmão, in the zone of shadows. As he walks along, he asks himself where this reassurance is coming from, when he knows full well that he is being pursued by the sword of Damocles, in the form of a letter of formal dismissal, for reasons more than justified, incompetence, deliberate fraud, premeditated malice, incitement to perversion. He asks, and imagines receiving a reply from the very offence that he committed, not from the offence in itself, but from the inevitable consequences, that is to say, Raimundo Silva, who finds himself at the precise location of the ancient Moorish city, has a multiple and kaleidoscopic awareness of this historical and topographical coincidence, no doubt thanks to his formal decision to have the crusaders refusing to help the Portuguese, thus leaving the latter to get along as best they could with their own meagre national forces, if they could already be described as national, since it is certain that seven years earlier, despite the assistance of other crusaders, they came face to face with the ramparts and did not even attempt to get any closer, simply carrying out forays, destroying orchards and kitchen-gardens, and doing other damage to private property. Well now, the only purpose of these minute considerations is to make it clear, however much it may cost to admit it in the light of crude reality, that for Raimundo Silva, until there is proof to the contrary or God Our Lord disposes otherwise, Lisbon continues to belong to the Moors, because, if you'll bear with the repetition, twenty-four hours have not elapsed since that fatal moment when the crusaders uttered that damaging refusal, and in such a short time it would have been impossible for the Portuguese to plan on their own the complicated tactics and strategies of siege, blockade, battle and assault, let us hope in diminishing order of duration when the time comes.

Obviously, the Café Graciosa, where the proof-reader is heading for at this moment, did not exist here in the year one thousand one hundred and forty-seven in which we find ourselves, under this June sky, magnificent and warm notwithstanding the fresh breeze coming in from the sea through the mouth of the straits. A café has always been the ideal place to catch up on the news, the customers sit there at their leisure, and this being a working-class district, where everybody knows each other and daily contact has reduced any formalities to the minimum, apart from a few simple pleasantries, Good morning, How are you, All well at home, said without paying much attention to the real meaning of these questions and answers, and soon moving on to the concerns of the day, which are wide-ranging and all of them serious. The city has become one great chorus of lamentations with the arrival of so many fugitives, ousted by the troops of Ibn Arrinque, the Galician, may Allah punish him and condemn him to darkest hell, and the wretched fugitives arrive in a pitiful state, the blood gushing from their wounds, crying out and weeping, many of them with stumps instead of hands, their ears or noses cut off with the most wanton cruelty, an advance warning from the Portuguese king. And it would appear, says the café-owner, that the crusaders are on their way by sea, damn them, rumour has it that two hundred ships are about to arrive, this time the situation is really serious, mark my words, Oh, the poor creatures, says a fat woman, wiping away a tear, for I've just come this minute from the Porta de Ferro, a wilderness of misery and misfortune, the doctors don't know where to turn, I saw people with their faces battered into blood and pulp, one poor fellow had his eyes gouged out, horrible, horrible, may the Prophet's sword fall on the assassins, It will, interrupted a youth who was leaning against the counter with a glass of milk in one hand, if left to us, We shall never surrender, said the café-owner, the Portuguese and the crusaders were here seven years ago and were sent packing with their tails between their legs, Too true, the youth continued, after wiping his mouth with the back of his hand, but then Allah is not in the habit of helping those who do not help themselves, and as for those five ships carrying crusaders anchored in the river for the last six days, I ask myself what we're waiting for before we attack and sink them, That would be just punishment, said the fat woman, in payment for all the misery they have caused our people, Scarcely in payment, rejoined the café-owner, since for every outrage committed against us, we have paid back in kind at least a hundredfold, But my eyes are like the dead doves that will never more return to their nests, said the muezzin.

Raimundo Silva entered, said good morning to no one in particular, and sat at a table behind the showcase where the usual tempting delicacies were on display, sponges, mille feuilles, cream cornets, tartlets, rice cakes, mokatines and, those inevitable croissants, in the shape dictated by the French word, a pastry that has risen only to collapse at the first bite and disintegrate until there are nothing but crumbs left on the plate, tiny celestial bodies which the huge wet finger of Allah is lifting to his mouth, then all that remains will be a terrible cosmic void, if being and nothingness are compatible. The fellow behind the counter, who is not the owner, puts aside the glasses he is washing and brings the coffee the proof-reader ordered, he knows him even though he does not patronise the café every day, only now and then, and he always gives the impression of whiling away the time, today he seems more relaxed, he opens a paper bag and takes out a thick bundle of loose pages, the waiter tries to find some space to deposit the cup of coffee and glass of water, he places the wrapped lump of sugar on the saucer, and before withdrawing, repeats the observation he has been making all morning that it has turned very cold, Fortunately, there isn't any fog today, the proof-reader smiles as if he had just received some good news. It is true, fortunately there is no fog, but a fat woman at the next table who is eating a mille feuille with her white coffee informs him that according to the weather report given by the Meteorological or Metrological Office, as the woman insists on pronouncing it, the mist will probably reappear by evening, who would have thought it, the sky now being so clear, this bright sunshine, a poetic observation not made by him, but inserted here because irresistible. Time, like fortune, is inconstant, said the proof-reader, conscious of the banality of those words. Neither the waiter nor the woman made any reply, this being the most prudent attitude to adopt when confronted with definitive statements, to listen and say nothing, waiting for time itself to tear them to shreds, although they often become even more definitive, like those of the Greeks and Romans, until finally consigned to oblivion when time finally comes to an end. The waiter turned back to washing glasses, the woman to what remained of her mille feuille, any minute now, furtively, because it is impolite, although irresistible, she will pick up the crumbs on her plate with her wet forefinger, but she will not lift all of them, one by one, because the crumbs of mille feuilles, as we know from experience, are just like particles of cosmic dust, endless, droplets of perpetual mist without remission. In this same café, we would find another youth, had he not died in the war, and as for the muezzin, we need only recall that we were just about to find out how he died of merciful fright, when the crusader Osbern, but not the same Osbern, came down on him, with raised sword, spilling fresh blood, may Allah take pity on his own creatures, wretched as they are notwithstanding.

While drinking his coffee, Raimundo Silva began searching for the pages of *The History of the Siege of Lisbon* that interested him, not the king's speech, nor the battle scenes, he has lost all interest whether *balear* or *balearic* is the correct adjective for those slings, and wants to know nothing more about capitulation and sacking. He has found what he was looking for, four sheets of paper which he separates from the pile and re-reads attentively, running a line over the more important references with a fluorescent yellow marker. The fat woman watches this strange operation with wary respect, and then quite unpredictably, with no direct relationship of cause and effect between another's action and one's own thoughts, she suddenly gathers the crumbs together into a little pile and with five chubby fingertips she scoops them up, squeezes them together and bringing them to her mouth, avidly devours them, smacking her lips. Disturbed by the noise, Raimundo Silva looked away, no doubt, disapprovingly, thinking to himself that the temptation to regress to certain childish habits is a constant trait in the human species, if Dom Afonso Henriques eats voraciously with his fingers, so what, it is the custom of the time, although certain innovations can now be seen, such as sticking a knife into a chunk of beef and bringing it to one's mouth, all that remains now is for someone to have the bright idea to add prongs to the tip of the knife, the invention is long overdue, after all, those absent-minded inventors need only take note of those pitchforks in rough wood with which farmers harvest and gather in their wheat and barley and load them on to carts, besides as experience has all too clearly shown, no one will progress in art or life if they succumb to the comforts of the court. But the woman in the café has no such excuse since her parents took great pains to teach her how to behave at table, yet here she is relapsing into her old habits which probably go back to those primitive times when Moors and Christians had similar habits, a somewhat controversial opinion, for some would argue that the followers of Mohammed were much more civilised, and that the others, out-and-out rustics who rejoiced in their stubbornness, knew little or nothing about good manners, but everything will change one day when they start to worship the Virgin Mary with such fervour that they soon forget Her Divine Son, not to mention their insulting disregard for the Eternal Father. And so we can see how, quite naturally, and without any effort, by passing quietly from one episode to another, we soar from that mille feuille eaten by a woman in the Café Graciosa, to Him who feels no hunger, yet who has endowed us with a thousand desires and needs.

Raimundo Silva puts the proofs of *The History of the Siege of Lisbon* back into the paper bag, with the exception of the four pages of interest which he folds and carefully tucks into the inside pocket of his jacket, he then goes up to the counter where the waiter is serving a glass of milk and a pastry to a young man who looks as if he is in search of work and whose earnest expression is that of someone who anticipates that this is the most substantial meal he is likely to have all day. The proof-reader is a sufficiently astute and sensitive observer to be able to take in all these details at a single glance, we might even speculate that one day he saw a similar expression in his own eyes when looking into the mirror at home, but no point in asking him, because we are much more interested in the present, and, from the past only some memory, not so much his as of the past in general, the part modified by that reckless word. Now it only remains to be seen where it will lead us, undoubtedly, in the first place, to Raimundo Silva, for the word, any word, has this facility or virtue to lead to the person who used it, and then, perhaps, who knows, to us who pursue it like hounds on the trail, considerations which are obviously premature, since the siege has not yet started, the Moors who come into the café sing in chorus, We shall conquer, we shall conquer, with the weapons we carry it is possible, but to achieve so much Mohammed will have to help as he best knows how, because we can see no weapons, and the arsenal, if the voice of the people is truly the voice of Allah, is not sufficiently stocked in proportion to their needs. Raimundo Silva says to the waiter, Look after this parcel for me, I'll collect it before you close, meaning the Café, of course, and the waiter sticks the parcel between two covered jars on the shelf behind him, It'll be quite safe here, he says, and it never occurred to him to ask why Raimundo Silva does not leave the parcel at home, since he lives so near, in the Rua do Milagre de Santo António which is only round the corner, but waiters, contrary to general opinion, are discreet fellows, they listen with saintly patience to the rumours going round, day in, day out, every day of their life, and it becomes tedious, while out of professional courtesy and rather than offend the clients who are their raison d'être, they show the greatest interest and listen attentively, but at heart, they are always thinking of something else, such as, for example, of what interest the proof-reader's reply might be if he were to give one, I'm afraid someone might ring. The young man has finished eating his cake and is now unselfconsciously using what remains of the milk to rinse out any crumbs still sticking to his teeth and gums, waste not want not, as our dear parents would say, but these words of sublime wisdom brought them no riches and, as far as we know, this was not the source of the lamented possessions of Godmother Benvinda, God forgive her if He can.

The waiter in the café is wise not to pay any attention to gossip. It is well known that when there are serious tensions on the international front, the first signs of instability and financial ruin are to be seen in the tourist industry. Now if the situation here in this city of Lisbon were one of imminent siege and attack, these tourists would not be arriving, the first this morning, transported in two buses, one full of Japanese with their binoculars and cameras, the other with Americans wearing anoraks and shorts in garish colours. They assemble behind the interpreters, and side by side, in two separate columns, they start climbing the slope, they are about to enter the Rua do Chão da Feira by the gate with the niche of St George, they will marvel at the saint and the terrifying dragon, ridiculously small in the eyes of the Japanese who are accustomed to somewhat more prodigious monsters of the species. As for the Americans, they will be deeply ashamed when forced to acknowledge that a cowboy from the Far West lassoing a wild heifer cuts a poor figure when compared with this knight in shining armour, invincible in every battle, although there is some suspicion that he abandoned these latest conflicts and is now living on past laurels. The tourists had already moved on and the street suddenly went quiet, we are even tempted to say into a state of torpor, if the word, which irresistibly insinuates into one's spirit and body the lassitude of a torrid summer, were not to sound incongruous on such a cold morning, however tranquil the place and quiet the people. From here the river can be seen over the merlons of the cathedral which resemble a game of ninepins above the bell-towers which the unevenness of the terrain has made invisible, and despite the great distance, you can sense the serenity out there and imagine the throbbing flight of seagulls over the gleaming highway of the waters. If it were true that there are five ships carrying crusaders out there, they would almost certainly have started to bombard the defenceless city, but no such thing will happen, because we know very well that from this side no harm will come to the Moors, once it has been said and subsequently written for posterity, that the Portuguese on this occasion cannot rely on help from those who have entered port simply to replenish their supply of drinking water and rest from the hardships of navigation and the agonies of tempests, before continuing their journey to oust the infidels, not in any old city such as Lisbon, but on that hallowed ground where God once walked, leaving the divine traces of his bare feet where no other has passed, and which the rain and wind have left undisturbed.

Raimundo Silva turned the corner leading into the Rua do Milagre de Santo António and passing in front of his house, perhaps because he was only semi-consciously listening to the sounds around him, had the fleeting impression that he could hear a telephone ringing, Could it be mine, he wondered, but the sound was coming from nearby, it might have been in the barber's shop on the other side of the street, and just then another possibility comes to mind, how careless of him, how utterly stupid to imagine that Costa would necessarily use the telephone, Who knows, he might be about to arrive at any minute, and his imagination, ever obliging, conjured up the scene, Costa at the wheel of his car, driving at full speed up the Rua do Limoeiro, the screeching of his tyres still hovering in the air as he takes the bend round the cathedral, unless Raimundo Silva gets out of the way, Costa will loom into sight with his engine roaring, braking abruptly at the entrance to his apartment and say breathlessly, Get in, get in, we must have a chat, no, I can't discuss these matters here, for despite everything Costa is well-mannered, incapable of creating a scene in public. The proof-reader waits no longer, he rapidly descends the Escadinhas de São Crispim and only pauses for breath after turning the bend where he is concealed from Costa's searching eyes. He sits on a step to recover from his fright, shoos away a dog that has come up to him, its nose outstretched to catch his scent, and removes from his inside pocket the four pages he has extracted from the bundle of proofs, he unfolds them and smooths them out on his lap.

The idea, which came to him as he watched the roof-tops descending like steps as far as the river, is to follow the lay-out of the Moorish fortifications according to the scant and rather dubious information provided by the historian, as he himself had the good grace to acknowledge. But here, right before Raimundo Silva's eyes is a fragment, if not of the indestructible rampart itself, at least of a wall occupying the same space where the other stood, and descending all the way down the steps beneath a row of broad windows surmounted by tall gables. Raimundo Silva, therefore, is on the outer side of the city, he belongs to the besieging army, and it would only take one of those windows to open for a Moorish girl to appear and start singing, This is proud Lisbon, Impregnable, Here the Christian will meet his perdition, and on finishing her song, she taps disdainfully on the window, but unless the proof-reader's eyes are deceiving him, the muslin curtain has been drawn back ever so discreetly, and this simple gesture was enough to mitigate any threat in those words, if we take them literally, for it might well be that Lisbon, contrary to all appearances, was not a city but a woman, and the perdition simply amorous, assuming that the restrictive adverb has some meaning here, and that this is not the only blissful perdition. The dog drew near once more, now Raimundo Silva looks at it nervously, who knows it might have rabies, for he once read, he no longer remembers where, that one of the signs of the dreaded disease is a drooping tail, and this one looks rather limp, probably because it has been ill-treated, for the animal's ribs are sticking out, another sign, but this one decisive, is that unsightly saliva trickling down the fauces and fangs, but this mongrel, is only drooling because of the smell of food being cooked here on the Escadinhas de São Crispim. The dog, let us rest assured, does not have rabies, perhaps if we were living in the time of the Moors, but nowadays, in a city like this, modern, hygienic, organised, even the sight of a stray dog comes as a surprise, it has probably escaped the net because of its preference for this remote, uphill route, which calls for nimble feet and the vigour of youth, blessings which do not necessarily coincide in dog-catchers.

Raimundo Silva goes on consulting the pages, mentally following the itinerary, and a stealthy glance at the dog suddenly reminds him of the historian's description of the horrors of famine endured by the beleaguered for months on end, neither dog nor cat survived, even the rats disappeared, but if this was so, then surely the man was right who said that a dog barked that serene dawn when the muezzin climbed the minaret to summon the faithful to morning prayers, and the man was mistaken who argued that because the dog was unclean, the Moors could not bear to have the animal in their sight, now let us concede that they banned dogs from their houses and deprived them of caresses and feeding-bowls, but never from vast Islam, for truly, if we are capable of living in harmony with our own impurities, why should we so vehemently reject the impurities of others, in this case, of the canine species, therefore, much more innocent than those of humans, who so thoroughly abuse the term dog, an insult hurled right and left at enemies, by Christians abusing Moslems, by Moslems abusing Christians, and by both parties abusing the Jews. Not to mention those whom we know best, those Portuguese noblemen coming yonder, so preoccupied and besotted with their hounds and mastiffs that they are given to sleeping with them, with as much or even greater pleasure than with their concubines, and yet, as you will see, the worst name they can call their most implacable enemy is Dog, there would appear to be no greater insult, except for Son of a Bitch. And all this has come about through the arbitrary criteria of men, they are the ones who create words, the animals, poor things, are unaware of these semantic subtleties as they listen to the quarrelling, Dog, says the Moor, You're the dog, retorts the Christian, and next minute they are fighting with lance, sword and dagger, while the hounds and mastiffs say to each other, We are the dogs, nor does it bother them in the least.

Having decided the route he must take, Raimundo Silva gets to his feet, shakes the dust from his breeches and begins to descend the steps. The dog has followed him, but keeps his distance, like someone accustomed to being stoned, and the man only has to bend down and pretend he is picking up a stone and the dog takes fright. At the bottom of the steps, the dog hesitated, and appeared to be asking himself, Should I or should I not go any further, but decided to carry on following the proof-reader who is making his way down the Calçada do Correio Velho. Somewhere around here, or a little further on, corresponding to the borders of the district of São Crispim, the rampart descended on the right, presumably as far as the famous Porta de Ferro, attributed by some to a certain Ferro, but of which no trace remains, perhaps if we were to remove this modern paving in the Largo de Santo António in front of the Cathedral, and dig deep down, we should discover the foundations of the period, the rusted remains of ancient weapons, the stench of a tomb, the entangled skeletons of warriors, not lovers, who shouted in unison, Dog, and then proceeded to kill each other. Cars pass up and down, the trams creak round the bend of the Madalena, they are on the 28 route, particularly esteemed by film directors, and yonder, turning in front of the Cathedral, goes another bus full of tourists, they must be French and imagine they are in Spain. The dog is wary about crossing, the world best known to him are those streets further up the hill, and although he can see the man looking back as he descends the Rua da Padaria, along which the walls of the rampart would have extended, centuries ago, as far as the Rua dos Bacalhoeiros, he does not dare to go on, perhaps the fear he now experiences is too unbearable as he recalls some terrifying event in the past, cats doused with cold water take fright, and dogs as well. The dog returns by the same route, returns to the Escadinhas de São Crispim, waiting for someone else to turn up.

The proof-reader is taking another look, he enters by the Arco Escuro in order to examine the stairway which the historian claims was one of the points of access to the battlements of the stockade, or rather, this stairway, the steps of which have only been in existence for three generations, is located where the original one stood. Raimundo Silva carefully examines the dark windows, the grimy façades eroded by saltpetre, the tiled insets, this one dated one thousand seven hundred and sixty-four, with St Anne teaching her daughter Mary how to write, and medallions on either side depicting St Martial, who wards off fire, and St Antony who restores earthenware jugs and is something of a wizard when it comes to finding lost objects. The inscription, in the absence of any authentic certificate, is the next best thing, if the date it carries, which we have no reason to doubt, is that of the year when the edifice was built, nine years after the earthquake. The proof-reader studies the information he has gathered and finds it has been much enriched, so when he returns to the Rua dos Bacalhoeiros, he will look with disdain upon those ignorant passers-by, who show no interest in the curiosities of the city and life, and who are quite incapable of making any connection between these two explicit dates. But shortly, when he arrives before the Arco das Portas do Mar, thinking to himself that the name deserved some other architectural commemoration, and not the prosaic name-plate of customs officials, reflecting at that moment on the discrepancy between the word and its meaning, he observed himself and disapproved of what he saw, After all, what right do I have to pass judgment on others, I have lived in Lisbon all my life and it has never occurred to me to come and see with my own eyes things described in books, things that I have often looked at time and time again, without actually seeing them, as blind as the muezzin, and were it not for this threat from Costa, I should probably never have thought of checking the lay-out of the wall, the gates, which I now recognise as belonging to the fortress of Dom Fernando, obviously by the time I have finished my stroll I shall know more, but it is also true that I'll know less, in other words, let's see if I can explain myself, this awareness of knowing more, brings me to an awareness of knowing little, besides, one is tempted to ask what it means to know, the historian was right, I ought to have been a philosopher, one of those admirable philosophers who can pick up a skull and spend the rest of their lives probing its importance in this world and wondering if there is any good reason why the world should concern itself with a skull, and now we come, ladies and gentlemen, tourists, travellers, or those of you who are merely curious, says the indispensable guide, to the Arco da Conceição, where once stood the celebrated fountain known as the Preguiça, whose refreshing waters have abated the thirst and any desire to work of so many people right up to the present day.

Raimundo Silva is not in a hurry. He studies the itinerary seriously, for his own satisfaction he makes detailed mental notes, complementary as it were, which attest to his own contemporaneity, there in the Calçada do Correio Velho a gloomy undertaker's office, white spume in the blue sky coming from a jet plane, like the extended backwash of a speed-boat on the blue sea, the Pensão Casa Oliveira Bons Quartos in the Rua da Padaria, the Restaurante Come Petisca Paga Vai Dar Meia Volta, right beside the Portas do Mar, the Cervejaria Arco da Conceição, nearby, the coat of arms of the Mascarenhas engraved on a cornerstone of one of the buildings of the Arco de Jesus, where there must have been a gate in the Moorish ramparts, as attested by the inscription on the wall, the Neoclassical entrance to the Palace of the Condes de Coculim, who were Mascarenhas, arsenals of weaponry, so much for all their achievements, a world of fleeting, transitory things, as all things without exception inevitably prove to be, for the white trail of the plane has evaporated and time will take care of the rest in due course, we need only have the patience to wait. The proof-reader entered the Alfama by the Arco do Chafariz d'El-Rei, he will lunch somewhere nearby, in an eating-house in the Rua de São João da Praça, over by the tower of St Peter, a traditional Portuguese meal of fried fish and rice with tomato sauce and salad, and with any luck, the tender leaves of a lettuce heart, where, something not many people know, nestles the incomparable freshness of the morning, the dew and mist, which are one and the same, but warrant repetition for the simple pleasure of writing both words and savouring the sound. At the entrance to the restaurant stood a gypsy girl, probably about twelve, with outstretched hand and saying never a word, simply staring at the proof-reader, who, lost in thought, did not recognise a gypsy but only a Moorish girl, when hunger was first making itself felt and when there was still someone to ask for alms, and cats and vermin felt their existence was assured until they died a natural death from disease or warfare amongst the species, after all, progress is a reality, nowadays no one in Lisbon hunts such animals for food, But the expression in the gypsy girl's eyes warns him that the siege is not yet over.

Raimundo Silva will peruse more slowly whatever remains to be inspected, another section of the wall in the Pátio do Senhor da Murça, the Rua da Adiça, where the wall rose up, and that of Norberto de Araújo, as the street was recently baptised, at the summit an imposing stretch of wall, eroded at the base, these are truly living stones, they have been here for nine or ten centuries, if not longer, from the time of the barbarians, and they survive, they intrepidly support the bell-tower of the church of St Lucy or St Brás, it makes no difference, at this spot, ladies and gentlemen, opened the ancient Portas do Sol, facing eastward, the first to receive the rosy breath of dawn, now all that remains is the square which took its name from this landmark, but the special effects of the aurora have not changed, for the sun, a millennium is like a tiny human sigh, sic transit, needless to say. The wall continued along these parts, at an obtuse angle, wide open, and continued right up to the walls of the fortress, thus enclosing the entire city, from the edge of the waters below to the point where it joins the fortress, head erect and strong joints, arms bent and fingers firmly clasped, like a woman supporting her pregnant womb. Feeling weary, the proof-reader goes up the Rua dos Cegos, enters the Pátio de Dom Fradique, time divides into two strands rather than disturb this village made of rock, it has been like this, in a manner of speaking, since the time of the Goths, Romans, or Phoenicians, then came the Moors, the first Portuguese, their children and their grandchildren, from whom we are descended, the power and the glory, the subsequent phases of decline, first, second and third, each of them divided into genera and subgenera. At night, in this space between the low-lying houses, the three ghosts gather, the ghost of the past, the ghost of the future and the ghost of things that might happen, they do not speak, they look at each other as if they were blind, and remain silent.

Raimundo Silva sits on a stone bench in the cool evening shade, he examines the pages for the last time and confirms that there is nothing more to see, he knows enough about the castle not to have to return there today, even if he is making a full inventory. The sky is beginning to turn white, perhaps a warning of that mist promised by the meteorological office, and the temperature drops rapidly. The proof-reader leaves the patio and heads for the Rua do Chão da Feira, in front of the Porta de São Jorge, even from here people can still be seen taking photographs of the saint. Less than fifty metres away, although invisible from here, is his house, and as this thought crosses his mind, he realises for the first time that he lives at the very spot where the Porta de Alfofa stood, whether on the inside or outside it is no longer possible to tell, so we cannot be sure whether Raimundo Silva is one of the besieged or an assailant, a future conqueror or hopeless loser.

There was no irate message from Costa awaiting him under the door. Darkness fell and the telephone did not ring. Raimundo Silva spent a peaceful evening searching his shelves for books that might tell him more about the city the Moors named Lissibona. It was late when he went out on to the verandah to check the weather. Mist, but not as dense as that of yesterday. He could hear two dogs barking, and for some reason, this made him feel even more tranquil. Dogs had been barking for centuries, therefore, the world was unchanged. He went to bed. Tired out from his exertions that day, he slept soundly, but he woke up several times, whenever he dreamt and went back to dreaming about a rampart with nothing inside, like a sack with a tight opening spreading its belly to the edge of the river, and all around, forested slopes, woods and valleys, streams, a scattering of houses, orchards, olive-groves, a broad estuary advancing inland. In the distance, the clear outline of the towers of Amoreiras.

IT TOOK THIRTEEN long and seemingly endless days before the publishers or someone acting on their behalf discovered the crime, and Raimundo Silva lived this eternity as if he had some slow-acting poison in his body, but ultimately as decisive as the most lethal toxicant, the perfect simile of death that each one of us goes through life preparing for and for which life itself serves as a protective cocoon, a propitious womb and ferment for cultivation. He made four visits to the publishers for no good reason, since his work, as we know, is freelance and can be done from home, exempt from the drudgeries that saddle ordinary employees, subjected to the chores of administration, editing, production, distribution and storage, a world under constant scrutiny and, by comparison, the task of proof-reader belongs to the realms of liberty. They asked him what he wanted, and he replied, Nothing, I just happened to be passing nearby and thought I'd call in. He lingered awhile, listening to conversations and studying the expression on people's faces, trying to pick up any thread of suspicion, a sly, provocative smile, a phrase wherein he could detect some hidden meaning. He avoided Costa, not because he had anything to fear, but simply because he had deceived him, Costa thus becoming that personification of outraged innocence we are incapable of confronting, because we have wronged someone and they still have not found out. We are tempted to say that Raimundo Silva goes to the publishers like the criminal returning to the scene of the crime, but that would not be entirely true, Raimundo Silva is certainly attracted to the place where his crime will be discovered and where the judges will convene to pass the sentence that will condemn him, prevaricator, exposed, false and defenceless.

The proof-reader is in no doubt that he is about to make a foolish mistake, that these visits will be remembered, when the time comes, as particularly odious expressions of a perverse malevolence, You knew the damage you had done, yet notwithstanding, you didn't have the guts, they would actually use the word guts, the frankness, the honesty, to own up of your own free will, they would use the words free will, you waited for events to take their course, perversely amusing yourself, yes perversely amusing yourself at our expense, and the banality of these final words will clash with the high moral tone of his severe reproof. It would be useless trying to tell them that they are mistaken, that Raimundo Silva was only looking for some peace of mind and reassurance. They still have not found him out, he sighs with relief each time he goes there, but any reassurance and peace of mind were of short duration, no sooner did he enter his apartment than he felt more beleaguered than Lisbon had ever been.

Not being superstitious, he was not expecting anything disagreeable to happen to him on the thirteenth. Only those obsessed with oracles are plagued by mishap and misfortune on the thirteenth day of the month, I have never allowed myself to be influenced by these absurd superstitions, and this would probably have been his answer if anyone had raised this hypothesis. This radical scepticism explains why his initial reaction was one of vexed surprise when he heard the voice of the director's secretary on the line, Senhor Silva, you are requested to attend a meeting at four o'clock this afternoon, she spoke the words in this curt manner as if she were reading from a written memo, carefully drafted to make sure that all the essential words were in place and any word eliminated that might diminish the effect of mental torment and confusion, now that surprise and annoyance no longer have any meaning when confronted with the evidence that the thirteenth of the month does not spare the strong-minded, while dominating the feeble. He slowly replaced the receiver and looked around him, with the distinct impression that he could see the apartment sway, Steady on, he said. At such moments, the stoic would smile, had this classical species not died out completely to give way to the evolution of the modern cynic, who, in his turn, bears scarcely any resemblance to his philosophical and pedestrian ancestor. Be that as it may, there is a wan smile on Raimundo Silva's face, his look of resigned martyrdom is tempered by a manly sorrow, this is what you mainly find in novels dominated by characters, by taking another look you learn so much.

The proof-reader asks himself whether he is troubled or not, and cannot come up with an answer. What he does find intolerable is to be obliged to wait until four o'clock in order to know what the editors have in mind for this irresponsible proof-reader, how they will punish his insolent disregard for sound historical facts which ought to be permanently reinforced and defended from any meddling, otherwise we shall lose any sense of our actuality and seriously undermine the concepts and beliefs derived therefrom, on which we rely for guidance. Now that the error has been discovered, it is pointless to speculate on the future consequences of the presence of that *Not* in *The History of the Siege of Lisbon*, whether fate had permitted a slower incubation, page against page, unobserved by the readers but invisibly burrowing a path like woodworms who leave a hollow shell where we expected to find a solid piece of furniture. He pushed the proofs he was revising to one side, not those of the novel Costa had left him on that famous day, this is a slim little volume of poems, and, resting his weary head in his hands, he remembered a story whose title and author escaped him, although he had an idea it was something like *Tarzan and the Lost Kingdom*, and where there was a city with ancient Romans and the first Christians, all hidden away in the African jungle, truly, the imagination of novelists has no limits, and this one, if all the rest tallies, can only be Edgar Rice Burroughs. There was an amphitheatre and the Christians were thrown to wild beasts, that is to say, to the lions, all the more feasible since Africa is where lions belong, and the novelist wrote, although without providing any proof or citing his sources, that the more nervous of those unfortunate creatures did not wait for the lions to attack, but actually ran, in a manner of speaking, into the arms of death, not in order to be the first to enter paradise, but simply because they did not have the strength of mind to bear this waiting for the inevitable. These reminiscences of books he had read in his youth made Raimundo Silva think, along the familiar paths pursued by one's thoughts, that it was within his power to precipitate the course of history, to accelerate time, to go immediately to the publisher, on some pretext or other, such as, At four o'clock I have a medical appointment, so don't beat about the bush and tell me what you want, this is the tone he would adopt in speaking to Costa, but needless to say, he did not go to any meeting with Production as the director's secretary called it, his case would be dealt with at the highest level and, ironically, this certainty pandered to his vanity, I must be mad, he muttered, repeating the same words he had spoken three days ago. If only I could find, amidst this confusion, some feeling that might prevail over all others, so that if he were subsequently asked, How did you feel in that terrible situation, he would reply, I felt worried, or indifferent, or amused, or troubled, or fearful, or ashamed, frankly, he does not know what he feels, he only wishes it were already four o'clock and time for that fatal encounter with the lion awaiting him with gaping jaws while the Romans applaud, the minutes are like this, although they usually step back in order to let us pass after brushing against our skin, but there will always be one ready to devour us. All metaphors about time and fate are tragic and at the same time futile, mused Raimundo Silva, perhaps not in these precise words, but since what really counts is the meaning, this is how he jotted it down, pleased to have thought of it. Yet he scarcely felt like eating any lunch, he had a lump in his throat, a familiar sensation, and a knot in his stomach, which is most uncommon, but conveys the seriousness of the situation. The charlady, this being her day, thought he looked odd and asked him straight out, Are you unwell, words which unexpectedly had a stimulating effect, for if his behaviour were giving strangers the impression that he was sick, then it was time to get a grip on himself, to overcome this malaise that was destroying him, so he replied, I feel fine, and at that moment it was true.

It was five to four when he walked into the publishers. This time he found all the things he had been looking for last time, whispering, furtive glances, sniggering, and also, on several faces, simply the puzzled expression of someone who is not entirely satisfied with the evidence, although forced to accept it. They showed him into the waiting-room outside the director's office and left him sitting there for more than a quarter of an hour, which goes to show the futility of fears which are in no sense punctual. He looked at his watch, the lion had obviously been delayed, nowadays it is extremely difficult to drive in the jungle even with Roman roads, but in this case, it is much more likely that someone may have thought it a good idea to have recourse to proven psychological tactics, to make him wait until his nerves became frayed, to push him to the edge of crisis, and leave him defenceless against the very first attack. Raimundo Silva considers that even so, taking into account the circumstances, he is reasonably calm, as if he had spent his entire life doing nothing except replacing true facts with lies, without really noticing the difference and learning to choose between the arguments for and against, accumulated throughout the ages by the endless discourse and sophistry that have flourished in the mind of homo sapiens. All of a sudden, the door was flung open and there stood, not the director's secretary as one might have expected, but the secretary of the Editorial Director. Please to accompany me, she said, and Raimundo Silva, despite having noticed the faulty syntax, perceived that his imagined calm was merely superficial, and tenuous, his knees were shaking as he rose from the sofa, the adrenalin stirring in his blood, the sweat oozing from the palms of his hands and from his armpits, and he could even feel a diffused colic, a sign that his entire digestive system was trying to expand, I am like a calf being led to the slaughterhouse, he thought to himself, and fortunately he was capable of self-disparagement.

The secretary allowed him to pass, Do go in, and closed the door. Raimundo Silva said, Good afternoon, two of those present replied, Good afternoon, the third, the Editorial Director, simply said, Take a seat, Senhor Silva. The lion is also seated and watching, we may assume the beast is licking its chops with bared fangs as it weighs up the texture and flavour of the pale Christian's flesh. Raimundo Silva crosses his leg, then uncrosses it at once, and at that moment realises he does not know one person who is there, a woman seated on the left of the Editorial Director. He recognises the Production Manager on his right, but he cannot recall ever having seen this woman before, Who can she be. He tries to get a better look, but the Editorial Director has started to speak, I imagine you know why we have sent for you, I have a fair idea, The Managing Director was anxious to deal with this matter personally but a matter of some urgency turned up at the last minute, obliging him to absent himself. The Editorial Director fell silent, as if wanting to give Raimundo Silva time to lament his misfortune, to have lost the opportunity of being interrogated by the Managing Director in person, but, confronted by the proof-reader's silence, he allowed a note of repressed annoyance to creep into his voice for the first time, although softened by a tone of voice that almost sounded conciliatory, I'm grateful to you, he went on, for having implicitly admitted that you were responsible, sparing us a disagreeable situation, should you have denied or tried to justify your action. Raimundo Silva thought they must now be waiting for him to say something more than simply, I have a fair idea, but before he could speak the Production Manager intervened, I still can't believe it, Senhor Silva, you have worked for so many years for this publishing house, and for an experienced professional like you to make such an error. It wasn't an error, interrupted the Editorial Director, it is useless extending a merciful hand to Senhor Silva, for we know as well as he does that the error was quite intentional, is that not so, Senhor Silva, What makes you think, Sir, that it was quite intentional, I trust you are not about to go back on what you intended to say when you came into this room, I'm not going back on anything, simply asking a question. The Editorial Director's annoyance became obvious, all the more so because of the irony in those words, I presume you are aware that the right to ask for an explanation and demand an apology, not to mention other measures we mean to take, is ours rather than yours, especially mine, as the Managing Director's representative, Quite right, Sir, I withdraw my question, No need to withdraw your question, we're convinced that the error was intentional because of the manner in which you wrote *Not* on the proof, in bold, neat lettering, unlike your usual handwriting which is brisk and fluent although perfectly legible. At this point, the Editorial Director suddenly fell silent, as if conscious that he was talking too much and, therefore, weakening his position as arbiter. There was silence and Raimundo Silva had the impression that the woman had not taken her eyes off him during all this time, Who can she be, but she said nothing as if this matter had nothing to do with her. For his part, the Production Manager, piqued at having been interrupted, appeared to have lost all interest in a discussion which, to all appearances, was getting nowhere. This idiot cannot see that this is no way to deal with such a case, he never stops talking, likes the sound of his own voice, and gives all the trump cards to Silva, who must be laughing up his sleeve, you only have to see how he handles the sudden silence, he should have been terrified and there he sits, calm personified. The Production Manager was wrong about Raimundo Silva being calm, if not about the rest, for the fact is that we do not know enough about the Editorial Director to form our own considered opinion. Raimundo Silva is not the least bit calm, he only looks calm, thanks to the disorientation provoked by the unexpected course of this dialogue which he had imagined would be literally catastrophic, the solemn formal accusation, his stuttering attempts to defend the indefensible, the vexation, heavy irony, the diatribe, threats, perhaps dismissal to cap all this or render it unnecessary, You're fired, and don't expect any references from us. Now Raimundo Silva perceives that he must say something, especially since the lion is not directly confronting him, he has moved up on one side and is absorbed in scratching his mane with a broken nail, perhaps no Christian will perish after all in this amphitheatre, even if there is no sign of Tarzan. He says, first addressing the Production Manager, then furtively eyeing the woman who remains silent, I've made no attempt to deny that the word was written by me nor did I ever mean to deny it once it came to light, but the important thing is not to have written it, the important thing, in my opinion, is to discover why I wrote it, I hope you're not going to tell me that you don't know, the Editorial Director said sarcastically, regaining control of the situation, It's true, Sir, I don't, That's a good one, this fellow commits a deliberate fraud, causes grave moral and material damage to the publishing house and the author, has not yet uttered a word of apology, and with the most innocent air imaginable, wants us to believe that some mysterious force, a spirit from beyond guided his hand while he was in a hypnotic trance. The Editorial Director smiled, rejoicing in his own eloquence, but trying to transform his smile into an expression of irrefutable irony. I don't believe I was in a trance, replied Raimundo Silva, I can clearly recall the circumstances in which everything happened, but this doesn't mean that I can explain how I came to make this deliberate mistake, Ah, so you confess it was deliberate, Naturally, Now you only have to admit that it was not a mistake, but blatant deception, and that you consciously hoped to prejudice the publishing house and ridicule the author of the book, I admit to deception, as for the rest, nothing could have been further from my mind, Perhaps a moment of agitation, suggested the Production Manager, as if trying to be helpful. Raimundo Silva expected a predictably brusque reaction from the Editorial Director, but it did not come, and then he realised the phrase had been foreseen, there would be no dismissal, everything would end up in words, yes, no, perhaps, and the sense of relief was so overwhelming, that he could feel his body weaken, his spirit unburden, now it was up to him to say the right words, such as, Yes, a moment of agitation, but we cannot forget that several hours elapsed before the proofs were delivered to Costa, and Raimundo Silva congratulated himself on the subtle manner in which he had slipped in that *cannot*, putting himself on the side of the judges, as if he were saying to them, Don't let us deceive ourselves. The Editorial Director said, Good, the book will be distributed bearing an errata, a somewhat absurd errata cautioning, Where there is a *Not* in the text it should be negated, where the text says the crusaders *did not* help, it should read, the crusaders *did* help, readers will be amused at our expense, but fortunately for us, we spotted the error in time, and the author has been most understanding, I even got the impression that he genuinely respects you, he spoke of a conversation you both had some time ago, Yes, we did have a conversation, it was about *deleatur*, About what, the woman asked, About *deleatur*, don't you know what it means, asked Raimundo Silva aggressively, Of course, but I didn't hear you the first time. The woman's intervention, which appeared to take everyone by surprise, seemed to warrant some deviation in their discussion, This lady, the Editorial Director informed him, from now onwards will be in charge of all the proof-readers employed by our publishing house, whether it is a question of deadlines and the rhythm of the work or the final checking of proofs to ensure accuracy, she will have full responsibility, but let us return to the matter in hand, the publishers have decided to treat this disagreeable episode as closed, and taking into account the good work and loyal service Senhor Silva has rendered during all these years, we are prepared to treat this lapse as the result of over-work, of mental fatigue, in a word, we shall treat the matter as settled, in the hope that it never happens again, however Senhor Silva must write a letter of apology to the publishers and another to the author, the latter has said it is not necessary, that one day, he himself will have a word with you about this matter, but we feel it is your duty, Senhor Silva, to write this letter, Of course, I shall write to him, Very well, the Editorial Director was obviously relieved, needless to say, for some time to come, your work will receive our special attention, not because we think you will deliberately set about altering texts, but to guard against the eventuality of any such sudden impulses ever recurring, and I don't have to tell you that we shall be less tolerant next time. The Editorial Director said no more, waiting for the proof-reader to make some declaration about his future intentions, at least those of which he was conscious, since any others, if they existed, were unconscious and, therefore, impenetrable. Raimundo Silva perceived what was expected of him, there is no denying that words demand words, which is why people say, One word leads to another, but it is no less true that, It takes two to pick a quarrel, let us imagine that the Pilgrim refused to satisfy the fatal curiosity of Esquire Telmo, most likely the matter would have been resolved and there would have been no conflict, drama, death, and widespread calamity, or let us suppose that a man has asked a woman, Do you love me, and she remains silent, simply looking at him, sphinx-like and distant, refusing to utter that No that will destroy him, or that Yes which will destroy both of them, then we must conclude that the world would be a better place if everyone were content with what they say, without expecting any reply and, moreover, neither demanding or desiring one. But Raimundo Silva feels obliged to say, I can understand that the publishing house should want to take precautions, who am I to criticise their decisions, in short, I wish to apologise and hereby promise that so long as I am in my right mind, it will never happen again, at this point he paused as if asking himself whether he should continue, but then he thought everything had been said, and shut up. The Editorial Director said, Good, and prepared himself to add the expected words, The matter is closed, now back to work, getting to his feet as he spoke and smiling as he offered his open hand to Raimundo Silva as a token of peace, but the woman seated on his left interrupted this magnanimous gesture, If you'll allow me, what surprises me is that Senhor Silva, that is his name, I believe, has not made the slightest attempt to explain why he behaved so irresponsibly, changing the meaning of a sentence, when as proof-reader it was his solemn duty to respect and safeguard the original text, which is why proof-readers exist. The lion suddenly reappeared, roaring, baring its terrifying fangs, its sharpened claws, now our only hope, abandoned in this arena, is that Tarzan will turn up at last, swinging from a liana and shouting, Ah-ah-ah-oe-oe, if my memory serves me well, and he might even bring elephants to assist him, since they have such a wonderful memory. Confronted with this unexpected attack, both the Editorial Director and Production Manager started frowning again, perhaps to avoid being accused of weakness by a fragile woman conscious of the professional obligations with which she had only recently been invested, and they stared at the proof-reader with fitting severity. They had failed to notice that there was nothing severe about the woman's expression, nothing but a playful smile, as if, at heart, she were enjoying the situation. Disconcerted, Raimundo Silva looked at her, she is still young, not quite forty, obviously tall, she has a pale complexion, brown hair, if the proof-reader were closer he might detect a few white hairs, and her mouth is nicely shaped and fleshy, but the lips are not thick, a strange encounter, and a hint of disquiet stirs inside Raimundo Silva, perturbation would be a better word, now we must choose the right adjective to accompany it, such as sexual, but we shall resist the temptation. Raimundo Silva cannot dally much longer before replying, although it is common in situations of this kind to say that time is at a standstill, something time has never been since the world began. The smile is still on the woman's face, but the brusqueness and hostility of her words cannot be ignored, not even the directors were so blunt, Raimundo Silva hesitates between responding with the same aggression or using the conciliatory tone his dependence on this woman would appear to warrant, it goes without saying that she has the means to give him a hard time in future on the merest pretext, so, having pondered as carefully as the little time at his disposal allowed, as well as taking into account the time lost in physiognomic observations, he finally replied, No one would be happier than I to find a satisfactory explanation, but, if I haven't found one after all this time, I doubt if I ever will, what I believe is that there must have been some inner struggle between my good side, if I really have one, and my bad side, which is common to all of us, a tussle between a Dr Jekyll and a Mr Hyde, if you will pardon this literary reference, or, to put it in my own words, between the inconstant temptation of evil and the spirit that upholds good, sometimes I ask myself what mistakes Fernando Pessoa must have made, whether of revision or otherwise, with that confusion of heteronyms, a hellish battle, I should imagine. The woman never stopped smiling as he delivered this speech, and she was still smiling when she asked him, Apart from Jekyll and Hyde, are you someone else, So far I have managed to be Raimundo Silva, Splendid, now let's see if you can stay that way, for the sake of the publishing house and harmony in our future relationship. Professional, I trust you're not suggesting it could be otherwise, I was simply finishing off your phrase, the proofreader's job is to propose solutions that will eliminate any ambiguity, either in matters of style or meaning, I presume you know that ambiguity is in the mind of the person listening or reading, Especially if the stimulus came to them from the person writing or speaking, Or he or she is one of those people who go in for auto-stimulation, I don't think so in my case, You don't think so, I rarely make peremptory statements, It was peremptory to write that *Not* of yours in *The History of the Siege of Lisbon*, and if you cannot justify the deception, at least explain it, because there can be no justification, Excuse me, we've been through all this before, Thanks for telling me, you've spared me the trouble of having to repeat what I think of your behaviour. Raimundo Silva opened his mouth to reply, but suddenly noticed the look of amazement on the faces of the directors and decided to hold his peace. Silence fell, the woman continued to smile, but perhaps because she had been smiling all this time, her facial muscles appeared to be twitching, and Raimundo Silva felt as if he were suffocating, the atmosphere in the office seemed to weigh on his shoulders, I detest this female, he thought, and deliberately eyed the directors as if making it clear that from now on he will only accept and consent to answer their questions. He knew that on this side the game had been won, the directors, both of them, were now getting to their feet and one of them repeated, We consider the matter closed, now back to work, but he did not extend his hand to Raimundo Silva, this dubious peace called for no celebration, when the proof-reader left the room, the Editorial Director commented to the Production Manager, Perhaps we should have dismissed him, it would have been simpler, and it was the woman who pointed out, We should have lost a good proof-reader, He's going to give us further trouble, judging from what we've just heard, Perhaps not.

On the way out, Raimundo Silva bumped into Costa who was coming from the printers. He curtly wished him good afternoon and was about to walk on, but Costa took him by the arm, gently, barely touching the sleeve of his raincoat, the expression in Costa's eyes was serious, almost pitiful, and his words accusing, Why have you done this to me, Senhor Silva, he asked, and Raimundo Silva, at a loss for an answer, simply shook his head childishly, But I haven't done anything to you. Costa shook his head, removed his hand, and set off down the corridor, he could not believe that this fellow did not realise he had offended him personally, and that this matter was really between the two of them, Costa and Raimundo Silva, the deceiver and the deceived, for them there could be no saving errata in extremis. On reaching the end of the corridor, Costa turned back and asked, Have they dismissed you, No, they have not dismissed me, Just as well, if they had given you the sack I should be even more put out, when all is said and done, Costa is a decent fellow, restrained in his use of language, he did not say sad or embittered, so as not to sound solemn, he said put out which is a common expression according to the dictionaries, yet incomparable, however much the purists may deny it. Costa is definitely put out, no other phrase could better express his state of mind, nor that of Raimundo Silva who, having asked himself for the umpteenth time, How do I feel, was able to give the same definite answer, I'm put out.

When he arrived home the charlady had already gone, leaving him a message, always the same message if he happened to be out, Everything is back in order, I've taken the washing with me to finish off the ironing, this show of zeal meant that she had taken advantage of his absence in order to leave earlier, but she would never admit to it, and Raimundo Silva, who was in no doubt about the hours she worked, accepted her explanation and said nothing. Certain harmonious relationships are created and endure, thanks to a complex system of little fibs and denials, a duet, as it were, danced with knowing gestures and posturings, which can be summed up in that proverb or maxim, to be more precise, that we can never hear too often, You know what I know, but let's keep it to ourselves. Not that there are any secrets, mysteries, skeletons in locked cupboards that need to be revealed when one speaks of the relationship between servant and master in this house where Raimundo Silva lives and where a woman is occasionally present, but only to do the chores, a woman whose full name he is never likely to need to know. But it is extremely interesting to see how the life of these two human beings is at once opaque and transparent, for Raimundo Silva there is no one closer, yet he has never shown any interest in knowing what existence this woman leads when she is not working, and as for her name, he only has to say, Senhora Maria, and she appears in the doorway to inquire, Senhor Raimundo, did you want something, Senhora Maria is short, thin, dark enough to be taken for a half-caste, and she has naturally curly hair of which she is immensely proud, just as well, for she is no beauty. When she says or writes, Everything is back in order, she is obviously abusing these words, for her idea of putting things in order consists of applying the golden rule whereby things only have to look neat and tidy, or, to put it in other words, no one should notice what has been overlooked or not been cleaned. The obvious exception is Raimundo Silva's study where untidiness seems to be in keeping with his work, that is how he sees it, unlike those proof-readers who are obsessed with tidiness, precision, geometrical harmony, and would give Senhora Maria a hard time, by pointing out, This paper is not where I left it, the papers in Raimundo Silva's office are always where he left them, for the simple reason that Senhora Maria is not allowed to touch them, and therefore can always protest, It's not my fault, whenever Raimundo Silva mislays books or proofs.

He crumpled the paper, disregarding the message, and threw it into the wastepaper basket. Only then did he remove his coat and change into a flannel shirt, trousers he wore indoors, a knitted waistcoat, not only because of the chilly weather, but because he feels the cold and is rarely warm enough, so much so that he has slipped a tartan dressing-gown over his clothes, bulky, but it could not be more comfortable, besides he is not expecting any visitors. Throughout the journey from the publishing house back to his apartment he had managed not to think, some find this impossible, but Raimundo Silva has mastered the art of floating vague ideas, like clouds that stay apart, and he even knows how to blow away any idea that gets too close, the important thing is that they should not come into contact thus creating a continuum or, something worse, if there is electricity in the mental atmosphere, with the inevitable storm bringing thunder and lightning. For a few moments he had allowed his thoughts to dwell on Senhora Maria, but now his brain was vacant once more. To make sure it stayed that way, he went through to the sitting-room where he kept the television and switched on the set. In there it was even colder. Thanks to a clear sky, the sun was still shining over the city, already from the direction of the sea, as it went down, casting a gentle light, bestowing a luminous caress to which the window-panes on the hillside would soon respond, first with flaring torches, then turning pale, dwindling to a tiny fragment of flickering glass, until finally extinguished as twilight gradually begins to sift its ashes between the buildings, concealing the gables, as the noise of the city down below dies away and withdraws beneath the silence spreading from these streets to on high where Raimundo Silva lives. The television has no sound, that is to say, Raimundo Silva has turned it off, there are only luminous images that move, not only on the screen, but also over the furniture, the walls, and over Raimundo Silva's face which looks without seeing or thinking. For almost an hour he has been watching video-clips of Totally Live, singers, for want of a better word, and the dancers wriggle their bodies, the former express every conceivable human feeling and sensation, some of them dubious, their faces speak for themselves, their words cannot be heard but that does not matter, it is incredible how a face can have so much mobility, twitching, leering, grimacing, scowling menacingly, an androgynous creature, false and obscene, mature women with a lion's mane, alluring girls with shapely hips, thighs and bosoms, others as slender as a reed and fiendishly erotic, mature gentlemen showing interesting wrinkles to add an air of distinction, all of this created by flickering light, all smothered in silence, as if Raimundo Silva had grabbed those throats, asphyxiating them behind a curtain of water, no less silent, the universal triumph of deafness. Now a man appears on his own, he must be singing although his lips scarcely move, the caption gave the name Leonard Cohen, and the image looks fixedly at Raimundo Silva, the movements of his mouth articulate a question, Why won't you listen to me, lonely man, no doubt adding, Listen to me while you can, before it's too late, one video-clip follows another, and they are never repeated, this isn't a disk you can play over and over again, I might be back but I can't say when, and you might miss me, so take your chance, take your chance, take your chance. Raimundo Silva bent over, turned on the sound, Leonard Cohen made a gesture as if to thank him, now he could sing, and sing he did, he sang of things only someone who has lived can sing of, and asks himself how much and for what, someone who has loved and asks himself who and why, and, having asked all these questions, he can find no answer, not one, contrary to the belief that all the answers are there and that all we have to do is to learn how to phrase our questions. When Cohen finished singing, Raimundo Silva turned the sound off again and then switched off the set. The sitting-room, located in the middle of the apartment, was suddenly plunged into darkest night, and the proof-reader can raise his hands to his eyes without anyone seeing him.

Anyone concerned with logic must now be asking himself how it is conceivable that during all this time Raimundo Silva has not given another thought to the humiliating scene in the director's office, or, if he did, why has it never been mentioned for the sake of giving some coherence to a character and verisimilitude to events. Now then, the fact is that Raimundo Silva did think, several times, about the disagreeable episode, but thinking can mean different things according to the circumstances, and the most he permitted himself was to remember, as we earlier explained using other words, when we referred to clouds in the sky and electricity in the atmosphere, the former unattached and the latter of minimum voltage. The difference is between an active thinking which goes burrowing around some fact, and this other form of thinking, if worthy of the name, which is inert and detached, when it looks it does not linger but passes on, convinced that what has not been mentioned does not exist, like the sick man who considers himself healthy because the nature of his illness has not yet been diagnosed. But anyone who imagines that these defensive systems last forever is much mistaken, there comes a moment in which the vagueness of one's thinking becomes an obsession, as a rule it only has to go on hurting a little more. This is what happened to Raimundo Silva as he was washing up the few dishes he had used during supper, it suddenly dawned on him that the publishers had not taken thirteen days to spot the deception, which not only absolved that old superstition but imposed the need for some new superstition, charging yet another day, hitherto innocent, with negative energy. When he was summoned to appear before the directors everything had already been exposed and discussed, What are we going to do with this rascal, asked the Managing Director and the Editorial Director telephoned the author to tell him about this ridiculous incident with profuse apologies, The fact is that you cannot trust anyone, whereupon the author replied, incredible as it may seem, It's not the end of the world, an erratum will solve the problem, and he laughed, What could this man be remembering, and Costa had an idea, There ought to be someone in charge of the proof-readers, Costa knows what is wrong, and the suggestion seemed such a good one that the Production Manager, as if he himself had thought of it, raised the matter with senior management who were so enthusiastic that before the thirteenth, the right person had been interviewed, appointed and installed, to the extent of being allowed to participate *ex officio* in the summary hearing that would consider this blatant misdemeanour, proven and finally confessed, although as confessions go there were far too many silences and mental reservations on the part of the culprit, an attitude which ended up irritating the new employee, the only possible explanation for her angry outburst as she launched one final attack, But I answered her question, muttered Raimundo Silva as he dried his hands and unrolled his sleeves once he had finished the washing up.

Now seated at his desk with the proofs of the volume of poems in front of him, he pursues the thought, although it might be more precise to say that he anticipates it, because, knowing as we do that thoughts are fleeting, if we content ourselves with pursuing some thought, we shall soon lose the trail, we shall still be inventing the flying machine only to find it has already reached the stars. Turning the thought over in his mind, Raimundo Silva tries to understand why from her very first words he could not repress his hostility, Don't you know the meaning of *deleatur*, and he is irked most of all by the memory of that tone of voice with which he threw the question, provocative, even rude, and then the final duel between sworn enemies as if there were some personal matter to settle, a long-standing grudge, when we know that these two have never met before, and if they did, they never noticed each other, Who can she be, Raimundo Silva wondered, and as the thought crossed his mind, he inadvertently slackened the rein with which he had been guiding the thought, enough for him to be able to pass in front and start thinking for himself, she is still a young woman, not quite forty, not as tall as he first imagined, pale complexion, brown hair worn loose, eyes the same colour, almost as dark, and a tiny, round mouth, tiny and round, tiny, round, round. Raimundo Silva stares at the bookcase in front of him, gathered there are all the books he has proof-read throughout his working life, he has not counted them but they constitute a library, titles, names, this one a novel, this a book of poems, this one a play, this one about the opportunism of politics, biographies, memoirs, titles, names, names, titles, some of them famous even today, others who enjoyed their hour of glory and then the clock came to a standstill, some still held in suspense by destiny, But the destiny we have is the destiny we are, murmured the proof-reader, replying to his previous thought, We are the destiny we have. Suddenly he felt hot even though the electric heater was off, he untied the cord of his dressing-gown, got up from his chair, these movements appeared to have some objective and yet, there can be no other explanation, they were merely the expression of an unexpected sense of wellbeing, an almost farcical vigour, a divine tranquillity without remorse. The apartment suddenly became small, even the window open to those three vast entities, the city, the river, and the sky, now looked like a blind peep-hole, and it is true that there was no mist and the night chill brought a reinvigorating freshness. It was not at that moment, but before then, that Raimundo Silva thought to himself, I wonder what she's called, it sometimes happens, we have a thought but do not wish to acknowledge or trust it, we isolate it along with lateral thoughts such as this latest one of having finally remembered that the woman's name was not mentioned even once, This colleague, the Editorial Director declared, will be in charge from now on, and, either because of an improbable lack of manners, or because of his own and everyone else's nervous state, never got round to introducing her, Senhor Raimundo Silva, Senhora So-and-So. These reflections had prevented Raimundo Silva from asking outright, What is her name, and now that he has asked he is unable to think of anything else, as if, after all these hours, he had finally arrived at his destiny, a word used here with its common meaning, in terms of a journey, without any ontological or existential derivations, simply that well-known expression of travellers, I've arrived, thinking they know what awaits them.

An explanation for Raimundo Silva's action is no longer expected or required. He went back into his study, opened José Pedro Machado's *Vocabulario*, sat down and slowly began perusing the columns of the section dealing with proper names beginning with the letter A, the first name is the personal name Aala, but the gender has been omitted, masculine, feminine, who can tell, a case of careless revision, or could it be a name common to both genders, be that as it may, no woman in charge of proof-readers could possibly be called Aala. Raimundo Silva dozed off over the letter M, his finger placed on the name Maria, undoubtedly the name of a woman, but a charlady, as we know, which does not rule out the hypothesis of a coincidence in a world where they are so easy to find.

THE LETTER WHICH Raimundo Silva wrote to the author of *The History of the Siege of Lisbon* contained the necessary *quantum satis* of excuses and a subtle touch of discreet humour which the cordial relations between the sender and the addressee permitted without any abuse of confidence, although in the end there must have been a lasting impression of genuine bewilderment, a serious questioning of the irresistible nature of certain absurd actions. The letter, like some meditation about human frailty, would break down any remaining resistance on the part of the author, who, on being informed of this damaging assault on his intellectual integrity, had replied to the Editorial Director's astonishment, It isn't the end of the world, of course, in real life you do not encounter such abnegation, but this reflection, needless to say, does not come from the historian, it is therefore merely introduced to augment the double meaning, and as relevant here as anywhere else or on any other page of this narrative. The waste-paper basket was soon filled with crumpled paper, discarded pages, drafts amended in all directions, the useless remains after having struggled all day with style and grammar, with those minute harmonies intended to balance the constituent parts of a letter, and an exasperated Raimundo Silva gave vent to his feelings, saying aloud, Is this what writers have to put up with, poor things, and he felt glad to be nothing more than a proof-reader.

Raimundo Silva was walking up the stairs to his apartment after taking his letter to the post office, when he heard the telephone ring. He made no attempt to hurry, partly because he was tired, partly because he felt indifferent and detached, most likely it was Costa wanting to know how he was getting on with the proofs of the volume of poetry or with the preliminary reading of the novel he had left him on that black day, Do you remember. He allowed enough time for Costa to give up, but the telephone went on ringing, it rang with gentle insistence, as if someone was determined to persist simply because it was his or her duty and not because they were counting on getting an answer. He was tranquilly inserting the key in the lock when he remembered it could not possibly be Costa who was calling, Costa had ceased to be his direct contact, poor Costa, an innocent victim, demoted in the hierarchy to the almost mechanical task of fetching and carrying, he who, whenever necessary, was capable of treating the proof-reading mob as equals. Raimundo Silva paused on the threshold of the study, and the telephone, as if sensing his presence, became twice as strident, like a pet dog delirious with excitement on hearing its master return, all it had to do was to jump down from the table and start leaping about, anxious to be patted and cuddled, its tongue out, panting, drooling with sheer pleasure. Raimundo has the odd acquaintance who rings from time to time, and there have been occasions when some woman or other has rung him because she wanted or pretended to want to speak to him and hear how he was getting along, but that was ages ago, calls from women were a thing of the past and there they remained, voices which, if they were to come to him now, would sound supernatural as if coming from another world.

He placed his hand on the receiver, waited a moment longer, as if giving the telephone one last chance to stop ringing, but finally picked up the receiver thinking he knew exactly what to expect, Is that Senhor Silva, asked the telephonist, and he laconically replied, Speaking, Since no one was answering I was just about to ring off, What can I do for you, I'm calling on behalf of Dr Maria Sara who wishes to have a word with you, just one moment. There was a pause, noises as the connection was being made, sufficient time to allow Raimundo Silva to gather his thoughts, She's called Maria Sara, so to some extent he had guessed correctly without knowing, for if it is true that he had fallen asleep with a revealing finger on the name Maria, it is also true that he had already forgotten and, on awakening, on raising his head from his hand spread out on the book, and then rubbing his eyes with both hands, he had culled from the page that precarious sign of orientation, he would only have those two limiting references at his disposal, and would know, at most, that what he was looking for had to be between Manuela and Marula, both names that could be ruled out immediately, because totally unsuited to the personality of this person or character. The telephonist said, I'm just connecting you, a phrase common to all telephonists, the jargon of their profession, yet they are words that promise results, as much for good as for evil. I'm just connecting you, she said, indifferent to the destiny that makes use of her services and pays no attention to what she is saying, I'm going to connect, dial, transfer, switch through, link, contact, plug in, put you in touch, in her mind it is simply a matter of making it possible for two people to communicate, but even this straightforward operation is not without its dangers and should be handled with care. But these warnings go unheeded, even though we are reminded daily that every word is a dangerous sorcerer's apprentice.

Raimundo Silva had slumped into a chair, suddenly feeling twice as tired, Trembling knees are a sign of old age, the obligatory quotation mocked him unjustly, a man who has just turned fifty is not old, perhaps in the past, but nowadays men take better care of themselves, there are lotions, dyes, creams, various skin conditioners, where, for example, would you find a man in the civilised world today, who after shaving would use alum, so severe on the skin, in this modern age cosmetics are queen, king and president, and if, as we have seen, he was unable to disguise the shaking in his legs, at least he has ways and means of contriving a look of composure in the presence of any witnesses. In their absence, Raimundo Silva's face starts twitching, while at the other end of the line, the composed Dr Maria Sara, no doubt with a graceful gesture, tosses her head to throw her hair back on the left side before putting the receiver to her ear, and at last she is ready to speak, We weren't introduced the other day, so let me introduce myself, my name is Maria Sara, yours, she was about to say, I already know, but Raimundo Silva, from force of habit, gave his name, but gave it in full, adding the Benvindo, and almost died of embarrassment there and then. Dr Maria Sara, however, despite having revealed nothing more about herself, ignored this confidence and addressed him as Senhor Silva, without ever suspecting how much balm she was pouring on to the proof-reader's wounded susceptibility, I'd like to discuss how we might organise our work, I'm having meetings with all the proof-readers in order to hear what they think, yes private meetings, I can think of no other way, tomorrow at midday, if that suits you, agreed, I'll expect you then, see you tomorrow. She then rang off but it took Raimundo Silva some time to regain his composure, now the apartment is filled with silence, only the faintest pulsation can be heard, which could be that of the palpitating city, the flowing river, or simply the proof-reader's heartbeat.

He awoke several times in the night with a start, as if someone had shaken him. He kept his eyes closed, trying to ward off insomnia, and soon he passed from uneasy torpor to another restless sleep, but without any dreams. As midnight approached it began to rain, the noise on the verandah roof was always the first sign, however light the rain, and Raimundo Silva's sleep was disturbed by the continuous patter of raindrops falling and reverberating, he slowly opened his eyes to greet the wan light that was just beginning to filter through the chinks of the shutters. As nearly always happens to anyone awakening at this hour, he went back to sleep, this time troubled by dreams, worrying if there would be enough time to dye his hair which badly needed doing, and whether he would be able to do it effectively enough to disguise the fact that it was dyed. It was after nine when he awoke, and immediately thought, I haven't time, then changed his mind. He went into the bathroom and, blinking his eyes, hair uncombed, his face wrinkled, he examined himself under the strong light of the two lamps, one on each side of the mirror. White roots were sadly visible, it would not be enough to ruffle his hair in order to hide them, the solution was really to dye them. He got through his breakfast in a matter of minutes, sacrificing his confirmed appetite for buttered toast, and went back into the bathroom, where he locked himself in to get on with the minting of false coin, in a word, to applying the product, as the instructions on the label described it. He always locked himself in, even though he might be all alone in the apartment when he dyed his hair, he did it in secret, which, as he ought to know, was no secret to anyone, and he would certainly have died of shame were he ever to be discovered carrying out what he himself considered a depressing operation. Like that of Dr Maria Sara, his hair, in more truthful times, was brown, but now it would be impossible to compare their respective hair tones, nature with nature, because that of Raimundo Silva has a uniform colour which bears a striking resemblance to a dowdy, moth-eaten wig, long forgotten then rediscovered in some attic, entangled amongst old pictures, items of furniture, ornaments, knick-knacks, the masks of another age. It was getting on for eleven-thirty before he was ready to leave, already very late, and unless he was fortunate enough to find a taxi right away, the situation would warrant another quotation, this time from an old saying, Ill often comes on the back of worse, a succinct and telling expression which could be transposed as, Out of one ill come many. He was truly fortunate to be living in the Rua do Milagre de Santo António, for only a miracle could have brought an empty taxi into such a deserted street on such a rainy day and it actually stopped when he hailed it without signalling back that it was heading elsewhere. Feeling cheerful, Raimundo Silva arrived at the publishers and made for the editorial department, but later, as he was depositing his umbrella, he realised he was being idiotic, his anxiety was showing in two quite different ways, the fear of going, the desire to arrive, the publishing house for him had become a loathsome place, and, on the other hand, It was not simply to arrive at midday on the dot that he had urged the taxi-driver to go faster, I'm in a hurry, running the risk of making an enemy of someone who had just shown himself to be instrumental in the working of a miracle. Descending into the lower part of the city took some time, to make headway amidst traffic held up by the rain was like thrashing about in treacle, Raimundo Silva perspired with impatience, it was already ten minutes past midday when he walked into the office, panting for breath, and in the worst possible frame of mind for a meeting to discuss new responsibilities and, almost certainly, to reopen the question of his recent fall from grace.

Dr Maria Sara rose from her chair and cordially came to greet him, How are you, Senhor Raimundo Silva, Sorry I'm late, in this rain the taxi took some time, It doesn't matter, make yourself comfortable. The proof-reader sat down, but made to get up again as Dr Maria Sara returned to her desk, Please, don't get up, and when she came back she was carrying a book which she placed on the low table, between the two sofas upholstered in soft black leather. Then she sat down, crossed her legs, she was wearing a skirt in a heavy material, pulled in at the waist, and she lit a cigarette. The proof-reader's eyes accompanied the movement which animated her upper regions, he recognised the face, the hair hanging loosely at shoulder-length, and was shocked to discover white hairs gleaming under the ceiling lamp, She doesn't dye them, he thought to himself, anxious to get out of the place as soon as possible. Dr Maria Sara had asked him if he wished to smoke, but he only heard her when she repeated the question, No thanks, I don't smoke, he replied, lowering his eyes and carrying away the image of a blouse with a plunging neckline, in a colour he was too perturbed to identify. Now he could not take his eyes from the table, he was fascinated, there lay *The History of the Siege of Lisbon*, turned towards him, no doubt deliberately, clearly showing the author's name, the title in bold lettering, an illustration in the centre of the cover with medieval knights with the emblem of the crusaders and on the ramparts of the fortification, disproportionately large drawings of

Moors, it was difficult to tell at this distance if it was a reproduction from some old manuscript or a modern design in medieval style, therefore, pseudo-naïf. He had no desire to go on looking at that provocative cover, yet he was so reluctant to confront Dr Maria Sara who at this moment must be staring relentlessly at him, like a cobra about to lunge and inflict one last fatal bite. But all she said, in a natural voice, with no particular intonation, deliberately neutral, as straightforward as the four words she uttered, This book belongs to you, she took a long pause and added, this time putting greater emphasis on certain syllables, Let me rephrase that, This is your book. Confused, Raimundo Silva raised his head, Mine, he asked, Yes, it's the only remaining copy of *The History of the Siege of Lisbon* that does not carry an erratum, the only copy which still claims that the crusaders refused to help the Portuguese, I don't understand, Don't you mean you're stalling until you decide how you should speak to me, Forgive me, that was not my intention, No need to justify yourself, you can't spend your entire life offering excuses, I was only hoping that you might ask me why I'm giving you this copy without any erratum, a book which preserves the deception, that makes no attempt to remove this error or falsehood, the choice of word is up to you, Then tell me, why are you giving me this book, Too late, I no longer feel like telling you, but she was smiling as she spoke, notwithstanding a certain tension in the way she moved her lips, I beseech you, he insisted, returning her smile, and he was surprised to find himself smiling in such a situation. To be smiling at a woman about whom I know almost nothing and who is almost certainly amusing herself at my expense. Looking somewhat nervous, Dr Maria Sara put out her cigarette and lit another, Raimundo Silva observed her closely, the scales were beginning to tip in his favour, but he could not understand why, much less the meaning of all this, he had not, after all, been summoned to discuss or simply receive instructions about new procedures for proofreaders, what was happening here made it obvious that the matter of the *Siege* had not been finally settled at that black hour on the thirteenth day when he had come here to be sentenced, But don't imagine you're going to subject me to any more vexation, he thought to himself, unwilling to recognise that he was misrepresenting the facts, the truth being that he had been spared the vexation of being dismissed under a cloud, and he certainly did not expect to be given a medal for good conduct or be promoted to head proof-reader, a rank that previously did not exist but had now apparently been created.

Dr Maria Sara quickly rose to her feet, it was interesting to see how she could move so quickly without losing a natural grace which eliminated any impression of brusqueness, and she went to her desk to find a sheet of paper which she handed to Raimundo Silva, From now on all the proof-reading will conform to these instructions, there is no radical departure from the way things have been done in the past and, as you will see, the most important thing is that where a proof-reader is working on his own, as in your case, the proofs will be given a final checking, which might be done by me or some other proof-reader, on the clear understanding that the criteria adopted by the first proof-reader must always be respected, all we are trying to do here is to carry out one final revision to avoid any errors and correct any inadvertent slips, Or intentional deviations, added Raimundo Silva, forcing a bitter smile, You're mistaken, that was an episode you couldn't even describe as locking the stable door after the horse has bolted, because I'm convinced that the thieves won't be back and that the door can stay unlocked, the rules you have there are based on common sense, they are not some penal code to dissuade and punish the offence of hardened criminals, Such as me, An isolated incident, which, as I've already told you, won't happen again, does not make someone into a criminal, Thanks for being so trusting, You don't need my trust, it's a question of basic logic and elementary psychology, something even a child would understand, But I do have my limitations, So does everyone else. Raimundo Silva made no reply, went on staring at the sheet of paper he was holding in his hands, but without reading it, because for an experienced proof-reader like him, it would be difficult to invent any surprise likely to make an impact beyond the time it would take to enunciate. Dr Maria Sara remained seated, but she had straightened up and was leaning ever so slightly forward, making it clear that for her part, the conversation was over, and that any second now, unless there was some good reason to act otherwise, she would be on her feet to say those final words, the ones we usually disregard, those phrases on parting which repetition and habit have robbed of any meaning, a comment which is no less repetitive, introduced here to echo a comment made elsewhere at some other time and not worth any further elaboration, see *Portrait of the Poet in the Year of his Death.*

Raimundo Silva carefully folded the sheet of paper twice, and tucked it into the inside pocket of his jacket. He then moved in such a way that he misled Dr Maria Sara, he appeared to be getting up, but no, he was simply preparing himself, so as not to half-finish the phrase he was about to utter, which, in a nutshell, more or less means that these moments, and moments are always many, even though the seconds of which they consist may be few, they have both lived with unstable equilibrium, the proof-reader compelled against his will to follow Dr Maria Sara's movement, as she herself changed her mind on realising that she had misunderstood his intention. Even more effectively than the theatre, the cinema would know how to show this subtle choreography of gestures, able even to decompose and recompose them successively, but our experience of communication has shown that this seeming wealth of visual images has not lessened the need for words, any words, even in the knowledge that they tell us so little about the actions and interactions of the human body, about the volition implied or actually there, about what we call instinct for want of a better name, about the chemistry of emotions, and all those other things, which precisely for lack of words, we shall refrain from mentioning. But since we are not dealing here with cinema or theatre, or even with life, we are forced to waste more time saying what we have to, especially since we are aware that after a first, second, and sometimes third attempt, only a minimum of the essentials will have been spoken, and even then subject to interpretations, inasmuch as, in a laudable attempt to communicate, we go back to the beginning in dismay, to the point of becoming incapable of getting near or distancing ourselves from the plane of focus, at the risk of blurring the outlines of the central motive, thus making it, let us say, unidentifiable. Fortunately in this case, however, we had not lost sight of Raimundo Silva, we left him in that vacillating movement that was to carry the phrase, not even Dr Maria Sara, rather subdued, if you will forgive the exaggeration, not through any loss of willpower, but because of one last and perhaps benevolent hope, the question is knowing whether the proof-reader is about to speak the right words, avoiding, above all, any cacophony, which arises when the word does not harmonise with the sound nor both word and sound with the intention, let us see how Raimundo Silva will solve the problem, Please, he said, and he had certainly made a good start, my reaction on receiving this book, my surprise on hearing that it carries no erratum, all of this is like having a sore, the whole body instinctively flinches if anyone touches the spot where it hurts, all I can say is that I want to erase this entire episode from my mind, You seem much less edgy than when you were here last time, Fires die out, victories lose their meaning, one gets tired of confrontation, and as I said, I'd like to forget what has happened, I'm afraid that may not be possible if you accept the suggestion I am about to make, A suggestion, Or a proposal, if you prefer. Dr Maria Sara took from a low bookshelf by her side a dossier which she placed on her lap, and told him, Here are all the filed reports about books which the firm has published or rejected in the past, This is ancient history, Tell me about it, Do you think there is any point, Yes, I have my own good reasons for believing so, Well, in those days the publishing house was only beginning to get established, any help they could get was welcome, and someone at that time thought that I could do more than only proof-read, for example being asked to write reviews and reports about manuscripts, I must confess it never occurred to me that these papers would still be here today. I came across them when I was inspecting the section of the archives related to my duties, After all this time, I can scarcely remember them, I've read all of them, You must have been amused by some of the rubbish I used to write, Not at all, on the contrary, your reports are excellent, carefully considered and nicely written, I hope you didn't find *not* constantly being substituted for *yes*, and Raimundo Silva was brave enough to smile, he could not resist it, but out of the side of his mouth so as not to appear over-confident. Dr Maria Sara also smiled, No, there were no such changes, everything was as it should be. She paused, casually leafed through the dossier, appeared to be still hesitating, and then went on to say, These were reports, and the fact that they are so well written and reveal, in addition to your flair for perceptive criticism, a kind of, how can I put it, lateral thinking is altogether rare, Lateral thinking, Don't ask me to explain, it's something I can sense rather than explain, and this is what made me decide to make a proposal, And what is it, That you yourself should write a history of the siege of Lisbon in which the crusaders do not help the Portuguese, therefore taking your deviation literally, the word I heard you use a moment ago, Forgive me, but I don't quite see what you're proposing, It couldn't be clearer, Perhaps that is why I can't see it, You still haven't got used to the idea, so naturally, your first reaction is to refuse, It's not a question of refusal, rather that the idea strikes me as being absurd, Tell me, do you know of any greater absurdity than this deviation of yours, Let's say no more about my deviation, Even if we were never to mention it again, even if this copy I've just given you were to carry the same erratum as all the others, even if this edition were to be completely destroyed, even so, the *Not* you slipped in that day will prove to be the most important act in your life, What do you know about my life, Nothing, apart from this, Then how can you have any opinion about the importance of the rest, True, but what I said wasn't meant to be taken literally, these are emphatic expressions which rely on the intelligence being addressed, I'm not very intelligent, There's another emphatic expression, which I accept for what it is worth, that is, nothing, Can I ask you a question, Go ahead, Tell me frankly, are you or are you not amusing yourself at my expense, Frankly, I am doing no such thing, Then why this interest, this proposal, this conversation, Because it isn't every day that you come across someone who has done what you did, I was in a state of agitation, Come on, Without wishing to be rude, I'm convinced your idea doesn't make sense, Then forget I ever mentioned it, Raimundo Silva got to his feet, adjusted his coat which he had never removed, Unless there is something else you wish to discuss, I'll be going, Take your book, it's the only copy of its kind. Dr Maria Sara wears no ring to suggest that she is married. As for her blouse, chemise, or whatever it is called, it looks like being made of silk, in a pale shade difficult to describe, beige, old ivory, off-white, whether it is possible that fingertips tremble differently according to the colours they touch or caress, we cannot say.

The rain had not subsided. At the front entrance of the publishing house, a bad-tempered Raimundo Silva glanced at the sky through the naked branches of the trees, but the sky was one great mass of cloud without any intervals of blue sky, and the rain was coming down in a steady drizzle, nothing more, nothing less. There will be no tomorrow, he murmured, repeating an old adage used by people acquainted with practical meteorology, but in which we must not put too much faith, because that day was followed by others, and for Raimundo Silva this is certainly not his last. As he awaited the unlikely respite promised by the meteorologists, employees were leaving the building on their way to lunch, it was already after one, the meeting had taken longer than expected. He was hoping Costa would not suddenly appear, forcing him to speak to him, listen to him, watch those accusing eyes, and at that moment it struck him that there was someone else whom he wanted to see even less, Dr Maria Sara, who, as it happens, is already descending in the elevator, and who on seeing him standing in the doorway, might think he is hovering there on purpose, using the rain as an excuse, in order to be able to carry on with their conversation elsewhere, in a restaurant, for example, where he would invite her, or the much more terrifying hypothesis, should she offer him a lift and take him home as an act of kindness, given this incessant rain, really, it's no trouble at all, get in, get in, you're getting soaked. Obviously Raimundo Silva does not know whether she possesses a car, but all the signs suggest that she does, she has that unmistakable air, the modern, outgoing woman, you only have to observe the controlled, methodical gestures of someone who knows how to handle the gears at just the right moment and who has learned how to assess distance and the size of a parking space at a glance. He heard the elevator stop and looked back quickly, to see the Editorial Director himself holding the door to allow Dr Maria Sara to pass, they were having a lively conversation, no one else was in the elevator, Raimundo Silva tucked the book in between his jacket and shirt, a protective reflex, and quickly opening his umbrella, scurried off, keeping as close as possible to the buildings, cowering like a dog being stoned, its tail between its legs, They must be going out to lunch together, he thought to himself. He could not get the thought out of his mind as he went down the street, trying to fathom why the thought had ever occurred to him, but he only met with a blank wall, without inscriptions, he himself an interrogation.

To get home he used two buses and a tram, none of which left him at the door, needless to say, but there was no other way of getting there, not an empty taxi in sight. In any case, the rain did not spare him, after all, you don't get any wetter falling into the ocean or into the village brook, that is to say that if Raimundo Silva had made the entire journey on foot he would not have got any wetter than he is at this moment, drenched from head to foot, soaked to the skin. During the journey, there was one unpleasant, not to say terrifying moment, should we prefer to dramatise the situation, when he began to imagine Dr Maria Sara in the restaurant, telling the Editorial Director the amusing story about the proof-reader, So I told him to write his own version of the siege and he was horrified at the idea, then he tried to assure me that the *Not* he introduced into *The History of the Siege of Lisbon* was not the outcome of any mental disorder, would you believe it, The man's a clown with that deadpan expression of his, but he's good at his job, there's no denying, and once he had committed this act of charity and forbearance with remarkable impartiality, the Editorial Director treats the matter as closed and passes to something closer to his heart, I say, Maria Sara, why don't we have dinner together one evening, then we might go on somewhere to dance and have a drink. On turning a corner, a sudden treacherous gust of wind turned the umbrella inside out, and Raimundo Silva got the full blast of the rain on his face, and that wind was a veritable cyclone, maelstrom, hurricane, it all happened so quickly, but terrifying while it lasted, only his book unharmed, safely tucked away between his jacket and his shirt. The whirlwind subsided, calm was restored, and the umbrella, despite the fact that one of the ribs is broken, can still be used, admittedly more as a symbol than adequate protection. No, thought Raimundo Silva, and stopped there, but we shall never know if this is the word Dr Maria Sara used to respond to the Editorial Director's invitation, or if this man who is climbing the Escadinhas de São Crispim, where there is no sign of the stray dog, is finally persuaded that there are people in this world so cruel as to exploit a poor, defenceless proof-reader in this way. Not to mention, that Dr Maria Sara might well be having her lunch at home.

Having changed his clothes, and more or less dried off, Raimundo Silva set about preparing lunch, he boiled some potatoes to accompany the tinned tuna for which he had opted after considering the few alternatives available, and, supplementing this frugal meal with the usual plate of soup, he felt more cheerful, his energy restored. As he ate, he had a curious feeling of alienation, as if, a purely imaginary experience, he had just arrived after a lengthy, drawn-out journey through distant lands where he encountered other civilisations. Obviously, in an existence so little given to adventures, any novelty, however insignificant for others, can seem like a revolution, even if, to cite only this recent example, his memorable desecration of the almost sacred text of *The History of the Siege of Lisbon* had not affected him in the slightest, but now he has the impression that his home belongs to someone else, and that he himself is the stranger, the very smell is different, and the furniture seems out of place or distorted by means of a perspective governed by other laws. He prepared a piping hot coffee, as usual, and with the cup and saucer in his hand, taking tiny sips, he went round the apartment to see if he could familiarise himself with it once more, he began with the bathroom, where there were still vestiges of the dyeing operation he had carried out, never imagining that it would later cause him embarrassment, then the sitting-room which he rarely used, with the television, a low table, a divan, a tiny sofa and a bookcase with glass-panelled doors, and then the study which brought him back into contact with things he had seen and touched a thousand times, and finally the bedroom with its bed made of old mahogany, a matching wardrobe, and the bedside table, furniture designed for a larger room and unsuited to this confined space. On top of the bed, where he had thrown it down on entering the apartment, lies the book, the last Iroquois of that decimated tribe, taking refuge in the Rua do Milagre de Santo António because of the inexplicable deference of Dr Maria Sara, inexplicable, say we, because it is not sufficient to have proposed, Write a book, only out of irony, for any connivance, with all the intimacy that word implies, makes no sense here, or could it be that Dr Maria Sara simply wants to see how far he is capable of going down the path of madness, since he himself spoke of mental disturbance. Raimundo Silva put the cup and saucer on the bedside table, Who knows, perhaps one of the symptoms is this impression of alienation, as if this were not my home and this place and these things meant nothing to me, the question remained in suspense, unanswered, like all questions that begin with the words, Who knows. He picked up the book, the cover illustration had actually been copied from an old manuscript, French or German, and at that moment, obliterating everything, he was invaded by a sense of fulfilment, of strength, he was holding something that was exclusively his, admittedly despised by others, but for that very reason, Who knows, prized all the more, after all this book is loved by nobody else, and this man has no one to love except this book.

As everyone knows, we spend a third of our short lives sleeping, and we can confirm this from our own experience, between going to bed and getting up, counting is easy, allowing for the wakeful hours of those who suffer from insomnia and, in general, the time devoted to the nightly sessions of the art of loving, still enjoyed and practised as a rule at dead of night, despite the increasing popularity of more flexible timetables which, in this and other particulars, appear to be guiding us towards the fulfilment of the golden dreams of anarchy, namely, that desired age in which each one of us can do as we please, provided we do not prejudice or restrict what pleases others. Yes, there is nothing simpler, but the fact that up to the present we have not succeeded in even identifying our neighbours amidst a multitude of strangers with any lasting certainty, goes to prove, were such proof necessary, what tradition has taught us, that the difficulty of achieving the simple is infinitely more complicated than any other task or skill, that is to say, it is less difficult to conceive, create, construct and manipulate an electronic brain than to find in our own the wherewithal to be happy, but, in the words of Jesus, one age succeeds another, and hope is the last thing to be lost, Alas, we might start losing it right away, because the time it will take to achieve universal happiness has to be counted in astronomical measurements, and this generation does not aim to live that long, disheartened as it clearly is.

Such lengthy circumlocution, made irresistible by the way in which words bring others in their wake, thus giving the impression that all they do is to obey the will of someone who will finally have to answer for them, but misleading him, to the extent of frequently leaving the point of the narrative abandoned somewhere without name or history, pure discourse, without reason or objective, whose fluctuation will transform it into the perfect stage set or backdrop for any old drama or fiction, this circumlocution, which began by probing the hours of sleep and wakefulness in order to finish off with a feeble reflection on the transience of human life and the longevity of hope, this circumlocution, let us conclude, will be justified if we suddenly ask ourselves how often in life a person goes to the window, how many days, weeks, months has that person spent there and for what reason. We usually go to the window to see what the weather is like, to examine the sky, to follow the clouds, to dream with the moon, to respond to someone's cry, to observe the neighbours, and also to occupy our roving eyes by distracting them, while our thoughts accompany the images they capture, born just as words are born, just like them. They are mere glimpses, instants, and lengthy musings about what cannot be seen, a smooth, blank wall, a city, the grey river or the water dripping from the eaves.

Raimundo Silva has not opened the window, he is watching through the window-panes, and is holding the book in his hands, opened at that false page, just as one speaks of false coinage minted by some forger. The dull patter of rain plays on the zinc roof of the verandah, and he does not hear it, although we would describe it, in an attempt to find a suitable comparison, as being like the distant sound of a cavalcade, a stamping of hooves on the soft, damp soil, a splashing of water from the marshes, a strange occurrence, inasmuch as wars were always suspended in winter, otherwise what would become of the men on horseback, scantily clad beneath their leather corslets and sleeveless coats of mail, with the drizzle penetrating the holes, rents and gashes, and the less said about the foot-soldiers the better, tramping practically barefoot in the mud and with their hands so frostbitten that they can scarcely hold the puny weapons with which they have come to conquer Lisbon, what a memory the king must have, to go to war in this appalling weather, But the siege took place in summer, murmured Raimundo Silva. Although less heavy, the rain on the verandah roof could now be heard clearly, as the sound of trotting horses returning to barracks grew fainter. With a rapid movement, surprising in someone not given to gestures, Raimundo Silva threw the window wide open, some of the drizzle sprinkled on to his face, but got nowhere near the book since he had taken the necessary precautions, and the same impression of brimming vitality took possession of him, body and soul, this is the city that was besieged, the ramparts descend over there all the way down to the sea, a name worthy of a river as wide as this one, and then they rise sharply until lost from sight, this is the Lisbon of the Moors, were the atmosphere less grey than on this winter's day we should have a better view of the olive-groves on the slope that goes down to the estuary, and also those on the other bank, at present invisible, as if covered by a cloud of smoke. Raimundo Silva looked and looked again, the universe murmuring beneath the rain, dear God, such sweet and gentle sorrow, may we never be without it, not even in moments of happiness.

CERTAIN AUTHORS, perhaps out of conviction or an attitude of mind not much given to patient investigation, hate having to acknowledge that the relationship between what we call cause and what we subsequently describe as the effect is not always linear and explicit. They allege, and with some justification, that ever since the world began, although we may have no way of knowing when it began, there has never been an effect without a cause, and every cause, whether because pre-ordained or by some simple mechanism, has brought about and will go on bringing about some effect or other, which, let it be said, is produced instantly, although the transition from cause to effect may have escaped the observer or only come to be more or less reconstituted much later. Going further, somewhat rashly, these authors argue that all the visible and recognisable causes have already produced their effects, and that now we need only wait for them to manifest themselves, and they also insist that all effects, whether manifest or about to be made manifest, have their inevitable causality, although our manifold limitations may have prevented us from identifying it in terms of establishing the respective relationship, not always linear or explicit, as we said at the outset. Putting it plainly, and before such laboured arguments draw us into more complicated problems, such as Leibniz's demonstration of the world's contingency or Kant's theory of cosmology, which would oblige us to ask whether God really exists or if He has been misleading us with vagaries unworthy of a superior being who ought to be able to do and say everything with the utmost clarity, what these writers claim is that there is no point in our worrying about tomorrow, because one way or another, everything that might happen has already happened, and as we have seen that is not quite the contradiction it might appear, because if the stone cannot be retrieved by the hand that threw it, we shall not escape the blow and wound if it has been well aimed and we do not get out of the way in time because we are distracted or unaware of the danger. In short, life is not only difficult, it is almost impossible, especially in those cases where in the absence of any apparent cause, the effect, if it can still be called that, raises questions, demanding that we should explain its basis and origin, and also its cause which in its turn it has started to become, inasmuch, as everyone knows, in this entire quadrille, it is up to us to find meanings and definitions, when we would rather close our eyes quietly and let this world go by, for it exercises much greater control over us than it allows us to exercise in return. If this should happen, that is to say, if we are confronted by what to all appearances looks like being an effect, and we can perceive no immediate or direct cause, the solution is to delay, to let time take its course, since the human species, about whom, let us remember, however absurd it may seem, we have no other opinion than that which it has of itself, is destined to await the effects for evermore, and go on seeking the causes for all eternity, at least, that is what it has done up to the present.

This conclusion, as providential as it is uncertain, allows us, by means of a subtle shift in the narrative plan, to return to the proof-reader Raimundo Silva at the precise moment when he is carrying out an act, the motives of which we ignore, distracted as we were in this exhaustive investigation of cause and effect, fortunately interrupted when it threatened to lapse into the traumas of existence and paralysing Angst. This action, like any other, is an effect, but its cause, probably just as obscure for Raimundo Silva, strikes us as being impenetrable, for it is difficult to understand, taking into account the details we know, why this man is pouring down the kitchen-sink that highly esteemed restorative lotion he had been using to mitigate the ravages of time. In fact, without a proper explanation, which only he himself could give, and not wishing to hazard any assumptions and hypotheses, which would be no more than reckless, foolhardy judgments, it becomes impossible to establish that desired and reassuring direct relationship which would convert any human life to an irresistible chain of logical facts, all of them braced to perfection with their points of support and calculated arrows. So let us content ourselves, at least for now, with the knowledge that Raimundo Silva, on the morning following his visit to the publisher, and after a night of relentless insomnia, went into his study, grabbed the concealed bottle of hair-dye, and within a second, barely enough time for any further hesitation, poured the entire contents into the sink and turning the tap on full, literally made that ingenious lotion, misnamed The Fountain of Youth, disappear in a flash from the face of the earth.

Having made this remarkable gesture, he then proceeded to follow the usual routine, mentioned here for the last time unless there should be any significant variation, such as shaving, having a bath, preparing something to eat, and then opening the window to air every nook and cranny in the apartment, the bed, for example, with the sheets drawn right back and already cold, without any vestige of restless insomnia, even less of the dreams he had when he finally fell asleep from sheer exhaustion, mere fragments, meaningless images where no light reaches, impenetrable even for the narrator, whom the ill-informed believe to know all the facts and to be holding all the keys, were this so, one of the good things the world still possesses would be lost, privacy, the mystery surrounding characters. The weather is still wet, but the rain much less heavy than yesterday, the temperature appears to have dropped, so he might as well close the window, especially now that the air has been freshened by the breeze coming in from the straits, Time to work.

The History of the Siege of Lisbon is lying on the bedside table. Raimundo Silva picked up the book, allowed it to fall open by itself, the pages are as we know them, there will be no further reading. He went and sat at his desk, where the unfinished book of poems awaits him, that is to say he still has to finish the proof-reading, and he has only read one third of the novel, amended the odd lack of agreement, suggested some clarifications, and even discreetly corrected several spelling mistakes, after all, Costa assured him there was no urgency. Raimundo Silva put these obligatory tasks aside and, with *The History of the Siege of Lisbon* before him, rested his forehead on arched fingers and stared hard at the book, but soon no longer seeing it, as became apparent from the distracted expression that came into his face. *The History of the Siege of Lisbon* soon joined the novel and book of poems, the top of the desk has a clean, smooth surface, *tabula rasa*, to use the correct expression, the proof-reader sat there staring for a while, the vague sound of rain coming from outside, nothing more, the city appearing no longer to exist. Then Raimundo Silva reached out for a blank sheet of paper, also clean and smooth, also *tabula rasa*, and, at the top, with the clear, neat handwriting of a proof-reader, he wrote *The History of the Siege of Lisbon*. He underlined the words twice, touched up the odd letter, and the next moment was tearing up the sheet, he tore it four times, any less and it might still have served some purpose, any more would have seemed an obsessive precaution. He took another sheet of paper, but not to write, since he scrupulously laid it out so that all four sides were parallel with the four sides of the desk, this meant twisting his entire body, what he wants is something he can ask, What am I going to write, and then wait for the reply, wait until his vision becomes blurred and he can no longer see the white, sterile surface of the page, nothing except a muddle of words emerging from the depths like drowned bodies just about to sink once more, they have not seen enough of the world, that is all they came for, they will return no more.

What am I going to write, this is not the only question, because another occurred to him almost immediately, just as peremptory and with such a sense of urgency that we might be tempted to accept it as the effect of a sudden reflex, but prudence tells us that we should not return to the debate in which we lost ourselves earlier, and which would require us, lest we end up mentally confused once more, to draw a distinction between essential and intimate relationships and casual relationships, this at the very least, since it would tell us whether Raimundo Silva after having asked, What am I going to write, then asked, Where shall I begin. You could say the first question is the more important of the two, inasmuch as it will determine the objectives and lessons of the book he is about to write, but Raimundo Silva is unable and unwilling to go so far back that he will end up having to draft *A History of Portugal*, fortunately brief having begun so few years ago and because its end is already in sight, which is, as has been said, *The Siege of Lisbon* and, because of the inadequate narrative framework in this story which only begins at that moment when the crusaders rejected the king's plea for help, then the second question assumes the character of a factual and chronological reference difficult to grasp, which is the same as asking in plain language, Where do I start from.

Yet it looks as if it might be necessary to step back a little, for example, to begin with the speech of Dom Afonso Henriques, which will permit, moreover, further reflection about the style and the words of the orator, perhaps even the invention of another speech, more in keeping with the age, the person and the place, or simply the logic of the situation, which because of its substance and detail, might justify that fatal refusal by the crusaders. This raises an earlier question, it would be useful to know the names of the king's interlocutors at that point, whom he was addressing, which people were present when he delivered his discourse. Fortunately, we can find out by turning to the primary sources, the writings of the chroniclers, the real *History of the Siege of Lisbon* sitting on Raimundo Silva's desk, it could not be more explicit, you only have to browse, search, discover, the information comes from a reliable source, some believe directly from the famous Osbern of Bawdsey, and so we learn that Count Arnold of Aarschot was there, the commander of the warriors from various regions of the German empire, Christian of Ghistelles was there, leader of the Flemings and the men from Boulogne, and that a third of the crusaders were led by four constables, namely, Hervey de Glanville with a contingent of men from Norfolk and Suffolk, Simon of Dover with ships from Kent, Andrew with recruits from London, and Saher of Archelle in charge of the others. We should also mention Willelmus Vitulus of Normandy and his brother Radulphus, neither name easy to pronounce, who were not in charge of any major army, yet were endowed with authority, military power and political influence which allowed them to participate in any discussions.

But the disadvantage with sources, however truthful they try to be, is their lack of precision in matters of detail and their impassioned account of events, we refer to a certain internal faculty of contradictory germination which operates within facts or the version of those facts as provided, sold, or proposed, and stemming like spores from the latter, the proliferation of secondary and tertiary sources, some copied, others carelessly transmitted, some repeated from hearsay, others who changed details in good or bad faith, some freely interpreted, others rectified, some propagated with total indifference, others proclaimed as the one, eternal and irreplaceable truth, the last of these the most suspect of all. Naturally, everything depends on the greater or lesser quantity of documents available for consultation, on how much or how little time one is prepared to devote to this irksome task, but, in order to get an updated idea of the nature of the problem in hand, we need only imagine, in this day and age in which Raimundo Silva is living, that he or one of us needs to verify some regurgitated truth, constantly being modified by dint of repetition, in the newspapers, yet notwithstanding, the country is small and the population little given to reading, scanning the titles alone gives them vertigo because, frankly, there are far too many of them, the *Diário de Notícias*, the *Correio de Manhã*, *O Século*, the *Capital*, *O Dia*, the *Diário de Lisboa*, the *Diário Popular*, *O Diário*, the *Comércio do Porto*, the *Jornal de Notícias*, *O Europeu*, the *Primeiro de Janeiro*, the *Diário de Coimbra*, and these are only the daily newspapers, because after glossing, summarising, commenting, forecasting, announcing, speculating, we have the weekly newspapers and magazines, *O Expresso*,

O Jornal, O Semanário, O Tempo, O Diabo, O Independente, O Sábado, and *O Avante*, and *Acção Socialista*, and *O Povo Livre*, and the list would be never-ending if, in addition to the most important and influential publications, we were to include all the newspapers and magazines published further afield, where people also have the right to exist and voice their opinions.

Fortunately the proof-reader has other things to worry him, he wants to know who those foreigners were, who during those hot summer days engaged in conversation with our King Afonso Henriques, it appeared that everything had been clarified by consulting *The History of the Siege of Lisbon*, beyond what had already been gathered from the manuscript attributed to Osbern and other ancient works of similar interest, such as Arnulfo and Dodequino, and marginally, the narrative account in the *Indiculum Fundationis Monasterii Sancti Vincentii*, but no, Sir, nothing has been explained, since, for example, in *The Chronicle of the Five Kings of Portugal*, which must have had its own good reasons for revealing so little, sometimes extracting, sometimes adding, no important foreigners are mentioned apart from Guillaume of the Long Arrow, Gilles de Rolim, and another Dom Gilles whose surname is not given, note that none of these men are mentioned in *The History of the Siege of Lisbon*, allegedly based on the testimony of Osbern, in similar cases one generally opts for the earliest of the documents because closer to events, but we do not know what Raimundo Silva will do, since he clearly likes the medieval flavour of the name Guillaume of the Long Arrow, a knight whose very name destined him to carry out the most incredible feats of chivalry. One expedient is to look for a solution in a work of greater authority, such as, in this case, the *Chronicle* of Dom Afonso Henriques himself, written by Fray António Brandão but, alas, this will not untangle the plot, only make it worse by referring to Guillaume of the Long Arrow as Guillaume of the Long Sword, and by introducing, according to the version of Setho Calvisio, a certain Euric, King of Damia, a bishop from Bremen, a duke from Burgundy, a certain Theodoric, Count of Flanders, and with reasonable likelihood, the aforementioned Gilles de Rolim, also known as Childe Rolim, and Dom Lichertes, and Dom Ligel, and the brothers Dom Guillaume and Dom Robert de La Corni, and Dom Jordão, and Dom Alardo, some of them French, others who were Flemish, Norman, or English, although it is doubtful whether in certain circumstances they would have revealed their nationality when questioned, considering that in those days and for some considerable time to come, a man, whether a nobleman or commoner, did not know his country of origin or still had not made up his mind.

But having reflected on these discrepancies, Raimundo Silva decided that ascertaining the truth would not be of much help, insofar as no more will be heard of these and other crusaders, however aristocratic or plebeian, once the king has made his speech, for whatever the consequences, the truth demands the negation inserted into this one and only copy of *The History of the Siege of Lisbon*. But since we are not dealing with unintelligent people, who, moreover, could rely on a multitude of clergymen to act as interpreters and spiritual counsellors, there must have been some serious motive behind their refusal to assist the Portuguese with the siege and capture of Lisbon, otherwise several hundred men would never have taken the trouble to disembark, while more than twelve thousand wait in the ships for the order to go ashore with weapons, coffers and knapsacks, and accompanied by the women travelling on board of whom no warrior should be deprived, even when engaged in holy wars, otherwise how could they possibly relieve and satisfy their corporeal needs. What that motive might have been, we must now investigate, if we are to give the slightest credibility and verisimilitude to this new account.

Let us see. The first hypothesis to come to mind is the climate, but this can be ruled out at once for, as we all know, foreigners, without exception, adore this warm sunshine, these gentle breezes, this incomparable blue sky, you only have to consider that we are already in late June, yesterday was the Feast of St Peter, and the city and the river were one and the same glory, but no one could tell whether beneath the gaze of the God of the Christians or the Allah of the Moor, unless both were enjoying the spectacle together and laying wagers. A second hypothesis could be the aridity of the land, a veritable desert, a scene of utter desolation, but such nonsense could only be conceived by someone unfamiliar with Lisbon and its immediate surroundings, a garden to regale any good man's soul, just look at all those orchards stretching along the banks of the resplendent estuary wending inland, in this Baixa nestling between the hill on which the city is perched and the one in front lying to the west, the perfect manifestation of just how skilful the Moors are in cultivating the land. A third and final hypothesis, to conclude, would be an outbreak of deadly pestilence, not unlike those plagues that from time to time decimate the population throughout Europe and its immediate frontiers, not excepting the crusaders, but a few endemic cases are no cause for alarm, a person can get used to anything, it is like living on the edge of a volcano, foolish comparisons if we think about it for earthquakes are rather more common on the earth, as we shall see more clearly within the next six hundred years or so. Here then are three hypotheses and not one of them plausible. Therefore, hard as we may find it to accept, the reason, cause, motive and explanation must be looked for, and perhaps even found, in the king's speech. There, and there alone.

Raimundo Silva will turn back the pages of the book until he comes to the harangue discussed earlier, in order to read between the lines, to eliminate any superfluous embellishments and proliferations and reduce the text to the bare essentials, and then, by somersaulting like an acrobat, by forcing himself to identify with the mentality of the people who bore these names, origins and characteristics, to feel welling up inside him a rage, indignation and displeasure that would give him the courage to say adamantly, Your Majesty, here we remain, notwithstanding that warm sun you have there, those fertile plains, those pure skies, that wondrous river where sardines leap, Your Majesty keep it and much good may it do you, farewell. As he read this for a second time, it occurred to Raimundo Silva that the crux of the problem might lie in those words, not entirely his own, as we have seen, with which Dom

Afonso Henriques tries to persuade the crusaders to carry out the operation on the cheap, telling them, presumably with an innocent expression on his face, Of one thing, however, we are certain, and that is that your piety will lead you to join us in this great crusade rather than any promise of financial rewards. This is what I, the crusader Raimundo Silva, heard with my own ears, and I was astonished that such a Christian king should have failed to observe those divine words, which as king he ought to have embraced as his guiding principle in politics, Render unto Caesar the things which are Caesar's; and unto God the things that are God's, which, here in our narrative, means that the King of Portugal should not confuse two quite separate issues, it is one thing for me to serve God, another that I should be justly rewarded on this earth for this and other services, especially when I am risking my skin in the enterprise, and not just my skin but everything it carries inside. Of course there is a blatant contradiction between this passage of the royal speech and that other coming immediately before, when he affirms that he considers at your disposal, that is to say, of the crusaders, all that our land possesses, but it is just possible that this was an expression of courtesy used at the time and which no well-educated person would have dreamt of taking literally, just as nowadays we say to people whom we have just met, I'm entirely at your disposal, imagine if they were to take us at our word and start treating us as if we were some flunkey.

Raimundo Silva has risen from his desk, he paces up and down the tiny space left in his study, moves into the corridor to rid himself as quickly as possible of another kind of tension that is getting a grip on him, and thinks aloud, This is not the problem, even though it may have provoked the conflict between the crusaders and the king, it is much more likely that all those disagreements, insults and feelings of mistrust, should we help, should we not help, stemmed from the question of payment for services, the king wants to make savings, the crusaders want rewards, but the problem I have to solve is different, when I wrote *Not* the crusaders went away, therefore my looking for an answer to the question is pointless, Why, in this history accepted as being true, must I myself invent another history so that it might be false and false so that it may be different. He got tired of pacing up and down the corridor, returned to his study, but did not sit down, scanned with nervous irritation the few lines that had survived the damage, six pages, one after the other had been torn up, and as for the amendments, they were like scars still waiting to heal. He realised that until he overcame the problem he would make no progress, and was surprised, accustomed as he was to books in which everything seemed fluent and spontaneous, almost essential, not because it was effectively true, but because any piece of writing, good or bad, always ends up appearing like a predetermined crystallisation, although no one can ever say how or when or why or by whom, he was surprised, as we said, for the following idea had never occurred to him, an idea which should have stemmed naturally from the previous idea, but, on the contrary, refused to emerge, or perhaps not even that, it simply was not there, did not exist even as a possibility. The seventh page was also torn up, the desk once more was clear, smooth, a *tabula* twice *rasa*, a desert, not a single idea. Raimundo Silva reached out for the proofs of the book of poems, he wavered for several more minutes between that nothing and this something, then, little by little, he began to concentrate on his work, time passed, before lunch the proofs had been revised and given another reading, ready for the publishers. Throughout the morning, the telephone had not rung, the postman scarcely ever calls at this address, and the calm in the street was rarely disturbed by the cautious passing of a car, tourist buses never come through this way, they turn into the Largo dos Lóios, and with all the rain there has been recently, few must have ventured all the way up here where there has been nothing to see except overcast skies. Raimundo Silva got to his feet, time to eat, but first he went to the bedroom window, the sky has finally cleared, it is no longer raining, and amidst the fleeting clouds patches of blue sky appear and disappear, a blue as intense as it must have been on that day, despite the difference in the time of year. For a moment, Raimundo Silva could not bring himself to go into the kitchen, heat up that eternal soup, forage amongst the tins of tuna and sardines, play about with a frying-pan or saucepan, not because he fancied eating something more elaborate, but simply, as it were, because of a sudden bout of mental apathy. But neither did he feel like going out to find a restaurant. To have to study the menu, to choose between a dish and the price, to sit amongst total strangers, to handle a knife and fork, all these actions, so easy, so commonplace, struck him as being intolerable. He remembered the nearby Café Graciosa where they serve toasted sandwiches with a cheese and ham filling, acceptable even for palates more discriminating than his, and with a glass of wine and coffee to finish off, his appetite will certainly be satisfied.

Having made up his mind, he left. His coat was still damp after the drenching of the previous evening, putting it on caused him to shiver, as if he were slipping into the skin of a dead animal, and the cuffs and collar were particularly uncomfortable, he ought to keep some dry clothes in reserve for such occasions, a necessity rather than a luxury, then he tried to recall whether Dr Maria Sara was wearing a long jacket or a coat when she stepped out of the elevator with the Editorial Director, but he could no longer remember, there had been no time to notice as he made his escape. This was not the first time he had thought about Dr Maria Sara throughout the morning, but before she had acted as a kind of vigilante, lodged somewhere in his mind, keeping an eye on him. Now she was someone who was moving, who was coming out of the elevator and engaged in conversation, under her coat or jacket she was wearing a tweed skirt belted at the waist, and a blouse or chemise, the name is not important since both words are of French origin, in a colour impossible to define, no, not impossible, because Raimundo Silva has already come up with the exact shade, the off-white of the sky at dawn, a colour that does not really exist in nature, since one morning can be so different from another, but that anyone who so wishes, can invent to his own liking and taste, even the blind muezzin unless he was conceived blind in his Moorish mother's womb.

In the Café Graciosa they did not serve wine by the glass. Raimundo had to wash down his buttered toast with a beer, not very appetising in this cold weather, yet somehow ended up by producing a similar effect in his body, a comforting sense of lassitude. An elderly man with white hair and the look of a retired officer was reading a newspaper at the next table. He did not appear to be in any hurry, he had almost certainly lunched at home and then installed himself here to have a coffee and read the newspaper which the owner of the Café, upholding an old tradition in Lisbon, provided for his customers. But what caught Raimundo Silva's attention was that white hair, how would he describe this shade of white, the crepuscular white of evening in contrast to the off-white of dawn, bearing in mind the man's advanced years, but that would be much too obvious, invention is all very well but it has to be justified. It has to be said, meanwhile, that Raimundo Silva was not simply preoccupied with the colour of the old man's hair, what worried him was the sudden thought that he could not really tell how many white hairs he himself might have, a fair amount or even a lot, when he had more than ten white hairs he started dyeing them, pursuing them with ferocious tenacity as if born for this one great battle. Disconcerted, stupefied, he foolishly began to wish that the time would pass quickly so that he might know his real face, the one that would appear like a new arrival, that would slowly approach, beneath hair that to begin with would be two grotesque strands, the artificial one ever more faded and short-lived, the natural one inexorably gaining ground at the roots, After all, mused Raimundo Silva, you could say that time inclines towards whiteness, and letting his imagination take over, he saw the world coming to an end, life extinguished like a huge white head swept away by the wind, leaving nothing behind except wind and whiteness. The retired officer took a mouthful of coffee, slurping as he drank, and then downed half of the brandy from the liqueur glass sitting in front of him, Aha, he exclaimed, then went on reading. Raimundo Silva felt secretly annoyed with this old fellow, almost envious of his apparent tranquillity, his ingenuous faith in the stability of the universe, it is true that the comforting effect of brandy is infinitely superior to that of beer, and note how in practice, brandy, as alcohol goes, is perfectly acceptable down to the very last drop while this beer is already going flat at the bottom of the glass, only fit for pouring down the sink like rancid water. He quickly ordered a coffee, No thanks, I don't need a digestive liqueur, the adjective used by waiters in restaurants here to describe a wide variety of cognacs and other fortified spirits, and many swear by their medicinal properties. In one gulp, the retired officer drank the rest of his brandy, Aha, and tapping the glass with the tip of his forefinger, he signalled to the waiter to pour him a refill. Raimundo Silva paid his bill and left, observing in passing that there were thin, yellowish strands in the old man's hair, perhaps the remains of dye, perhaps the definitive sign of senility, like old ivory that darkens and starts to split.

Raimundo Silva has not visited the castle in months, but he is on his way there now, he has just made up his mind, although he thinks that may be why he decided to go out in the first place, otherwise the idea would not have occurred to him so naturally, at heart, let us assume, he felt a certain repugnance, an irresistible reluctance to enter the kitchen, but he did it all the better to deceive himself, he feared that to the suggestion, Let's visit the castle, he might churlishly have replied, To do what, and this is precisely what he was unable or at a loss to confess deep down. Savage gusts rent the air, the proof-reader's hair is windswept, the lapels of his coat flap like wet sheets. It is ridiculous to go to the castle in such weather, to climb those exposed towers, he could even be blown off one of those stairways without a handrail, the advantage is not to have anyone there, to be able to enjoy the place without any onlookers, to see the city, Raimundo Silva wants to see the city, although he cannot think why. The vast esplanade is deserted, the ground flooded with puddles of water transformed by the wind into tiny waves, and the trees creak as they are shaken about by the wind, this is almost a cyclone, an exaggeration permissible in a city which in the year nineteen hundred and forty-one suffered the as yet modest effects of the tail-end of a hurricane which people still speak of today when they complain of the damaging consequences there will be a hundred years hence in the wake of the great fire that destroyed the Chiado. Raimundo Silva goes up to the wall, looks way down into the distance, the rooftops, the upper regions of the façades and gables, to the left the muddy river, the triumphal arch of the Rua Augusta, the tangle of intersecting streets, the odd corner of a square, the ruins of the Carmo, as well as those resulting from the fire. He does not linger there, and not because he is greatly troubled by the wind, he vaguely knows that this unusual outing has a purpose, he has not come here to contemplate the towers of the Amoreiras, it was nightmare enough to have them appear in a dream. He entered the castle, he never ceases to be surprised that it should be so small, almost like a toy castle, another Lego or Meccano set. The high walls reduce much of the wind's impact, breaking it down into many contrasting currents that penetrate the arches and passageways. Raimundo Silva is on familiar territory, he will climb to the ramparts near São Vicente, from there to examine the lie of the land. And there is the mound of the Graça, facing the highest of the towers, and the descent to the Campo de Santa Clara, where Dom Afonso Henriques encamped his soldiers, our own men and the first parents of the nation, because their ancestors who were born much too soon, could not possibly have been Portuguese. This is an aspect of genealogy that is often overlooked, the need to examine what for all its lack of importance, gave life, place and occasion to the importance acquired by what we now consider to be important.

This was not the place where the meeting took place between the crusaders and the king, it must have been further down on the other bank of the estuary, but what Raimundo Silva is looking for, if the phrase has any meaning, is an impression of something visually tangible, something he would not be able to define, yet capable, for example, of transforming him this very moment into a Moorish soldier watching the shadowy forms of the enemy and the glinting of swords, but which, in this instance, by means of some secret mental circuit, hopes to receive, as tangible evidence, the detail missing from the narrative, namely, the indisputable reason for the crusaders' departure after that decisive *Not*. The wind continues to buffet Raimundo Silva, obliging him to hold on to the battlements in order to keep his balance. For a moment, the proof-reader feels utterly ridiculous, becomes aware of his theatrical, or better still, cinematographic posturing, his coat has become a medieval cloak, his flowing hair plumes, and the wind is no longer wind, but a current of air produced by a wind-machine. And just at that moment, as he became somewhat defenceless and innocent because of the irony directed at himself, there finally surfaced clearly in his mind and with no less irony, the much sought-after motive, the reason for that *Not*, the ultimate and irrefutable justification for his assault on historical truth. Now Raimundo knows why the crusaders refused to help the Portuguese to besiege and capture the city, and he is about to return home to write *The History of the Siege of Lisbon*.

IT IS STATED in *The History of the Siege of Lisbon*, the other one, that there was much excitement amongst the crusaders when it was announced that the King of Portugal was coming to make proposals whereby he hoped to enlist the support of those brave warriors who had set their sights on rescuing the Holy Land. Drawing on the providential source of Osbern, never actually written by Osbern, the author also states that nearly all of those people, both rich and poor, to quote his very words, on hearing that Dom Afonso Henriques was approaching, went to meet him in festive mood, so we are led to believe, otherwise they might as well have awaited his arrival, without further ado, as is the custom at such gatherings, that is to say, in the rest of Europe, when the king arrives, the people rush to shorten his journey and welcome him with cheers and applause. Fortunately, we were given this explanation right away, to chasten national pride, lest we should naively imagine that the Europeans of that time, like those of today, allowed themselves to fall completely under the spell of a Portuguese king of recent vintage, who was arriving on horseback with a troop of soldiers, Galicians like himself, some of them nobles, others clergymen, all of them rustic and uneducated. For we know that the monarchy at that time still had enough prestige to bring crowds out on to the road, saying to each other, Let's go and see the king, let's go and see the king, and the king is this bearded gentleman, smelling of sweat, with miserable weapons, and the horses are no thoroughbreds but simply unkempt beasts of burden, destined to die in battle rather than execute graceful voltes in some riding school, but despite there being so little to see in the end, one must not lose the opportunity, for when a king comes and goes, who knows whether he will ever return.

And so Dom Afonso Henriques arrived, and the leaders of the crusaders whom we have already mentioned, except where there are no reliable sources, were lined up with some of their men to greet him, since most of the soldiers were still confined to the ships until their masters decided their fate, not excluding their own. The king was accompanied by the Archbishop of Braga, Dom João Peculiar and the Bishop of Oporto, Dom Pedro Pitões, both well-versed in Latin, and enough dignitaries to form a royal cortege with some decorum, namely, Fernão Mendes, Fernão Cativo, Gonçalo Rodrigues, Martim Moniz, Paio Delgado, Pêro Viegas, also known as Pêro Paz, Gocelino de Sousa, another Gocelino called Sotero or Soeiro, Mendo Afonso de Refoios, Múcio de Lamego, Pedro Pelágio, or Pais da Maia, João Rainho, or Ranha, and others whose names have not been recorded but who were there. Both parties finally met up and having gone through the endless formalities of being introduced, for not only were the names and surnames of everyone given, but also a list of their achievements and personal qualities, the Bishop of Oporto announced that the king was about to make a speech, and swore before the laws of God and man that he would faithfully interpret his words. Meanwhile, the riders had dismounted from their mules, the king had climbed on to a boulder where he could be seen by everyone, and from where, moreover, he could see over the heads of the crusaders and get a splendid view of the entire estuary, the abandoned orchards destroyed by the Portuguese who for the last two days had stripped them of all the vegetables and fruit. Up there on the fortress, tiny human forms could be seen on the battlements, and, descending, the city wall, with its two gates on this side, that of Alfofa and that of Ferro, shut and bolted, you could sense the disquiet of the Moors on the other side, for the moment in safety, as they wondered what was about to befall them, the river cluttered with ships and a large crowd gathered on the hill opposite, standards and pennants fluttering in the breeze, a fine spectacle, some fires burning, who knows for what reason, because the weather is warm and it is not yet time for eating, the muezzin listens to the explanations being given by a nephew and starts to fear the worst, another way of saying that the bad is still more or less bearable. The king then raised his powerful voice, Although we may live in this God-forsaken corner of the earth, we have heard good things about you, that you are men of great strength and unequalled when it comes to using weapons, and who would doubt it, judging from your impressive physique, and as for your skill in waging war we need only consider the list of your achievements, both religious and secular. Despite the difficulties we face, caused as much by this ungrateful soil as from the many deficiencies in the Portuguese character yet to be fully formed, we try to do our best, neither fish nor fowl, moreover we have had the misfortune to be landed with these Moors, people who have no great wealth if compared with those of Granada and Seville, all the more reason for getting them out of here once and for all, and this raises a question, a problem, I would ask you to consider, and it is the following, What we would need, in a manner of speaking, is some voluntary assistance, that is to say, you would remain here for some time to help us, and once this proved to be no longer necessary, you would be rewarded with some symbolic token of our appreciation and proceed to the Holy Land where you would be rewarded a hundredfold, both in material goods since the wealth of the Turks cannot be compared with that of the Moors, and in spiritual goods, which pour down on the believer the moment he sets foot on that soil, and let me warn you Dom Pedro Pitões that I know sufficient Latin to judge how the translation is going, as for you crusaders, I beseech you, don't get annoyed, what I meant by a symbolic token of our appreciation was that in order to guarantee our nation's future we are anxious to preserve all the riches we possess here in the city, which will come as no surprise, yet how true the proverb that says or will come to say, No one helps the poor like the poor themselves, people reach an understanding by talking to each other, you tell me how much you want for your services and we shall see if we can meet your price, although the truth that passes through these lips dictates that I have my own good reasons for believing that even if we should reach no agreement, we shall be able to overcome the Moors and take the city on our own, just as three months ago we captured the city of Santarém with a ladder and half a dozen men, and once the army went in they took the sword to men, women and children, no matter their age or whether they were armed or defenceless, the only survivors were those who managed to escape and they were few, now then, if we succeeded in Santarém, we shall also succeed in besieging Lisbon, and if we tell you these things, it is not because we despise your aid, but lest you should judge us lacking in strength and courage, not to mention that we Portuguese have faith in the succour of Our Lord Jesus Christ, be quiet Afonso.

Let no one think that anyone in the entourage or in that gathering of foreigners had the insolence to tell the king to be quiet, addressing him only with his name at baptism, as if they had once supped from the same plate, those were simply the words of someone talking to himself, just as one says, Shut your trap, which, as anyone accustomed to listening and searching for those subtle meanings that come to say more than the words themselves well knows, really means that the person who spoke is dying to say what he had apparently decided to suppress. Even so, he must reckon with the benevolent curiosity of others in order to remove this tactical obstacle, by raising, for example, a question more or less in these terms, Come now, out with the rest, don't leave us in suspense, but it might turn out otherwise, it depends on the person and the circumstances, in this case the intervention came from Guillaume Vitulo, that evil-looking fellow, who might or might not have been the one with the Long Sword, and with unseemly bluntness, he dared to express his doubts, Our Lord Jesus Christ helps all Christians alike, and so He should, otherwise it would be the end of religion if some were to be treated like sons and others like stepsons. Several crusaders looked disapprovingly at this meddler, but more because of the manner than the substance of his intervention, because when it came to the latter there must have been general agreement that in the king's speech, in addition to a reprehensible avariciousness that might have spoiled everything, there was much petulance and pride, he sounded more like a bishop than a simple king who does not even have the right to use that title since it is not recognised by the pope, who three years ago did him the great honour of treating him as dux, and he should consider himself fortunate. The silence did not last as long as this explanation might lead you to believe, but it lasted long enough for the atmosphere to become tense and increasingly hostile, Dom Afonso Henriques was displeased at this lack of confidence, and was about to open his mouth, almost certainly to speak his mind, when Saher of Archelles, one of the more diplomatic crusaders, struck a conciliatory note, That the Portuguese should have captured Santarém with a ladder, we are in no doubt, God assisting as on that memorable occasion when He allowed the walls of Jericho to fall to the sound of trumpets, not even blown by seven warriors but by seven priests, nor is it so very surprising that the Portuguese should have carried out such carnage, when in that same city of Jericho not only were men, women, children and the elderly slaughtered, but also the oxen, sheep and donkeys, what we find really odd is that any man, even though a king, should rashly invoke the name of the Lord, whose will, as we know, only manifests itself where and when He so wishes, not in response to prayers, pleas and supplications, and as for the question of sons and stepsons, I have nothing to say.

Dom Afonso Henriques was favourably impressed not only by this apt quotation from the Bible but also by the conciliatory tone adopted by Saher of Archelles, the substance of his words as suspect as those of Guillaume of the Long Arrow, but unlike the latter, he had chosen his words carefully, and after conferring for a few minutes with the Archbishop of Braga and the Bishop of Oporto which meant descending from the boulder, he got back on to it and said, Gentlemen, you should know that this Portuguese land on which you stand, not here, but further south, and as recently as eight years ago, was the scene of a miraculous appearance of Our Lord Jesus Christ, and since I am not Joshua nor my people Hebrew, this had a different impact on enemies more formidable than those watching us from yonder as they tremble with fear, a victory to match that of Jericho and other such resounding victories, and, if we were able to carry off this mighty feat, there is no reason why the Saviour of the World should not reappear before the walls of Lisbon, wherefore, God willing, our military skills would be as useless as yours, and our joint forces would be nothing other than astonished witnesses of God's power and majesty. As the king was speaking, the Archbishop and Bishop nodded approvingly, and as he brilliantly rounded off his speech, both of them applauded rapturously, their enthusiasm shared by all the other Portuguese who were present. Bewildered, the crusaders eyed each other, momentarily at a loss for words, until finally Gilles de Rolim decided to speak out, telling them, I agree, Your Majesty, that Our Lord Jesus Christ could easily do all of these things, but what we want to know at this stage, is not what He might do, but what He did, therefore we would ask you to give us a detailed account of this great victory, which, as far as we have understood, would suffice to justify the long, arduous journey we have made to this land, yours, and for the present still that of the Moors. The king conferred once more with the Archbishop and the Bishop, and, having all three agreed, he told them, Now then, listen.

The telephone rang. It has one of those old-fashioned bells that are enough to awaken the dead, and Raimundo Silva was so deeply lost in thought, that the unexpected fright caused his hand to jerk leaving a scrawl on the paper, as if the world had suddenly accelerated and skidded beneath his pen. He waited, then asked, Who is speaking, and immediately recognised the voice of the telephonist at the publishers, I'm putting you through to Dr Maria Sara's extension, she replied. As he waited, he looked at his watch, ten to six, How the time has passed quickly, it was true, the time had passed quickly, but to think it had no other purpose than to serve as a precarious safeguard, like a screen of thin smoke scattered and swept away by the breeze, while Raimundo Silva pauses to think, How the time has passed quickly, that other time, this one into which he had suddenly been launched, would give him the illusion of allowing himself to slow down, a pause sustained on a vibration, his right hand appearing to tremble slightly as it rests on the paper. Then he could hear the telephonist, incorrigible as ever, say, You're connected Dr Maria Sara, Raimundo Silva clenched his fist, time became blurred, confused, then became diffused, flowed in its natural current, Good afternoon, Senhor Raimundo Silva, Good afternoon, Dr Maria Sara, How have you been, Fine, and how are things with you, Going very well, thank you, I'm still organising the work here, and I simply wanted to ask you how you are getting on with the proofs of that book of poems we gave you, I've just finished correcting the proofs this very minute, I have been working on them all day and can bring them to your office tomorrow, Ah, so you've been working on them all day, Well not quite all day, I spent about two hours reading the novel Senhor Costa left with me, You've had a busy day, In fact I have nothing better to do, An interesting phrase, Perhaps, but it was unintentional, it slipped out without my thinking, There's probably some advantage in this, What do you mean by this, To speak without thinking, to act without thinking, On the contrary, I've always considered myself a reflective person, that is how I see myself, someone who reflects on things, Even though given to impulses, Do me a favour, Dr Sara, if I'm to be subjected to constant reminders about past errors, I'd better look for work with some other publishing house, Forgive me, I didn't mean to hurt your feelings, I promise not to say another word on the subject, Many thanks, Now then, why don't you bring me those proofs tomorrow, and as for the novel, once you have another free day to devote to reading, perhaps you might be able to finish the work and deliver it without delay, Don't worry, it won't take me long, I'm not in the least worried, I know I can rely on your cooperation, I've never let anyone down who put their trust in me, Then you won't disappoint me, Trust me, Until tomorrow

Senhor Raimundo Silva, Until tomorrow, Dr Sara. The hand holding the telephone glided slowly through the air, descended slowly, and after replacing the receiver lingered there, as if reluctant to be separated from it or awaiting some word that could not be spoken. Raimundo Silva would have done better to concern himself with those words that had been uttered, for example, anyone else would have seen that Dr Maria Sara was not convinced that he had spent the whole day working on the book of poems, even allowing for the feasible assumption that he had devoted two hours to reading the novel, however since she had no possible means of knowing how he had occupied his time during the day, she resorted to guessing, typical of women, all of them think of themselves as being sybils and sorceresses, and end up deceiving themselves like the most common of those feeble men whom they generally regard with ironic and indulgent benevolence. But what troubled Raimundo Silva most of all was that she should have said, and in all seriousness, without altering her tone of voice, Then you won't disappoint me, obviously she was only referring to the more than proven professional competence of someone who throughout his working life, pardon the repetition, but this is always overlooked, the working life of someone who only made one mistake, and the same was discovered, acknowledged and fortunately excused. Now then, having clearly excluded those motives of a more intimate nature which relations between them rule out from the outset, that leaves the strong possibility of an indirect reference to that famous suggestion that he should write *A New History of the Siege of Lisbon*, a suggestion to which he found himself doubly committed, not just because he had already made a start on the work, but also because he had replied just as seriously, Trust me, and at that moment he did not know what he was saying.

Raimundo Silva looked at the sheet of paper, Listen, then picked up his biro to carry on with the narrative, but realised that his mind was vacant, yet another blank page, or one covered with indecipherable alternatives or crossings-out. Given the declaration made by Dom Afonso Henriques, all that remained for him to do was to relate the miracle of Ourique in his own words, introducing, as you might expect, a predictable note of modern scepticism, authorised moreover by the great Herculano de Carvalho, and giving free rein to the language, without overdoing it, because proof-readers tend not to take all that many risks with texts closely scrutinised by public opinion. The tension, however, had been broken, or been substituted by another, perhaps the impulse would return later, during the hours of night, like some new inspiration, without which we can achieve nothing according to those who should know. Raimundo Silva has heard that in similar cases it is preferable not to force what we call nature, to allow the body to follow the soul's weariness, above all that they should not fight each other, however heroic and edifying tales of such battles may be, and this is wise advice, although not that most favoured by those who have firm ideas about what each of us should do, even though they themselves are not inclined to put them into practice. The king continues to say, Now then, listen, but it is a cracked disk that turns round and round, hypnotically turning round. Raimundo Silva rubs his tired eyes, the page in his brain is blank, the paper page is half-written, with his right hand he reaches out for *The Chronicle of Dom Afonso Henriques* written by Fray António Brandão, which will serve to guide him when, tonight or tomorrow, he resumes the narrative, and, incapable of writing at present, he reads in order to acquaint himself with the details of this mythical episode, he is on the second chapter, The gifts brought by the courageous prince, Dom Afonso Henriques, were not of sufficient quality to allow him to rest, nor did his thoughts occupied with the greatness of the enterprise in hand give him much cause for tranquillity and reassurance. And so to shake off his disquiet, he took up the Holy Bible which he kept in his tent, and on starting to read, the first thing he came across was the victory of Gideon, the illustrious leader of the Jewish people, who with three hundred soldiers routed the four Midianite kings and their armies, putting to the sword a hundred and twenty thousand men, not counting the even greater number who perished in the end. Delighted with the outcome of this encounter, and treating this victory as an auspicious forecast of further triumphs, he became even more determined to wage war and, with inflamed heart, his eyes turned towards Heaven, he poured out the following words: As you well know, my Lord Jesus Christ, it was in your service and in order to exalt your holy name that I embarked on this war against your enemies; You, who are all powerful, help me to win this war, inspire and fortify my soldiers so that we may overcome these enemies who blaspheme your most holy name. Having thus spoken, he fell into a gentle slumber, and began to dream that he was seeing an old man of venerable appearance, who told him not to lose heart because he would undoubtedly win that battle, and as a clear sign of God's love and favour he would see the Saviour of the World with his own eyes before entering into battle. Lulled as he was into this pleasant dream, neither fully asleep or fully awake, his aide João Fernandes de Sousa entered the tent and informed him that an old man had arrived seeking an audience, and as far as one could tell, it was a matter of some importance. The prince ordered that if he were a Christian, he should be brought before him, and the moment he saw him, he recognised him as being the same old man he had just seen in his dreams and this greatly consoled him. The venerable old man repeated to the prince the same words he had heard in his dream, and confirming his victory and the appearance of Christ, he added that he should have every confidence in the Lord who loved him, and who would cast his merciful eyes on him and his descendants unto the sixteenth generation, when his descent would dwindle, but even then the Lord would watch over, and protect them. In the name of that same Lord he warned him that on the following night when he heard the bell ring at the hermitage where he had been living for the last sixty years, under the special protection of the Almighty, he should leave the camp, because God wished to show him the greatness of his mercy. On hearing this sovereign message, the Catholic prince received it with all due respect and with the deepest humility gave infinite thanks to God. The old man took his leave and returned to his hermitage, and the prince, awaiting the promised sign, spent the night in fervent prayer until the second vigil, when he heard the bell ring; then taking up his shield and sword he went outside the encampment, and, raising his eyes to heaven, he saw the most glorious resplendence towards the east, which gradually spread and grew bigger. In the middle he could see the redeeming sign of the Holy Cross, and nailed thereon the Redeemer of the world, surrounded by a throng of angels, in the guise of the most handsome youths dressed in shining white robes, and the prince noticed that the Cross was enormous and raised some cubits from the ground. Startled by this wondrous vision, and with the fear and reverence due in the presence of the Saviour, the prince laid down his arms, removed his royal robes, and prostrated himself barefoot on the ground and, with much weeping, he began to beseech the Lord to protect his vassals, and said: What merits have you found, my God, in so great a sinner, that you should favour me with such sovereign mercy? If You are doing this in order to increase my faith, it seems unnecessary, because since receiving Baptism I have acknowledged you as the one, true God, Son of the Holy Virgin, of human descent and the Eternal Father through divine generation. Better that the infidels should witness this wondrous manifestation of your glory, so that by abominating the error of their ways, they might come to know you. Whereupon the Lord, in gentle tones the prince has no difficulty in hearing, spoke these words: I have not appeared to you like this in order to increase your faith but in order to strengthen your resolve in this enterprise, and to lay the foundations of your Kingdom on solid rock. Take heart, for not only will you win this battle, but all the others you may wage on the enemies of the Catholic Faith. You will find your people ready for war, and they will earnestly entreat you as their king to take up arms; do not hesitate to accept, but heed their petition, for I am the founder and destroyer of the world's Empires, and in you and your descendants I wish to found a great kingdom for myself that will spread my name far and wide. And so that your descendants may know from whose hand they have received this kingdom, you will buy your arms at the price I paid for mankind, the price paid for me by the Jews, and this kingdom will be sanctified and loved by me for the purity of its Faith and its exemplary piety. On hearing this singular promise, Dom Afonso prostrated himself on the ground once more and, giving praise to the Lord, asked him, What have I done, my God, to be worthy of so much compassion? But if this is your holy will, cast the eyes of your mercy on the successors you have promised me, protect the Portuguese people from all perils, and should you decide to punish them, I implore you to inflict that punishment on me and my descendants, and spare this people whom I love as an only child. All this the Lord graciously accepted, assuring him that he and his people could count on his mercy, for they had been chosen as his labourers so that they might reap a great harvest far and wide. Hereupon the vision disappeared, and the Infante Dom Afonso, his resolve and happiness understandably restored, made an inspection tour of the camps before withdrawing into his tent.

Raimundo Silva closed the book. Although weary, he felt like reading on and following the sequence of battles before the Moors were finally routed, but Gilles de Rolim, speaking on behalf of the crusaders who were present, told the king that, having been informed of the memorable prodigy performed by Our Lord, Jesus Christ, in the remote region south of Castro Verde, at a place called Ourique in the province of Alentejo, they would give him their reply next morning. Whereupon, after complying with the usual greetings and formalities of protocol, they, too, withdrew to their tents.

THE KING SLEPT BADLY, his restless sleep constantly interrupted, yet heavy and gloomy as if he should never forget it, and it was a sleep without dreams or nightmares, no old man of venerable aspect announcing some pleasant miracle, I am here, no woman crying out, Don't ill-treat me, I'm your mother, nothing except a dense, mysterious blackness that seemed to enshroud and quell his heart. He awoke feeling thirsty and asked for water which he drank in great gulps, and then looked out of the tent to study the night sky, impatient with the slow movement of the stars. There was a full moon, one of those moons that transform the world into a ghostly apparition, when all things, living and inanimate, whisper mysterious revelations, each expressing its own, and all of them discordant, therefore we never come to understand them and we suffer the anguish of almost but never quite knowing. The estuary shone between the hills, the river carried the gleaming waters as if ablaze, and the bonfires burning on the terraces of the castle and the huge torches distinguishing the various ships of the crusaders were like dying flames in that luminous darkness. The king looked to one side, then to the other, he tried to visualise those Moors and Franks watching the bonfires of the Portuguese encampment, to imagine their thoughts, fear and scorn, to fathom their next move and military strategy. He lay down once more on the bearskin with which he usually covered his pallet, and tried to sleep. The voices of men on patrol could be heard, now and then, the sound of weapons, the lantern inside the tent cast dancing shadows, then the king sank into silence and infinite darkness, he was asleep.

The hours passed, the moon descended and disappeared, night turned to night. Then the stars covered the entire sky, sparkling like reflections on the water, creating space for the Milky Way leading to Santiago, later, much much later, the first light of morning broke through behind the city, black against the light, little by little the minarets faded, and when the sun appeared, still invisible from this spot where we are standing, familiar voices could be heard echoing amongst the hills, those of the muezzins summoning the followers of Allah to prayer. The Christians are not such early risers, aboard the ships there is no sign of life, and the Portuguese encampment, save for the weary sentinels who are nodding off, continues to be immersed in a deep sleep, a lethargy interrupted by grunts, sighs, murmurings, which only much much later when the sun is already up, will free their limbs and untie their voices, the contrite and irrepressible morning yawn, the interminable stretching causing bones to creak, one day more, one day less. The fires have been lit and the cauldrons are now suspended over the flames, the men draw near, each with his wooden bowl, the guards arrive in a state of exhaustion, others who have rested disperse throughout the encampment as they chew one last mouthful of food, while at the same time, near the tents, the nobles nourish themselves on much the same food, unless we are talking about meat which is the main difference in their diet. They eat from large wooden platters along with the priests who have celebrated Mass before breaking their fast, and together they try to predict what the crusaders will decide to do, someone suggests they will not join them unless they are promised more generous rewards, another feels they might be content simply to serve for the greater glory of God, if compensated for their labours with a token sum of money. They keep a watchful eye on the ships in the distance, probe the manoeuvres of the sailors, look out for any signs, in the hope of discovering whether the crusaders are planning to stay or, on the other hand, are already weighing anchor.

The king is waiting. He fidgets impatiently on the seat placed in front of his tent, he is fully armed, with only his head uncovered, and he sits there in silence, looking and waiting, nothing more. It is mid-morning, the sun is high in the sky, beads of sweat trickling down under his armour. The king is visibly annoyed yet anxious not to show it. A canvas awning erected over his head flaps gently in the breeze, in harmony with the royal standard. A silence different from that of night, but perhaps even more disquieting because during the day we expect movement and noise, a silence of foreboding hovers over the city, the river and the surrounding hills. The crickets are chirping but this is a sound from another world, the grating of the invisible saw cutting away at the world's foundations. Up on the walls, behind the battlements, the Moors are also watching and waiting.

At last there is a movement of boats between the three main galleys anchored at the mouth of the estuary, from each of them descend people who step into the boats, and now they are heading this way, you can hear the beating of oars on the smooth water, the splashing of spade oars, the general picture is almost one of pure lyricism, a clear blue sky, two small boats approaching without haste, all we need is a painter to record these subtle colours of nature, the dark city rising up the hill and surmounted by the castle, or, changing our perspective, the Portuguese encampment against a background of irregular hills, ravines, slopes, scattered olive-groves, some stubble, the vestiges of recent fires. The king is no longer there, he returned to his tent, because, being a royal personage, he does not have to wait for anyone, the crusaders have to assemble, waiting respectfully and then Dom Afonso Henriques, armed from head to foot, will appear to hear their message. Some of the high-ranking warriors who had conferred with the king now began to approach, their demeanour forbidding and impenetrable, we can already tell that they are about to refuse to help the Portuguese, but the latter are still in a state of holy ignorance, they nourish, as the saying goes, high hopes, it is difficult to imagine how they can justify such a grave decision, for there must have been a reason, otherwise they will be accused of being thoughtless and inconsiderate. The delegation includes Gilles de Rolim, Ligel, Lichertes, the La Corni brothers, Jordão, Alardo, also a German hitherto unmentioned, whose name is Heinrich, a native of Bonn, a knight of high repute and moral standing, as he will come to prove, and a learned English monk whose first name is Gilbert, and as spokesman, Guillaume Vitulo, he of the Long Sword or the Long Arrow, fear struck in the hearts of the Portuguese when they saw that he would do the talking, for they were well aware of his hostility towards the king, there are such enmities, for no good reason we take a dislike to someone and nothing will change our mind, I can't stand the fellow, I can't stand the fellow, and there is nothing more to be said.

Dom Afonso Henriques emerged from his tent accompanied by his advisers Dom Pedro Pitões and Dom João Peculiar, and it was the latter, who after consulting the king, extended words of welcome to the emissaries, speaking in Latin, of course, with no detriment to the words themselves, and told them the king was anxious to hear the answer they had brought, which he had no doubt would be most profitable for the greater glory of Our Lord Jesus Christ. An astute form of words for since we obviously do not know what most befits God, we leave it to His judgment to choose, while we humbly resign ourselves if that choice is not in our best interests, and, on the other hand, not to overstate our gratitude if it turns out to be everything we could have wished for. The eventuality that God might be indifferent to yes and no, good and evil, cannot enter heads such as the ones we were given, for when all is said and done, God always has to serve some purpose. However this is not the moment to be pursuing such tortuous meanders, because Guillaume of the Long Sword, already adopting an attitude of blatant insolence quite out of keeping with his subordinate rank, is insisting that since the King of Portugal can count on so much favour and assistance from Our Lord Jesus Christ, such as, for example, during those critical moments during the battle of Ourique, then surely the Lord would take it amiss if the crusaders, who were after all in transit, should presume to take His place in this new enterprise, therefore the Portuguese would be well-advised to go alone into battle, for their victory was assured and God would appreciate this opportunity to show His might, as and when it might be sought. Guillaume Vitulo having spoken in his native language, the Portuguese listened throughout, pretending to understand as happens on such occasions, never suspecting for a moment that the decision was contrary to their own interest and advantage, but they found out soon enough when the friar accompanying the Knight of the Long Sword reluctantly began translating, his lips refusing to articulate words of such sarcasm, and others which demand a second hearing, given the undertones of blasphemous doubt cast on the divine power to quell or curtail wars, to propose or dispose, to grant or withhold victory, to allow one man to overcome a thousand, things only become difficult when Christians are fighting Christians, or Moors are struggling against Moors, although in the second case, this is a problem for Allah to resolve, so let him get on with it.

The king listened in silence, and silent he remained, his hands grasping the hilt of his sword, held to the right, the tip of the blade resting firmly on the ground as if he had already taken possession of this territory. And it was Dom João Peculiar who, crimson with holy indignation, uttered the phrase that ought to have shamed the provocateur, Thou shalt not tempt the Lord thy God, a phrase understood by all, even by those weak in matters of doctrine, because rather than simply show his contempt for the Portuguese, Guillaume Vitulo, in other circumstances and with different words, had, in fact, done nothing more than repeat Satan's wicked ploy when he said to Jesus, If you be the Son of God, cast yourself down, for the angels will protect you and you will come to no harm, whereupon Jesus replied, You shall not tempt the Lord your God. These words ought to have shamed Guillaume but he felt no remorse, and even appeared to be sneering with contempt. Then Dom Afonso Henriques asked, Is this the crusaders' final decision, It is, replied the other, Then be gone, and may God accompany you to the Holy Land, where, unless I am mistaken, you will no longer have any excuse for evading battle as on this occasion. It was now Guillaume Vitulo's turn to raise his hand to the sword that gave him his name, and this might have had the most dire consequences if his companions had not intervened, not so much physically as with the words spoken by one of them, this was Gilbert, the only member of the delegation who could outshine the interpreters when it came to expressing himself in Latin, as fluent as any learned high-ranking prelate, and these were his words, Your Majesty, Guillaume Vitulo is telling the truth when he says that the crusaders refuse to stay here, but he has failed to mention the material considerations which have prompted their refusal, after all, it's up to them, however some have decided to remain and these are the men you see here who have come with the delegation, Gilles de Rolim, Ligel, Lichertes, the La Corni brothers, Jordão, Alardo, Heinrich, and myself, the most insignificant and lowly of all and at your service. Dom Afonso Henriques was so pleased that his wrath soon passed, and, there and then, ignoring any niceties of protocol, he went up to Gilbert and embraced him, showing his disdain in passing for the insolent Guillaume who is truly well-named, and said aloud, This being your decision, I promise that you will be the first Bishop of Lisbon once the city becomes Christian, and as for you others who have chosen to stay with me, I can assure you that you will have no cause to complain of my magnanimity, whereupon he turned away and entered his tent. Here the waters parted, that is to say, Guillaume remained isolated, even the friar accompanying him moved three cautious paces away, looking suspiciously for any signs of a cloven hoof or goat's horns on this rash fanatic who had been put in his place.

Combining what was effectively written with what for the moment only exists in his imagination, Raimundo Silva arrived at this crucial climax, and he has made considerable progress, if we recall that besides his more than once confessed lack of preparation for anything other than the meticulous task of proof-reading, he is a man who writes slowly, forever conscious of agreements, sparing in the use of adjectives, painstaking in matters of etymology, punctilious in observing the rules of punctuation, which goes to show that everything that has been read here in his name, in the final analysis, is nothing more than a free version and adaptation of a text which probably has little in common with this one and that as far as we can foresee, will be kept back until the very last line, and out of reach of the lovers of naive history. Besides, we only have to see that the version at our disposal already consists of twelve extremely compact pages, and it is obvious that Raimundo Silva who has none of the characteristics of the writer, neither the vices nor the virtues, could not possibly within thirty-six hours have written so much with so many variations, as for the literary merits of what he wrote, there is nothing to be said, because this is history, consequently science, and because of the lack of what might strictly be called authoritative sources. These precautions are worth repeating so that we may bear in mind the importance of not confusing appearances with reality, but we do not know how or why we should doubt, when we thought we were certain of some reality which looks and sounds convincing, that it might simply be another version among many, or, worse still, be the only version and proclaimed as such.

It is the middle of the afternoon, time to pay a visit to Dr Maria Sara who is waiting for the proofs of the book of poems. The cleaner is tidying up the kitchen, or doing the ironing, he scarcely notices her as she goes quietly about her work, perhaps thinking that writing or correcting what has been written has something to do with religion, and Raimundo Silva who has not left the house all day, went and asked her, What is the weather like, since he never has much to say to her, he seizes the slightest opportunity, or invents one, therefore he did not go to the window as usual, and he should have done, today being such a special day, perhaps they already know in the city that the crusaders are going away, espionage is not an invention of modern warfare, and Senhora Maria replies, It's fine, a synthetic expression, which only means, in fact, that it is not raining, for by constantly saying, It's fine, but cold, or, It's fine, but windy, we never say nor ever will say, It's fine, but raining. Raimundo Silva goes in search of the complementary information, whether there is any threat of rain, or wind such as yesterday, and what the temperature is like. He can go out without any protection other than what is normal, his coat, dry as can be and now quite presentable, of the two scarves he possesses, the flimsy one. He went to the kitchen to settle the weekly accounts with Senhora Maria, she looked at the money and sighed, a habit of hers, as if on receiving the money she were already beginning to be parted from it, in the beginning Raimundo Silva used to get nervous, she appeared to be putting on a sad expression to show her displeasure at being so badly paid, therefore he felt quite uneasy until he was sufficiently informed about standard rates of payment amongst the lower middle class to which he belongs, coming to the conclusion that he was reasonably well off, one could not honestly say that he was exploiting the labour of others, but just in case, he increased her wages, but he could not cure her of that sighing.

There are three main routes connecting the street in which Raimundo Silva lives to the city of the Christians, one that follows the Rua do Milagre de Santo António, and depending on which street of the trifurcation he chooses, he might end up in Caldas and the Madalena, or in the Largo da Rosa and its immediate surroundings, the Costa do Castelo above, the Escadinhas da Saúde and the Largo de Martim Moniz below, and, in the middle, the steep Calcada de Santo André, the Terreirinho and the Rua dos Cavaleiros, another route takes him through the Largo dos Lóios in the direction of the Portas do Sol, and finally, the most common route of all, down the Escadinhas de São Crispim which soon brings him to the Porta de Ferro, where the tram is waiting that will take him to the Chiado, or where he sets off, still on foot, for the Praça da Figueira, if he has to use the underground, as is the case today. The publishing house is situated near the Avenida do Duque de Loulé, much too far away for him to start climbing the Avenida da Liberdade at this late hour, he usually walks up on the right-hand side, for he has never liked the other side, he cannot explain why, although this impression of liking or disliking may not be constant, it has its ups and downs, whether it be here or there, but somehow he feels happier on the right-hand side. One day, even while telling himself that he was being obsessive, he took the trouble to mark out on a map of the city those stretches of the Avenida which he liked and those he disliked, and he discovered to his surprise, that the agreeable part on the left side was more extensive, but taking into account the degree of satisfaction, the right side prevailed in the end, so that he would often go up on this side and look across at the pavement on the other side, wishing he were there. Obviously he does not take these little obsessions too seriously, he is not a proof-reader for nothing, only a few days ago, while holding a conversation with the author of *The History of the Siege of Lisbon*, he argued that proof-readers have had wide experience of both literature and life, giving to understand that what they did not know or wish to learn about life, literature more or less taught them, especially when it comes to foibles and manias, for as everyone knows normal characters do not exist, otherwise they presumably would not be characters, which, summed up, may imply that Raimundo Silva may have looked in the books he proof-read for some striking features that, with the passage of time, would come to instil, in combination with any natural traits, this coherent and contradictory totality we normally refer to as character. Now that he is standing on the Escadinhas de São Crispim, eyeing the dog who is watching him, he might well ask himself which fictional character it most resembles at this moment, a pity it is not a wolf or some other animal, for then St Francis would immediately come to mind, or a pig, and then it might be St Antonino, or a lion, and then it might be St Mark, or an ox, and then it might be St Luke, or a fish, and then it might be St Antony, or a lamb, and then it might be St John the Baptist, or an eagle, and then it might be St John the Evangelist, we could not simply describe the dog as being man's best friend, because the way the world is going it might well be his one and only remaining friend.

On condition that its friendship is returned, Raimundo Silva thinks to himself in the presence of this gaping mongrel, it is more than evident that the inhabitants of São Crispim have no liking for the canine species, perhaps because the people in this district are the direct descendants of the Moors who saw it as their religious duty to abhor the dogs roaming the streets at that time, although both men and dogs are the brothers of Allah. The dog, with more than eight centuries of ill-treatment in its blood and genetic legacy, raised its head from afar to give a pitiful howl, a voice of unabashed frustration and despair begging for food, howling or stretching out a hand is not so much public degradation as inner abnegation. Raimundo Silva has no fixed appointment, Until tomorrow, was all Dr Maria Sara had said, but it is already getting late, worst of all is this dog preventing him from going on his way, the howl has turned to wailing, unlike what happens to humans who weep first then start howling, and what this dog is begging, pleading, supplicating and craving for, as if this simple man were God Himself, is a morsel of bread or a bone, rubbish-bins nowadays are difficult to open or tip over, hence my desperate need for something to eat, kind Sir. Torn between going on and feeling remorseful about having done so, Raimundo Silva decides to return home to find something that a famished dog dare not refuse, as he goes upstairs he looks at his watch, It's getting late, he repeated to himself, bursting into the apartment and giving the cleaner, whom he caught watching television, the fright of her life, but without appearing to notice he made straight for the kitchen, rummaged in drawers, peered into pots and pans, opened the fridge, Senhora Maria could not summon the courage to ask, What are you looking for, or even register any surprise as well she might, for as we know, she was caught in the act, watching television when she should have been getting on with her work, and now she tries to collect herself, the television has been switched off and she is now busily moving furniture and making the most awful din as she puts on a show of frenetic activity, busying herself to no purpose, while Raimundo Silva, if he actually noticed that she was taking liberties, did not give it another thought, he was so worried about being late and making a favourable impression when he puts the fruits of his plunder before the dog, these he carries wrapped up in newspaper, a bit of cooked sausage, a slice of fatty ham, three morsels of bread, pity there is no bone to pacify the poor mongrel for there is nothing better while digesting than a bone to stimulate the salivary glands and to strengthen a dog's teeth. The door has slammed, Raimundo Silva is already descending the stairs, no doubt Senhora Maria has gone to the window to watch him leave, then gone back into the sitting-room to switch on the television, she had even lost five minutes of the soap opera, what's been happening.

The dog had not moved, but simply lowered its head, its nose almost touching the ground. Its protruding ribs, like those of some crucified Christ, tremble in the joints of its spine, this animal is an utter fool, refusing to leave the Escadinhas de São Crispim where it has suffered starvation, despising the riches of Lisbon, Europe and the World, now these are facile judgments, this is not a case of stubbornness but rather of timidity, therefore worthy of our respect, the fearless never see any difficulties, for example, what confusion there would be in this dog's mind on discovering that the familiar one hundred and thirty-four steps suddenly had one more, not that any such thing has happened, this is merely a hypothesis, how wretched the mongrel would feel confronted with this unsurmountable abyss, for we have not forgotten how difficult the dog found it to follow this man the other day all the way to the Porta de Ferro, better not to repeat certain experiences. Standing three paces away, Raimundo Silva watches the dog go up to the parcel opened out on the ground, and the animal, wary of being landed a kick, cannot decide whether it should keep an eye on him, or pounce on the food, its very smell provoking unbearable pangs of hunger, the saliva rushes to its teeth, oh god of dogs, why have you condemned so many of us to a miserable existence, it is always the same, we blame the gods for this and that, when it is we who invent and fabricate everything, including absolution for these and other crimes, Raimundo Silva can see that the dog is afraid, he moves away, the animal advances a little, its nose quivering with desire, one minute the food was there and gone the next, swallowed up in a flash, and with its long, pale tongue the dog is licking the grease soaked into the paper. Fate has confronted Raimundo Silva with this sad spectacle, Dr Maria Sara already forgotten, and suddenly he finds himself identified with the fictional character who was missing, none other than St Rock who was assisted by a dog, and it was time the saint repaid the favour, thus proving the assertion that everything is reciprocated in this life, even if in reverse, from a human angle, needless to say, for when it comes to dogs, who can tell how they see Raimundo Silva, let us say, a living being with a human face, so that we may finally complete the aforementioned collection of apocalyptic animals and let Raimundo Silva also become the St Matthew who was missing, but how will he cope with such a heavy burden.

But it cannot be all that heavy, if we observe the speed at which he began descending the steps, having suddenly remembered Dr Maria Sara who is waiting for him, now he will need to take a taxi in order to get there in time, and he cannot afford such luxuries, damn dog, me playing the Good Samaritan, you can be sure I wouldn't have gone back home to look for food had it been an old woman begging on the Escadinhas de São Crispim, well, perhaps if it were an old woman, but certainly not for an old man, interesting to see how generosity itself, assuming that is what we are talking about, varies according to the situation and the circumstances, with our frame of mind and mood at that moment, generosity, if you will forgive the comparison, is rather like a piece of elastic, it stretches, contracts, is capable of embracing all humanity or the selfish individual who only knows how to be generous with himself, however an act of charity is always good for the soul, the mongrel remained there, deeply grateful, although it was so famished that this food would barely suffice to fill a hollow tooth, poor little creature, an expression of pity, for the dog is not all that small, what breed, all of them, except for the most timid of them that never appear on the streets, and if they do they are on a leash and wearing a cache-sexe, this one at least is free, enjoys pursuing stray bitches but will not get much enjoyment if he never leaves the Escadinhas de São Crispim, if he never leaves the Escadinhas de São Crispim. At this point Raimundo Silva consciously interrupted the musings in which he had been absorbed as the taxi carried him, he had become aware of a sudden malaise, not physical, rather as if someone asleep inside him had suddenly awoken and called out on finding himself plunged into total darkness, therefore he repeated, to allow his fear to pass, If he never leaves the Escadinhas de São Crispim, who am I talking about, he asked himself, the taxi was climbing the Rua da Prata and he was inside it, after all, he belonged to the land of men, not that of dogs, and he could always leave the Escadinhas de São Crispim whenever he wanted or needed to, such as now, when he is on his way to the publisher to speak to Dr Maria Sara who is in charge of the proof-readers, to deliver the final proofs of the book of poems, and then he may decide not to go back home just yet, he has finished proof-reading the book, although such a slender little volume that it scarcely passes for a book, he will do what he usually does, eat in some restaurant, go to the cinema, although he probably does not have enough money for such an ambitious programme, he does some mental arithmetic, the taxi-meter, he tries to remember how much he has in his wallet, and he is in the middle of these calculations when he realises he will not go out this evening, he must not forget that he has started on a new book, no, no it is not the novel delivered by Costa, he looked at his watch, almost five o'clock, the taxi goes up the Avenida do Duque de Loulé, stops at traffic lights, drives on, drop me off here, please, and when Raimundo takes out the money to pay, he can see at a glance that he does not have enough money to go to a restaurant and the cinema, either one or the other, but the one without the other is not much fun, I'll eat at home and get on with my work, he means *The History of the Siege of Lisbon*, at one time he would have said it outright, when he was proof-reading a book with this title, in the days when he was innocent.

The lift is ancient and cramped, perfect for intimate encounters were it not for the transparency of the glass doors and the side panels, nevertheless there is an interval between two floors, and so long as you keep an attentive eye on the flights of stairs, going up on the one side, going down on the other, it is always possible to touch hands or even steal a furtive kiss, if you are feeling desperate. In all the years he has worked here, Raimundo Silva has used this mechanical cage, sometimes on his own, at others accompanied, and never before today, as far as he can remember, had he ever been assailed by such disquieting thoughts, it is true that in the beginning he preferred to use the stairs because he did not have the patience to wait when the lift was slow in coming, and also because he was still nimble on his feet and sound of heart, capable of competing with the junior staff in all the offices, including the staff in Editorial, although here the average age has always been on the high side. It is not much of a climb, only two floors, but bearing in mind that this is an old building where each floor is almost twice as high as those built today, similar in this respect to the very old building he inhabits in Castelo, in other words this is nothing new, the high has always been followed by the low and the low by the high, probably one of life's laws, even our own father once gave the impression of being a giant and now it is we who look over his shoulder, and he gets more and more decrepit from year to year, poor man, but let us say no more, so that he may suffer in silence. It strikes Raimundo Silva as being absurd that he should be remembering his deceased father in this elevator, just as he was beginning to be assailed by erotic thoughts, the truth is that the person who thinks only knows what he is thinking and not why he thought it, we think from the moment we are born, I suppose, but do not know what our first thought might have been, the one from which all others have subsequently come, the definitive biography of each one of us would be to ascend the river of thoughts to its primeval source, and presumably change our life, were it possible to retrace their course, to suddenly have another thought and pursue it, so that we might arrive at the day in which we find ourselves, unless by choosing another life we made it shorter, and that the life in question was not that of a proof-reader, and we would go up in another lift, perhaps to speak to someone other than Dr Maria Sara. As it happened, Raimundo Silva was standing on the side where he had seen the Editorial Director descend with the new employee appointed to supervise the work of the proof-readers, and we catch him looking at the empty space with severe disapproval, as if he were about to reprimand the woman who had stood there for her immoral conduct, for as you ought to know these are things one does not do in a lift, one does not do, I repeat, for I am well aware that there are people who do these things, and even worse, It was only a little groping, Mr Proof-reader, it was only a little kiss, Mr Proof-reader, No matter, that was more than enough, in the name of my own, incurable envy, I denounce you, during the last few centimetres of his ascent, Raimundo Silva moved to the centre of the elevator, there was no room for the others, they had to get out, thoroughly ashamed of themselves if there is any shame left in this world, most likely they are laughing at this hypocritical moralist, They're no good because they're still green, said the vixen.

To look, see and observe are different ways of using the organ of sight, each with its own intensity, even when there is some deterioration, for example, to look without seeing, when someone is distracted, a common situation in traditional novels, or to see and not notice, when the eyes out of weariness and boredom avoid anything likely to tax them. Only by observing can we achieve full vision, when at a given moment or successively, our attention becomes concentrated, which may just as easily result from a conscious decision as from an involuntary state of synaesthesia, whereby what is seen pleads to be seen once more, thus passing from one sensation to another, arresting, slowing down the process of looking, as if the image were about to be produced in two different places in the brain with a temporal discrepancy of a hundredth of a second, first the simplified sign, then the exact design, the clear, imperious definition of a thick handle in polished brass on a dark varnished door which suddenly becomes an absolute presence. Time and time again, Raimundo Silva has stood at this door waiting for them to open up from within, the click of the buzzer, and never as today has he been so keenly and almost terrifyingly aware of material things, a handle that is not simply a smooth polished surface, but an object whose density can be perceived until coming up against this other density, that of wood, and it is as if all of this were sensed, experienced, felt inside the brain, as if the senses, this time all of them and not just his vision, were observing the world after finally observing a handle and a door. The buzzer has clicked, fingers have pushed the door, inside the light seems overpowering, and although not true, Raimundo Silva feels as if he were floating in space without any bearings, just like those sets saturated with light that are much in vogue in films about the supernatural and extra-terrestrial apparitions with dazzling lighting effects, he waits for the telephonist to shriek in terror or fall into an ecstatic trance if he should manifest himself outwardly in a proliferation of sensitive tentacles or bright rays of ineffable beauty, the kaleidoscopic vibration into which, for a fleeting instant, his sensibility has been transformed. But the telephonist, whose duties, in addition to managing the switchboard, include pressing the button to release the lock and receiving anyone who arrives, gives him a little wave while she finishes a conversation on the telephone, and then friendly, familiar and unsurprised, greets him with, Hello, Senhor Silva, she has known him for many years and each time she sees him she finds him no different than one might expect with the passage of time, if asked within the next few minutes how she found the proof-reader, she would reply, although not with total conviction, Difficult to say, perhaps a little nervous, this is what she would say and nothing more, either she is not very observant or Raimundo Silva is his old self again, if anyone could really tell from outward appearances what was going on inside a person, even by observing them closely, I'd like to speak to Dr Maria Sara, he said, and the telephonist, who is also called Sara but without the Maria and who feels very proud of this semi-coincidence, informs him that Dr Maria Sara is in the director's office, she does not even have to say which director, she means the Editorial Director, it has always been the same, the others, from the Managing Director down to Costa, are people of no importance, and Raimundo Silva, somewhat brusquely for him, tells her to ask whether she can see him or whether he should leave the proofs of the book of poems here at the reception desk, she will know what he is referring to. Sara listens to what Dr Maria Sara is saying, nods her head, the dialogue is brief, but perhaps because of whatever keen vision he still possesses, although now only a pale shadow of what it was on the other side of the door, Raimundo Silva observes, strand by strand, the telephonist's blonde hair, a colour resembling that of crushed straw, she keeps her head lowered, she cannot imagine the ferocity in his expression, ferocity is perhaps too strong a word, obviously the man bears the woman no malice, it is his eyes that are being irresponsible, he is simply waiting to be given instructions, he has come quite some distance and in haste, perhaps only to be told to leave the proofs in reception, as if he were an errand boy delivering a letter that requires no answer, Dr Maria Sara would like you to wait in her office, the telephonist has raised her head and is smiling, Many thanks, Sarita, she has always been called Sarita, and the name stuck even after she married and became a widow, some people are extremely fortunate, the women, of course, for as a rule, men have had little time to be boys and some never were, as is known and has been written, while others have never stopped being boys but dare not admit it.

Raimundo Silva did not have long to wait, three or four minutes at most. He had remained standing, looking around him, with the strange impression of entering this office for the first time, it is not surprising, he had no memory of being in this office before, most likely it had been used by the administration before the recent alterations, nor, as he now noticed to his amazement, had he retained those images when summoned by Dr Maria Sara, he could no longer remember, for example, if that vase with a white rose had been standing on the desk or that work-schedule on the wall where he could read his own name on the top line and below it the names of all the other proof-readers who worked for the publishing house, their names marked alongside the abbreviated titles of books, dates, coloured symbols, a simple geometrical square, a map, as it were, of the city of proof-readers, some six in all. We can picture them, each in his own home, in Castelo, in Avenidas Novas, perhaps in Almada or Amadora, or Campo de Ourique, or Graça, poring over the proofs of some book, reading and correcting, and Dr Maria Sara thinking about them, changing a date, substituting a green symbol for a blue one, very soon now the names themselves will no longer matter, be no more than a little diagram that will provoke ideas, associations, reflections, but for the moment each of these names represents an item of information that has to be assimilated, first Raimundo Silva, then Carlos Fonseca, Albertina Santos, Mário Rodrigues, Rita Pais, Rodolfo Xavier, this being an office one might expect them to be arranged in alphabetical order, but not at all, no Sir, Raimundo Silva appears on the top line, and perhaps there is a simple explanation, namely, that when the work-schedule was drawn up, he was Dr Maria Sara's main concern.

Whereupon, she walks in, and says, Sorry to have kept you waiting, the sound of the door and her voice startled Raimundo Silva, caught unawares, and he turned round hastily, It doesn't matter, I only came to, he does not finish the sentence, it is as if he were also seeing this face for the first time, how often had he thought about Dr Maria Sara in recent days, and in the end, he had no image of her in his mind, her name alone had occupied all the available space in his memory, progressively displacing her hair, eyes, features, the gestures she made with her hands, all he could remotely recognise was the softness of that silk, not because he had ever touched it, as we know, nor was he having recourse to former sensations in order to imagine morbidly what touching it might be like, impossible as it may seem, Raimundo Silva knows everything about this silk, its sheen, the soft texture of the material, the floating pleats, like sand dancing, although its present colour is not as before, it, too, immersed in the mists of memory, at the risk of being disrespectful by citing the national anthem. I've brought you the proofs, as we agreed, said Raimundo Silva, and Dr Maria Sara took them from him, in passing as it were, now she is seated at her desk, having invited the proof-reader to be seated, but he replied, No, I won't bother, and averted his gaze to the white rose, so close to her that it can see into her most tender heart, and, since one word leads to another, he is reminded of a verse he had once revised, a line that spoke of the intimate murmur that makes roses bloom, he had been struck by the beauty of those words, one of those felicitous expressions to be found even in mediocre poets, The intimate murmur that makes roses bloom, he repeated to himself, and he could hear, incredible as it may seem, the ineffable caress of petals, or was it a sleeve rubbing against the curve of her breast, dear God, take pity on men who spend their lives imagining things.

Dr Maria Sara replied, As you wish. Only these three words, in a tone of voice that did not augur any further conversation, and Raimundo Silva, who could probe the meaning even of words half-spoken, understood, on hearing these three words, that he had no more business here, he had come to deliver the proofs, he had handed them over, all he had to do now was to take his leave, Good afternoon, or to ask, Do you need anything more of me, a common enough expression, as capable of expressing humble subordination as restrained impatience, and which, in this instance, using the appropriate tone of voice, might be turned into an ironic gibe, the unfortunate thing is that the person addressed often hears the phrase without noticing the intention behind it, they only have to be leafing through published proofs with a professional eye, even more attentive when checking the proofs of verses which require special care. No, I cannot think of anything more at present, she said, rising from her chair, and it was just then that Raimundo Silva, without meditating or premeditating, detached as he was from the act and its consequences, gently touched the white rose with two fingers, and Dr Maria Sara looked at him in astonishment, she could not have been more startled had he caused that flower to appear in an empty vase or pulled off some similar sleight of hand, but most unexpected of all, is that a woman so sure of herself should suddenly become perturbed to the point of blushing, it happened in a flash, but flagrant, it seems quite incredible that anyone should blush so in this day and age, what could she have thought, if she thought anything, it was as if the man, on touching the rose, had brought out a hidden intimacy in the woman, spiritual rather than physical. But the most extraordinary thing of all is that Raimundo Silva also blushed, and for much longer than she did, he felt so utterly ridiculous. How shameful, he said or is about to say to himself. In similar situations, when courage is lacking, and don't let's ask, Courage for what, the only salvation is to escape, our instinct for self-preservation is a wise counsellor, the worst comes afterwards, when we repeat those horrible words, How shameful, we have all experienced these horrors and punched the cushion with rage and humiliation, How could I have been so stupid, and there is no answer, probably because we would have to be very intelligent to be able to justify our stupidity, just as well that we are hidden by the darkness in the room, no one can see us, even though night possesses, and that is why we fear it so much, this evil power of making even the most petty irritations seem monstrous and irremediable, let alone a disaster of this order. Raimundo Silva turned away abruptly, with the vague idea that he had nothing more to live for and that he would never again return to this establishment, It's absurd, absurd, he repeated in silence and he had the impression of saying it a thousand times as he made for the door, In two seconds I'll be out of this place, gone, far away, when at the very last moment he was detained by Maria Sara's voice, surprisingly calm, in such stark contrast to what is happening here this very moment, that it was as if the meaning of her words had vanished into thin air, had he not been so conscious of the absurdity of it all, he might have pretended that he had misunderstood, however he had no choice but to accept that she really had said, I'm leaving in five minutes, I only have to settle some business with the Editorial Director, can I offer you a lift. With his hand gripping the door-handle, he tried desperately to appear natural, and how much effort it cost him, one part of him commanded, Be off with you, the other eyed him like a judge and decreed, You won't get a second chance, all the blushings and surprises had lost any importance in comparison with the dramatic step taken by Maria Sara, but in which direction, dear God, in which direction, and this is how we humans are made, for notwithstanding the confusion of sentiments with which he was struggling, it is clear that he was still sufficiently indifferent to be able to recognise the annoyance the expression, can I offer you a lift, had caused him, a trite colloquialism altogether unsuited to the occasion and reminding him of some popular ditty, a spontaneous and irresistible jingle, lift, ride, ditty, Maria Sara could have said, I'll take you wherever you like, but she probably did not remember, or thought the better of using such an ambiguous phrase, I'll take you wherever you like, I'll take you wherever I like, how true that an elevated style tends to elude us when we need it most. Raimundo Silva managed to let go of the door and stand firm, an observation which might appear to be in dubious taste were it not the expression of an amicable irony as we wait for him to reply, Many thanks, but I don't want to take you out of your way, now here it should be said the sonnet is about to suffer with the correction and it only remains to the ill-starred proofreader to bite his tongue if this tardy sacrifice would serve any purpose, fortunately, Maria Sara paid no attention, or pretended not to have understood the mischievous duplicity of the phrase, at least her voice was not trembling when she said, I won't be a minute, do take a seat, and he did his best to prevent his voice from trembling when he replied, I won't bother, I prefer to stand, from the way he had spoken earlier it seemed that he was refusing the offer, now he appears to be accepting. She goes out only to return within five minutes, meanwhile it is to be hoped that both of them recover the rhythm of their breathing, their sense of appraising distances, the regularity of their pulse, which will certainly be no small feat after such perilous exchanges. Raimundo Silva looks at the rose, it is not only people who do not know why they are born.

One day, perhaps because of some lighting effect reminiscent of this bright chilly afternoon which is already fading, someone will say, Do you remember, first the silence inside the car, awkward words, a tense and expectant glance, protestations and avowals, Drop me off in the Baixa, please, I'll catch a tram from there, Whatever next, I'm taking you home, it isn't any trouble, But you're going out of your way, The car is, not me, It's quite a climb up to the district where I live, At the foot of the castle, So you know where I live, In the Rua do Milagre de Santo António, I saw the address on your file, afterwards a certain but still hesitant sense of relief, body and soul semi-relaxed, but his words ever cautious until the moment Maria Sara said, I think we're where the Moorish city once stood, and Raimundo Silva pretending not to notice the allusion, replied, Yes, we are, and tried to change the subject, but she persisted, Sometimes I try to imagine what it must have been like, the people, the houses, their way of life, and he remained silent, now obdurately silent, feeling that he hated her as one detests an invader, and he was on the point of saying, I'll get out here, my apartment is nearby, but she neither stopped nor replied, and they kept silent for the remainder of the journey. When the car came to a halt outside the front door, Raimundo Silva, although unsure as to whether this was an act of politeness, felt he ought to invite her up, and then repented, It is rather tactless, he thought, besides I mustn't forget that she is my boss, whereupon she said, Perhaps another time, it's getting late. We could debate for hours about this historic phrase, for Raimundo Silva could swear that the words she spoke just then were different, and no less historic, It is not yet time.

During these last few days, had the muezzin been sleeping heavily, no doubt he would have been roused, if not altogether prevented from sleeping, by the tumult of an entire city living in a state of alert, with armed men up on the turrets and battlements, while the people are all excited, gathered in the streets and marketplaces, asking if the Franks and Galicians are about to attack. They naturally fear for their lives and possessions, but even more distressed are those who have been forced to abandon their homes outside the wall, for the moment being defended by the soldiers, but where the first battles will inevitably be fought, if this should be the will of Allah, praised be his name, and, even if Lisbon should overcome the invaders, this prosperous and thriving suburb will be reduced to ruins. High on the minaret of the largest mosque, the muezzin raised the same shrill cry as he did each day, knowing that he will no longer awaken anyone, at most the innocent children will still be asleep, and contrary to custom, when the final echo of the call to prayer is still hovering in the air, the murmurings of a city at prayer can already be heard, truly there was no need for anyone who had barely dozed off to come out of his sleep. The sky displayed all the beauty of a July morning, the breeze was soft and gentle, and, if experience is anything to go by, we are going to have a warm day. Having finished his prayer, the muezzin prepares to descend, when suddenly from down below comes the most dreadful and alarming uproar that the blind man is panic-stricken and for one moment thinks that the tower is collapsing, the next that those accursed Christians are storming the walls, only to realise in the end that they are cries of jubilation coming from everywhere and setting the city ablaze, the muezzin can now say that he knows what is meant by light, if it has the same effect on the eyes of those who can see as these joyful sounds have on his hearing. But what could be the cause for this rejoicing. Perhaps Allah, moved by the fervent prayers of the people might have sent the angels from his tomb, Munkar and Nakir, to exterminate the Christians, perhaps he might have dropped the inextinguishable flames of heaven on to the armada of the crusaders, perhaps, out of earthly humanity, the King of Evora, warned of the dangers threatening his brothers in Lisbon, has sent word by messenger, Let the villains stew there, for my soldiers from the Alentejo are already on their way, that is how we refer to people who come from beyond the Tagus, pointing out in passing, that the inhabitants of Alentejo existed before the Portuguese. At the risk of bruising his fragile bones on the steps, the muezzin descends the narrow spiral stairway in haste, and when he reaches the bottom, he is overcome by vertigo, he is a poor old man who gives the impression of wanting to bury himself underground, an illusion of ours based on past examples, now he can be seen struggling to get to his feet, while questioning the darkness all around him, What happened, tell me what happened. Next moment arms reach out to lift him up, and a strong, young voice is almost shouting, The crusaders are leaving, the crusaders are withdrawing. The muezzin fell to his knees with fervour and emotion, but everything in its own good time, Allah will not be offended if the thanks due to him are a little slow in coming, first the faithful must give vent to their feelings of joy. The Good Samaritan lifted the old man off the ground and set him firmly on his feet, straightened his turban which had been knocked sideways in the heat of his descent and collapse, and he told him, Don't worry about your turban, let's go to the rampart and watch the infidels scatter, now these words, spoken without any conscious malice, can only be attributed to the fact that the muezzin's blindness is caused by amaurosis, look, he is watching us, that is to say, he has his eyes fixed in our direction yet cannot see us, how sad, it is difficult to believe that such transparency and clearness are, in the final analysis, the outer surface of absolute opacity. The muezzin raises his hands and touches his eyes, But I cannot see, at this moment the man recognises him, Ah, you're the muezzin, and makes as if to move away, but quickly changes his mind, Never mind, Come with me to the rampart, I'll explain what's happening, kindly acts such as these we used to refer to as Christian charity, which goes to show once more to what extent words become ideologically disoriented.

The man pushed his way through the crowd huddling together as they tried to force their way up the stairway leading to the battlement, Make way for the muezzin, make way for the muezzin, my brothers, he pleaded, and people moved back and smiled with pure fraternal love, but so that all might not be roses, or because all is not roses, there was one suspicious onlooker who cursed this kind deed, he did not have the courage to show his face, but shouted from one of the back rows, Just look at that crafty old fellow trying to push in front of everyone else, and the muezzin who knew this was not the case, replied in the direction from which the voice came, May Allah punish you for such malice, and Allah must have taken careful note of the muezzin's words, because the slanderer will be the first man to die in the siege of Lisbon, even before any Christian, which tells us a great deal about the Almighty's wrath. And so the old man and his protector made it to the top, and by using the same strategy of warning and petition, favourably received by all, they were able to occupy an excellent vantage point, with an open view of the estuary, the wide river, the immense ocean, but it was not this particular splendour that caused the man to exclaim, Ah, such wonder, before saying to the muezzin, If only I could give you my eyes so that you might see what I can see, the fleet of the crusaders sailing down the river, the smooth water glistening as only water can, and all blue, the colour of the sky overhead, the oars move slowly up and down, the ships resembling a flock of birds that drink as they fly close to the surface, two hundred migratory birds named galleys, long-boats, and cargo-ships, and who knows what else, for I am a man of the earth, not the sea, and how swiftly they go, carried by the oars and the tide they anticipated so that they are now departing, those in front must have already felt the wind, they are about to raise their sails, ah, how wonderful if they should turn out to be white, this is a day for celebration, muezzin, yonder on the other bank, our brothers from Almada are waving, as happy as we are, also saved by the will of Allah, He who reigns supreme, the Merciful One, the Eternal, the Living God, The Comforter, the Merciful, thanks to Whom we have been liberated from the terrifying threat of those dogs sailing out of the straits, crusaders they are and may they be crucified, let the beauty of their departure perish and be forgotten with their demise, and may Malik, the custodian of hell, imprison and castigate them for evermore. Those present applauded this final rebuke, except for the muezzin, not because he disagreed, but because he had already done his duty as a moral vigilante, when he prayed that the suspicious and outspoken mischief-maker should be punished, besides it would scarcely be fitting for someone entrusted with summoning his brothers to prayer to be spreading curses, to invoke punishment once daily is more than enough for a simple human being, and we do not know if God Himself can withstand such enormous responsibility for all eternity. Therefore the muezzin remained silent, besides he was blind and unable to see for himself if there was any real cause for so much rejoicing, Have all of them gone, he asked, and his companion, after pausing long enough to check, replied, The ships, certainly, What exactly do you mean, is there something else apart from the ships, It's just that they are lying way out on the margin of the estuary and now they're heading for the Galician encampment, about a hundred men are disembarking, taking arms and baggage with them, it isn't easy to count them from here, but there can't be more than a hundred. The muezzin remarked, If these men have stayed behind, they have either definitely made up their mind not to join the crusade, and have exchanged their lands for this one, or, in the event of there being a siege and battle, they will side with

Ibn Arrinque when he attacks us, Do you really believe, muezzin, that with so few men of his own and this small contingent who will join him, that Ibn Arrinque, damn him and his offspring, will lay siege to Lisbon, He once tried with the help of the crusaders and failed, now he'll be anxious to show that he did not need them, the latter serving as witnesses, The spies report that the Galician has no more than some twelve thousand soldiers, scarcely enough men to surround and subdue a city, Perhaps not, unless they starve us into submission, So the future looks black, muezzin, It does, but then I'm blind. At this point another man who was with them stretched out his arm and pointed, Things are moving in the encampment, the Galicians are leaving, So you were mistaken, after all, said the muezzin's companion, Only when you can tell me that there is not a single Christian soldier to be seen anywhere, can I be sure that I was mistaken, Don't worry, I'll stay here to keep watch and then I'll come to the mosque to report, You're a good Moslem, may Allah grant you in this life and for all eternity the rewards you so richly deserve. Let us say here and now, in anticipation, that once again Allah will heed the muezzin's plea, because, as far as this life is concerned, we know that this man whom we have improperly called the Good Samaritan will be the penultimate Moor to die in the siege, and as for eternal life all we can do is to wait for someone who is better informed to come and tell us, when the time comes, what kind of prize that was and for what. For our part, we are taking this opportunity to show that we are also capable of exercising kindness, charity and friendship, now that the muezzin has asked, Who'll help me to go down the stairs. The proof-reader Raimundo Silva is also going to need someone to help him to explain how, after having written that the crusaders did not stay for the siege, some of them appear to have disembarked, about a hundred men, if we are to believe the calculation made by the Moors, from a distance and at a glance. Their presence certainly comes as no surprise, for we already knew ever since that unfortunate episode when Guillaume of the Long Sword spoke so rudely to the king, that several foreign nobles declared there and then that we could count on them, but no one explained the reason for this decision, nor did Dom Afonso Henriques express any desire to know, at least not in public, and, if it was clarified in private, private it remained, nothing has been recorded, nor would it have any bearing on subsequent events. Be that as it may, what Raimundo Silva cannot do is to carry on with his version, in other words, that no crusader was prepared to negotiate with the king, since the Authorised History is there to inform us that, discounting the odd exception of whom we have no details, those gentlemen truly prospered on Portuguese soil, we need only recall, so that no one may think we are speaking in vain or disproving the maxim, Look out for number one, our good king gave Vila Verde to the Frenchman, Dom Alardo, to Dom Jordãno, also French he gave Lourinhã, and to the La Corni brothers, who subsequently changed their name to Correia, was granted Atouguia, but where there is some confusion is with Azambuja, for we have no way of knowing if it was given immediately to Gilles de Rolim or later to one of his sons with the same name, this time it is not a question of there being no records, but the imprecision of those that do exist. Now then, so that these people and others may claim their benefices, it was necessary to begin by making them disembark, and so, there they are, prepared to win them with their arms, thus more or less conciliating the proof-reader's decisive *Not* with the *Yes*, or *Perhaps* and the *Even So* with which our national history has been written. We will be told that the men gathered there and others who have not been mentioned, will be little more than a half-dozen and that they are greatly outnumbered by the men advancing on the encampment, therefore it is only natural that we should be curious to know who these men are and if they, too, will have their labours rewarded with titles and property. I am aware that this is irrelevant and should be treated with contempt, but it is a sign of sound moral upbringing to be tolerant of blameless ignorance and patient with the reckless, therefore let us make it clear that the majority of these men, apart from a few mercenary conscripts, are servants who came as henchmen to do the loading and unloading, and whatever else might require to be done, without forgetting the three women brought along as concubines or mistresses to serve the particular needs of three nobles, one of them with the expedition from the outset, the others picked up wherever they happened to disembark to replenish their supplies of water, because, frankly speaking, no one has ever discovered better fruit or learned of its existence in unknown territories.

Raimundo Silva put down his biro, rubbed his fingers where the pen had left a crease, then with a slow, weary movement, he leaned back in his chair. He is in the room where he sleeps, seated at a small table which he has placed beside the window, so that by looking to the left he can see the surrounding roof-tops, and here and there, between the gables, the river. He has decided that when proof-reading the work of others he will go on using the study which has no windows, but what he is writing at present, whether it turns out to be the history of the siege of Lisbon or not, he will write in daylight, the natural light falling on to his hands, on to the sheets of paper, on to any words that might appear and remain, for not all words that appear remain, in their turn casting light on our understanding of things, as far as possible, and where, were it not for them, we would never arrive. He jotted down this thought, if it can be called that, on a loose sheet of paper, hoping to use it later, perhaps in some pondered statement about the mystery of writing which will probably culminate, following the definitive lesson of the poet, in the precise and sober declaration that the mystery of writing lies in the absence of any mystery whatsoever, which if accepted, might lead us to the conclusion that if there is no mystery about writing, neither can there be any mystery about the writer. Raimundo Silva amuses himself with this farcical display of profound meditation, his memory as a proof-reader is filled with snatches of verse and prose, the odd line or fragment, and even whole sentences with meaning, hover in his memory like tranquil and resplendent cells coming from other worlds, the sensation is that of being immersed in the cosmos, of grasping the real meaning of everything, without any mystery. If Raimundo Silva could line up in the correct order all the separate words and phrases he has memorised, he would only have to say them, record them on tape, and there he would have, without the tiresome effort of having to write it, the *History of the Siege of Lisbon* he is still pursuing, and, were the order different, the history, too, would be different, and the siege, and Lisbon, and so on and so forth.

The crusaders are already on the open sea, ridding us of the pressing and awkward presence of thirteen thousand participants, however Raimundo Silva's task was not made much easier for there are at least as many Portuguese, and, if their numbers were to be combined, they are still greatly outnumbered by the Moors inside the city, including the fugitives from Santarém who have finished up here, trying to take shelter behind these fortifications, poor wretches, wounded and humiliated. How is Raimundo Silva to cope with all these people, is the formal question. We suspect he would prefer to take each of them separately, study their lives, their precedents and consequents, their loves, quarrels, the good and bad in them, and he would pay special attention to those who are soon to die, because who could foresee that closer to our own time there would be another opportunity to leave some written record of who they were and what they did. Raimundo Silva is well aware that his limited gifts do not match up to the task, in the first place because he is not God, and even if he were, neither God nor Jesus for all his fame never achieved anything like this objective, in the second place because he is not a historian, a human category which is closer to divinity in its way of looking at things, and in the third place, an initial confession, he never had any talent for writing creative literature, a weakness that will obviously make it difficult for him to manipulate with any conviction this imaginary fable in which we all participate. On the Moorish side, the most he has achieved so far is to have a muezzin appear from time to time and who finds himself in the least favourable situation possible, because being something more than a minor figure, there is not enough to transform him into a character. On the Portuguese side, leaving aside the king, the archbishop, the bishop and a number of well-known nobles who only intervene as the bearers of aristocratic names, what is patent and indiscernible is a great confusion of faces that cannot be identified, thirteen thousand men who speak who knows how and who, presumably possessed of feelings, express them so remotely from our way of thinking that they are closer to their Moorish enemies than they are to us who are their legitimate descendants.

Raimundo Silva gets up and opens the window. From here, if the information given in *The History of the Siege of Lisbon* which he proof-read is correct, he can see the location where the English, the Aquitanians and the Bretons set up camp, yonder to the south, on the hillside of Trindade and all the way up to the ravine of the Calçada de São Fransisco, give or take a metre, there stands the church dedicated to the Holy Martyrs, which is well-named. Now, in *The New History*, it is the encampment of the Portuguese, for the moment reunited, as they wait for the king to decide whether we remain or depart, or what. Between the city and the encampment of the Lusitanians, to give them the name they themselves never used, we can see the wide estuary, so vast, winding inland, that to go around it on foot would mean passing along the eastern strait, near the Rua da Palma, and, along the western strait, near the Rua das Pretas, quite a trek across the fields which only yesterday were carefully cultivated, and now, in addition to being stripped of their crops, are trampled and scorched as if the horsemen of the Apocalypse had passed through with hooves of fire. The Moor had declared that the Portuguese encampment was moving, and so it was, but soon they came to a halt once more because Dom Afonso Henriques wished to receive with his entire army the approaching crusaders who were heading the dwindling posse of soldiers who had disembarked, thus paying them special honour, all the more so since the departure of the others had made him so angry. Familiar as we are with these encounters and assemblies between personages of lineage and influence, it is time to see who else is there, whose soldiers are these, ours, dispersed between the Carmo and the Trindade, awaiting orders, without the consolation of a cigarette, there they are seated or at a standstill or strolling among friends, in the shade of the olive-trees, for with the recent good weather, few tents have been set up, and most of the men have been sleeping in the open air, their heads resting on their shields, absorbing the night's warmth from the soil before warming it in return with the heat of their own bodies, until that day when they will lie side by side, one cold corpse against another, may it be slow in coming. We have good reason to take a close look at these men, poorly armed if one thinks of the modern weapons used by Bond, Rambo and Company, in our search for someone here who might serve as a character for Raimundo Silva, because the latter, timid by nature or temperament, averse to crowds, has lingered at his window in the Rua do Milagre de Santo António, without plucking up the courage to go down on to the street, and his behaviour is ridiculous, if he was not capable of going out alone, he could have asked Dr Maria Sara to accompany him, a woman, as we have seen, who is capable of taking decisive action, or, perhaps as a more romantic and interesting sign of solidarity, if not of blindness, he might have taken the dog on the Escadinhas de São Crispim with him, what a pretty picture that would make, a rowing-boat crossing the placid estuary, over no man's waters, and a proof-reader rowing, while the dog, sitting astern, inhales the fresh air and, now and then, bites as discreetly as possible the fleas pinching its sensitive parts. So let us leave in peace this man who is not quite ready to look, even though he spends his life revising proofs, and who only occasionally, because of some passing psychological disturbance, notices things, and let us find him someone who, not so much for his own merits, ever questionable, as for some sort of fitting predestination, may take his place in the narrative quite naturally, so that people will come to say, as one says of self-evident coincidences, that they were made for each other, However, easier said than done. It is one thing to take a man and lose him in a crowd, as witnessed elsewhere, another to search for a man in a crowd and, as soon as he is spotted, to say, That's the one. There are very few old men in the encampment, this is an age when most people die young, besides their legs would soon give way and their arms weaken in battle, for not everyone has the resistance of Gonçalo Mendes da Maia, the Warrior who even at the age of seventy gives the impression of being in his prime, and will only at ninety be struck down by the sword of the King of Tangiers and finally die. Let us go searching and listening, what a strange language our people speak, one more problem to add to all the others, for it as difficult for us to understand them as it is for them to understand us, even though we belong to the same Portuguese motherland, so who knows, perhaps what we nowadays refer to as a conflict of generations is nothing more than a question of differences in the language we use. Here there is a circle of men seated on the ground underneath a leafy olive-tree, which, judging from the gnarled trunk and general signs of age, must be at least twice as ancient as the Warrior, and while he wounds and massacres, the tree is content to produce olives, both of them serving the purpose for which they were born, as the saying goes, but these words were invented for olive-trees rather than for men. The ones who are here, for the moment, do nothing except listen to a tall, short-bearded youth, with black hair. Some give the impression of having heard the story a thousand times before, but listen patiently, they are soldiers who were at Santarém at the time of the famous siege, the others, judging from their rapt attention, must be new recruits who have joined the army along the way, and like the others, the sold paid three months in advance, from sold comes soldiering and from soldiering soldier, and, until the war begins, they assuage their thirst for glory with the glorious deeds of others. This man will have to be acknowledged by name, undoubtedly he possesses one like the rest of us, but the problem is that we shall have to choose between Mogueime which he assumes to be his name, and Moigema as he will later come to be known, do not think that such mistakes only occurred in ancient and uncivilised tomes, we have been told that someone in this century spent thirty years saying his name was Diogo Luciano, until the day when he needed to consult some papers only to discover that his real name was Diocletian, and he gained nothing from this exchange, even though the latter was an emperor. You must not discount this question of names, Raimundo could never be José, Maria Sara would not wish to be Carlota, and Mogueime does not deserve to be called Moigema. That said, we can now draw near, sit on the ground if you wish, and listen.

Mogueime narrates, It was at dead of night as we were waiting for dawn to break in a hidden and secluded valley so close to the town that when we heard the sentinels on the wall call out, we quietly took up the reins, making sure the horses did not neigh, and when the quarter moon appeared and our captains were sure that the guards were dozing off, we left, leaving the pages behind in the valley with the animals, taking a byway we were able to reach the fountain of Atamarma, so called because of the sweetness of its waters, and travelling on we approached the wall just as the patrol was passing so that we were forced to wait once more, silent as could be in a field of wheat, and when Mem Ramires, as commander of the soldiers who were with me, thought the moment was right, we lost no time in climbing the slope, the plan was to secure a ladder against the wall by sending it up on a spear, but ill-fortune decreed, or Satan, that we should run into difficulties, the ladder slipped and came crashing down with the most awful din on the roof of a pottery, everyone was in a panic, if the guards were to awaken the enterprise was in danger of failing, we got back down concealed by the shadow cast by the wall, and then, since the Moors were giving no sign of life, Mem Ramires summoned me as the tallest man there, and ordered me to climb on to his shoulders, and I secured the ladder on top, then he climbed up, with me behind him, and another behind me, and as we waited for the rest of the men to follow, the guards woke up and one of them asked, *Menfu*, which means, Who goes there, and Mem Ramires, who speaks Arabic as well as any Moor, replied that we were with the patrol and had been ordered to return, and the Moor, having come down from his turret, had his head cut off and thrown down, thus reassuring our men that we had entered the stronghold, but the other guard realised who we were and began shouting at the top of his voice, *Anauchara, anauchara*, which in their language means, An assault by the Christians, at this point there were ten of us on top of the wall as the patrol came running and swords clashed on both sides, Mem Ramires called out, invoking the help of Santiago, the patron saint of Spain, and the king, Dom Afonso, who was down below, shouted back, Santiago and the Holy Virgin Mary come to our assistance, before going on to say, Kill all of them, let no man escape, in a word, the usual incitements, meanwhile elsewhere, twenty-five of our men scaled the wall and rushed to the gates which they only managed to open after smashing the locks and bolts with an iron mallet, and then the king entered with his men, and falling to his knees at the entrance, began giving thanks to God, but rose quickly to his feet when he saw the Moors rushing to defend the gates, but the hour of their death had come and, advancing pell-mell, our soldiers massacred them along with their women and children, and their numerous livestock, and there was so much blood that it flowed though the streets like a river, and this was how Santarém came to be won, a battle in which I took part, and others who are here with me. Some of those named, nodded their heads in agreement, no doubt they would have their own deeds to relate, but being men who are always at a loss for words, firstly because they do not have enough words, secondly because words never come to mind when needed, they remained as they were, seated in silence in a circle and listening to this fellow who was much more loquacious and skilful in the incipient art of speaking Portuguese, disregard this gross exaggeration, for we must have the most advanced language in the world if eight and a half centuries ago, a simple soldier could already concoct such an eloquent speech, where not even the felicities of narration are missing, the alternation of long and short sentences, the sudden break, the transition from one plane to another, the element of suspense, and even a hint of irreverent satire in making the king get to his feet in the middle of his prayers of thanksgiving, in case the scimitar might fall before he can say amen, or, having recourse for the thousandth time to the inexhaustible treasury of popular wisdom, Trust in the Virgin rather than flee, and much good may it do you. One of the recruits, whose only experience of war had been to watch the army file past, but endowed with a sharp mind and commonsense, on seeing that none of the old guard were prepared to speak up, said what everyone else must surely have been thinking, It's fairly obvious that Lisbon is going to be a harder bone to crack, an interesting metaphor which recalls the story about the dog and the dogs, for it would take lots and lots of them to get their teeth into those tall, massive walls confronting us from afar and where weapons and white burnouses are gleaming. This warning plagued the spirits of our companions with dark omens, when it comes to wars you can never tell who is going to lose their life, and there really are fortunes that happen once and nevermore, the Moors would have to be quite mad to settle down to sleep when the fatal hour arrives, we wager that this time it will not be necessary for a sentinel to call out, *Menfu*, for they know perfectly well who is there and what they want. Fortunately this gloom was dispelled by the presence of two pages who had stayed behind to look after the horses in that hidden and secluded valley of Santarém, and they were frolicking about and laughing their heads off as they recalled what they along with others had done to a number of Moorish women who had fled the town and been guided here by destiny, a black destiny, for after being raped over and over again, they were butchered without mercy, as befitted infidels. Mogueime in the meantime disapproved, using his authority as a front-line combatant, for it may be all right, in the heat of battle, to kill women indiscriminately, but not like this, after having abused them sexually, it would have been more Christian to have let them go, a humanitarian attitude the pages contested, arguing that these women should always be put to death, raped or otherwise, so that they would conceive no more of those damn Moorish dogs. It seemed that Mogueime might have no answer to such a radical statement, but from some hidden recess of his mind he extracted a few words which left the pages speechless, Perhaps you have massacred the sons of Christians in those wombs, and they were at a loss for words, because they might well have replied that they are only Christians if the mother, too, is Christian, what must have silenced them was a sudden awareness of their importance as apostles, leaving traces of Christianity wherever they sowed their seed. A clergyman who happened to be passing, a military chaplain, would finally clarify this issue, erasing any doubts from souls and strengthening convictions and faith, but all the clergy are with the king, awaiting the foreign nobles, and now they must have arrived, judging from the cries of acclamation, each man celebrates as best he can, within limits, on this occasion so much for so little.

As for Raimundo Silva, whose main concern is to defend as best he can the unorthodox theory that the crusaders refused to take part in the conquest of Lisbon, he will be as satisfied with one character as with another, although, obviously, being a somewhat impulsive fellow, he cannot avoid sudden feelings of sympathy or aversion, peripheral, as it were, to the crux of the matter, which often allow acritical preferences or personal antipathies to prevail over rational judgments, or, as in this case, historical facts. He was drawn more by young Mogueime's lack of inhibition than his powers of narration as he listened to his account of the attack on Santarém, more by his humanitarian sentiments than any literary skills, indicative of a sound morality untainted by the negative influences of the milieu, that had led him to take pity on the Moorish women, and it is not because he does not care for the daughters of Eve, however degenerate, for had he been in the valley, instead of striking down their husbands with his sword, he would have indulged his flesh as avidly as the others, but to slit the throats of these women a minute after having kissed and bitten them with sheer pleasure, never. Therefore Raimundo Silva assumes Mogueime as his character, but believes certain points ought to be clarified beforehand, so that there will be no misunderstandings that might later prejudice, once the bonds of inevitable affection that tie the author to his worlds become binding, prejudice, as we were saying, the full assumption of causes and effects that must tighten this knot with the double force of necessity and fatality.

It is necessary, in effect, to know who is lying here and who is telling the truth, and we are not thinking about the question of names, whether it is Mogueime or Moqueime as some will get round to calling him, or Moigema, as has been said, names are certainly important, but only become so once we know them, until then, a person is simply a person, and nothing more, we look at him, he is there, we recognise him somewhere else, I know him, we say, and leave it at that. And if we eventually come to know his name, it is more than likely that of his full name we shall limit ourselves to choosing or accepting, with more precise identification, only a part of it, which goes to prove that if the name is important, not all of it has the same importance, that Einstein should have been called Albert is of no real interest, just as we are indifferent to the fact that Homer had other names. What Raimundo Silva would dearly love to confirm is whether the waters of the fountain of Atamarma were really as sweet as Mogueime claimed, announcing the future lesson of *The Chronicle of the Five Kings of Portugal*, or whether they were, in fact, bitter, as expressly stated by Fray António Brandão, whom we mentioned earlier, in his esteemed *Chronicle of Dom Afonso Henriques*, who actually goes so far as to say that it was because the waters were so bitter that the fountain was called Atamarma, which if put into the vernacular and made intelligible would strictly be called the Fountain of the Bitter Waters. Although it may not be the most important problem to resolve, Raimundo Silva took the trouble to reflect long enough to conclude that, logically, although as we well know reality does not always follow the straightforward path of logic, it would not make sense, waters on land generally being sweet, to presume to distinguish a fountain by the properties associated with fountains, just as we would not call a fountain surrounded by ferns, a fountain of maidenhairs, then he thought, until he had further evidence of other fountains, historical and authenticated, that the waters of Atamarma must have been bitter, and, continuing to think, that one day he will find out by the most practical means, namely, by drinking them, whereby he will finally reach the firm conclusion, in terms of experimentation and probability, that they are brackish, thus satisfying everyone, since you could say that brackish is somewhere between sweet and bitter.

Raimundo Silva is less concerned, however, with names and taste buds as may appear, despite the extent and duration of these latest debates, perhaps simply indicative of that oblique thinking Dr Maria Sara thought she could detect, even before she really got to know him. What really worries the proof-reader, now that he has accepted Mogueime as his character, is to find him in contradiction, if not in flagrant falsehood, a situation for which there can be no other alternative than the truth, inasmuch as there is no space left here for a new fountain of Atamarma capable of offering in conciliation, waters that are neither yea nor nay. Mogueime described, and explained quite clearly, how he climbed on to Mem Ramires's shoulders to secure the ladder between the battlements, which, moreover, would serve to demonstrate, on the basis of historical evidence, what we might imagine those ages to have been, so close to the golden age that they still retained the brilliance of certain deeds, in this case that a nobleman from the court of Dom Afonso should have loaned his precious body as support, plinth and pedestal for the thoroughly plebeian feet of a soldier with no other apparent merit than that of having grown more than the others. But what Mogueime said, and, on the other hand, is confirmed by Fray António Brandão, contradicts the earliest version of *The Chronicle of the Five Kings*, where it is written, no more no less, that Dom Mendo was most anxious lest he should arouse suspicions by making a noise so he paused for a moment in silence and then asked the young Mogueime to bend over and he climbed on to his back with the king's approval and hoisted the ladder against the wall, and notwithstanding the lexical and orthographical peculiarities of the original text, it is quite clear that Mogueime, obeying orders, bent over so that Mem Ramires might climb on to his shoulders, and all the interpretations and linguistic casuistry of this world cannot justify a different reading. Raimundo Silva has the two versions of the text before him, he compares them, there can no longer be any doubt, Mogueime is a liar, as we can logically deduce both from the difference in their rank, the one a common soldier, the other a captain, as from the particular source on which he relies, the much earlier *Chronicle of the Five Kings*. People who are only interested in broad historical syntheses are certain to find these issues far-fetched, but we have to consider Raimundo Silva, who has a task to complete and who from the outset finds himself struggling with the problem of coping with such a dubious character, this Mogueime, Moqueime or Moigema, who, as well as being unable to prove his identity, is probably abusing the truth which, as an eyewitness, it is his duty to respect and transmit to posterity, namely, to us.

But as Jesus said, let him who is without sin cast the first stone. It is, in fact, very easy to make accusations, Mogueime is lying, Mogueime lied, but those of us here present, who know rather more about the lies and truths of the last twenty centuries, with psychology nurturing souls, and the much misinterpreted psychoanalysis, together with all the rest which it would take some fifty pages to list, should not hold the defects of others up to ridicule, when we tend to be so indulgent with our own, the proof being that there is no recorded evidence of anyone who, as a severe and intransigent judge of their own actions, carried that judgment to the extreme of stoning their own body. Besides, returning to the quotation from the gospel, we are entitled to question whether the world at that time was so hardened by vice that its salvation could only be brought about by the Son of a God, for it is the episode itself about the adulteress which illustrates that things were not going all that badly there in Palestine, not like today when they are at their worst, consider how on that remote day not another stone was thrown at the hapless woman, Jesus only had to utter those fatal words for aggressive hands to withdraw, their owners declaring, confessing and even proclaiming in this manner that, yes, Sir, they were sinners. Now a people that was capable of acknowledging its sins in public, however implicitly, could not have been entirely lost, it preserved intact an inner principle of kindness, thus authorising us to conclude, with the minimum risk of being proved wrong, that there was some precipitation in the coming of the Saviour. Today, His coming would have done some good, for not only do the corrupt persevere on the path of corruption, but it becomes increasingly difficult to find any reason for interrupting the stoning once it gets under way.

At first sight, it will not appear that these moralising digressions are in any way related to the reluctance Raimundo Silva has shown in accepting Mogueime as a character, but their usefulness will become apparent when we remember that Raimundo Silva, assuming that he is immune from any greater faults, is habitually guilty of another, certainly no less serious, yet tolerated everywhere because so very widespread and accessible, and that is deception. Besides, he knows there is no real difference between lying about who climbed on to whose back, whether I climbed on to that of Mem Ramires or Mem Ramires on to mine, and, to give but one example, the mundane act of dyeing one's hair, everything, in the final analysis, is a question of vanity, the desire to keep up appearances, both physically and immorally, it being possible even now to imagine a time in which all human behaviour will be artificial, disregarding without further thought sincerity, spontaneity, simplicity, those most excellent and shining qualities of character which were so difficult to define and put into practice in times long since past when, although conscious of having invented falsehood, we still believed ourselves capable of living the truth.

Halfway through the afternoon, during a pause between coping with the problems of the siege and the trivialities of the novel which the publisher is waiting for, Raimundo Silva went out for a break. This was all he had in mind, to take a little stroll, amuse himself, mull over ideas. But on passing a florist's shop, he went in and bought a rose. White. And now he is returning home, a trifle embarrassed to be seen carrying a flower in his hand.

WITHOUT ANY WARNING, Japanese aeroplanes suddenly made a surprise attack on the United States fleet that was docked in Pearl Harbour, an act of destruction, as everyone knows, that was nothing out of the ordinary regarding the loss of human lives, if we compare it with Hiroshima and Nagasaki, but with catastrophic consequences in terms of material losses, battleships, aircraft-carriers, destroyers, and the rest, a serious financial loss, thirteen ships sunk in all without a single shot being fired seriously, apart from the usual manoeuvres. One remote cause of this naval disaster was having lost, at some hour in that night of ages that guards secrets, having lost, as we were saying, the gentlemanly custom of declaring wars with three days' notice, in order to give the enemy enough time to prepare themselves or, if they preferred, to seek refuge, also so that anyone who might decide to break the truce should not be accused of having sullied military honour. Those times are gone for ever. Because, when all is said and done, it is one thing to attack at dead of night, without either drums or trumpets, but having sent a message, and another to arrive surreptitiously and with blackened weapons, enter gates that have been carelessly left unlocked, and massacre everyone in sight. We know that no one can escape his destiny, and it is obvious that the women and children of Santarém were fated to die that night, this had been agreed between the Allah of the Moors and the God of the Christians, but at least the poor wretches could not complain that they had not been warned, if they remained it was of their own free will, for our good king had despatched Martim Moab along with two companions to the town of Santarém to warn the Moors that there would be war in three days' time, so there was no guilt on the part of Dom Afonso Henriques when he told his men, before engaging in battle, Kill regardless of sex or age, no matter whether a babe in arms, some senile old man, a young maiden, or a decrepit old woman, because he imagined, having given the notice prescribed in the code, that they might be expecting to find only Moorish warriors awaiting them, all male and in their prime.

Now then, in this episode with which we are concerned, namely, the Siege of Lisbon, any warning would have been superfluous, not only because the peace, in a manner of speaking, had been broken since the capture of Santarém, but also because the objectives of whosoever had assembled this huge army on the hills beyond were clear for all to see, and he had only been prevented from adding several more divisions because of a typographical error aggravated by feelings of resentment and wounded pride. But even so, formalities have to be observed and respected, adapting them to every situation, therefore the king determined that Dom João Peculiar together with Dom Pedro Pitões, and a fair representation of nobles, backed up by the appropriate number of armed men, should enter into discussions with the city governor, as much for the pomp and ceremony as for reasons of security. With a view to avoiding the unpleasant surprise of some irreparable betrayal, they decided not to cross the estuary, for one does not have to be a strategist like Napoleon or Clausewitz to realise that if the Moors were to lay hands on the messengers and the latter tried to escape, the estuary would prevent any kind of rapid withdrawal, if the Moorish frigates had not already surrounded and destroyed the flat-boats used for disembarking. So our men took the circuitous route they had been advised to take, along the Rua das Taipas below as far as Salitre, then, with the natural fear of anyone entering the enemy camp, they went skidding through the mud in the direction of the Rua das Pretas, followed by much climbing and descending, first up the Monte de Santa Ana, then along the Rua de São Lázaro, they then forded the brook that comes from Almirante Reis, before embarking on yet another climb, what a silly idea, to set out to conquer a whole city with all this climbing and descending, along the Rua dos Cavaleiros and the Calçada de Santo André as far as the gate we now call the Porta de Martim Moniz for no good reason. It was a long trek, worse in this heat, despite their early morning start, the hide of the mules is covered in scum, and the horses, few in number, are in a similar if not worse state, insofar as they are more delicate animals and do not have the same resistance as hybrids. As for the infantry, although sweating profusely, they do not complain, but as they wait for the gate to be opened, they must be quietly hoping that after all the effort of cutting their way through the undergrowth, there will be no fighting to be done. Mogueime is here, as it happened he was sent with the detachment, and ahead, close to the archbishop, we can also see Mem Ramires, it is an interesting coincidence that two of the main protagonists in the siege of Santarém should join forces at this historic hour, both of them equally influential in the outcome of events, at least until we can verify which of them served as a stepping stone for the other. The people convened for these formal discussions were all Portuguese, the king having deemed it inappropriate that foreigners should be involved in reinforcing an ultimatum, although, it should be said in passing, there are still grave doubts as to whether the Archbishop of Braga had any Portuguese blood in him, but then, even in those remote times we already had the reputation we have enjoyed to this day, of extending a warm welcome to outsiders and providing them with duties and benefices, and this Dom João Peculiar, let's face it, repaid us a hundredfold in patriotic deeds. And if, as is also claimed, he really was Portuguese, and from Coimbra, we may see him as a pioneer of our migratory vocation, of our magnificent dispersion, for he spent his entire youth studying in France, and here we should draw attention to the marked contrast in the fortunes of recent emigrants to that country, *plutôt* restricted to filthy and heavy labour. One unmistakable foreigner, but considered separately, because here on a special mission, and neither a political nor military figure, is that sandy-haired, freckled friar over there, whom we have just heard being called Rogeiro, but whose real name is Roger, which would leave open the question as to whether he is English or Norman, were this of any relevance to the matter in hand. The Bishop of Oporto had warned him to be prepared to write, which suggests that Roger or Rogeiro joined the expedition as a chronicler, as becomes clear when he starts removing writing materials from his knapsack, only the stylus and writing-tablets, because the swaying of his mule would spill the ink and cause his lettering to sprawl, all of this, as you know, the mere speculation of a narrator concerned with verisimilitude rather than the truth, which he considers to be unattainable. This Rogeiro does not know a word of either Arabic or Galician, but in this case ignorance will be no impediment, because the entire debate, lead where it may, will inevitably end up in Latin, thanks to the translators and simultaneous interpreters. The Archbishop of Braga will speak in Latin, one of the friars in the group will translate it into Arabic, unless it is thought preferable to consult Mem Ramires, the representative of an illustrious army, who has shown more than sufficient competence, then the Moor will reply in his own language, which the same friar or one of his companions will translate into Latin, and so on and so forth, what we do not know is whether there is anyone here entrusted with translating into Galician a summary of what is said, so that the Portuguese might be able to follow the debate in a single language. What is more than certain, with all these delays, is that if the speeches turn out to be long, we shall be here for the rest of the afternoon.

Terraces, battlements and communication trenches are crowded with dark, bearded Moors making threatening gestures, but in silence, refraining from hurling insults, after all, the Christians might withdraw as they did five years ago, in which case they might as well save their breath. The two panels of the gate were opened wide, reinforced by iron bands and nails, and a number of Moors emerged at a slow pace, one of them, getting on in years, could be the governor, a title which serves for everything and which in this case is used in the absence of any certainty about his precise title and the difficulty of choosing the right one from amongst several possibilities, besides it is just possible that they have sent out an *alfaquí*, *cadi* or *amir*, or even a *mufti*, the rest being functionaries and soldiers, their numbers strictly the same as those of the Portuguese outside, this explains why the Moors were slow in coming out, first they had to organise their delegation. We are usually led to believe that civil, military and religious authorities in ancient times were endowed with stentorian vocal organs, capable of being heard from afar, so much so that in historical narratives when some chief has to harangue his troops or other multitudes, no one is surprised that he should have been heard without difficulty by hundreds and thousands of noisy onlookers, often quite restless, when everyone nowadays knows how much work is involved in installing and tuning electronic sound equipment so that people in the back rows can hear perfectly, without any of those distortions or blurring of sound that would obviously affect the senses and change the meaning of what is being relayed. Therefore, contrary to custom and convention, and with the deepest regret at having to contradict the much applauded traditions of spectacle and historical stage sets, we are obliged out of love for the simple truth to declare that the envoys on both sides were only a few paces away from each other, and they spoke at close range as this was the only way of making themselves heard, while those looking on, whether the Moors in the fortress or the Portuguese with the delegation, awaited the outcome of this diplomatic colloquium, or whatever news the messengers might rapidly communicate as it was taking place, the odd phrase or snatch of rhetoric, sudden anxieties or dubious hopes. So it is established once and for all, that the exchanges in the debate did not echo over hill and dale, the heavens were not moved, the earth did not shake, nor the river turn back, in fact, human words have never been capable of making such an impact, not even words of threat and war such as these, contrary to what we might have believed by innocently trusting in the far-fetched descriptions given in the epics.

As the archbishop spoke, Rogeiro summarised his words in shorthand, later adding any rhetorical flourishes before addressing them afar to Osbern, wheresoever he might be and whosoever he might have been, adding in the meantime his own embellishments, the fruit of his own vivid imagination, We have come here to make peace, were the archbishop's opening remarks, and he continued, For we have thought that since all men, both you and we, are offspring of the same nature and the same origin, it seems wrong that we should pursue this more than regrettable conflict, and we wish to reassure you that we have not come here to conquer the city or take it from you, this ought to convince you of the goodwill of Christians in general, who even when they exact what is rightfully theirs, do not steal from others, and if you should argue that this is precisely what we came for, we can reply that we are only claiming this city as our rightful possession, and if you had any sense of natural justice, without any further pleas on our part, you would take your baggage, money and possessions, your women and children and return to Moorish territory from whence you came, leaving us with what is ours, no, let me finish, I can see you shaking your heads back and forth, showing with a gesture what you still have not put into words, bear in mind that you who belong to the race of the Moors and the Moabites fraudulently stole from your and our kingdom the land of Lusitania, destroying, even to this day, towns and villages and churches, for the past three hundred and fifty-eight years you have unjustly taken possession of our cities and lands, but after all, since you have occupied Lisbon for all this time and were born here, we are prepared to be generous and only request that you should hand over the keep of your castle, each of you will continue to enjoy your former freedom because we have no wish to drive you from your homes, where, I promise, you may observe your own customs, unless, through conversion, you wish of your own free will to join the ranks of the one true Church of God, I speak these words in friendship, a city as prosperous and seemingly contented as Lisbon excites much envy, take a look at those encampments, those ships, the hordes of men conspiring against you, therefore, I implore you, do not allow your fields and fruits to be destroyed, think of your riches, take pity on your own people, accept the peace offered while we are still in a generous frame of mind, for you ought to know that peace without a struggle is preferable to that achieved with much bloodshed, just as the health one has never lost is preferable to health drawn and rescued by force from serious and almost fatal illness, I am not telling you these things at random, observe how grave and dangerous the illness is from which you are suffering, because unless you take decisive action, one of two things will happen, either you will succeed in overcoming your illness or you will succumb, and instead of trying to look for other alternatives, be on your guard, for you have reached your end, so look after your health while there is still time, remember the Roman motto, The gladiator takes counsel in the arena, and do not tell me that you are Moors and not gladiators, for all I can say is that the motto applies as much to you as to them once you are about to die, that is all I have to say to you, if you have something to say, speak up, and be brief.

These did not sound like the words of a shepherd of souls, this chilling disdain you could sense lurking beneath the blandishments and honeyed words, before finally coming out with a blunt warning, however, before proceeding any further, let us repeat, this time with special emphasis, the somewhat unexpected acknowledgement of the fact that everyone here, whether Christian or Moor, is offspring of the same nature and the same origin, which leads us to assume that God, the father of nature and responsible for the origin from which all other origins have come, is unquestionably the father and creator of these estranged sons, who, in fighting against each other, deeply hurt the undivided love of their common father, and we could go so far as to say, without exaggerating, that it is over the helpless body of God the Father that his creatures battle unto death. The Archbishop of Braga's words clearly implied that God and Allah are one and the same, and going back to the time when nothing and no one had a name, there were no differences then between Moors and Christians apart from those that are apparent between one man and another, colour, girth, physiognomy, but what the prelate probably overlooked, nor should we expect so much of him, bearing in mind the backwardness and widespread illiteracy at that time, is that problems always arise the moment God's intermediaries are invoked, be they Jesus or Mohammed, not to mention the minor prophets and evangelists. We can be only too grateful that an Archbishop of Braga should have immersed himself so deeply in theological speculation, armed and equipped as he was for war, with his coat of mail, his broadsword dangling from the pommel of his saddle and his helmet with a nose-piece, arms which might well prevent him from reaching any conclusions based on humanitarian logic, because even at that time it was possible to see to what extent the artefacts of war can bring a man to think differently, something we are much more aware of today, although we are still incapable of removing the arms of those who tend to use them instead of their brains. However, nothing could be further from our thoughts than to offend these men who are still so little Portuguese that they are about to engage in combat in order to create a motherland that may serve them, openly whenever necessary, by treachery whenever expedient, for this is how motherlands have emerged and prospered, without exception, which explains why once the stain of ignominy has descended on all of them it can pass as an adornment and symbol of mutual absolution.

By allowing our mind to dwell on these somewhat hazardous thoughts, we lost the opening words of the Moorish governor's reply, and we are sorry, because as far as the herald could make out and summarise, he had started out by casting some doubt about the propriety or even the simple geographical relevance of the allusion to the kingdom of Lusitania. We are sorry, we repeat, inasmuch as the controversial question of boundaries and, more importantly, the question as to whether we really are the descendants and historical heirs of the famous Lusitanians, might perhaps have received, as reasoned by such illustrious men as the Moorish scholars at that time, some clarification, even if they were to reject it because damaging for the pride and patriotic pretensions of those who feel that they might as well be dead unless they can prove that they have two or three drops of the Lusitanian chief Viriato's blood in their veins. And it is not improbable that, having decided we have even less than this inheritance from Lusitania, and that consequently André de Resende should feel less inclined to derive lusiad from Luso, we are almost convinced that Camoens could not have found a better solution than to mundanely call his epic, *The Portuguese*. Since we are Portuguese, even if it profits us little. And now, before the rest of his speech is also lost, let us listen attentively to the Moorish governor, noticing at once how composed he sounds, speaking in the tone of voice of someone quietly discussing self-evident facts from which he has no intention of departing, How can you expect us, he asked, to believe you when you insist that you are only demanding that we should hand over the keep of our castle, that you have no desire to drive us from our homes, when we recall how you behaved in Santarém, where you inflicted the most atrocious death, even robbing the aged of the little life they had left, beheading defenceless women like innocent lambs and butchering little children whose suffering left you completely unmoved, now do not try to tell me that you have blotted these tragic events from your memory, for if it is true that we cannot confront you with the corpses of Santarém, we can certainly summon all the wounded, disfigured and mutilated who still had the strength to seek refuge in our city, these same people whom you are now about to exterminate once and for all, and us along with them, because you were not satisfied with that initial crime, but make no mistake, we never had any intention of peacefully handing over Lisbon or surrendering it to your control, even if you were to allow us to remain here, for surely you must agree that it would be most ingenuous on our part if we were to exchange certainty for uncertainty, security for instability, trusting only in your word which is worth so little. The Bishop of Oporto reacted violently, as if he were about to interrupt the Moor, but the Archbishop cautioned him, Be quiet, let us hear him out, you will have the final word. The Moor continued, This city was once yours, but now it is ours, and in the future it may be yours once more, but that is up to God who chose to give it to us and will take it from us whensoever He wishes, because no rampart is impregnable against His holy will, of this we are convinced, and we desire only what is pleasing to God, who has rescued us from your hands on so many occasions, wherefore it is only right that we should never cease to worship Him and marvel at His irrevocable designs, not only because He holds power over all evils, but also because it is His sublime reason that submits us to disasters, sorrows and injuries, so be gone from here, only by force can the gates of Lisbon be opened, and as for these inevitable disasters promised us, should they ever occur, that is something for the future, and to torment us with what has yet to come is nothing more than madness and a deliberate provocation of misfortune. The Moor paused as if searching for other arguments, but probably thinking it pointless, he shrugged his shoulders and concluded, Remain here no longer, do whatever you like, as for us we shall obey God's will.

Raimundo Silva was favourably impressed by these thoughtful words, not simply because the Moor was leaving it to God to resolve the differences which in his holy name and solely on his behalf bring men to fight each other, but because of the Moor's admirable serenity in the face of possible death, which, being ever certain, becomes fatalistic, as it were, when it comes in the guise of the possible, that sounds like a contradiction but you only have to think about it. Comparing the two speeches, it saddened the proofreader that a simple Moor deprived of the light of the true faith, even though bearing the title of governor, should outshine the Archbishop of Braga in prudence and eloquence, despite the prelate's wide experience of codicils, bulls and dogmas. It is only natural that we should prefer to see our own side always gain the upper hand, and Raimundo Silva, although suspicious that there might be more Moorish blood than that of Aryan Lusitanians in the nation to which he belongs, would have liked to applaud Dom João Peculiar's reasoning rather than find himself intellectually outwitted by the exemplary speech of an infidel whose name has been forgotten. However, there is still a possibility that we might finally prevail over the enemy in this rhetorical joust, and that is when the Bishop of Oporto, also armed, begins to speak and, resting his hand on the hilt of his broadsword, he says, We addressed you in friendship, in the hope that our words would fall on friendly ears, but since you have shown annoyance at what we had to say, the time has come for us to speak our mind and tell you how much we despise this habit of yours of waiting for events to take their course and evil to strike, when it is clear for all to see how fragile and weak hope can be, unless you trust in your own valour rather than in the misfortunes of others, it is as if you were already prepared for defeat, only to speak later about the uncertain future, take heed that the more often an enterprise turns out badly, the harder we have to try to make it succeed, and all our efforts against you having been frustrated so far, we are now making another attempt, so that you may finally meet the destiny awaiting you when we enter these gates you refuse to open, yes, live in accordance with God's will, that same will is about to ensure us victory, and there being nothing more to add, we are withdrawing without any further formalities, nor do we expect any from you. Bidding them farewell with these offensive words, the Bishop of Oporto took up the reins of his horse, although in terms of rank, he was not entitled to take this initiative, he had acted out of pique, and was now taking the entire party with him, when the Moor unexpectedly spoke up, without any trace of the intolerable stoicism that had sent the prelate into a rage, now he spoke with the same arrogance and pride, and here is what he had to say, You are making a grave mistake if you confuse patience with cowardice and fear of death, no such mistake was made by your fathers and grandfathers whom we defeated a thousand and one times in armed combat throughout the length and breadth of Spain, and beneath this very soil you tread lie the corpses of those who thought they could challenge our domain, can you not see that your days of conquest are over, your bones will be broken against these walls, your grasping hands cut off, so be prepared to die, for as you well know, we are ever prepared.

There is not a cloud in the sky, the warm sun shines on high, a flock of swallows flies back and forth, circles with much twittering over the heads of these sworn enemies. Mogueime looks up at the sky, gives a shudder, perhaps brought on by the wild screeching of the birds or the Moor's threats, the heat of the sun affords him no comfort, a strange chill makes his teeth chatter, the shame of a man who with a simple ladder brought down Santarém. The silence was broken by the Archbishop of Braga's voice giving an order to the scribe, You must make no mention, Fray Rogeiro, of what the Moor said, words thrown to the wind when we had already departed and were descending the slope of Santo André on our way to the encampment where the king awaits us, he will see, as we draw our swords and raise them to the sunlight, that battle has commenced, and that is something you can certainly write down.

DURING THOSE FIRST DAYS after he had thrown away the dyes which for years had concealed the ravages of time, Raimundo Silva, like an ingenuous sower waiting to see the first shoot break through, examined the roots of his hair, day and night, with obsessive interest, morbidly relishing his anticipation of the shock he would almost certainly get once the natural hairs began to appear amongst the dyed ones. But because one's hair, from a certain age onwards, is slow in growing, or because the last dyeing had tinged, or tinted, even the subcutaneous layers, let it be said in passing that all of this is no more than an assumption imposed by the need to explain what is, after all, not very important, Raimundo Silva gradually lost interest in the matter, and now combs his hair without another thought as if he were in the first flush of youth, although it is worth noting a certain amount of bad faith in this attitude, a certain falsification of self with oneself, more or less translatable in a phrase that was neither spoken nor thought, Because I can pretend that I cannot see, I do not see, which came to be converted into an apparent conviction, even less clearly expressed, if possible, and irrational, that the last dyeing had been definitive, like some prize conceded by fate in recompense for his courageous renunciation of the world's vanities. Today, however, when he has to deliver to the publisher the novel which he has finally read and prepared for the printers, Raimundo Silva, on entering the bathroom, slowly put his face to the mirror, with cautious fingers he pushed back the tuft of hair on his forehead, and refused to believe what his eyes were seeing, there were the white roots, so white that the contrast in colour seemed to make them whiter still, and they had an unexpected appearance, as if they had sprouted from one day to the next, while the sower had fallen asleep from sheer exhaustion. There and then, Raimundo Silva repented the decision he had taken, that is to say, he did not quite get round to repenting, but thought that he might have postponed it a little longer, he had foolishly chosen the least opportune moment, and he felt so vexed that he wondered whether there might be a bottle which he had forgotten and was still lying around somewhere, with some dye left, at least just for today, tomorrow I'll go back to sticking to my resolution. But he did not start searching, partly because he knew he had thrown out the lot, partly, because he feared, assuming that he found something, that he would have to make another decision, as it was quite possible that he might decide against it and end up playing this game of coming and going for lack of the willpower to refuse to succumb once and for all to the weakness he acknowledges in himself.

When Raimundo Silva wore a wristwatch for the first time many years ago, he was a mere adolescent, and fortune pandered to his immense vanity as he strolled about Lisbon and proudly sported his latest novelty, by crossing his path with that of four different people who were anxious to know the time, Have you the time, they asked, and generous fellow as he was, he did indeed know the time and lost no time in telling them so. The movement of stretching out his arm in order to draw back his sleeve and display the watch's shining face gave him a feeling of importance at that moment that he would never experience again. And least of all now as he makes his way to the publishing house, trying to pass unnoticed in the street or amongst the passengers on the bus, withholding the slightest gesture that might attract the attention of anyone who, also wanting to know the time, might stand there staring in amusement at that unmistakable white line of the parting on the top of his head while waiting for him to overcome his nerves and disentangle his watch from the three sleeves that are covering it today, that of his shirt, his jacket and his coat, It's half past ten, Raimundo Silva finally replies, furious and embarrassed. A hat would come in handy, but that is something the proof-reader has never worn, and if he did, it would only resolve a fraction of his problems, he certainly has no intention of walking into the publishers wearing a hat, Hello there, how is everyone, the hat still stuck on his head as he marches into Dr Maria Sara's office, I've brought you the novel, obviously, it would be best to act as if the colours in his hair were all quite natural, white, black, dyed, people look once, do not look a second time, and by the time they look a third time, they notice nothing. But it is one thing to acknowledge this mentally, to invoke the relativity that conciliates all differences, to ask oneself, with stoic detachment, what a white hair on earth means in the eyes of Venus, another dreadful moment is when he has to confront the telephonist, to withstand her indiscreet glance, to imagine the giggles and whisperings that will while away idle moments in the next few days, Senhor Silva has stopped dyeing his hair, he looks so comical, before they used to mock him because he dyed it, but then there are people who always find something to amuse themselves at the expense of others. And suddenly all these foolish worries disappeared because the telephonist Sara was saying to him, Dr Maria Sara isn't here, she is ill and hasn't come to work for the last two days, these simple words left Raimundo Silva divided between two conflicting sentiments, relief that she should not see his white hair reappearing, and deep distress, not caused by her illness, of the seriousness of which he was still unaware, it could be a flu without complications, or a sudden indisposition, the sort of complaint that affects women, for example, but because he suddenly felt lost, a man risks so much, subjects himself to vexations, just to be able to hand over in person the original manuscript of a novel, and there is no hand there, perhaps it is resting on a pillow beside a pale face, where, until when. Raimundo Silva realises in a second that he has lingered so long in handing over the work in order to savour, with unconscious voluptuousness, the anticipation of a moment that was now eluding him, Dr Maria Sara isn't here, the telephonist had informed him, and he made as if to leave, but then remembered that he ought to entrust the original manuscript to someone, to Costa presumably, Is Senhor Costa here, he asked, suddenly realising that he was deliberately standing in profile to avoid being observed by the telephonist, and, irritated by this show of weakness, he turned around in order to confront all the curiosities of this world, but young Sara did not as much as look at him, she was too busy inserting and pulling out plugs on the old-fashioned switchboard, and all he got was an affirmative gesture as she nodded vaguely towards the inner corridor, all this meaning that Costa was in his office, and that as far as Costa was concerned, there was no need to announce this visitor, something Raimundo Silva did not need to be told because before the arrival of Dr Maria Sara all he had to do was to walk straight in and look for Costa who, as Production Manager, could be found in any of the other offices, pleading, remonstrating, complaining, or simply apologising to the administration, as he always had to do, no matter whether he was responsible or not for any slip-ups in the schedule.

The door of Dr Maria Sara's office is closed. Raimundo Silva opens it, peers inside and feels a knot in his stomach, not so much because of her absence as because of a dispiriting sense of emptiness, of final abandonment, suggested perhaps by the tidy arrangement of objects which, it occurred to him one day, is only tolerable when disturbed by a human presence. Over the desk drooped a withered white rose, two of its petals having already been shed. Raimundo Silva nervously shut the door, he could not stay there in case someone appeared, but this idea of an empty office, where a single life, that of a rose, was slowly withering, close to death because of a progressive depletion of cells, filled him with evil premonitions, with dark omens, all quite absurd, as he would subsequently reflect, What have I got to do with this woman, but not even this feigned detachment will put his mind at rest. Costa received him cordially, Yes, Dr Maria Sara is ill, I'm looking after things, superfluous words, all of them, Raimundo Silva already knew that Maria Sara was ill, that Costa should be dealing with her work was only to be expected, and, as for the rest, no need to worry, he could not care less about the novel's immediate or future destiny, what he needed was some information that no one was likely to give him unless he asked, after all, an employee on sick leave scarcely justifies the publication of hourly medical bulletins. So at the risk of rousing Costa's curiosity as to why he should be so interested, Raimundo Silva finally plucked up the courage to ask, Is it serious, Is what serious, the other asked in return, having failed to grasp what he was talking about, Dr Maria Sara's illness, now Raimundo Silva is worried at the thought that he might be blushing at this very moment, Oh, I shouldn't imagine so, and steering the conversation towards more professional matters, Costa added, introducing a subtle note of irony, directed both at the absent Dr Maria Sara and the proof-reader who is present, Even if she were to stay at home for a while, you may rest assured that work will proceed as normal. At this point Costa ever so slightly averted his eyes, a hint of smiling malice creeping into his expression. Raimundo Silva frowned, waiting for some further remark, but Costa had already turned to the novel, was leafing through it as if searching for something he could not quite define, but his attitude was not altogether conscious, and now it was the proof-reader's turn to smile as he remembered that day when Costa had leafed through another book, the erroneous proofs of *The History of the Siege of Lisbon*, their falsification finally frustrated, yet the cause of these radical changes, these outrageous alterations, a new siege, an encounter no one could have foreseen, certain feelings that slowly began to stir, like the impenetrable waves of a sea of mercury. Suddenly, Costa became aware that he was being observed, thought he understood why, and like someone carrying out tardy revenge, asked, Have you by any chance inserted the odd *Not* this time, and Raimundo Silva answered with tranquil irony, Put your mind at rest, this time I put in a *yes*. Costa abruptly pushed aside the bundle of page proofs and said drily, If there is nothing else I can do for you, he left the phrase in suspense, with invisible dots of suspension, but thanks to his lengthy experience as a proof-reader, Raimundo did not need them in order to know that it was time for him to leave.

Young Sara takes advantage of a quiet moment to give all her attention to a fingernail that had broken a few minutes earlier in that infernal bustle of inserting and pulling out plugs, she has already repaired the damage and is now deeply absorbed in gently smoothing the nail with her file, she is certainly not going to reply to Raimundo Silva as he would wish, having had the bright idea whilst walking down the corridor perhaps helped by the dialectic parrying with Costa, these are the advantages of an intellectual gymnastic exercise, but now we shall see if it will serve any purpose, the question being the following, Do you know if Dr Maria Sara is well enough to receive telephone calls, it's just that I have some business, another interrupted phrase, an anxious look, in fact, he could not have chosen a worse moment, the inevitable annoyance of someone who has just broken a long, oval-shaped fingernail, and besides the number will have to be traced in the telephone directory, assuming the telephonist is willing to divulge it, Just my luck, muses Raimundo Silva, that this should have happened, the broken nail, the file, Ah, Senhor Silva, if only you knew the trouble I have with these nails, how I wish they would get rid of this old contraption and give me a modern push-button electronic switch-board, whether she is well enough to receive telephone calls, I cannot say, but here is her number if you'd like to write it down. She knew it by heart, one of her little vanities, to memorise as many numbers as she could, to boast of her memory, Sara has a phenomenal memory, and just as well, because she had to repeat the number twice, Raimundo Silva was in such a muddle, first of all because he could not find anywhere to write, then he got the numbers mixed up, hearing six instead of three, at the same time as his brain pursued a nagging question he could not resist raising in a tone of voice feigning nonchalance, Obviously if no one has called her from here, then she isn't receiving any calls, No calls have passed through me, but the administration may have called her on a direct line, of course, the direct line does not pass through the telephonist, one can speak at will by means of a direct line and Raimundo Silva seems to remember there having been a direct line in the Editorial Director's office. Young Sara has finished repairing her broken nail and critically appraises the result, bearing in mind the seriousness of the damage, she has done her best and is moderately satisfied, which may explain why she asks him, If you wish, I can call her from here, leaving Raimundo Silva speechless, he shook his head vigorously, and just at that moment, divine providence, the switchboard signalled an incoming call, two signals that were almost simultaneous, the world went into its routine orbit, or so it will seem to anyone who does not know that Raimundo Silva is already carrying Maria Sara's telephone number in his pocket, and this makes a vast difference to the universe.

Contrary to his habitual thriftiness, he returned home by taxi, no great surprise, for he could not wait to get back to his desk, pick up the telephone and dial Maria Sara's number, tell her, I heard you were ill, I trust it's nothing serious, I've just delivered the novel to Costa, I'm glad to know you're feeling better, you're right, you have to be healthy to succumb to illness, a silly expression, but that's life, at least half the things we say don't make much sense, no, Costa hasn't given me any more work, well, it doesn't really matter, I need a rest, yes, a rest, so that I can put my papers into some order, sort out my life, in a manner of speaking, obviously, what I do is to think that I am thinking about life and I'm not really thinking about anything, but I didn't mean to bore you with my personal problems and difficulties, yes, in coping with life, I wish you a speedy recovery and hope to see you back at work soon, goodbye for now. But Senhora Maria, despite this not being her day, has turned up for work, she explains that she has to take her nephew to the doctor tomorrow when she should have been coming here, so she decided to come today instead, Raimundo Silva had no idea that his charlady had a nephew, My sister can't afford to stay off work, That's fine, it doesn't make any difference, and he shut himself away in his study in order to use the telephone. But his courage failed him. Even with the door shut, he would feel uneasy about making a simple call to find out about the state of health of someone higher up the ranks, How have you been, Dr Maria Sara, perhaps it would be different, certainly easier, if his superior were a man rather than a woman, although Raimundo Silva would have to admit, if called to account, that whenever any of the other directors had been ill in all these years, our proof-reader had never once remembered to ring up and inquire about their precious health. In brief, what Raimundo Silva appeared not to want, for some obscure, not to say, clear reason, if we take into account what we have learned of this man's personality, withdrawn, indecisive, was that Senhora Maria should suspect that her employer was holding a telephone conversation with a woman. The outcome of this absurd conflict will be to request that his lunch should be left on the kitchen table while he goes out to rid himself of two obsessive presences, that of the telephone and that of Senhora Maria, both clearly innocent and oblivious of the war in which they have become involved. Raimundo Silva is eating the usual plate of soup with beans and greens, while a meat and potato stew, already heated up, is waiting on the stove, when the voice of Senhora Maria can be heard asking from the other room, Can I throw out this withered rose, and almost in a panic, he replies, No, no, leave it alone, I'll deal with it, he could not hear the charlady's closing remarks, but she made some comment, which may not have been resentful but sounded very much like it, a further reminder that it is impossible to deceive a woman, even if only a charlady, when a rose, a white rose if you please, suddenly appears in a man's apartment where no flower has ever been seen before, and it is just possible that what Senhora Maria said was, There's a Moorish ship on the coast, a historical and popular saying expressing grave suspicion, dating from the time when the Moors who had already been driven out of Portuguese territory were forever attacking our shores and coastal towns, and nowadays a mere rhetorical reminiscence, but serving some purpose, as has just been seen.

Without the help of the crusaders, who are already way out on the open sea, Raimundo Silva finds himself deprived of the military weight of these twelve thousand men in whom we had placed so many hopes, leaving him with no more than roughly the same number of Portuguese, not nearly enough men to constitute a vanguard capable of surrounding the entire city, and being in full view of the Moors, they will find it impossible to move away together, to carry out an attack, for example, on one of the gates, without their movements alerting those inside that they have sufficient time to reinforce the position about to be attacked by those on the outside who have to pass over hill and dale and a fair amount of water. It becomes necessary, therefore, to reconsider their strategy, and in order to examine the theatre of operations *in loco*, Raimundo Silva once more climbs up to the castle from whose lofty towers he can survey the terrain, rather like a chessboard, where the pawns and knights will fight each other, objectively speaking, beneath the gaze of the king and bishops, perhaps with the assistance of several additional towers, built, if the suggestion of one of the foreigners who remained with us should be taken up, Let's raise them to the height of the walls and push them up close, so that all we have to do is to jump over and kill the infidels, It sounds easy, replied the king, but we must see if we have enough carpenters, Don't let that worry you, retorted the other, that Heinrich who bore his name and was a man of great piety, fortunately we live in an age when every man can turn his hand to anything, sow grain, harvest the wheat, mill it, bake bread, and eventually eat it, unless he dies beforehand, or, as in this case, construct a wooden tower and climb it, sword in hand, to kill the Moor or be killed by him.

As the debate proceeds, inconclusively as yet, but with a clear forecast of losses, Raimundo Silva mentally verifies the location of the gates, that of Alfofa, on top of whose wall he lives, that of Ferro, that of Alfama, that of Sol, which look directly on to the city, and the gate known as Martim Moniz, the only gate of the castle facing on to the open countryside. So it is obvious that the twelve thousand soldiers of King Afonso will have to be divided into five groups in order to cover all the gates with the same manpower, and for five, read six, because we must not forget the sea, which is not really the sea, but a river, however by force of habit the Moors always referred to it as the sea, and this is what we call it even today, now then, things being so, we are talking about the groups, what we have here is the absurd situation of two thousand men for each battle front. Not to mention, God help us, the problem created by the estuary. As if the steepness of the various points of access were not enough, with the exception of the Gate of Alfama, which is at ground level, there was this estuary getting in the way and complicating even more the already difficult deployment of the troops, scattered for the moment along the heights and slopes of the Monte de São Fransisco as far as São Roque, where they are resting, replenishing their strength in the gentle shadows, but if no attack could be launched from such a distance, nor arrows reach their target, this would scarcely be a siege worthy of the name with that unguarded estuary down below, giving free passage to reinforcements and supplies from the other side, for it was most unlikely that the fragile line of the naval blockade about to be set up would prove a lasting obstacle. This being the case, there would appear to be no other solution than to move four thousand men to the other side, while the others will follow the route taken by the emissaries João Peculiar and Pedro Pitões, before finally taking up positions in front of the three gates facing north and east, namely that of Martim Moniz, that of Sol and that of Alfama, as previously explained and now repeated here, to satisfy the reader and round off the discourse. Returning to that cautious and vacillating phrase of Dom Afonso Henriques, everything sounds so easy, however, a quick glance at the map will soon expose the complexity of the problems of strategy and logistics which have to be faced and resolved. The first problem is directly concerned with the number of ships available, these are scarce, and this is where the assistance of the crusaders would be most useful, with their entire fleet and those hundreds of boats and other service vessels, which, if they were here, in the twinkling of an eye would be able to transport the soldiers to form the most extensive line of attack imaginable, obliging the Moors to disperse along the riverbank and therefore weaken their defence. The second, and most pressing problem right now, is to decide the point or points of disembarkation, a matter of crucial importance, because they have to take into account not only the greater or lesser proximity of the gates, but also the hazards of the terrain, from the swamps at the mouth of the estuary to the precipitous rock faces defending the access to the gate of Alfofa from the southern side. The third, fourth and fifth problems, or sixth and seventh, could also be listed were it not for the fact that all of them follow on, more or less in mathematical order, from the first two, so we shall simply mention one further detail, but of considerable importance because of what it tells us about the veracity of other details in this narrative, the aforementioned detail being the very short distance separating the Porta de Ferro from the shore of the estuary, no more than a hundred paces, or, in modern measurements, some eighty metres, which rules out any possibility of disembarking here, because as the flotilla of canoes, with their heavy load of men and arms, would come crawling forward awkwardly in mid estuary, the city walls on this side would already be garrisoned with soldiers, while others, stationed at the water's edge, would be waiting for the Portuguese to approach in order to riddle them with arrows. And so Dom Afonso Henriques will tell his chief of staff, It isn't easy, after all, and as they discuss other possible tactics let us recall that fat woman in the Café Graciosa, at the outset of these events, commenting on the wretched state of the people fleeing from the advancing forces, who said she had seen them enter, covered in blood, through the Porta de Ferro, which at the time people accepted to be true, because testified by an eyewitness. But let us be logical. Undoubtedly, because of its proximity to the shore of the estuary, the Porta de Ferro would be used mainly for the river traffic of people and merchandise, which obviously would not deter fugitives from entering, were it not for the fact that it was located, in a manner of speaking, at the southern tip of the wall, thus making it the most distant of all the points of access for anyone ousted from the north or from the region of Santarém. That some unfortunates, driven out of the territory between Cascais and Sintra, should have reached the city along routes that ended up at the estuary, and, on arriving there, should still have found ferrymen to transport them to the shore on this side, is quite possible. Such cases, however, would be rare, and scarcely authorise the fat woman to make special reference to the Porta de Ferro, when she herself was so close to the Porta de Alfofa, which even the least attentive observers of maps and topographies would recognise as being more appropriate, as it was no less true of the gates of Sol and Alfama, to receive this sad invasion. And what is most curious is that no one among those present should have contradicted this inaccurate version of the facts when the evidence was so readily available, which only goes to show how lacking in curiosity some people are and how slow their minds work, when confronted with such a dogmatic statement, wheresoever it may come from and whatever its reliability, whether from a fat woman or Allah, not to cite other well-known sources.

The king said, Having heard your wise opinions and after considering the advantages and disadvantages of the various plans proposed, it is my sovereign will that the entire army should move from this place and go off to besiege the city from closer by, for here we shall never achieve victory even if the world were to end, so we shall proceed as follows, a thousand men experienced in navigation will go in the barges since we do not have enough vessels for any more, even counting the boats the Moors were unable to take inside the walls or destroy and which we had captured, and these men will be entrusted with cutting off all communications by sea, making sure that no one may enter or leave, and the remaining body of troops will be concentrated on the Monte da Graça, where we shall finally divide, two fifths moving to the gates on the eastern side, another two fifths to those on the western side, and the rest will remain over there to guard the northern gate. Then Mem Ramires intervened, pointing out that since the task was much more arduous and dangerous for the soldiers being sent to attack the gates of Alfofa and Ferro, because stuck, as it were, between the city and the estuary, it would be prudent to reinforce them, at least until such time as they were able to consolidate their positions, for there would be the most terrible disaster if the Moors were to make a sudden incursion and push the Portuguese back to the sea, where we would be forced to choose between drowning or being slaughtered, caught, as the saying goes, between sword and fire. The king was impressed by this advice, and there and then appointed Mem Ramires captain of the western group, postponing the nominations for other commands until later, As for me, destined as I am by nature and my royal obligations to be the commander of all of you, I shall also assume under my direct orders a body of the army, namely the one on Monte da Graça where the general headquarters will be. It was now the turn of the Archbishop Dom João Peculiar to intervene to say that God would be displeased to find that those killed in this battle for the conquest of the city of Lisbon were being buried here and there throughout these hills and valleys, when they should be receiving a Christian burial on consecrated ground, and that since from the time of their arrival here, some had already died because of illness or in some brawl, and had been buried somewhere outside the encampment, the cemetery which, in effect, had already been started, should be established there. At this point, Gilbert from England spoke up on behalf of the foreigners, arguing that it would be indecent, because confusing, that in the aforesaid cemetery, the Portuguese should be buried alongside the crusaders, because the latter, should God will that they lose their lives in these parts, had every right to be considered martyrs, just as those who were even now sailing to meet their deaths in the Holy Land were promised martyrdom, so that in his opinion not one but two cemeteries ought to be consecrated, allowing each dead man to be buried alongside his peer. The king liked this suggestion, although resentful mutterings could be heard amongst the Portuguese, who even at the hour of death saw themselves being deprived of the glories of martyrdom, and without wasting any time, they were soon all on their way to mark out the provisional boundaries of the two cemeteries, postponing their consecration until the territory was finally rid of these living sinners, and orders have already been given that in due course those first stray corpses should be disinterred and reburied elsewhere, all of them, as it happened, Portuguese. Once he had carried out this inspection, the king closed the meeting, duly recorded with all the appropriate formalities, and Raimundo Silva returned home as evening began to draw in.

To Raimundo Silva's annoyance, Senhora Maria was no longer there, not because she might have left half the chores unfinished, but because there was now no one to come between him and the telephone, no indiscreet witness who, with her presence, might absolve him from the cowardice, or timidity, a less offensive word, that had overwhelmed him on confronting that other self who, with such subtle cunning, had persuaded the telephonist at the publishing house to divulge Maria Sara's number, and, as we saw, one of the world's best kept secrets. But this other Raimundo Silva is an unpredictable fellow, he has his days, or not even that, simply hours or seconds, at times he erupts with a force that seems capable of moving worlds, both outside and within, but it never lasts, no sooner does that force come than it is gone, a fire that is barely alight when it dies out. The Raimundo Silva who is here before the telephone, incapable of lifting the receiver and dialling a number, was the man, at the top of the castle with the city stretching out below, the man, we insist, to plan the best possible tactics for the mammoth task of besieging and capturing Lisbon, but he is now close to repenting that moment of reckless bravado when he gave in to another person's wishes, and he is about to search in his pockets for the paper on which he jotted down the number, not to use it, but in the hope that he might have lost it. He has not lost it, the piece of paper is there, crumpled up in his open hand, as if, and this is what it was, even though Raimundo Silva does not remember, he were afraid of losing it during all that time he had spent searching and fumbling. Seated at his desk, with the telephone beside him, Raimundo Silva imagines what might happen if he were to decide to dial the number, what conversation would he engage in other than the one he had invented beforehand, and as he considers the various possibilities, it occurs to him, and it is absurd that it should occur to him for the first time, that no one knows anything about Maria Sara's private life, whether she is married, a widow, spinster or divorcee, if she has any children, if she lives with her parents, or with only one of them, or neither, and this unknown reality becomes threatening, it shakes and demolishes the fragile architecture of the dream and foolish hopes he had been building for several weeks on sandy terrain without any solidity, Suppose I were to dial the number and a man's voice answers telling me she cannot come to the telephone, that she is in bed, but if I should like to leave some message or inquiry, not really, I only wanted to know if she is feeling better, yes, I'm a colleague of hers and as I spoke I would be asking myself once more if the word colleague is appropriate in the case of a professional relationship between a proof-reader and his boss, and as our conversation came to a close, I would ask, To whom am I speaking, and he would reply, I'm her husband, now it is true that she does not wear a wedding ring but that does not mean anything, there are plenty of married couples around who do not wear rings and consider themselves just as happy, or they are unhappy and then it does not matter, besides the man's reply would be the same whatever the circumstances, He would say, I'm her husband, even if he were not, he most certainly would not say, I'm her companion, the word companion is no longer used, and even more unlikely, I'm the man she lives with, a vulgar expression no one would use, but there is something about Maria Sara that tells me she is not married, it is not just the absence of a wedding ring, it is something difficult to define, the way she speaks, the way she pays attention while giving the impression that her mind is elsewhere, and when I say married, I also mean living with a man, or to have a man although not actually living with him, what is usually referred to as an affair, or a casual relationship, without any ties or commitments, the most common situation of all nowadays, although I cannot claim to have much experience of such blessings, I simply observe the world and learn from those who know, ninety per cent of the knowledge we claim to possess comes to us in this way, not from first-hand experience, and therein also resides the merest premonition, that nebulous information wherein occasionally shines that sudden light we call intuition, now then, my premonition and intuition tell me that there is no man in Maria Sara's life, impossible though it may seem for one so pretty, no raving beauty, but most appealing, as for her body, the first impression is good, but bodies can only be judged when they are naked, this is sound advice, judge on the evidence, better still afterwards, once you know what was covered and have found it to your liking.

Everyone agrees that the powers of imagination are infinite, as this instance has once more proved, when Raimundo Silva began to feel his own body, what was happening inside it, first the sensation of a weak earth-tremor, almost imperceptible, then a sharp palpitation, insistent, urgent. Raimundo Silva looks on, with half-closed eyes he follows the process as if he were mentally recalling a familiar page, and he remains quiet, waiting, until his blood little by little recedes like the tide abandoning a cavern, slowly, from time to time still tossing fresh waves in rebellion, but it is futile, the tide ebbs, these are the final assaults, finally there is nothing but the quiet trickling of rivulets of water, the algae spread limply over the rocks where tiny crabs scurry in terror to take shelter, leaving signs on the wet sand that are barely discernible. Now in a pleasant state of semi-numbness, Raimundo Silva asks himself where these grotesque little creatures might have come from and what they are trying to tell him with their strange, disconcerting movements, as if nature had initiated its predictable general upheaval, In future, we'll all be crabs, he thought, and suddenly he could visualise the soldier Mogueime on the bank of the estuary, washing blood from his hands and watching the crabs of that time escape, to the right, into the darkest depths, their earthen colour merging with the shadows of the water. The image quickly disappeared, another came, like passing slides, once more it was the estuary, but now there was a woman washing clothes at the water's edge, Raimundo Silva and Mogueime knew who she was, they had been told she was the concubine of the aforementioned knight Heinrich, a German from Bonn, picked up in Galicia when some crusaders disembarked there to replenish their supplies of drinking-water, one of their servants abducted her, now the knight has been killed in ambush along with his servant, and the woman goes around, more or less with any man whom she chances to meet, we say more or less, but with caution, because sometimes she has been taken against her will, two fellows who tried it were discovered several days later stabbed to death, those responsible were never found, with such a large gathering of men, it is difficult to avoid disorder and violence, not to mention that it might have been the work of Moors who had infiltrated the encampment and were secretly carrying out treacherous assaults. Mogueime got close to the woman, and a few paces away, sat on a rock and watched her. She did not turn round, she had seen him out of the corner of her eye as he approached, she recognised him from his appearance and familiar gait, although she did not yet know his name, only that he was Portuguese, having heard him speak Galician on one occasion. The swaying movement of the woman's hips perturbed Mogueime. Besides, he had his eye on her ever since the knight's death, and even long before then, but a common soldier, and medieval at that, would never dare to pursue another man's woman even if a concubine. He had felt angry and resentful when he then saw her carried off by others, but she had not stayed with any of them, however much they loved her, like those men stabbed to death who had desired her so much that they wanted to take her by force. To take her by force himself was never Mogueime's intention, especially here in this wilderness in full view of everyone, soldiers who were off duty, stable-lads washing down their masters' mules, a truly peaceful scene which seemed remote from the imminent siege and assault on the city, especially if, as now, we turn our backs on the city and castle and contemplate the tranquil surface of the waters of the estuary as it wends its way inland where the broad swell of the river cannot reach, and ahead the hills with trees scattered here and there on terrain that is yellowish one minute and dark green the next depending on whether it is covered by perennial scrub or pasture scorched by the sun. It is midday and the heat is intense, eyes have to be averted from the water in order not be dazzled and blinded by the constant glare of the sun, but not the eyes of Mogueime who goes on staring at the woman. She now straightens up, raises and lowers her arm to beat the clothes, the sound of smacking travels over the water, an unmistakable sound, then another smack, and another, and then silence, the woman rests both hands on the white rock, an ancient Roman sarcophagus, Mogueime looks without moving, at that moment the wind carries the shrill cry of a muezzin, almost muffled in the distance, yet still intelligible for anyone who, although not familiar with the Arabic language, has been listening to that cry for almost a month, three times a day. The woman turns her head slightly to the left as if trying to hear the muezzin's invocation more clearly, and Mogueime being on this side, a little way behind, it was inevitable their eyes should meet. Any physical desire Mogueime might have felt died instantly, his heart beating fast as if in panic, it is difficult to probe the matter any further for one has to take into account the primitive nature of feelings at that time, there is always the risk of falling into an anachronism, for example, to put diamonds on crowns of iron or invent subtleties of refined eroticism in bodies that are content to go all the way after making a quick start. But Mogueime had already shown himself to be somewhat different from the common soldier when the debate took place about the conquest of Santarém and the rape and beheading of the Moorish women, and if it is true that at the time he betrayed a tendency to let his imagination run riot, then, ironically enough, it could be that for this very same reason, if truth is to prevail, we will find the difference in his nature stemming from doubt, from the subsequent re-ordering of a fact, from the oblique verification of his motives, from an ingenuous questioning of the influence each one of us has over the actions of others without knowing it, an influence deliberately denied by those who claim to be entirely responsible for their own actions. With his bare feet on the rough wet sand, Mogueime feels the weight of his whole body, as if he had become part of the rock on which he is seated, now the royal trumpets might well give the signal to attack but in all likelihood it will not be heard, what is echoing in his head, however, is the cry of the muezzin, he continues to hear it even while watching the woman, and when she finally averts her eyes the silence becomes absolute, true there are sounds all around but they belong to another world, the mules pant and drink from a freshwater stream that flows into the estuary, and probably because he could not find any better way of embarking on what has to be done, Mogueime asks the woman, What is your name, how often we must have asked each other that question since the world began, What is your name, sometimes going on to give our own name, I'm called Mogueime, to open up the conversation, in order to give before receiving, and then we wait until we hear the reply, when it comes, when the question is not met with silence, but not on this occasion, My name is Ouroana, she said.

The paper with the telephone number is still lying there on his desk, nothing could be easier, dial six numbers, and hear a voice at the other end of the line, a few kilometres away, so simple, it no longer matters whether it is the voice of Maria Sara or that of her husband, what is important is to note the differences between then and now, in order to speak, or to kill, it is necessary to get close, that is what Mogueime and Ouroana did, she arrived from Galicia, brought by force to the siege, the concubine of a crusader who is now dead and subsequently washerwoman for the nobility in order to earn a living, while he, having conquered Santarém, came in search of greater glory, before the imposing walls of Lisbon. Raimundo Silva dials five numbers, he only needs one more but cannot make up his mind, he pretends that he is savouring the foretaste of pleasure, a shiver of fear, he tells himself that if he wanted to, he could complete the number, only one to go, but he declines, muttering, I cannot, and he replaces the receiver as if getting rid of a heavy load threatening to crush him. He gets to his feet, thinks, I'm thirsty, and goes to the kitchen. He fills a glass with water from the tap, drinks slowly, relishes the coolness of the water, it is a simple pleasure, perhaps the simplest of all, a glass of water when one is thirsty, and as he drinks he can picture the stream flowing towards the estuary, and the mules stirring the water's surface as they drink, seven hundred and forty years ago, the stable-lads spur them on with a whistle, how true that there is not much that is new under the sun, not even King Solomon was capable of imagining how right he was. Raimundo Silva put down his glass, turned round, there was a note lying on the kitchen table, the usual and quite superfluous explanation from the charlady, Goodbye for now, I've left everything in good order, but not this time, not a word about her obligations, a quite different message this time, A lady rang, she wants you to call this number, and Raimundo Silva does not have to dash into the study to know that it is the same number as that on the crumpled piece of paper which had been so difficult to find. Or not to lose.

RAIMUNDO SILVA'S MOTIVE for not telephoning Maria Sara was as simple as it was tortuous, a statement which gives the immediate impression of not being very precise, inasmuch as these adjectives should be applied with greater rigour to the reasoning with which the aforesaid motive was obliged to conform. As in the classic detective novels, the nub of the question lay in the time factor, that is to say, the fact that Maria Sara's call came during Raimundo Silva's absence, at an unspecified hour, which might have been exactly one minute after he went out, or one minute just before the cleaner left, another unspecified hour, to mention only these final minutes. In the first instance, more than four hours must have passed before Raimundo Silva became aware of the message, in the second instance, judging from her normal practice, some three hours. All things considered, this means that Maria Sara, if she was waiting for a return call, had time to think that Raimundo Silva had probably returned home very late, at an hour at which it would have been in bad taste to telephone anyone at home, especially if indisposed. Although, a restrictive expression but not ironic, her illness was not so serious as to prevent her from personally making a telephone call to this apartment near the castle, where Raimundo Silva searches in vain for an answer to the inevitable question, What does she want from me. He spent the rest of the afternoon and evening working out endless variations on this theme that went from the simple to the complicated, from the general to the particular, from any request for information, which would be absurd in view of the circumstances, to the even greater absurdity of wishing her to declare her love for him, just like that, over the telephone, as if no longer able to resist such sweet temptation. His irritation with himself at having allowed this mad thought to carry him to this hypothesis reached such an extreme that, in a fit of temper, he grabbed the white rose which was already withering in the vase and threw it into the rubbish-bin, before slamming the lid in a gesture of finality, I'm a fool, he said aloud, but failed to explain whether this was because he had allowed his thoughts to run riot or because he had ill-treated an innocent flower that had bloomed for several days and deserved to be allowed to fade quietly, to wilt, its scent lingering and the last traces of whiteness concealed in its inner heart. Meanwhile it should also be said that, already in bed at dead of night and unable to sleep, Raimundo Silva got up and went to the kitchen, pulled out the rubbish-bin from under the cooker and retrieved the defiled rose which he gently cleaned and rinsed under a trickle of water in order not to disturb the limp petals before putting it back in the vase, resting its drooping corolla on a pile of books placed one on top of the other, the last one, by an interesting coincidence, being *The History of the Siege of Lisbon*, a copy not for sale. Raimundo Silva's final thought before falling asleep was, Tomorrow I'll ring her, a peremptory declaration so very much in keeping, so long as it is just a promise, with his vacillating nature, as if it had been spoken with a genuine sense of purpose by someone more decisive, the fact is that not everything can be achieved today, a firm intention is enough unless we leave it until the day after tomorrow.

The following morning, Raimundo Silva awoke with a clear idea as to how the troops should finally be deployed on the ground for the assault, including certain strategic details of his own making. A good sleep, assisted by intermittent dreams, had dispelled, once and for all, any remaining doubts, natural in someone who had never been trained to cope with the hazards and dangers of a real war, not to mention the onerous responsibilities of being in command. It was more than obvious that any so-called surprise element was now out of the question, that sudden attack taking the enemy by surprise before they can respond or show any reaction, especially when they find themselves unexpectedly besieged, because by the time they realise what is happening it is already much too late. With all this flaunting of military force, this coming and going of envoys, these manoeuvres to surround the city, the Moors are all too aware of what to expect, proof of which are those terraces swarming with soldiers, those walls spiked with lances. Raimundo Silva finds himself in an interesting situation, that of someone who is playing chess on his own and knows the final outcome beforehand, prepared to play as if he did not know and determined, moreover, not to favour consciously either the one side or the other in this contest, the black or the white, here the Moors or the Christians, according to the colours. And he has shown this quite openly, as can be seen from the sympathy, not to say esteem, with which he has treated the infidels, especially the muezzin, not to mention the respect he has shown when describing the city's spokesman, his eloquence and nobility when compared with a certain coldness, impatience, and even cynicism, that always comes to the surface whenever he refers to the Christians. However, we should not conclude that Raimundo Silva's sympathies are reserved entirely for the Moors, his attitude should be seen as one of spontaneous charity because, much as he might try, he cannot forget that in the end the Moors will be defeated, besides since he, too, is a Christian, though not a practising one, he deplores certain forms of hypocrisy, envy and infamy that are given carte blanche in his own camp. In a word, the game is on the table, so far only the pawns and several knights have moved, and in Raimundo Silva's wise opinion an assault should be carried out simultaneously on the five gates, Lisbon has two less than the city of Thebes, with the objective of testing the military strength of the besieged and, with any luck, one of their battalions may prove to be weak, which would soon secure our victory and greatly reduce the number of innocent victims on both sides.

Meanwhile, before embarking on this enterprise, he must make a telephone call. To prolong silence for yet another day would not only be impolite but create difficulties for any future relationship between them, professional, of course. Therefore Raimundo Silva will make the call. But first he will ring the publishing house because it is feasible, even very likely, that having recovered from her brief spell of illness, Maria Sara is back at work today, which might even be the reason for the call taken by the cleaner, perhaps to ask him to come to her office next day to discuss, without further delay, another proof-reading assignment. Raimundo Silva is so convinced that this was her reason for calling that when the telephonist tells him she is not there, She's ill, Senhor Silva, don't you remember me telling you yesterday, he replies, Are you sure she's not back at work, do check, the secretary takes offence and rebukes him, I know who is here and who is not, She might have arrived without you noticing, I see everything, Senhor Silva, nothing escapes me, and Raimundo Silva trembled on hearing those prophetic words which sounded threatening, as if she were warning him, I'm nobody's fool, or, Don't imagine you can pull the wool over my eyes, and without even attempting to pursue the insinuation, he blurted out some mollifying phrase and rang off. Dom Afonso Henriques harangues his troops gathered on the Monte da Graça, he speaks to them about the motherland, as it was known even at that time, about their native land, about the future awaiting them, the only thing he did not mention was their ancestors because few existed so far, but he warned them, Bear in mind that if we do not win this war, Portugal will be finished before it has even got under way, which will make it impossible for so many kings yet to come to be Portuguese, so many presidents, so many soldiers, so many saints, and poets, and ministers, and farm-labourers, and bishops, and navigators, and artists, and workers, and clerks, and friars, and directors, all in the masculine gender, without, however, forgetting all those Portuguese women, queens, saints, poets, ministers, farm-labourers, clerks, nuns, and directors, therefore, if we want to include all these people in our history, along with all the others whom I shall not mention otherwise my speech will be too long, and since we do not yet know all of them, if we want to include them then we had better make a start by capturing Lisbon, so let us be off. The troops acclaimed the king, and then, under orders from their lieutenants and captains they marched off to take up their positions, their leaders carrying strict instructions that at noon next day, while the Moors were at prayer, the assault should be carried out simultaneously on five fronts, may God protect all of us, for we are fighting in His name.

Raimundo Silva must have whispered a similar plea, transposed into the first person singular, as he set about dialling the number of his destiny, but in a whisper so low that it scarcely passed his lips, a plea as tremulous as that of any adolescent, he himself now has more food for thought, if he thinks, whether his body is not simply one huge kettledrum where the bell of the telephone rings and rings, not the bell, the electronic signal, awaiting the sudden interruption of the call, and a voice that says, Speaking, or, What can I do for you, perhaps Hello, perhaps Who's calling, there is no lack of possibilities amongst the conventional phrases and their modern variants, however, dazed as he was, Raimundo Silva was unable to hear what was being said, only that it was a woman speaking, so he asked disregarding any niceties, Is that Dr Maria Sara, no, it was not, Who's speaking, it was as if Raimundo Silva wanted to know his editor's voice, this was not a truth beyond question, but served as a simple form of identification, we are certainly not going to suggest that he introduced himself as Raimundo Benvindo Silva, proof-reader, working for the same publishing house, and even if he had, the reply would have been the same, Wait a moment, please, I'll see if Dr Maria Sara can take your call, never had a moment been so brief, Don't ring off, I'm carrying the telephone through, then silence. Raimundo Silva could visualise the scene, the woman, almost certainly her maid, removing the plug from the socket, childishly cradling the telephone in her bosom with both hands, that is how he pictured her, and entering a bedroom in shadows, then stooping down to reconnect the telephone to another socket, How are you, her voice taking him by surprise, Raimundo Silva had expected to hear the maid say something more, such as, I'm passing the telephone to Dr Sara, that would have meant a further postponement of three or four seconds, but instead this direct question, How are you, reversing the situation, for surely it was up to him to express interest in her state of health, I'm fine, thank you, and quickly added, I wanted to know if you're feeling better, How did you know I've been ill, At the office, When, Yesterday forenoon, So you decided to ring to see how I am, Yes, Many thanks for being so thoughtful, you're the only proof-reader to have shown any interest, Well, I felt I had to, I hope I haven't disturbed you, On the contrary, I'm deeply grateful, I'm feeling better, I think probably tomorrow or the day after, I'll be back at the office, Well, I mustn't tire you, I wish you a speedy recovery, Just before you ring off, how did you find my telephone number, Young Sara gave it to me, Ah, the other Sara, Yes, the telephonist, When, As I told you, yesterday forenoon, And you waited until today to call me, I was afraid of disturbing you, But you overcame your fear, I suppose so, otherwise I wouldn't be speaking to you right now, Meantime, you should have been told that I wanted to speak to you. For two seconds, Raimundo Silva thought of pretending that he had not received the message, but before the third second passed, he found himself answering, Yes, Therefore I can assume that you couldn't help calling me once I had taken the initiative, You may assume what you please, that's up to you, but you must also assume that if I asked the telephonist for your number it wasn't just to carry it around in my pocket, waiting for who knows what, there was another reason, What, Simply a lack of courage, Your courage appears to have been limited to that little proof-reading episode you don't like me mentioning, In fact, I'm only telephoning to inquire about your state of health and to say I hope you'll soon be better, And don't you think it's time you asked me why I called you, Why did you call me, I'm not sure that I like your tone of voice, Words are more important than the way they're spoken, I would have assumed that your experience as a proof-reader must have taught you that words mean nothing unless spoken in a certain tone of voice, The written word is mute, Reading gives it a voice, Except when read in silence, Even then, unless Senhor Raimundo Silva believes the brain is a silent organ, I'm only a proof-reader, like the shoemaker, I make do with carpet-slippers, my brain knows me, I know nothing about my brain, An interesting observation, You still haven't answered my question, What question, Why did you telephone me, I'm no longer certain that I feel like telling you, So, I'm not the only coward, I don't recall having said anything about cowardice, You spoke about a lack of courage, That's not the same thing, The two sides of a coin are different, but the coin is one and the same, Valour is only to be found on one side, This conversation is getting beyond me and I suggest we drop the subject, besides it's most unwise to argue like this, given your state of health, This cynicism doesn't become you, I'm not being cynical, I know, so stop pretending, Seriously, I don't think we know what we're talking about, Speak for yourself, Then explain it to me, There's no need for any explanations, You're evading the question, It's you who are evading the question, you're hiding from yourself and want me to tell you what you already know, Please, Please what, I think we ought to ring off, this conversation has got out of hand, You're to blame, Me, Yes, you, You're much mistaken, I like things to be clear, Then try being clear and tell me why you are so aggressive whenever you speak to me, I'm never aggressive with anyone, I don't have this modern vice, Then why are you aggressive with me, It isn't true, Since the first day we met, should you need reminding, Circumstances, But those circumstances have changed yet you've gone on being aggressive, Forgive me, that was never my intention, Now it's my turn to ask you not to use such meaningless words, Agreed, I'll say no more, Then listen, I telephoned you because I was feeling lonely, because I was curious to know if you were working, because I wanted you to take an interest in my health, because, Maria Sara, Don't say my name like that, Maria Sara, I like you, a long pause, Is that so, It's the truth, You took your sweet time before telling me, And perhaps I might never have got round to telling you, Why not, We're different, we belong to different worlds,

What do you know about all these differences between us and our worlds, I can guess, observe, draw my own conclusions, These three operations can just as easily lead us to draw the right or the wrong conclusions, Agreed, and my biggest mistake right now is to have confessed that I like you, Why, Because I know nothing about your private life, whether you are, Married, Yes, or, In any way spoken for, to use an old-fashioned expression, Yes, Well, let's imagine that I am already married or engaged, would that prevent you from being fond of me, No, And if I really were married or engaged to someone else, should that prevent me from being fond of you, if that was how I felt, I don't know, Then you should know that I am fond of you, a long pause, Is that true, Yes, it's true, Listen Maria Sara, Tell me, Raimundo, but first you should know that I got divorced three years ago, that I ended an affair three months ago and haven't had any more affairs since, that I have no children but would dearly love to have them, I live with a married brother, and the person who answered the telephone was my sister-in-law, and you don't have to tell me who took down my message, she's your cleaner, and now, Mr Proof-reader, you may speak, pay no attention to this wild outburst, it's just that I'm brimming over with joy, Tell me, why do you like me, What can I say, I just like you, And aren't you afraid that once you get to know me, you won't like me any more, It sometimes happens, in fact, it happens quite a lot, So, So, nothing, it takes time to get to know each other, I like you, I believe you, When can we see each other, As soon as I can get up from this bed of pain, Where's the pain, All over, What is actually wrong with you, Nothing serious, or rather, the worst flu I've ever experienced, From where you are, you can't see me, but I'm smiling, Now that's really something, I don't believe I've ever seen a smile cross your lips, Can I confide that I love you, No, simply say that you are fond of me, I've already said so, Then keep the rest for the day you truly love me, should that day ever come, It will come, Let's not bank on the future, better to wait and see what it has in store for us, and now this weak, feverish woman asks to be left in peace to rest, to recover her strength in case it occurs to someone to call back again today,

To speak to you, Or you, for the phrase could just as easily refer to either of us, Ambiguity isn't always a defect, So long, Let me leave you with a kiss, The time will come for kisses, For me it has been slow in coming, One last question, Tell me, Have you started to write your *History of the Siege of Lisbon*, Yes, I have, Good, for I'm not sure that I could have gone on liking you if you'd said no, Goodbye.

The word she used was, Goodbye. Lying down in her bedroom, Maria Sara slowly replaces the receiver at the same time as Raimundo Silva, seated at his desk, does the same at his end. With a billowing movement, she indolently buries herself between the sheets, while he leans right back in his chair. The two of them are happy, so happy that it seems quite unfair to detach ourselves from the one in order to speak of the other, as we shall be more or less obliged to do, although, as we see in another more fanciful tale, it is physically and mentally impossible to describe the simultaneous actions of two characters, especially if they are far away from each other, to suit the whims and preference of an author who is always more preoccupied with what he believes to be the objective interests of his narrative than with the wholly legitimate aspirations of this or that character, however secondary, and with giving preference to his modest sayings and tiniest actions over the actions and words of his protagonists and heroes. And speaking of heroes, take for example those marvellous encounters between the knights of the Round Table or the Holy Grail with wise hermits or mysterious maidens who crossed their path, once having entertained us to yet another edifying episode, the knight would move on to fresh adventures and reunions, and of necessity, we the readers would move on with him, often abandoning for evermore the hermit on one page, the maiden on another, when we should have liked to know more about the fate awaiting them, whether some queen, out of love, would rescue the hermit from his hermitage, whether the maiden, instead of remaining in the forest to await the next knight errant, would go looking for a man somewhere in this wide world. When dealing with Maria Sara and Raimundo Silva, things get very complicated, since both of them are crucial characters, just as their gestures and thoughts will become crucial, from amongst which, given the insurmountable problem, we have no other solution than to choose something that the reader might consider to be essential, for example, in the case of Maria Sara, to observe that there was also a certain voluptuousness in her movement which we earlier described simply as being indolent, and that Raimundo Silva has parched lips as if a sudden fever, a raging fever, had taken possession of his body as he began trembling from head to foot, the outcome of all that nervous tension during their conversation, deceptively relaxed as they briefly made their farewells, and now humming like stretched wires, or, respecting the beauty and emotion of that moment, an Aeolian harp plucked by the wind, as ferocious as any cyclone. It is also worth mentioning that when Maria Sara went on smiling, her expression that of someone who was genuinely happy or looking the part, her sister-in-law asked her out of curiosity, Who is this Raimundo Silva who has got you into such a nervous state, and still smiling, Maria Sara replied, I still haven't discovered. Raimundo Silva has no one to talk to, he simply smiles, now little by little he regains his composure, he has finally got to his feet, a rejuvenated man emerges from the study and heads for the bedroom, and looking into the mirror he does not recognise himself, but so very conscious of being what he sees there that on observing the white line at the roots of his hair, he merely shrugs his shoulders with genuine indifference, at most a trifle impatient, perhaps because truth progresses so slowly. Maria Sara checks the time on her watch, it is too soon to expect him to ring back or for her to telephone him, the real test of wisdom is to bear in mind that even feelings must learn how to use time. Raimundo Silva checks the hour on his watch and goes out. He lost no time in heading for the nearest florist to buy four roses, in the most delicate shade of white he could find. This involved him in an animated dialogue with the assistant to ensure that they were just as he wanted them, and in the end, he had to give her a more generous tip than usual, especially for him, because the assistant was not easily persuaded by the various arguments he used, first trying to convince her that the difference between two and twelve roses is purely arithmetical and irrelevant, then making mysterious and veiled allusions to the fulfilment of a promise he swore never to reveal, much as he would like to confide in her, What else could he do to recompense so much patience and kindness. With that reassuring tip already in her apron pocket, the assistant allowed herself to be impressed, and, as the conversation continued, no one could be blamed for thinking that money had nothing to do with the enthusiasm with which she responded to the customer's unusual request, yes, unusual, for no matter how you look at them, two roses are not twelve, nor even an orchid, for the latter can stand on its own, and even prefers it so. Rather than miss her call which would be twice as frustrating, Raimundo Silva returned home by taxi, ran upstairs, a gymnastic feat which prevented him from breathing for several minutes, Such imprudence, he thought to himself, climbing the Calçada da Glória like this at my age, he said *glória* without thinking, then amused by his own excesses, physical as well as verbal, he went to remove the withered rose from the vase, change the water, and then began arranging the two roses with the painstaking artistry of a Japanese floriculturist.

From the window, clouds could be seen slowly passing, dark and heavy, in the violet evening sky. Although advanced, spring had not yet decided to open its doors to the heat, to the warm southern wind, that encourages us to unfasten our collars and roll up our sleeves, to some extent, Raimundo Silva is going to live in two ages and in two seasons, blazing July that causes the weapons surrounding Lisbon to shine and glow, and this damp, grey April, sometimes with glinting sunshine that makes the light as hard as that of a bright, impenetrable diamond. He opened the window, rested his elbows on the parapet of the verandah, felt at peace with the world despite the inclement weather, fortunately his apartment was protected from the north wind blowing at this moment in sudden little gusts that come round the corner and brush against his face like a cool caress. He gradually begins to feel chilly and wonders if he should not go back inside, when he suddenly turns numb, literally numb, on remembering that from where he is standing he will not hear the telephone if Maria Sara should ring. He rushed back inside and dashed into the study as if trying to hear those final bleeps, the telephone was there, silent, as black as ever, but no longer a threatening animal, an insect armoured with prickly spines, more like a cat asleep, curled up in its own warmth, and once awake, no longer a danger with those claws of a tiny and often lethal wild beast, but waiting for an outstretched hand where it is all too ready to rub itself voluptuously. Raimundo Silva went back inside, sat at the small table near the window without putting on the light, and waited. He rested his forehead in his hands, a characteristic gesture of his, and with his fingertips distractedly scratching at the roots of his hair where another story might be written, because this one already started can only be read by those with perceptive and open eyes, not by a blind man, however keen his sense of touch, for his fingers cannot tell him about this latest colour appearing in certain hairs. Although evening is drawing in, the shadows in the room would not be so deep, were it not for the verandah, which even on clear days shuts out the light, and even now plunges the room into the darkness of night, while immediately outside, between the slow rents in the clouds, the nearby sky still allows itself to be pierced by the last rays which the sun, passing behind the sea, casts into the upper regions of space. Erect in the slender vase, the two roses seem even whiter in the purplish darkness of the room, Raimundo Silva's hands add several indecipherable black lines to the last written page, perhaps in Arabic, if only we had paid attention to the muezzin's cry, the sun lingered on for one long minute, settled on the bright horizon, waiting, then sank from view, too late now for any words. Raimundo Silva's indistinct form gradually merges with the denseness of the shadows while the roses still absorb from the window the almost imperceptible light preserved in the window-panes and bathe therein, at the same time releasing an unexpected scent from the intimate depths of their corollas. Raimundo Silva slowly raises his hands and reaches out to touch them, first the one, then the other, as if two cheeks were touching, a prelude to the gesture that follows, his lips slowly drawing close to the petals, the flower's multiple mouth. Now the telephone must not ring, let nothing interrupt this moment before it is ready to end, tomorrow the soldiers gathered on the Monte da Graça will advance like two pincers, to the east and west, as far as the margin of the river, they will pass under the gaze of Raimundo Silva who lives in the tower north of the Porta de Alfofa, and whenever he looks out on to the terrace, curious, holding a rose in his hand, or two, they will shout up to him from below that it is too late, that this is no longer a time for roses, but for final bloodshed and death. Along this side, in the direction of the Porta de Ferro, will descend the battalion of troops captained by Mem Ramires, amongst his men is Mogueime and when the leader sees and finally recognises him beneath the beard everyone wore at that time, he will call out to him amiably with a broad, medieval smile, Hey there, my friend, I'm afraid these walls are much too high for me to be able to climb back on to your shoulders and throw up a ladder as we did in Santarém to our own benefit and that of our king, and Mogueime, treated with familiarity, but with no intention of questioning his leader's version of the relative position of the constituent parts of that now famous human ladder, reacts as philosophically as that soldier on his way to war who calls out to the general passing in his jeep, If we ever see each other again, it will be a sign that we have both won the war, but if either of us should fail to turn up, then he has lost it, and now raise your shield, your Majesty, for there's a shower of arrows coming this way. Raimundo Silva switched on the table-lamp, the sudden light momentarily appeared to obliterate the roses, then they reappeared as if they had reconstituted themselves, but without any aura or mystery, contrary to what is commonly believed because of those famous words circulated by a botanist, A rose is a rose is a rose, whereas a poet would simply have said, A rose, before contemplating it in silence.

The telephone rang at long last. Raimundo Silva jumped to his feet, pushing back his chair which swayed and fell as he reached the passageway, just ahead of someone who observed him with gentle irony, Whoever would have thought, my dear fellow, that anything like this could happen to us, no, say nothing, save your breath, it's a waste of time trying to answer rhetorical questions, we've often discussed this, go, be off you, I'm right behind you, I'm never in a hurry, whatever might be yours one day, will also be mine, I'm the one who always arrives later, I live each moment lived by you, as if I were inhaling your scent of roses preserved only in memory, or, less poetically, your plate of greens and beans, wherein your infancy is constantly being reborn, yet you cannot see it, and would refuse to believe it were you to be told. Raimundo Silva pounced on the telephone, in a moment of doubt he thought, And suppose it isn't her, but it was her, the voice of Maria Sara telling him, You shouldn't have done it, Why not, he asked in dismay, Because from now on I shall be expecting roses every day, I'll see that you're not disappointed, I'm not talking about roses, roses, About what then, No one should be able to give less than they have given before, roses shouldn't appear today and a wilderness tomorrow, There won't be any wilderness, That's only a promise, how can we be sure, How true, we don't know, just as I didn't know that I would send you two roses, while you, Maria Sara, don't know that I have two roses exactly the same as yours here in a vase, on a table where there are written pages about the history of a siege that never happened, beside a window that looks on to a city that does not actually exist as I picture it, It would be nice to see where you live, You probably wouldn't approve, Why not, I can't say, it's a simple apartment, not even that, nothing fancy, me and a few items of furniture that don't match, lots of books, they're my whole life, yet I'm always the outsider, even when I correct a printing error or some mistake made by the author, rather like someone strolling in a park who feels obliged to keep the place tidy and lifts any litter in sight, then not knowing where to put it, shoves it into his own pocket, that's all I carry with me, dry withered leaves, no fruit worth eating, May I come and visit you, There's nothing I'd like better, he paused for a second before adding, Right now, but, as if regretting what he had just said or feeling he had been tactless, he corrected himself, Forgive me, that was unintentional, and when she remained silent he came out with words he would never have imagined himself ever capable of saying, direct, frank, explicit in themselves, and not because of any game of cautious insinuation, Of course it was intentional, and I'm sorry. She laughed, cleared her throat, My problem in this situation is to know whether I should have blushed before or if I should be blushing now, I can recall having seen you blush once, When, When I touched the rose in your office, Women blush more easily than men, we're the weaker sex, Both sexes are weak, I was also blushing, How come you know so much about the weakness of the sexes, I know my own weakness, and something about the weakness of others, if books are to be trusted, Raimundo, Tell me, As soon as I'm on my feet again, I'll come and see you, but . . . , And I'll be waiting for you, Such fine words, What do you mean, Once I arrive there, you must go on waiting for me, just as I shall go on waiting for you, meanwhile we still don't know when we shall arrive there, I'll be waiting, Until soon, Raimundo, Don't be long, What will you be doing once we ring off, Camp in front of the Porta de Ferro and pray to the Most Holy Virgin that the Moors don't decide to attack at dead of night, Are you afraid, Trembling with fear, Is it that bad, Before engaging in this battle, I was a simple proof-reader whose only concern was to mark in a *deleatur* correctly in order to make it clear to the author, There seems to be some interference on the line, What you are hearing are the cries of the Moors shouting threats from up there on the battlements, Look after yourself, Don't worry, I haven't come all this way to die before the walls of Lisbon.

IF WE ACCEPT and rely on the facts as written by the aforementioned Fray Rogeiro in his letter to Osbern, then Raimundo Silva will have to be told not to deceive himself about the presumed easiness of camping, without further ado, in front of the Porta de Ferro or any other gate, for this perverse race of Moors is not so timorous as to have locked themselves in with seven turns of the key without putting up a struggle, relying on a miracle from Allah who is capable of dissuading the Galicians from their evil intentions. Lisbon, as we said before, has houses outside its walls, many houses and villas and not simply for summer retreats, but more like one city surrounding another, and if it is known that, within days, when the encirclement finally becomes a geometrical reality, the military headquarters will be comfortably installed here and all the dignitaries, both military and religious, thus spared the relative discomfort of the tents, now they will have to fight hard in order to expel the Moorish hordes from these delightful suburbs, from street to street, from patio to patio, from terrace to terrace, a battle that will last at least a week, and which the Portuguese only managed to win because they were more numerous on that occasion and because the Moors had not sent out all their battalions and the troops inside could not intervene in the confrontations with catapults and beasts for fear of wounding their brothers who, willingly or otherwise, had sacrificed themselves by fighting on the front line. Therefore do not let us censure Raimundo Silva, who, as he himself has never tired of telling us, is merely a simple proof-reader exempt from military service and with no experience of warfare, notwithstanding that amongst his books there is an abridged edition of the works of Clausewitz, bought from an antiquarian bookseller years ago and never opened. Perhaps he wanted to abbreviate his own narrative, considering that, after so many centuries, what counts are the main episodes. Nowadays people have neither the time nor the patience to keep historical data and minutiae in their heads, that might have been all right for the contemporaries of our King Dom Afonso the First, for they clearly had less history to learn, a difference of eight centuries in their favour is no joke, the advantage we enjoy is having computers, we can feed any encyclopaedia or dictionary into them, and hey presto, we no longer need to rely on our memory, but this way of understanding things, let's say it before someone else says it for us, is totally reactionary and quite unacceptable, because the libraries of our parents and grandparents served this very purpose, so that the neopallium should not become overloaded, it already does a great deal for its size, minuscule, buried deep down in the brain, surrounded by circuits on all sides, so when Mem Ramires said to Mogueime, Get ready, for I'm going to climb on to your shoulders, you might think this phrase was not the work of the neopallium, wherein there resides not only the memory of ladders and good soldiers, but also the intelligence, convergence or relationship between cause and effect, something no computer can boast of, because despite knowing everything, it understands nothing. Or so they say.

Lisbon is surrounded at last, the dead have already been removed for burial, the wounded transported with them in the same ships to the other bank of the estuary and from there, carried uphill, some to the cemeteries, others to field hospitals, the latter indiscriminately, the former according to social rank and nationality. In the encampment, if we discount the sorrow and mourning for the losses suffered, and not all that demonstrative, because these people are stoical and not much given to tears, you can detect much confidence in the future and an exalted faith in the intercession of

Our Lord Jesus Christ, who on this occasion need not take the trouble of appearing as He did in Ourique, He has already worked enough wonders by making sure that the Moors, in the haste of their retreat, should have left behind to satisfy the appetite of their enemy, that is to say, ours, generous stocks of wheat, barley, corn and vegetables to feed the entire city, and which for lack of space were stored in open caves halfway up the slope, between the Porta de Ferro and the Porta de Alfofa. And when this fortunate discovery was made, Dom Afonso with a wisdom rare in one so young, at the time he was only thirty-eight, a mere stripling, uttered those famous words which immediately entered the thesaurus of Portuguese sayings, He that saveth his dinner, will have the more for supper, before prudently giving orders that these supplies should be requisitioned before it became necessary to invent another maxim, Better belly burst than good food lost, the best time for rationing is when there is plenty, he concluded.

A week had passed since Raimundo Silva had made his mistaken forecast, that of his first strategy, when he thought that by noon on the day after the troops moved from the Monte da Graça, there would be a simultaneous attack on all the city gates, in the hope of finding a weak spot in the enemy's defence where an entry could be forced, or, of attracting reinforcements to the spot, thus leaving the other fronts unprotected with the obvious consequences. There is nothing more to be said. On paper, all plans seem more or less feasible, however reality has shown its irresistible urge to deviate from what is written on the page and to tear up all plans. It was not simply the fact that the Moors had converted the outskirts into strongholds, this problem had just been solved, although with numerous casualties, the question now is knowing how to penetrate securely locked gates, defended by posses of warriors perched on the towers that flank and protect them, or how to attack the Moors at such a height, beyond the reach of ladders and where the guards are never asleep. In a word, Raimundo Silva is in an excellent position to judge the difficulties of the enterprise, because from his verandah he can see that he would not even need to have an accurate aim to kill or wound any Christians who might try to get near this Porta de Alfofa, were it still here. The news spreads throughout the encampment that disagreements are brewing between their leaders, divided between two operational proposals, the one favouring an immediate assault with all the means at their disposal, starting with a heavy bombardment to drive the Moors off the battlements and ending with the use of huge battering-rams to storm the gates until they cave in, the other less adventurous that defends the setting up of a blockade so tight that not even a rat could leave or enter Lisbon, or, to be more precise, let those who wish leave, but let no one enter, for we shall finally bring the city to its knees. The opponents of the first proposal argue that the outcome, that is to say, the victorious entry into Lisbon, is based on a false premise, namely, the assumption that the bombardment would be enough to drive the Moors off the battlements, This, dear friends, is what is known as counting your chickens before they're hatched, the chances are that the Moors won't budge an inch, besides all they have to do is to provide themselves with some form of cover, a roof of some kind to afford them shelter, so that in all safety they might shoot us at their ease from above or douse us with boiling oil, as is their wont. Those in favour of an immediate attack insist that to wait for the Moors to succumb to famine would scarcely be worthy of nobles of such high lineage as those present and that it was already an act of undeserved charity to have suggested that they should withdraw, taking with them all their wealth and possessions, now only blood can wash from Lisbon's walls this infamous stain that for more than three hundred and fifty years has contaminated these places which must now be restored to Christ. Having listened to the arguments of both factions, the king finds their proposals unacceptable, for while recognising that it scarcely befits his dignity to wait for the fruit to fall from the tree when ripe, he is not convinced that an attack launched at random will have any effect, even if he were to storm the Moorish gates with all the battering rams in his realm. Then the knight Heinrich asked to be allowed to remind everyone present that in all the sieges mounted throughout Europe, mobile wooden towers were used to the best possible effect, that is to say, mobile up to a point, because to move anything so gigantic into place requires a multitude of people and animals, what matters is that at the top of the tower, once it has reached the right height, we shall build a cat-walk, which, well-protected from any assaults, will gradually advance towards the wall where our men, like an irresistible torrent, will launch themselves, carrying the nefarious rabble before them without mercy or recourse, and he ended this explanation by telling them, This is only one, amongst many, of the modern strategies Portugal will adopt from other parts of Europe to good effect, although at first you might encounter some difficulty in understanding such modern technology, I myself know enough about building these towers to teach everyone here, Your Highness need only give me orders, confident as I am that when the day comes to distribute honours my contribution will be recorded alongside that of other benefactors on whom Portugal, notwithstanding the defections verified, relied at this decisive moment in her history.

Having listened to these wise words, the king was about to announce his decision when two other crusaders, one from Normandy, the other French, got to their feet and asked to be allowed to intervene, explaining that they, too, were experienced in building towers and were willing to show, there and then, how their competence, not to mention the superiority and economy of their methods, both in terms of design and construction, were just right for this initiative. As for their conditions, they, too, confided in the king's magnanimity and gratitude, thus offering their support to the knight Heinrich, and making his words theirs on the same grounds. This unexpected turn in the debate displeased the Portuguese, whether they were in favour of waiting or of taking immediate action, although for different reasons, both factions only in agreement that they should reject the hypothesis, though alarmingly feasible, that foreigners should get the upper hand, while those who belonged here were reduced to anonymous manual labour, without any right to have their name inscribed on the honorary roll of benefactors. It was true that this idea of building towers was not entirely rejected by those who argued for a passive siege, because it was becoming quite obvious that they could not be built amidst the tumult and confusion of battle, but patriotic pride had to be given precedence over these considerations, and so they ended up making common cause with those urging prompt and direct action, thus hoping to postpone any acceptance of the foreigners' proposals. Now then, the proof that Dom Afonso Henrique truly deserved to be king, and not just king, but our king, is that like Solomon, another example of enlightened despotism, he knew how to merge conflicting theories into a single strategic plan, by arranging them into a harmonious and logical sequence. First of all, he congratulated those in favour of an immediate attack for their courage and daring, then praised the engineers of towers for their commonsense, enhanced by the modern gifts of invention and creativeness, and finally expressed his gratitude to the others for their admirable wisdom and patience, the enemies of unnecessary risks. This done, he concluded, I have therefore determined that operations will be carried out in the following order, first, a general assault, second, should that fail, the German, French and Norman towers will advance, third, should all fail, to keep up the siege indefinitely, they will have to surrender sooner or later. The applause was unanimous, either because it is only to be expected when a king speaks, or because everyone present was reasonably satisfied with the decision taken, which came to be expressed with three different sayings or mottoes, one for each faction, the partisans of the first group said, The lamp that goes before illuminates twice, those in the second group retorted, The first corn goes to the sparrows, while those in the third group quipped ironically, He who laughs last, laughs best.

The evidence provided by most of the events that have so far constituted the main core of this narrative has convinced Raimundo Silva that it was pointless trying to impose his own point of view even when it stemmed directly, as it were, from that negative introduced into a history which, until he made the change, had remained prisoner of this particular fatality we call facts, whether they make sense in relation to other facts, or inexplicably surface at a determined moment in our state of consciousness. He recognises that his freedom began and ended at that precise moment when he wrote the word *Not*, that from then on a new and no less imperious fatality had got under way, and that he has no other choice than to try and understand what, having initially appeared to stem from his initiative and reflection, is now seen to have resulted from a mechanism that was, and continues to be, external, of whose functioning he only has the vaguest idea and in whose activity he only intervenes with the aleatory handling of levers and buttons the real function of which escapes him, aware only that this is his role, to be the button or lever moved in their turn at will by the emergence of unexpected impulses, or if predictable and even self-induced, totally unpredictable as regards their consequences, whether immediate or remote. Therefore we can confirm, since he effectively never foresaw that he would write a new history of the siege of Lisbon, as narrated here, that he suddenly finds himself confronted with the outcome of a necessity as implacable as that other, from which he thought he could escape by the simple inversion of a sign only to find himself falling for it once more, now negatively, or, to speak in less radical terms, as if he had written the same music lowering all the notes half a tone. Raimundo Silva is seriously thinking of bringing his narrative to a full stop, of returning the crusaders to the Tagus, they cannot be far away, perhaps somewhere between the Algarve and Gibraltar, thus allowing the history to materialise without variations, as a mere repetition of the facts, as they appear in manuals and *The History of the Siege of Lisbon*. He considers that the tiny tree of the Science of Errors he planted has already given its true fruit, or promised it, which was to make this man encounter this woman, and if this has been accomplished let this new chapter begin, just as one interrupts the diary of a sea-voyage at the moment of discovering uncharted land, obviously it is not forbidden to continue writing the diary kept on board, but that would be another story, not that of the voyage which has ended, but that of the discovery and what was discovered. Raimundo Silva suspects, however that such a decision, if he were to take it, would not please Maria Sara, that she would look at him with indignation, not to say an unbearable expression of disappointment. This being so, there will be no final stop in the meantime, only a pause until the announced visit takes place, besides, at this very moment, Raimundo Silva would be incapable of writing another word, since he has lost all composure as he starts imagining that Mogueime on the eve of the planned mass assault, on setting eyes on Lisbon's walls shining in the glow of the flares on the terraces, might have turned his thoughts to a woman he had seen several times in recent days, Ouroana, the concubine of a German crusader, who at this very hour is probably sleeping with her master, up there on the Monte da Graça, almost certainly inside a house on a mat stretched out on cool tiles where no Moor will ever rest again. Mogueime felt stifled inside the tent and came out to get some air, Lisbon's walls illuminated by the bonfires appeared to be made of copper, Let me not die, My Lord, without having savoured life. Raimundo Silva now asks himself what similarities there are between the picture imagined and his relationship with Maria Sara, who is nobody's concubine, if you'll pardon that indelicate word which is no longer relevant in describing sexual mores, after all what she said was, I ended an affair three months ago and since then there have been no more affairs, the situations are obviously different, and we can assume all they have in common is desire, felt as deeply by Mogueime at that time as by Raimundo now, such differences as exist, are purely cultural, yes, Sir.

As he turned over these thoughts in his mind, Raimundo Silva was distracted from his worries by the sudden memory that never at any time had Maria Sara shown any curiosity in his emotional life, to use a phrase that embraces everything. Such indifference, at least formally there was no other name for it, provoked a feeling of resentment, After all, I'm not all that advanced in years, what does she think, and suddenly he realised that he sounded almost childish, yet forgivable since it is well known that men, all of them, are children at heart, his pique aggravated by the ill humour of someone who feels that his virility has been offended. Male pride, foolish pride, he muttered, and the lapidary eloquence of this sound precept was not lost on him. In fact, Maria Sara's attitude might be attributed to her natural discretion, some people are quite incapable of forcing the doors of another's privacy, yet on reflection, this cannot be said of Maria Sara who at all times, from the very beginning, took up the reins and the initiative without a moment's hesitation. So there must be another explanation, for example, Maria Sara might feel that her frankness should be spontaneously repaid, and, this being so, she might even now be harbouring evil thoughts, such as, Mistrust the man who does not speak and the dog that does not bark. Nor should we rule out the possibility, more in keeping with modern attitudes to morality, that she might consider any eventual liaison he might have as a matter of no importance, in the manner of, I only have to show what I am feeling, no need to find out beforehand if the gentleman is free or not, it's up to him to say. In any case, anyone who has taken the trouble to go through the staff files in order to find a proof-reader's address, might just as easily have used the opportunity to check his marital status, even if the information were out of date. Single is what appears on Raimundo Silva's file, were he to have married later, it is certain that no one would have remembered to register his change of status. Besides, as everyone knows, between the status of bachelor and married, or divorced, or widower, there are a number of other possible situations, before, during and after, capable of being summed up in the replies each of us finds when asked, Whom do I love, independently of loving anyone, naturally including here all the main and secondary variants, whether active or passive.

During the next two days, Maria Sara and Raimundo Silva chatted frequently on the telephone, repeating things they had already said, sometimes marvelling at some new discovery and searching for words to express it better, a feat, as we know, that is practically impossible. It was in the afternoon of the second day that Maria Sara announced, Tomorrow I'm going back to work, I'll leave an hour earlier and call at your apartment. From that moment, Raimundo Silva began to confirm everything that has been said about the childish nature of men, restless, as if he felt the need to get rid of excess energy, impatient of time becoming one of the slowest moving things of this world, capricious too, or stubborn, as Senhora Maria mentally called him, on seeing her cleaning routine upset by the quite absurd demands of a man who was usually so accommodating. She first became suspicious that there might be Moors on the coast when she saw the rose in the vase, and this became a near certainty, albeit a certainty without any object, when the roses became two, finally turning into a firm conviction before the somewhat unseemly agitation of someone who had been on the point of showing a forefinger covered in dust gathered on a door ledge, thus repeating that disagreeable tradition of housewives obsessed with cleanliness. Raimundo Silva only became aware that he must control himself when Senhora Maria asked him provocatively, Would you like me to change the sheets today or can it wait until Friday as usual. Men are not only childish, they are also transparent. Just as well Raimundo Silva was not in the bedroom at that moment, otherwise Senhora Maria would have seen him become flustered, although all she needed as confirmation that she had touched on a sore point was the unmistakable tremor in his voice, readily identified by someone with her keen hearing. I can see no reason for changing the domestic routine, a phrase that failed to deceive her and served to provoke another worry, vague and devious, that tried to check the only words with which he could sincerely express himself, too crude to be introduced into his interior monologue, If we were to end up in bed, will the sheets be clean enough, he would ask, and he does not know the answer, he can hear Senhora Maria with just the right note of facetiousness, no more no less, I thought you'd want them changed, he sheepishly remains silent, if she wants to change the sheets that is up to her, fate will decide. Only when the cleaner departs will he go and investigate only to discover that the sheets have been laundered, for all her faults, Senhora Maria is a kind-hearted soul, but he cannot make up his mind whether to be pleased or disgruntled. What a complicated life.

Shortly after five, the bell rang. A light, rapid ring, which caused Raimundo Silva to rush to the door as if afraid that it would ring but once only and never again, only in Beethoven's symphony does destiny summon more than once, in life it is different, there are times when we had the feeling that someone was out there waiting, and when we went to see there was no one, and at other times we arrived just a moment too late, not that it mattered, the difference here being that we can go on asking ourselves, Who could it have been, and spend the rest of our life dreaming about this. Raimundo Silva will not need to dream. Maria Sara is there on the threshold and makes her entrance, Hello, she said, Hello, he replied, and both of them lingered in the narrow passageway, rather gloomy now that the door is closed. Raimundo Silva switched on the light, murmuring, Excuse me, as if he had divined a suspicious and equivocal thought going through Maria Sara's mind, What you want is to take advantage of the dark, you think I don't see through you, frankly this much desired visit has got off to a bad start, these two who could be so intelligent and witty on the telephone, have said nothing to each other so far apart from, Hello, it is difficult to believe that after so many implicit promises, this game of roses, these courageous steps she had taken, who can tell whether she is disappointed at the manner in which she is being received. Fortunately, in such difficult situations, the body is quick to understand that the brain is in no fit condition to give orders and acts of its own accord, generally doing what is necessary and by the shortest route, without words, or using only those that have preserved some hint of innocence and spontaneity, this was how Raimundo Silva and Maria Sara found themselves in the study, she has not yet sat down, her hand in his, perhaps neither of them aware that they have been like this since she arrived, all they know is that they are holding hands, his right hand holding her left hand, Maria Sara looks for a chair, and that is when Raimundo Silva, as if there were no other way of detaining her even for an instant, raises her hand to his lips, and it worked, yes, Sir, for the next moment Maria Sara was looking straight at him and he drew her gently towards him, his lips barely grazing her forehead, close to the roots of her hair. So close, and then so far, for she drew back without being brusque, saying as she did so, This is a visit, remember. He gently released her, I remember, he said, and pointed to a chair, There's a little sitting-room next door with more comfortable chairs, but I think you'll feel more at ease in here, and with these words, he went and sat at his desk in the only remaining chair, the two of them separated by the table as if they were in a consulting room, Tell me what's wrong, but Maria Sara said nothing, they both knew that it was up to him to speak, even if only to welcome her. And he spoke. The words came out in a uniform tone, practically devoid of any modulations of persuasion or insinuation, each word intended to count in its own right, because of the naked meaning it might have at that moment and in those circumstances. I've lived alone in this apartment for many years, there are no women in my life except when the urge becomes irresistible, and even then I feel I'm on my own, I'm a person without any special qualities, normal even in my defects, and I haven't wanted much from life apart from keeping in good health which is a blessing, and not to be without work, these have been my only ambitions and I realise that I might be asking too much, but what I now want from life is something I cannot remember ever having, that taste of life that must surely exist. Maria Sara listened without taking her eyes off him, except for one fleeting moment when her concentration was replaced by an expression of surprise and curiosity, and when Raimundo stopped talking, she said, We're not here to discuss a contract, and besides, there's no need to tell me things I already knew, This is the first time I've mentioned the details of my private life, The things we consider private are nearly always known to everyone, you cannot imagine what one can find out from two or three apparently disinterested conversations, Have you been going around asking questions about me, Only the usual routine inquiries about the proof-readers working for the publishing house simply to form some impression, but people are usually prepared to say more than has been asked of them, they only need a little encouragement, a little prompting without them noticing, I could see you had this ability when we first met, But I only exploit it for the right reasons, Don't think I'm complaining. Raimundo Silva ran his hand over his forehead for a second, then said, I used to dye my hair but no longer, white roots are not a pretty sight, forgive me, in time my hair will get back to its natural colour, Mine has stopped being natural, because of you I went to the hairdresser today to have these venerable white hairs tinted, They were so few I shouldn't have thought it worth the bother, So you did notice, I looked at you closely enough, just as you must have looked at me and asked yourself how a man of my age could be without white hairs, No such question entered my mind, it was obvious that you dyed your hair, who did you think you were deceiving, Probably only myself, Just as I've decided to start deceiving myself, It comes to the same thing, What do you mean by the same thing, Your reason for dyeing your hair, mine for no longer dyeing it, Explain yourself, I stopped dyeing my hair in order to be as I am, And what about me, why have I tinted my hair, To go on being as you are, Smart thinking, I can see that I'll have to practise mental gymnastics daily in order to keep up with you, I'm no more intelligent than you are, simply older. Maria Sara smiled quietly, Irremovable evidence that clearly worries you, Not really, our age only matters in relation to that of others, I suspect I'm young in the eyes of someone who is seventy, but I'm in no doubt that a youth of twenty would consider me an old man. And in relation to me, how do you see yourself, Now that you've tinted the few white hairs you possess and I'm allowing all of mine to show, I've become a man of seventy in the presence of a girl of twenty, You can't count, there is only a difference of fifteen years between us, Then I must be thirty-five, They both laughed and Maria Sara suggested, Let's come to an agreement, What agreement, That we say no more about people's ages, I'll try not to bring up the subject again, You'd better do more than try if you want to hold a conversation with me, I'll speak to the mirror, You can speak to yourself if you wish to, but that isn't why I came here, I suppose it would be presumptuous to ask why you came, Or impolite, I'm not expressing myself very well, a phrase suddenly slips out and spoils everything, Forget it, you haven't spoilt anything, the fact is that we're both terrified, Suppose I were to get up and give you a kiss, Don't, but if you do, give me no warning, From bad to worse, any other man in this situation would know exactly what to do, Any other man in this situation would have another woman here, I give up, I told you it was only a visit, and I asked you to be patient, I'm prepared to wait but I know what I want, I concede it's important to know what one wants, everybody has these words on their lips, but in my opinion it is much better to want what one knows, it takes more time, of course, and people don't have the patience, Once again, I give in, so what do you suggest I do, You can start showing me your apartment, Tell me how you live and I'll tell you who you are, On the contrary, I'll tell you how you shouldn't live if you tell me who you are, Let me try and tell you who I am, And I'll try to discover how we should live. Raimundo Silva rose to his feet, Maria Sara did the same, he sidled round the desk, drew close, but not too close, he merely touched her on one arm, as if indicating that the visit was about to begin, yet she lingered, looked at the table, the objects on top of it, the lamp, papers, two dictionaries, Is this where you work, she asked, Yes, this is where I work, I see no signs of a certain siege, You're about to see them, the fortress is not simply this study.

We know that there is not much more than this, the bathroom, which until a few weeks ago was also a cosmetics laboratory, the kitchen where he toasted bread and ate the same old frugal meals, the study where we are right now, the sitting-room, inhospitable and abandoned, this door that leads into the bedroom. With his hand on the door-handle, Raimundo Silva appears to hesitate in opening it, he holds back respectfully as if observing some superstition, decidedly a man of another age, who is fearful of offending a woman's modesty by confronting her with the libidinous vision of a bed, even if she herself had asked, Show me your apartment, which allows us to assume that she knew very well what to expect. The door is finally opened, it's the bedroom with its heavy mahogany furniture, in front, standing lengthwise, the bed, the thick, white bedspread, under the pillow, the immaculate folds of the sheet, light filtering in through the window and softening the outline of things, as well as a silence that seems to breathe. We are in April, the evenings are drawn out, the days slow in passing, this probably explains why Raimundo Silva does not switch on the light, not to mention his reluctance to spoil the onset of twilight, which in its turn, makes him feel uneasy lest Maria Sara should misunderstand his intentions, we know all too well, from experience or hearsay, how often one can be dazzled along the path of obscurity, in the depths of darkness. Maria Sara immediately spotted the two roses in a vase on the tiny table by the window, and the sheets of paper, one half-written in the middle, to the left a little pile of sheets, now Raimundo had to switch on the lamp to create an atmosphere, but decided not to, he was standing right at the foot of the bed, as if he were trying to hide it from view, and waited for words, trembling as he tried to imagine what words might be spoken, he was not thinking of gestures or actions, only of words, here, in this room.

Maria Sara went up to the table. For several seconds she remained there without moving, as if waiting for the guide to follow on with a detailed description, he might say, for example, Look at the flowers, and she would have to avert her eyes, show some interest in the roses, the matching pair of those others in her apartment, and then she would make an understanding allusion, a discreet expression perhaps of loving sentiments, Our roses, accentuating the pronoun, but he remains silent and she does nothing except look at the half-written page, she does not need to be told that these are the signs of the siege, still indecipherable in the dim light despite the chronicler's neat handwriting. She realises that Raimundo will not speak, much as she would wish and at the same time does not wish that he should say something, that anything should break this uncanny silence, but that something should happen to prevent another world from irrupting into the one in which we find ourselves, perhaps death itself, the only other world, in fact, which, poised between the Martian and the terrestrial, will always have something in common with life. At just the right moment, she drew back the chair a little and sat down, with her left hand she switches on the lamp, the light covers the table and casts a halo of faint and impalpable mist over the entire room. Raimundo Silva has not moved, he tries to analyse the vague impression that with her gesture Maria Sara has just taken material possession of something previously possessed in her mind, and he suddenly thinks that, however long he may live, he will never experience another moment such as this, no matter how often she might return to this apartment and this room, even if, an absurd idea, they were to spend the rest of their lives here. Maria Sara has made no attempt to touch the paper, her hands are folded in her lap, and she reads from the first line, ignorant of what has been written on the previous page, and on the pages before that, where the history begins, she reads as if these ten lines embraced everything she had to know about life, a final judgment, one last summary, or, on the contrary, sealed orders where she will find instructions about the new route to be navigated. She finished reading, and, without turning round, asks, Who is this Ouroana, and this Mogueime, who is he, their names were written there and little else, as we know. Raimundo Silva took two short steps in the direction of the table and came to a halt, I'm still not sure, he said and fell silent, after all, he should have guessed that Maria Sara's first words would be to inquire who these two were, these, those, whosoever else, in a word, us. Maria Sara seemed satisfied with the reply, she was an experienced enough reader to know that the author only knows what his characters have been, even then not everything, and very little of what they will become. Raimundo Silva said, as if he were replying to an observation made aloud, I doubt whether they could be called characters, People in books are characters, objected Maria Sara, As I see them they belong somewhere in between, free in a different way, so that it would not make sense to talk either about the character's logic or about the contingent necessity of the person, If you can't tell me who they are, at least tell me what they do, He's a soldier who took part in the conquest of Santarém, she was picked up in Galicia to become a crusader's concubine, So there's a love intrigue, If you can call it that, Why the uncertainty, It's just that I don't know how people loved at that time, that's to say, I'm capable of imagining their feelings, but I have no idea or any certain knowledge of how the common man and woman expressed their feelings in those days, language, in this case, would not have been an obstacle, both of them spoke Galician, Invent a love story without any amorous words, *sans mots d'amour*, assuming such a thing is possible, From what I've seen and read, I very much doubt it, at least in real life, And what about this Ouroana, as the concubine of a crusader who was presumably a nobleman, how does she come to end up with Mogueime, Life takes many twists and turns, we humans even more so, and the last of them is death, crusader Heinrich, as he is called, will soon meet his death, Oh, so this crusader of yours is the same character mentioned in that other *History of the Siege of Lisbon*, Precisely, Then you'll also narrate the miracles he worked after his death, Too good an opportunity to miss, The miracle of the two mutes, Yes, but with a slight modification, and Raimundo Silva's reply was accompanied by a smile. Maria Sara rested her hand on the small pile of paper, May I look, she asked, Surely you don't want to read this right now, besides I've a long way to go yet, the history is incomplete, I shouldn't have the patience to wait, besides there aren't all that many sheets, Please, not today, But I'm curious to know how you solved the problem of the crusaders' refusal, Tomorrow, I'll make some photocopies and bring them to your office, Fine, that's settled, since I cannot persuade you otherwise. She got up, Raimundo Silva was very close, It's getting late, said Maria Sara, looking towards the window, Could you open it, she asked, Don't worry, said Raimundo Silva, I won't do you any harm, bearing in mind that you're paying me a visit and nothing more, You might also bear in mind that you're talking nonsense, I want some air and would like to see the view of the city from here, that's all.

There was a gentle twilight, the coolness of evening barely perceptible. Side by side, their elbows resting on the balcony, Maria Sara and Raimundo Silva watched in silence, conscious of each other's presence, the arm of the one feeling the arm of the other, and, little by little, the warmth of their blood. The pounding of Raimundo Silva's heartbeat echoed in his ears, that of Maria Sara threatened to shake her from head to foot. His arm drew closer, hers remained where it was, expectant, but Raimundo Silva dared go no further as fear crept in, I might make a mess of things, he thought, he could not see clearly, or did not want to, what was there to mess up, but this very uncertainty only served to increase his panic. Maria Sara could feel his entire being recoil like a snail withdrawing ever deeper into the protection of its shell, and she remarked cautiously, It's a nice view. The first lights appeared in the windows where the last rays of daylight still lingered, the street-lamps had just come on, someone in the nearby Largo dos Lóios spoke in a loud voice, someone replied, but the words were incomprehensible, Raimundo Silva asked, Did you hear them, Yes, I did, It was difficult to make out what they were saying, The same here, I didn't understand a word they said, We'll never know to what extent our lives would change if certain phrases, heard but elusive, had been understood, Much better, in my opinion, to start by not pretending that we did not understand those other words which were clear and direct, You're quite right, but there are some people, the dreamers, who prefer doubt to certainty, who are much less interested in the object than in its traces, in the footprints in the sand rather than in the animal that left them behind, You are clearly one of them, Up to a point, although I must remind you that it was not my idea to write this new history of the siege, Let's say that I sensed I had the right person before my very eyes, Or that, wisely, you prefer not to be responsible for his dreams, Would I be here if this were true, I suppose not, The difference being that I do not look for footprints in the sand, Raimundo Silva knew that he did not need to ask what it was that Maria Sara was looking for, now he could put his arm around her shoulders, as if unintentionally, a simple gesture, nothing other than fraternal for the moment, allowing her to react, perhaps gently relax her body, perhaps, as one might say, curl up, letting her body curve ever so slightly to one side, her head a trifle bent, awaiting the next gesture. Or she might become tense, protesting silently, anxious that he should see that it was still too soon, So when, Raimundo Silva was asking himself, forgetful of the fear he had felt, After what we've just said, what we've explicitly promised each other, the logical thing would have been, at least, to embrace and kiss, yes, at the very least. He straightened up as if suggesting that they should go back inside, but she continued to lean over the balcony, and he asked her, Don't you feel cold, No, not at all. Fighting back his impatience, he went back to his former position, without knowing what he could talk about, perversely imagining that she was amusing herself at his expense, it was all so much easier when he telephoned her at home, but he could not very well say to her, Go home and I'll call you. Then it occurred to him that he might get out of this embarrassing situation if he were to touch on some neutral topic, That building over there occupies the very spot where one of the towers defending the gate in this locality once stood, you can still see the markings on the ground, And the other tower, where was that, for there must have been two, Right here, where we are, Are you sure, Not absolutely sure, but there is every indication that I'm right, considering what we know about the former plan of this section of the walls, Well then, here on this tower, what are we, Moors or Christians, For the time being, Moors, we're here precisely to prevent the Christians from entering, We won't succeed, nor will it be necessary to await the end of the siege, have you seen the tiled panels depicting the miracles of St Antony at the entrance to the street, Abominable, You mean the miracles, No, the tiles, Why is this street called the Milagre de Santo António, when on the panels alone there are three, I can't answer that, perhaps the saint worked a special miracle for the city fathers, Milagres de Santo António would certainly sound nicer, but the one thing we mustn't do is to imagine that St Antony might have helped with the conquest of Lisbon in any military sense for he wasn't even born then, Two of the miracles on the panels are familiar, the apparition of the Child Jesus and that of the broken pitcher, the third one I don't recognise, there's a horse or a donkey, I didn't pay much attention, It's a donkey, How do you know, I have it here in a book, an old manuscript dating from the eighteenth century which describes all the miracles including this one, Tell me about it, You'd better read it for yourself, Another time, When, I can't say, tomorrow, after tomorrow, one day. Raimundo Silva took a deep breath, he could not pretend that he had not understood these words and he swore in his heart that he would definitely remind Maria Sara of them, as a definite promise demanding to be fulfilled. He felt so happy, so relaxed and free, that without thinking, he placed his hand on her shoulder and said, No, I'll read you the story about the donkey, come inside, Is it long, Like any story it can be told in ten words, or a hundred, or a thousand, or never end.

Raimundo Silva closed the window and went to his desk. Maria Sara could hear him muttering, It isn't here, where the devil have I put it, and then he went into the sitting-room, opened and closed the doors of the bookcase, finally announcing, Here it is. He reappeared with a quarto manuscript bound in leather, old in appearance, almost certainly the original text, and he came back with the satisfied expression of someone who has searched and found, but not just the book, You'll be more comfortable sitting down, he said, whereupon she sat on the chair by the table, her hand resting on the sheet of paper where the names of Ouroana and Mogueime were written, he remained standing, looked much younger, and happy, Now listen carefully, for this is interesting, I'll start with the title, here it goes, Sun Risen in the West and Set at Sunrise, St Antony, the Greatest Portuguese Luminary in the Firmament of the Church Between the Minor Constellations in the Sphere of Fransisco, A Historic and Panegyrical Précis of His Exemplary Life and Prodigious Deeds, Written and Offered to the Most Serene, August, Sublime, and Sovereign Family of the Royal House of Portugal, Whose Illustrious Names and Surnames are

Complimented and Adorned with the Sacred Denominations of Fransiscos and Antónios, by the most Reverend António Teixeira Alveres of His Majesty's Council, May God Protect him, Judge of the Royal Court of Appeals, Member of the General Council of the Holy Office of the Inquisition, Doctoral Canon in the Cathedral of Coimbra, and Distinguished Emeritus Professor in the Faculty of Canon Law, etcetera, Brás Luís de Abreu, from the left bank of the Tagus, Member of the Holy Office of the Inquisition, whew. Maria Sara laughed, If I've understood correctly, the author of this admirable work is this Brás Luís de Abreu, from the left bank of the Tagus, Yes, you've understood correctly, congratulations, now listen, page one hundred and twenty-three, pay attention, I'm about to start, On hearing the news that some Provinces of that Realm, the realm in question being France, had become infected by this disease, this heretical depravity, as explained several lines above, António de Lemonges left for Toulouse, a city as rich in trade as in vices, and worst of all, a pestilent hotbed of the Sacramental Heretics who deny the real presence of Christ in the Consecrated Host. The Saint was no sooner placed in this den of apostasy than he began to descend into the area of conflicts, only so that he might ascend in the chariot of triumphs. Fired with the burning zeal of God's glory and the infallible truths of his faith, he hoisted the flags of doctrine on the banners of charity, on the shields of penance the arms of the Cross, and transformed into the Evangelical Trumpet of the Divine Word, he raised voices to eradicate vices. His implacable hatred for the Heretics was matched only by his untiring activity driven by zeal. Everything was sacrificed on the altars of Faith, victims of his cruelty, like someone who with so many truths had exposed life for death, his affections for martyrdom. Those Birds of ill omen who, living in the dark night of their errors, only surrender their obstinate pride to the weapons of light, took care to concoct secret poisons against his life, diabolical wiles against his honour, infernal machinations against his reputation, seeking, as far as the powers of their malice would permit, to discredit and obscure the lights of so much doctrine, the triumphs of so much Sanctity.

St Antony began to preach to the applause and admiration of all Catholics, and all the more so because, recognising that he was a Foreigner, they heard him speak in their own language with such eloquence and ease that he appeared to have become naturalised in an idiom which, like him, had taken root in people's affections. The news soon spread of the wonderful effect his words were having on Souls, and the Preaching Heretics, once they saw the damage being done to their reputation by this new preacher who was attracting many converts, with that arrogance and presumption so characteristic of this rabble, decided to engage in a mercurial debate with Antony, relying on their specious fallacies to achieve a resounding victory.

So far no signs of the donkey, said Maria Sara. At that time the paths of the world were awkward and those of writing even more so, observed Raimundo Silva, and he went on, To achieve their objective, they enlisted the services of a distinguished Dogmatist from Toulouse, the most capable and respected of scholars, named Guialdo, fearless, presumptuous and overbearing, deeply versed in Holy Scripture and with an excellent command of Hebrew, a sharp wit and fiery temperament, and well-prepared for the most testing debates. The Saint did not reject the letter of challenge in order to satisfy the duel of Faith, putting all his trust in God as the only Agent of his cause. He fixed the day and the place for the contest. A huge crowd gathered of both Catholics and Sectarians. The Heretic spoke before Antony, for Malice has always prevailed on the world stage, ranting on with vain ostentation about his ill-used learning, and introducing torrents of verbiage with all the loquaciousness of captious syllogisms. The Saint listened patiently to this flood of words, full of artifice, devoid of truth, and then proceeded to refute his depraved errors, with so many quotations from Holy Scripture, enhanced by such clear reasoning, by such convincing arguments and pertinent words that the Heretic's obstinacy was soon overcome, as much for the worn-out discourses of reason, if he had not held out firmly, as for the diabolical caprices of the will. I shall not go into detail about the subtle arguments with which Antony ennobled this battle of wits, because superior to the narrative, they succumb to the silence of history like the mysteries of fame, suffice it to say that he spoke so wisely that he surpassed himself, his success all the more glorious as it had appeared to be impossible. Now listen carefully, Maria Sara, you can already hear the sound of the donkey's hooves. The perverse Dogmatist found himself humiliated and confounded on seeing himself defeated in the presence of those very same followers who with so much pride had hoped to see his deceptions prevail. And on seeing the artificial mesh of his fraudulent sophistries undone, he began to test the Saint's modesty and humility with this malicious discourse, Now then, Father Antony, enough of speeches, conceits and disputes, time we turned to deeds, and since as a beloved son of the Roman Catholic Church you believe in miracles, which as confirmation of the Articles of Faith were in remote times the most powerful motives for cautious belief, I should acknowledge my acceptance of the article of faith proclaiming the Real Presence of Christ's body in the Sacrament if God were to work some miracle. Antony, who in order to emerge victorious from all conflicts, always had God by his side, confidently replied, I'm happy to oblige, and confide in the mercy of my Lord Jesus Christ, who, in order to win over your soul and that of so many others, with shameful blindness following the impious Dogmas of their errors, will manifest his divine power on behalf of Catholic truth. Responding to this bold and holy resolution, the Heretic told him, It must be left to me to choose the miracle. I keep a donkey on my property. If the donkey after not having eaten or drunk for three days, will, in the sight of the Sacred Host, not so much as look at food however much it is coaxed, I shall firmly accept Christ's presence in the Holy Sacrament as an infallible truth. Moved by Divine inspiration, the Saint at once saw in the proposed event a cause for quiet confidence in victory, and the only disquiet to invade his heart was that of excitement. And confident that this was so much God's cause, he felt certain of victory, preparing for the contest both with the arms of Humility, and the escutcheon of Prayer.

I feel quite nervous, said Maria Sara, with the solemnity of the moment, and with the vernacular, but this so-called escutcheon strikes me as being the most awful gallicism, Just so, and lest we forget that flaws are to be found everywhere, let us continue, The appointed day arrived, a vast crowd assembled on both sides, that of the Catholics, confident but humble, that of the Heretics, not simply incredulous but presumptuous. Antony celebrated the Holy Sacrifice of the Mass in the nearest Church, and taking the Consecrated Host into his hands with all due reverence, went out to where the starving Beast stood warily. They brought before its eyes and up close to its mouth a ration of ripe barley, as the Saint said aloud in a commanding voice, In the virtue and name of Jesus Christ, Whom I am holding in my unworthy hands, I order you, irrational creature, to reject this sustenance so that you may pay due homage to your Creator and mankind might be persuaded to abandon its wilful stubbornness and embrace the truths of the Roman Catholic Faith, convinced by the less stubborn instinct of Beasts. Antony had not quite finished uttering these words, when the foul beast, belying its true nature by rejecting the food it had started to devour, and overcoming its pressing hunger, came up to the Saint and kneeling before him, paid homage to Christ in the Blessed Sacrament, to the astonishment and wonder of all those present. All gathered there, witnessed this wondrous spectacle with tears in their eyes, but with varying reactions, for what were tears of devotion and tenderness in the Catholics, were tears of compunction and remorse in the Heretics. The Catholics celebrated the triumphs of Faith while most of the Heretics deplored the errors of the Sect, only one or two rebels, in the face of the evidence, clung to their cherished absurdities and appeared to court disgrace. But they could not deny their amazement, so that those very men who before the contest were predicting triumphs, were so petrified by events that they became like the first statues erected to commemorate the victory.

Raimundo Silva paused to observe, The following paragraph describes the conversion of Guialdo along with his relatives and friends, I'll spare you this passage, but what you must hear is the peroration, How admirable the enduring virtue of St Antony. A virtue capable of transforming Beasts into humans to confound Mankind. David complained that the irrational servants were only familiar with the stable where they found sustenance, while ignoring their Lord who provided for them, but on this occasion by order of St Antony, the ingratitude of its nature forgotten, this grateful living creature scorned sustenance and the stable in order to worship the true Lord who had given it both life and nourishment. Oh blessed Animal. You have now shown that judicious Beasts do exist, for you have given due warning to so many brutish Men. Once in Bethlehem, you refrained from munching the hay in order to protect the new-born Jesus, now in Toulouse you refrain from eating barley in order to worship God in the Holy Sacrament. You ignored the hay in the Manger in order to adore the Child Jesus made manifest in the house of bread, you ignored the barley during the contest in order to venerate Christ concealed in the substance of bread. You have thus shown yourself capable of reason and deserve our applause. Your instinct may be fantasy, but has all the appearance of discourse, your notions may not be reasoning, yet seems akin to understanding. Deprived of memory, you appear to know what you are venerating, deprived of willpower, you show affection for what you adore, without understanding, you appear to discover judgment in what you know. St Antony worked two miracles in you with a single prodigy that might be infinitely prodigious in this one portent. He made your brute instinct look like a rational idea because you adored, he made your bestial hunger look like penitential abstinence because you did not eat. There were not simply two surprises, because there were many more brutes present on this occasion. Guialdo was blind in his acceptance of that mystery, slow to show Faith in that presence, but Antony's faith opened his eyes before this singular miracle, Guialdo's faith stirred when confronted with this wonder never before witnessed. Behold how a single action by sovereign St Antony brought about three incredible miracles, because thrice refined in virtue whereby one became triple, because thrice miraculous in its works in that single miracle it became a wondrous superlative. Amen.

Raimundo Silva closed the formidable book with a gesture of mock solemnity and repeated, Amen. Does this amen appear in the author's discourse, or was it introduced by you, asked Maria Sara, An oratorical bombast such as this demanded no less, What a strange world it must have been, that such things should have been believed and written, I'd prefer to say in which such things are not written, but believed even today, We're positively mad, Do you mean us, No, I was referring to people in general, I'm one of those people who thinks that human beings have always been mentally deranged, As platitudes go, that isn't bad, Perhaps it will sound less like a platitude if I tell you that in my opinion, madness is the result of the shock produced in man by his own intelligence and we still haven't recovered from the trauma three million years later, So, according to this hypothesis of yours, we're going from bad to worse, I'm no fortune-teller but I fear so. He went to put the book on the table just as Maria Sara was getting to her feet, they stood facing each other, neither can escape nor wants to. He took her by the shoulders, the first time he had touched her in this way, she raised her head, her eyes were shining brightly, caught by the dim light of the lamp, and whispered, Say nothing, not a word, don't tell me that you like me, that you love me, simply give me a kiss. He drew her gently towards him without their bodies touching, and slowly leaned forward until his lips touched hers, at first the merest touch, the most delicate contact, and then, after some hesitation, their mouths quickly opened, their sudden kiss total, intense, and eager. Maria Sara, Maria Sara, he murmured, not daring to use other words, but she made no reply, perhaps she still did not know how to say Raimundo, for anyone who thinks it is easy to pronounce a name for the first time when you're in love, is much mistaken. Maria Sara drew back, he tried to hold on to her, but she shook her head, moved away, slipped quietly from his arms, I must go, she said, give me my coat, it's in the study, and my bag, please. When Raimundo Silva returned, she was holding a sheet of paper in her hand and smiling, The world is full of such madmen, she said, and Raimundo Silva replied, Mogueime, I can see him below, in front of the Porta de Ferro, awaiting the order to attack, Ouroana, now that dusk has fallen, will be summoned to the knight Heinrich's tent so that he might take his pleasure, as for us, we're the Moors up here on a tower where we think we can watch destiny advance. Maria Sara took her coat, without putting it on, and her bag, and made for the bedroom door. He accompanied her, tried once more to detain her, No, she said, losing no time in opening the door on to the landing, from where she announced, I'll be back tomorrow, there's no need to bring me the photocopies at the office, and please, no telephone calls.

Raimundo Silva scarcely ate any dinner and stayed up late writing, when the time came to go to bed he realised he would be incapable of turning down the covers, of lying on those laundered sheets, or so much as disturbing the pillow on top of the bolster. He took two extra covers from the wardrobe and carried them into the sitting-room, improvised a bed on the narrow divan and settled down to sleep.

It is generally considered a show of unsurpassable bravura when a man condemned to death himself gives the firing squad the order to shoot, and even the most peaceful or cowardly of us, attended by favourable circumstances, at some time must have dreamed of this glorious demise, especially if someone survived to tell the tale, for glories without anyone to narrate them are valued less. In fact, it is necessary to have come into the world with nerves of steel, or, if shaky and cracking, to be possessed of a patriotic or similar zeal beyond the ordinary, to cry out with a hoarse and then for ever afterwards silent voice, Fire, somehow alleviating the conscience of the assassins from any sense of guilt, while elevating our own conscience in one last glow to the sublime heights of sacrifice and total abnegation. It is possible that the common spectacle of such gestures, especially when transferred to the screen, contributes to an exaltation capable of turning the most mediocre person into a hero, only by chance absent from the scene of the drama, precisely because they decided to come to the cinema today, to see, one minute feigned, the next real, how the famous actor simulated death or how, with the realism of a documentary, an executed man without a name died for good. There is no hint of malice in this doubt, only what we assume to be true, that no one condemned to the electric chair, gallows, guillotine, garrote or stake will have given the order to switch on the current, open the trap-door, release the blade, turn the screw, or spark the match, perhaps because such deaths are so undignified, including those with the longest tradition in art, perhaps because they lack the military factor, the institution of arms, where heroism is more readily found, for even when the condemned man was no more than a common civilian, the shots he received in the chest turned out to be a ransom for his mediocrity and were the viaticum, the safe-conduct, thanks to which he will be permitted, when the time comes, to enter the paradise of heroes, without any wrangling over meaning and cause, for there one loses any notion of these differences on earth.

This lengthy circumlocution had no other justification than to show how, in all innocence, it can happen that a person gives voice to his own death, even if it should not be imminent, and how, in this case, words spoken in piety are transformed into enraged serpents that would not turn back for anything in this world. It was noon, and the muezzins had climbed up on to the balcony of the minarets to summon the faithful to prayer, because although the city is under siege and plunged into the turmoil of warfare, the rites of worship must not be neglected, and although the muezzin of the great mosque knew that he could be seen on all sides by the Christian soldiers, especially by those besieging the nearby Porta de Ferro, he remained unconcerned, firstly because he was not so close that he might be hit by a stray javelin, secondly because his own words would protect him from any danger, *La ilaha illa llah*, he was about to cry out, Allah is the one and only God, and what good would it do him if he were not in the end. At this moment, positioned before the five gates, the Portuguese forces no sooner hear this cry than they launch a general and simultaneous attack, the first of the three strategic points, as we know, drawn up in the definitive plan of combat, as established by our good king after consulting his chief of staff. Out of habit, we might be tempted to describe this ironic touch of putting the order to attack into the mouths of the unsuspecting Moors as Machiavellian, but Machiavelli was not even born at this time nor did any of his ancestors, contemporary or preceding the conquest of Lisbon, distinguish themselves internationally in the art of deception. The utmost care has to be taken in the use of words, never using them before the epoch in which they came into the general circulation of ideas, otherwise we shall immediately be accused of an anachronism, which, amongst the reprehensible acts in the terrain of writing, is second only to plagiarism. In fact, if we had been as important a nation then as we are today, then it would not have been necessary to wait three centuries for Machiavelli to enrich the practice and vocabulary of political astuteness, and without further ado, we would describe this ingenious stroke as obsolete, Allah is the one and only God cries the muezzin, and, as one man, the Portuguese, shouting their heads off to summon their courage, advance steadily on the city gates, even though the most ordinary observer, so long as he is impartial, could not fail to notice a certain lack of conviction in the advancing armies, as if disbelieving that with so little they might get so far. It is true that the bows and the crossbows fired a veritable shower of arrows and other missiles over the battlements in order to drive back the guards and to give some respite to the assailants on the front line so that they might attempt to break down the gates with axes and hammers, while others, manning the heavy battering-rams, push them forward in a regular rhythm, but the Moors refused to give way, firstly because they were protected by the shelters they had built, and then, when these began to burn, set alight by flaming torches tied to the larger javelins, they came crashing down on to the heads of the Portuguese, who were forced to retreat, scorched like pigs after slaughter. Once they had put out some of the more dangerous fires, which meant that some of Mem Ramires's soldiers had to dive into the waters of the estuary, from where they emerged shivering and pleading for ointments, the artillery launched another barrage of missiles, this time more cautious, and preferring to use stones and missiles of hardened clay, for those fiendishly wicked Moors hit us back with our own munitions, causing at least one Portuguese soldier to die, showing that no man escapes his destiny, when a javelin was thrown back which he himself had been the first to aim.

From the balcony of the minaret, the muezzin heard the fateful turmoil, so different from the uproar of animated voices that had reached his ears in that very same spot, when the crusaders departed. This time he did not need to come rushing down to find out what was happening, he knew all too well that the battle was starting up again after the pause following the loss of the nearby suburb, but he was not worried, the cries he heard coming from his brethren were not those of despair and defeat, but of courage, that is how they sounded to him, and he knew he was right because, being blind, he had been compensated with the keenest of hearing which did not abandon him even in old age. On the other minarets throughout the city, the muezzins were probably hearing the same uproar, some six, eight, ten blind men assigned to other mosques and perched between heaven and earth in total darkness. All of them were responsible for this attack, they were the ones who had given the order, but, innocent as they were, they did not connect the words spoken with their obvious effect, each of them no doubt saying to himself, what a coincidence, and preferring to think, as the echoes of their holy summons to prayer continued to hover in the air, although already mingled with the howls and curses of the combatants, that it was as if the palpable presence of Allah were protecting the city, an enormous cupola made from the myriads of other vibrant little cupolas that were descending all the way down the slope from the castle as far as the river, while all around, the God of the Christians appears to have been lacking in enough shields to defend his sceptical soldiers from the missiles raining down from on high. Startled by the commotion, dogs are barking on these slopes, they run for shelter and start burying bones, their instinct must serve some purpose when even people endowed with judgment can foretell evil times ahead.

This allusion to Moorish dogs, that is to say, the dogs that still lived with the Moors at the time, clearly in their condition as the most impure of animals, but who would soon begin to feed with their foul flesh on the emaciated bodies of the human creatures of Allah, this allusion, as we were saying, reminded Raimundo Silva of the dog on the Escadinhas de São Crispim, unless, on the other hand, it was an unconscious memory on his part, that led to the introduction of the allegorical picture with that brief commentary about judgment and instinct. As a rule, Raimundo Silva boards the tram at the Portas do Sol, although the distance is greater, and he comes back the same way. If we were to ask him why he does it, he would reply that because he has such a sedentary occupation, it is good for him to walk, but that is not entirely true, the fact is that he would not mind descending the hundred and thirty-four steps, gaining time and benefiting from those sixty-seven flections of each knee, if, out of male pride, he did not also feel obliged to climb up them with the inevitable weariness everyone suffers if they pass this way, as we can see from the small number of mountaineers around. A reasonable compromise would be to go down that way as far as the Porta de Ferro and come back up by the longer but easier route, but to do this would mean acknowledging, all too clearly, that his lungs and legs are no longer what they were, a mere assumption, because the period when Raimundo Silva was in his prime does not come into this history of the siege of Lisbon. On the two or three occasions that he took this route down in recent weeks, Raimundo Silva did not encounter the dog, and thought to himself that, tired of waiting for even the barest ration from the miserly neighbours, the dog had emigrated to richer pastures, or had simply given up the ghost when it could wait no longer. He remembered his act of charity and told himself that he could have done it more often, but when it comes to dogs, you know what it is like, they live with the fixation of acquiring a master, to encourage and feed them is to have them at your feet for evermore, they stare at us with that neurotic anxiety and there is no other solution than to put a collar round their neck, pay for a licence and take them home. The alternative would be to leave them to die of hunger, so slowly that there would be no room for remorse, and, if possible, on the Escadinhas de São Crispim, where no one ever passes.

News arrived that another burial site had been consecrated on a plain facing the fortress, beneath the slope on the left-hand side of the royal encampment, because of the work involved in transporting corpses across ravines and marshes as far as the Monte de São Fransisco, who arrived more battered than a load of fish and, in this hot weather, smelling worse than the living. As with this new site for burial, the cemetery of São Vicente is divided into two sections, Portuguese on one side, foreigners on the other, to all appearances a waste of space yet responding, in the final analysis, to that desire for occupation inherent in human nature, and in this sense serving both the living and the dead. When his hour comes, knight Heinrich will end up here, for whom that other hour is at hand when he will prove the tactical excellence of the assault towers, now that direct attacks on gates and walls have met with failure, the first item on the strategic plan. What he does not know, nor could anyone have told him, is that the moment the hopeful eyes of the soldiers are upon him, with the exception of the envious who already existed even then, this very moment, on the threshold of glory, will be that of his unfortunate death, unfortunate in military terms, let's say, because to that other and greater glory, was finally destined he who had come from so far away. But let us not precipitate. The thirty native casualties who lost their lives during the attempted assault on the Porta de Ferro still have to be buried, their corpses will be transported by boat to the other bank of the estuary then carried uphill on improvised litters made from rough pieces of wood. On the edge of the common grave they will be stripped of any clothing that might be used by the living, unless they are much too bloodstained, and even these will be snatched up by the less scrupulous and squeamish, so that generally speaking the dead are lowered into their grave as naked as the earth that receives them.

Lined up, with their bare feet touching the first fringe of mud kept moist and soft by the high tides and waves, the corpses are subjected to the stares and taunts of the victorious Moors up on the battlements, as they lie there waiting to be carried on board. There is some delay in transporting them because there are more volunteers than are actually needed, which may seem surprising when the task is so painful and lugubrious, even if we take into account the enticement of being rewarded with clothing, but in fact everyone is trying to get hired as a boatman or drover, because just recently, there alongside the cemetery, prostitutes have gathered from the ravines and outlying districts where they were awaiting the outcome of the war, if it were to be a case of *veni, vidi, vici*, any precarious arrangement would do, but if it turned out to be a long, drawn-out siege, as looks likely, forcing them to look for greater comfort, they would select some shady spot out of the heat where they might rest from their labours, and set up some wattle huts and use branches to make an awning, for a bed requiring nothing more than an armful of hay or entwined plants which in time will turn to humus and merge with the ashes of the dead. It would not take much learning to observe, as much today as in those medieval times, despite the Church's disapproval of classical similes, how Eros and Thanatos were paired off, in this case with Hermes as intermediary, for it was common practice to use the clothes of the dead to pay for the services of women who, being in the infancy of their art and the nation as yet in its early stages, still accompanied the raptures of their clients with genuine pleasure. Confronted with this, the following discussion will come as no surprise, I'll go, I'll go, which is not a sign of compassion for their lost comrades nor a pretext to escape the contingencies on the front line of battle for a few hours, but rather the insatiable cravings of the flesh, their gratification dependent, would you believe it, on the likes and dislikes on the part of some sergeant-major.

And now let us take a little stroll past this line-up of filthy, bloodstained corpses, lying shoulder to shoulder as they await embarkation, some with their eyes still open and staring heavenwards, others who with half-closed eyelids appear to be suppressing an irresistible urge to burst out laughing, a grim spectacle of festering sores, of gaping wounds devoured by flies, no one knows who these men are or might have been, their names known only to their closest friends, either because they hailed from the same place, or because thrown together as they faced the same dangers, They died for the fatherland, the king would say if he were to come here to pay his last respects, but Dom Afonso Henriques has his own corpses there in his encampment without having to travel all this way, his speech, were he to make it, should be interpreted as that of someone contemplating on equal terms all those who more or less at this hour await despatch, while important matters are being discussed, such as who should be hired as crew or assigned to the cemetery as grave-diggers. The army will not need to inform the relatives of the deceased by telegram, In the fulfilment of his duty, he fell on the field of honour, undoubtedly a much more elegant way of putting it than by simply explaining, His head was smashed in by a heavy stone that some bastard of a Moor threw down from above, the fact is that these armies do not as yet keep a register, the generals, at best, and somewhat vaguely, know that at the outset they had twelve thousand men and that from now on what they must do is to discount so many men each day, a soldier in the front line scarcely needs a name, Listen, simpleton, if you draw back, you'll get a thick ear, and he did not draw back, and the stone came hurtling down and he was killed. He was called Galindo, it's this fellow here, in such a sorry state that even his own mother would not recognise him, his head smashed in on one side, his face covered in congealed blood, and on his right lies Remígio, pierced with arrows, two side by side, because the two Moors who targeted him at the same time had the eye of an eagle and the strength of Samson, but the delay is no disadvantage, their turn will come within the next few days when they too will be exposed to the sun as they await burial inside the city, which being under siege means they cannot get to the cemetery where the Galicians have carried out the most wicked acts of profanation. In their favour, if such a thing can be said, the Moors only have the farewells of their families, the loud lamentations of their womenfolk, but this, who knows, could be even worse for the morale of the soldiers, subjected to a spectacle of tears of sorrow and suffering, of mourning without consolation, My son, my son, while in the Christian encampment only the men are involved, for the women, if there are any, are there for other reasons and purposes, to open their legs for the first man who turns up, whether a soldier be dead or at his post, any differences of length or width are not even noticed after a while, except in exceptional cases. Galindo and Remigio are about to cross the estuary for the last time, if they have ever crossed it before in this sense, for the siege being in the early stages there is no lack of men here who did not get to relieve themselves of secret humours, they entered death full of a life that profited no one. With them, stretched out at the bottom of the boat, one on top of the other, packed tightly because of the confined space, there are also the corpses of Diogo, Gonçalo, Fernão, Martinho, Mendo, Garcia, Lourenço, Pêro, Sancho, Álvaro, Moço, Godinho, Fuas, Arnaldo, Soeiro, and those who still have to be counted, some who have the same name, but not mentioned here so that no one starts complaining, He's been named already, and it would not be true, we might have written, Bernardo is in the boat, when there were thirty corpses with the same name, for we shall never tire of repeating, There is nothing in a name, as proved by Allah himself who despite his ninety-nine names, has only succeeded in being known as God.

Mogueime, too, is in the boat, but alive. He escaped unharmed from the assault, not as much as a scratch, and not because he sheltered from the fighting, on the contrary, one could swear that he was always in the line of fire, handling the battering-rams like Galindo, although the latter was less fortunate. To be sent to the funeral is as good as an official summons, an act of commemoration with the troops on parade, a day off duty, and the sergeant is in no doubt how his men will use their time between going and returning, his great disappointment is not to be able to be part of the retinue, he is going with his captain Mem Ramires to the prince's encampment, where the leaders have been convened to weigh up the outcome, clearly negative, of the assault, which only goes to show that life in the superior ranks is not always a bed of roses, not to mention the more than likely hypothesis that the king would put the blame for this fiasco on his captains, who in their turn would criticise the sergeants, who, poor things, could scarcely excuse themselves by accusing the soldiers of cowardice, for as everyone knows, any soldier owes his worth to his sergeant. If this should happen, there is every chance that permits for burial will be refused, for when all is said and done, these corpses who sail alone have only one route and the time has come to begin the story of the phantom ships. From the hillside opposite, the women at the gates watch the boats approach with their cargo of dead bodies and desires, and any woman who might be indoors with a man will fidget disloyally in order to get rid of him quickly, for the soldiers accompanying these funereal gondolas, perhaps because of an unconscious need to balance the fatality of death with the demands of life, are much more passionate than any soldier or civilian on routine duty, and as we know, generosity always increases in proportion to the satisfaction of ardour. However little a name may be worth, these women, too, have a name, in addition to the collective title of whore by which they are known, some are called Tareja like the King's mother, or Mafalda, like the queen who came from Savoy last year, or Sancha, or Maiores, or Elvira, or Dórdia, or Enderquina, or Urraca, or Doroteia, or Leonor, and two of them have precious names, one who is called Chamoa, another known as Moninha, enough to make one feel like rescuing them from the streets and taking them home, not out of pity, as Raimundo Silva did with the dog on the Escadinhas de São Crispim, but in order to try and discover what secret links a person to a name, even when that person scarcely matches up to the name itself.

Mogueime is making this crossing with two declared aims and one that is private. Much has already been said about the declared purpose of the journey, the open trenches are there to receive the dead and the women with open legs to receive the living. His hands still soiled with the dark, moist earth, Mogueime will unfasten his breeches and, pulling up his jacket without taking off any clothes, he will go up to the woman of his choice, she too with her skirt hitched up and bundled round her belly, the art of making love has yet to be invented in these newly-conquered lands, the Moors are said to have taken all their knowledge about love with them, and if any of these prostitutes, being Moorish in origin, has been forced by circumstances to offer her services to foreigners, she will reveal nothing of the amatory skills of her race, until she can begin to sell these novelties at a higher price. Needless to say, the Portuguese are not entirely ignorant in this matter, after all the possibilities depend on means more or less common to all races, but they obviously lack refinement and imagination, have no talent for that subtle gesture or prudent interruption, in a word, are devoid of civilisation and culture. Do not forget that as the hero of this story, Mogueime is more competent and refined than any of his comrades. Lying next to him, Lourenço grunted with pleasure and Elvira screamed, and Mogueime and his whore responded with the same vehemence, Doroteia is determined not to be outdone by Elvira in expansive prodigality, and Mogueime, who is enjoying himself, has no reason to keep quiet. Until the poet Dom Dinis becomes king, let us content ourselves with what we have.

When the boats returned to the other bank, much more swiftly, Mogueime will not return with them. Not because he has decided to desert, any such idea would never have crossed his mind, given his reputation and the fact that his place is already assured in *The Grand History of Portugal*, these are not things to be thrown away lightly in a reckless moment, after all, this is the same Mogueime who took part in the conquest of Santarém, enough said. His secret objective, which he will not confide even to Galindo, is to go from here, along the routes that were described when the army moved from the Monte de São Fransisco to the Monte da Graça, as far as the king's encampment, where he knows the crusaders have their separate tents, where he hopes, by some happy coincidence, to find the German's concubine around some corner, she is called Ouroana and she is forever in his thoughts, although he has no illusions that he could ever win her favours, for a soldier without any rank can only aspire to a common prostitute, concubines are reserved for the pleasure of gentlemen, at most swopped around, but always amongst equals. Deep down, he does not believe that he will have the good fortune to see her but how he would love to feel once more that throbbing in the pit of his stomach he has experienced on two occasions, despite everything he has no cause for complaint, for with so many randy men on the prowl, the women are kept under guard, even more so if they go out to get some fresh air, as proved by Ouroana who was always accompanied by one of knight Heinrich's servants, armed as if for battle, although merely a member of the domestic staff.

There are enormous differences between peace and war. When the troops were camped here while the crusaders decided whether they would stay or leave, and there was no warfare apart from the brief skirmish or exchange of arrows and insults, Lisbon looked almost like a jewel resting against the slope and exposed to the voluptuaries of the sun, sparkling all over, and surmounted on high by the mosque of the fortification, resplendent with green and blue mosaics, and, on the slope facing this side, the neighbourhood from where the population had not yet withdrawn, a scene that could only be compared with the ante-chambers of paradise. Now, outside the walls, the houses have been burnt down and the walls demolished, and even from a distance you can see the onslaught of destruction, as if the Portuguese army were a swarm of white ants as capable of gnawing wood as stone, although they might break their teeth and the thread of life in this arduous task, as we have seen, and it will not stop here. Mogueime is not sure if he is afraid of dying. He finds it only natural that others should die, in war this always happens, or is it for this reason that wars are fought, but were he capable of asking himself what he really fears at this time, he would perhaps reply that it is not so much the possibility of meeting his death, who knows, perhaps in the very next assault, but something else which we shall simply call loss, not of life in itself, but of what might happen in life, for example, if Ouroana were to be his the day after tomorrow, unless destiny or Our Lord Jesus Christ should ordain that he must die tomorrow. We know that Mogueime has no such thoughts, he travels by a more straightforward route, whether death comes late or Ouroana comes soon, between the hour of her arrival and the hour of his departure there will be life, but the thought is also much too complicated, so let us resign ourselves to not knowing what Mogueime really thinks, let us turn to the apparent clarity of actions, which are translated thoughts, although in the passage from the latter to the former, certain things are always lost or added, which means that, in the final analysis, we know as little about what we do as about what we think. The sun is high, it will soon be midday, the Moors are certain to be observing any movements in the encampment, watching to see whether the Galicians will stage another attack like that of yesterday when the muezzins summon the faithful to prayer which only goes to show how little respect these heartless creatures have for the religion of others. In order to shorten his journey, Mogueime fords the estuary at the level of the Praça dos Restauradores, taking advantage of the low tide. Soldiers from the detachment assigned to the Porta de Alfofa roam these parts, seeking some distraction from the horrors of battle and trying to catch small fish in the estuary, they have certainly come a long way, and even in those days there was the saying, Out of sight, out of mind, but the allusion here is not to interrupted love affairs, but a question of finding some respite away from the arena of warfare, a sight the more delicate find unbearable once the heat of battle is over. And to avoid any desertions, commanding officers patrol the area, like shepherds or their dogs guarding the flock, there is no other solution, for the soldiers have been paid until August and there is much to be done, day by day, until this period expires, save for any impediment resulting beforehand because another period of expiry has been completed, that of life. Mogueime cannot ford the second branch of the estuary, for it is deeper, even when the tide is out, so he goes up the embankment until he comes to the freshwater streams, where one day he will see Ouroana washing clothes and he will ask her, What is your name, a mere pretext to start up a conversation, for if Mogueime knows anything about this woman, it is her name, he has said it to himself so often that, contrary to appearances, it is not only the days that go on repeating themselves, What is your name Raimundo Silva asked Ouroana, and she replied, Maria Sara.

It was almost seven o'clock in the evening when Maria Sara

arrived. Raimundo Silva had been writing until five, his attention constantly distracted, with great difficulty he would compose two or three lines and then start staring out of the window, clouds in the sky, a pigeon that would settle on the balcony from time to time, looking at him through the window-pane with its fierce crimson eye, shaking its head with movements that were at once rapid and fluent, the wastepaper basket which he had brought through from the study was full of torn-up sheets of paper, a disaster, if all the days from now on were to turn out like this, there was every danger that his history would never be finished, the Portuguese remaining before this invincible city of Lisbon until the end of time, without the courage to conquer it or the strength to relinquish it. During the day he had to resist the temptation to telephone a thousand times, which contributed to distracting him even more from what he wanted to write, the outcome being that in terms of work he had advanced no more than a page, and even so, thanks to that benevolence that so often leads us to tolerate what has no other merit than that of not being insufferable. He has spent the last half-hour out on the verandah, now and then showing himself without dissembling, like someone who is waiting and does not care who knows or comments, but nearly always leaning against the inner frame of the window, with half of his body concealed, and gazing furtively towards the Largo dos Lóios where Maria Sara will park her car. He saw her appear on the corner of the building with the murals of St Antony, walking at a steady pace, neither quickly nor slowly, she was wearing a jacket and skirt he had seen before, her bag over one shoulder, her hair dancing freely in the breeze, and desire brought a sudden knot into the pit of his stomach, not as happened to Mogueime, for the latter had felt his heart pound. He perceived that this was genuine desire, that yesterday it had been more like a convulsive and constant throbbing throughout his entire body that might be resolved by means of rapid physical contact that probably, if consummated, would leave signs of frustration or, worse still, of disenchantment. He went to open the door and stepped out on to the landing, Maria Sara was already climbing the stairs and was looking up with a smile, and he smiled back, Why so late, he asked and she replied, You know what the traffic can be like, yesterday was different because I left the office earlier, and on reaching the landing she gave him a quick kiss on the cheek and entered the apartment. The nearest door, as we know, is that of the bedroom, there would be no point, things being as they are, in looking for another, all the more so because this bedroom is not simply a bedroom but also, however provisional, a work-room, and for this reason, we repeat, somehow neutralised. But Raimundo Silva removed the bag from her shoulder, slowly, as if he were removing her clothes, it was an unpremeditated gesture, one of those moments when intuition helps out where science has sometimes forgotten, Yesterday, when you said goodbye, you somehow sounded more friendly, Forgive me, I need a little more time to get used to being on intimate terms, Maria Sara replied, Would you prefer to go through to the study, No, we're fine here, but you have nowhere to sit, Wait, I'll go and fetch a chair. When he returned, Maria Sara was reading the last page of the manuscript, You haven't made much progress, she said, And why should that be, asked Raimundo Silva, Yes, why should that be, she replied, this time without smiling, and looking at him as if awaiting some reaction, Take a look at the bed, What about the bed, and in another tone of voice, she said, I seem to be alone in dropping the formalities, It's probably more difficult for me to be familiar, but let's try again, you've asked me to look at the bed and I'm asking you, What about the bed, Do you notice anything different from yesterday, It's the same bed, Of course it's the same bed, what I want you to tell me is whether it looks as if it has been slept in, being a woman you won't find it difficult to see that the folds of the sheets have not been disturbed, that there isn't a crease on the bolster or pillow, that the bedcover is pristine and all the fringes straight, Yes, it's true, Just as my cleaner left it yesterday, So you didn't sleep here last night, No, Why not, where did you sleep then, Let me answer the second part of the question first, I slept through there on a divan, But why, Because I'm like a child, an adolescent whose grey hairs have come much too soon, because I could not bring myself to sleep here alone, that's all. Maria Sara put the sheet of paper down on the table, went up to him and embraced him, You will never need to tell me that you love me, Oh yes, I will, But not like this, I'll put it into words, And I want to hear them, I know I shall forget most of them, the moment, the place, the hour, but I shall never forget this, or that moment when you touched the rose. They were in each other's arms but still had not kissed, they looked at each other and smiled a lot, their expression one of happiness, and then their smile slowly withdrew, like water being sucked up and savoured by the earth, until they both became serious, staring at each other, a sudden, subtle shadow hovered in the room, it came only to disappear, and then immense and powerful wings enfolded Maria Sara and Raimundo Silva, drawing them together as if they were one body, and their kiss began, so different from the kiss they had shared here yesterday, they were and they were not the same two people, but to say this is to have said nothing, because no one knows what a kiss is really like, perhaps some impossible deglutition or diabolical communion, perhaps the beginning of death. It was not Raimundo Silva who led Maria Sara to the bed, nor did she gently draw him there as if distracted, they simply found themselves there, seated first of all on the edge of the mattress, crumpling the white bedcover, then he tilted her back and they went on kissing, her arms round his neck, his right arm supporting her head while his left arm appeared to hesitate, not knowing what to do, or knowing but not daring, as if an invisible wall had been erected between them at the eleventh hour, guided by a wise hand, he touched Maria Sara's waist, went down as far as the small of her back until it came to rest ever so gently on the curve of her thigh, only to travel slowly up her body once more as far as her breast, now his knowing fingers recognise the soft texture of this blouse he was touching for the first time, the sensation was fleeting and instantly mitigated by the disturbing awareness that beneath a man's clumsy hand there was this miracle of a breast. Dazed by this contact, Raimundo Silva raised his head, he wanted to look, see, know, be certain that it was his own hand that was there, now the invisible wall was really collapsing, beyond stood the city of the body, streets and squares, shadows and light, a melody that comes from who knows where, infinite windows, an interminable peregrination. Maria Sara placed her hand on that of Raimundo Silva, and he kissed it profusely until she withdrew it taking his hand with her, and her erect breast, still covered, offered itself to his kisses. It was she herself who, without haste, unbuttoned and removed her blouse, beneath the white lace of her bra her skin was like lace in the palest gold, the nipples rose-coloured, dear God, then Raimundo Silva's hand was back, gentle, violent, and with one resolute gesture he uncovered her breast, elastic and dense. Maria Sara moaned when his lips eagerly sucked her nipple, her whole body shuddered, and then more deeply because Raimundo Silva's hand had come to rest on her belly, before descending almost naturally to her sex, where it twitched, persistent and invasive. They were still dressed, she only with her jacket open and her blouse unbuttoned, and it was Raimundo Silva who covered her breast once more, so delicately that Maria Sara's startled eyes became moist with tears. The shadows in the room suddenly lit up, no doubt because over by the straits the evening clouds had opened up, and the last rays of sun were coming through the window, oblique, casting over that side of the wall a flickering light the colour of cherries, which in its turn sent an invisible vibration throughout the entire room, a sudden pulsation of atoms aroused by the waning light, as if the world had just been born and was still without strength, or had aged from so much living, its strength gone forever. Maria Sara and Raimundo Silva, either out of modesty or intuition, did not undress completely, they kept their private parts covered and she was still wearing her bra. Lying together under the covers, they trembled. He held her hands and kissed them, she repeated the gesture, with an undulating movement their bodies came together, so close that their breathing merged, then their mouths touched and their kiss became an avid devouring of lips and tongues, while the hands of the one pursued the body of the other, they held each other tightly, hugged, caressed, then their words could be heard, disconnected, convulsive, breathless, my darling, I love you, how was this possible, I don't know, it had to be, embrace me, I want you, that ancient murmur, which, with these and other words sweeter still, or crude, or rough, or brutal, has pursued from the beginning of time, if we may be allowed to repeat the expression, the ineffable. Raimundo Silva's hand struggled clumsily with the fastener of her bra, but it was Maria Sara who with the merest touch and movement of her shoulders undid it, releasing her breasts from their prison and offering them to his eyes, his hands and mouth. Then they undressed completely, the one helping or encouraging the other, Undress me, they said, when, in fact, they were already naked, but now they could touch, fondle and probe each other, Raimundo Silva suddenly threw back the covers and there was Maria Sara, her breasts, belly, swollen sex, long thighs, and he, without any sense of shame, his fears forgotten, exposing himself to the light, little as there was, only the white sheet was shining as if flooded by moonlight, night was slowly descending over the city, it seemed as if the external world had settled down to await some new miracle, yet no one noticed when it happened, here, when these two came into sexual contact for the first time, when for the first time they moaned with pleasure in each other's arms, when they called out in muffled tones, when all the floodgates opened over the earth and its waters, and then calm, the broad estuary of the Tagus, two bodies drifting side by side, holding hands, the one says, Oh, my love, the other, May this last forever, and suddenly they were both afraid of the words they had spoken, and they embraced, the room was dark, Switch on the light, she said, I want to know if this is real.

MARIA SARA SPENT THE NIGHT at Raimundo Silva's apartment. After having asked him to switch on the light and confirmed with all her senses that she really was there, naked and with this naked man beside her, looking at him and touching him, and offering herself freely to his eyes and hands, she said, between two kisses, I'm going to call my sister-in-law. Wrapping the white bedspread around her, she ran barefoot to the study, from the bedroom, Raimundo Silva could hear her dial the number, and then, It's me, followed by silence, most likely her sister-in-law was expressing her surprise that she had not been in touch sooner, asking her, for example, Has something turned up, and Maria Sara who had so much to tell, replied, No, I simply wanted to warn you that I won't be coming home tonight, which really was most unusual, bearing in mind that this was the first time anything like this had happened ever since she went to live at her brother's house after her divorce. Further silence, her sister-in-law's discreet surprise at these words which immediately made her an accomplice, Maria Sara laughed, I'll explain later, and tell my brother he needn't play the protector of widows and virgins, for that would scarcely be appropriate in my case. At the other end of the line her sister-in-law would naturally have expressed her concern, I hope you know what you're doing, the least one can say in similar situations, and Maria Sara replied, for the moment, all I need to know is that this is real, and after another pause, she simply said, Yes, it is, and that was sufficient for Raimundo Silva to surmise that Maria Sara's sister-in-law had asked, Is it the proof-reader, and Maria Sara replied, Yes, it is. After having rung off, she remained there for several moments, suddenly everything had taken on an air of unreality, this furniture, these books, and through there in the bedroom there was a man lying on the bed, she could feel a cold caress pass over the inside of her thighs, and thinking to herself, It's his caress, she shivered and drew the bedspread more closely around her, but this gesture made her aware that she was completely naked, and now the memory of recent sensations tussled with a vexing thought she could not shake off, Suppose he were still lying naked on top of the bed, the thought stopped there, or it was she who refused to pursue it any further, but clearly this was a threat, a decision taken, even if it was not very explicit who was under threat. She was surprised he had not called her, he must have heard her ring off, silence seemed to be taking over the apartment like some furtive and disquieting foe, and then she thought she had found an explanation, he did not know what to call her, yes, he would say Maria Sara, but the problem was not in the words, it was in the tone with which they were said, how to choose between the commanding tone of someone who believes himself already the proprietor of a body and the expression of loving tenderness that we would not describe as affected, but which was much too self-conscious to sound natural. She headed back to the bedroom, thinking to herself, as she made her way along the corridor, He's covered up, he's covered up, as anxiously as if the future of all the words and actions that had been said and done here depended on this. Raimundo Silva had drawn the covers up over his shoulders.

They dined in a restaurant in the Baixa, she asked how the history of the siege was coming along, Reasonably well, I'd say, considering how absurd it is, How soon do you expect to finish it, Three lines would be sufficient if I were to adopt the formula of then they married and lived happily ever after, or as in our case, the Portuguese with supreme effort took the city, or I set about listing the arms and baggage, and then I shall never get to the end, one alternative would be to leave the text as it stands, now that we have met each other. I'd rather you finished it, you must resolve the lives of that Mogueime and Ouroana, the rest will be less important, in any case we know how the story must end, the proof being that here we are dining in Lisbon, being neither Moors nor tourists on Moorish territory, The boats probably passed this way carrying the corpses of those who lost their lives when storming the city gates, When we return home I'm going to read it from the beginning, Unless we happen to be doing something more interesting, We have all the time in the world, dear Sir, Besides the history is brief, you will have read all of it within half an hour, I restricted myself, as you will see, to what I thought essentially stemmed from the fact that the crusaders went away without helping the Portuguese, And would make a good novel, Possibly, but when you set me this task, you knew that I was nothing more than an ordinary, run-of-the-mill proof-reader with no other qualities, But enough to take up the challenge, Provocation might be the better word, All right, let's call it provocation, What did you have in mind when you talked me into this, what were you looking for, At the time, I didn't see things too clearly, however much I might have justified them to myself, or to you, if you had asked for some explanation, but it's now quite obvious that I was looking for you, For me, for this thin, serious man with badly-dyed hair, as sad as a dog without a master, A man to whom I felt attracted the moment I saw him, a man who had deliberately committed an error he was obliged to correct, a man who had realised that the distinction between *no* and *yes* stems from a mental operation that is only thinking about survival, A good enough reason, It's a selfish reason, And socially useful, Undoubtedly, although everything depends on who the owners are of that *yes* and *no*, Let's be guided by norms based on consensus and authority obvious as it is that any variation in the authority varies the consensus, You give no leeway, Because there can be no leeway, we live cooped up in a room and paint the world and the universe on its walls, Don't forget that men have already gone to the moon, Your claustrophobic little room went with them, You're a pessimist, Not quite, I'm simply a sceptic of the radical kind, A sceptic is incapable of love, On the contrary, love is probably the last thing in which the sceptic can still believe, He can, Rather let us say he has to. They finished their coffee, Raimundo Silva asked for the bill, but it was Maria Sara who, with a quick gesture, drew a credit card from her wallet and placed it on the saucer, I'm your boss, I can't allow you to pay for the dinner, there would be no more respect for the hierarchy if underlings were to start outshining their superiors, I'll allow it this time, but don't forget that I'll soon be an author, and then, Then you won't pay under any circumstances, whoever heard of an author treating his editor to dinner, really, you know very little about public relations, I've always been led to believe that editors lunch and dine off their wretched authors, Such shameful slander, a base display of class hatred, As a simple proof-reader, I'm not involved in this conflict, If the idea upsets you, No, not at all, you can pay, but my reasons for allowing it are not what you think, What are they then, Simply that with this long, drawn-out history of the siege, I've scarcely done any proof-reading, and since you're responsible for the precarious state of my finances, it's only right that you should pay and in recompense, I'll make you some toast for breakfast tomorrow, You're going to leave me with a terrible debt on my hands.

Maria Sara had parked her car in the Largo dos Lóios and they both fancied the idea of a walk on such a mild evening. Before descending the Limoeiro, they lingered on the belvedere to watch the Tagus, this wide, mysterious inland sea. Raimundo Silva had put his arm round Maria Sara's shoulder, he knew this body, he knew it, and from knowing it came this feeling of infinite strength, and, on the other hand, a feeling of infinite emptiness, of indolent weariness, like a great bird hovering over the world and postponing the moment to settle. Now they were returning home, slowly, the night seemed interminable, there was no need to run in order to arrest the hours, or hasten them on, for this is all time permits. Maria Sara said, I'm curious to read what you've written, you could be right when you say you're on the way to becoming an author, Surely you didn't take me seriously, One can never tell, one can never tell, our best clothes are not simply there to attract stains, If I'm already condemned to the punishments of hell, just think what my fate would be as an author, Worse than hell, I suppose there is only limbo, Agreed, but I'm rather too old for limbo, and, since I'm baptised, should I escape the punishments, I won't escape the rewards, for it is said there are no alternatives, here stood the Porta de Ferro, they demolished it some two hundred years ago, what was left of it, of course, as for the Moorish gate, no one knows what it was like, Don't change the conversation, the idea is a good one, What idea, That your history of the siege should be published, By our publishing house, Why not, You'd make a hopeless Editorial Director, allowing feelings to cloud your judgment, But starting from the principle that the book was good enough, And do you think that our bosses would agree after seeing themselves ridiculed, If they have any sense of humour, I've never given it a thought, which could be my fault for being slow on the uptake, Finish the book then we'll see, there's nothing to be lost in trying, What I have there at home is not a book, only a few dozen pages with separate episodes, It's a start, Very well, but on one condition, Such as, That I should proof-read my own book, But why, when everyone knows that the author is the last person to be trusted with checking his own work, So that I don't find someone inserting a *yes* where I've written *not*. Maria Sara laughed and said, I really do like you. And Raimundo Silva replied, I'm doing my utmost to make sure you go on liking me. They were climbing the Calçada do Correio Velho, that very same route he always tried to avoid, but today he felt elated and relaxed, and any fatigue he felt was somehow different, demanding not so much rest as further exertions. At this hour the street was deserted, the place and circumstances were propitious, Raimundo Silva kissed Maria Sara, there is nothing more common nowadays than kissing in public, but we must bear in mind that Raimundo Silva belongs to a much more circumspect generation that was not given to showing its feelings, let alone its desires. His boldness, after all, would go no further, the street was empty and badly lit, but it's a start. They went on climbing, paused at the foot of the Escadinhas de São Crispim, there are a hundred and thirty-four steps, said Raimundo Silva, and as steep as those of the Aztec temples, but once we get to the top we're almost home, Who's complaining, let's go, If you look up there, under those large windows there are still traces of the wall built by the Goths, at least, according to the experts, And you're now one of them, Nonsense, I've simply done a little reading, I've amused or educated myself little by little, discovering the difference between looking and seeing, between seeing and observing, Sounds interesting, It's elementary, I even imagine true knowledge depends on our awareness of the change from one level of perception, as it were, to another, Barbarian, more Goth than anyone, the person moving from one level to another is me ever since we started clambering up this mountain, let's rest for a moment on this step until I get my breath back. These words and what followed suddenly reminded Raimundo Silva of that day, when terrified of being confronted by an indignant and threatening Costa, he had rushed down the Escadinhas and sat on one of these steps, hiding from those accusing eyes he imagined, not only his cowardice but also the shame it would cause him. One day, when he feels more confident about this love affair springing up between them, he will tell Maria Sara about these base traits in his nature, although, on the other hand, he might decide to say nothing rather than tarnish any positive image he might one day give of himself, and preserve. But even at this moment, when he still has not taken any decision about what he will finally do, he can sense the discomfort of a neglected scruple, the remorse that anticipates failure, a mental thorn. He promises that he will not forget this premonitary warning of his conscience, and suddenly becomes aware of the silence that has come between them, perhaps a constraint, but no, Maria Sara's expression is tranquil, serene, touched by the light of a waning moon that somehow dilutes the shadows in this place where they find themselves and where there are no street-lamps, a constraint inside him, for no other reason than knowing that he is hiding something, let us say not so much the shame of fear, but fear of shame. If

Maria Sara does not speak it is because she feels that she should remain silent, if Raimundo Silva is about to speak it is because he does not wish to explain the real reason for his being silent, Some time ago there was a dog here, a mastiff, that disappeared, and departing from this statement, he began telling the tale of his encounter with the animal, adding enough imaginative detail to make it sound more real and authentic. It refused to leave this spot, on two or three occasions I fed it and I believe some neighbours were also giving it food but not all that much, because the poor beast always looked famished. I don't know what became of it, whether it found the courage to go wandering off in search of life, or perished right here for want of nourishment, I now feel I should have done something more, after all, it wouldn't have cost me anything to feed it some scraps every day or buy it some of this dog-food you find on sale everywhere nowadays, at no great expense. For several more minutes, Raimundo Silva repeated his responsibilities and omissions, conscious, in the meantime, that he was covering up with false remorse his real remorse, the latter suspect, the one to come uncertain, then suddenly, he fell silent, he felt ridiculous, childish, all these scruples because of a stray dog, all it needed now was for Maria Sara to make some off-hand comment, for example, Poor beast, and that is precisely what she said, Poor beast, before getting to her feet and saying, Let's go.

Seated at the little table where he has written *The History of the Siege of Lisbon*, looking at the last page as he awaits that providential word that by means of attraction or repulsion will reactivate the interrupted flow, Raimundo Silva was no doubt saying to himself, like Maria Sara on the Escadinhas de São Crispim last night, Let's go, write, push ahead, develop, abbreviate, annotate, perfect, but without any of the gentle modulation of that other Let's go, which, incapable of remaining suspended in space, went on reverberating inside them like an echo slowly becoming louder until transformed into glorious song when the bedclothes were drawn back once more to receive them. The memory of that splendid night distracts Raimundo Silva, the surprise of awakening in the morning and seeing and feeling a naked body beside him, the ineffable pleasure of touching it, here, there, softly, as it were one great rose, saying to himself, Slowly, don't awaken her, let me come to know you, rose, body, flower, then those eager hands, that prolonged, insistent caress, until Maria Sara opens her eyes and smiles, when they said together, My love, and embraced. Raimundo Silva searches for the word, on any other occasion these same words would have served, My love, but it is doubtful whether Mogueime and Ouroana would have used them, not to mention that at this stage, they still had not met, let alone declared such sudden feelings whose expression seems beyond their understanding.

Meanwhile, the unwitting instrument of destiny, knight Heinrich debates in his intimate forum, whether he should take Ouroana with him to Mem Ramires's quarters, or leave her behind in the royal encampment, under the care and vigilance of his trusted squire. But he is so accustomed to having this squire with him that he does not feel inclined to dispense with his services, so after giving the matter careful consideration, he summoned him and told him to prepare their baggage and arms because early next morning they will descend from these sheltered heights in order to join the troops gathered at the Porta de Ferro, where, under his command and authority, they will build an assault tower, Let's see who finishes first, us, or the French, or the Normans, at the Portas do Sol and the Porta de Alfama. And what about your concubine, Ouroana, what will you do with her, asked the squire, She will come with me, There are many dangers, down there the Moors and Christians are directly facing each other, Later we'll see what's to be done, since I'm certain that these infidels have not dared to engage in battle outside the walls. Having thus agreed, the squire went to warn Ouroana and to organise the move, five of his armed bodyguards would also accompany knight Heinrich, because this German was not such a great lord as to have a private army at his disposal, his speciality was more in the line of engineering, which nearly always depends on having a large number of men to build the machines, and always on the engineer's knowledge, skill and imagination.

Early next morning, as stated before, after attending holy mass, knight Heinrich went to kiss the king's hands, Farewell, Your Majesty, I'm going to build the tower. Standing a little way off, were his squire and armed bodyguards who were not entitled to speak with the king, and Ouroana in her litter, more to satisfy her master's vanity than to display the fairness of her complexion, for in the fields of Galicia where she had been abducted, she was the daughter of peasants and like them she laboured, tilling the soil. Dom Afonso Henriques embraced the knight, May the Holy Virgin Mary accompany and protect you, he said, and help you to erect this tower the likes of which has never been seen before in these parts, you will be working with ship's carpenters, the only suitable men we could find for the job, but if they should prove to be as good apprentices as you are reputed to be a master, then any further sieges I undertake with assault towers will only be carried out by native craftsmen without hiring any foreign labour, Your Majesty, many reports have reached my country praising the humility, frugality and spirit of abnegation of the Portuguese, ever ready and willing to serve family and fatherland, now if to so many rare qualities they were to add some intelligence and much greater strength of character and willpower, then I can assure Your Royal Highness that no tower will be beyond their capabilities, whether it is built tomorrow or at any other time. These reassuring sentiments made a deep impression on the king, especially coming from whom they came, and such was his satisfaction, that taking knight Heinrich on one side, he confided his private concern, You must have noticed that some of my chiefs of staff are unhappy with this idea of using assault towers, they're traditionalists who cling to old-fashioned methods of warfare, so if any of them try to put up obstacles or delay the work on some defeatist pretext or other, tell me at once, for as I take pride in being a modern king, I am determined to proceed with this enterprise without further delay, all the more so because this war has drained my finances and the last thing I want is to find myself obliged to pay the soldiers their wages at the end of August when the three months expire, for although our troops earn little, all told it comes to a tidy sum, it would indeed be fortunate if we were to succeed in capturing the city in the meantime, so you can imagine how much I'm relying on these towers, therefore you have all my support and encouragement to forge ahead with this plan, and have no fears about being generously rewarded, for you have all those possessions of the Moors with which to pay yourselves ten times as much. Knight Heinrich assured the king that he could put his mind at rest, with God's help he would secure victory, he would reveal nothing about the treasury's difficulties, and under no circumstances should he worry about rewarding him for his services, For the best reward, Your Majesty, is in heaven above, and to gain the citadel of paradise other towers are needed, those erected by good works, such as this pledge of ours not to leave a single Moor alive if they stubbornly go on refusing to surrender. The king took his leave of the knight, thinking to himself that he must bear him in mind, for such a man would make as good a bishop as a general, and if this business of the towers should succeed he will suggest that he should become naturalised and be rewarded with lands and a title to start a new life.

It soon became clear that knight Heinrich had no intention of wasting time for no sooner had he arrived at the Porta de Ferro than he was discussing with Mem Ramires the number of men he needed for this ambitious project, starting at once with the felling of the trees in those parts, some produced by nature, others planted by the Moors themselves, who could not have foreseen that they were literally providing wood for their own sacrifice, these are, let us repeat once more, the ironies of destiny. But we must go no further with these descriptions, without first mentioning the excitement caused by the arrival of the knight and his retinue, and little wonder, for here was a foreign technician, a German, if you please, which is to be a technician twice over, some, sceptical by nature or persuaded by others, were cautious about the enterprise and its outcome, others felt it was wrong to condemn something that had not yet had time to prove its worth, finally the practical and impartially-minded prevailed by acknowledging from the evidence that it was preferable to fight the Moors in direct confrontation and at the same height rather than have them up there throwing down stones and taking advantage of the laws of gravity, with us down below suffering the effects. Detached from these polemical matters relating to the military-cum-industrial enterprise that was under way, and with eyes only for the woman arriving on a litter, Mogueime could scarcely believe his good fortune. Never more would he need to go prowling around the encampment of Graça, in constant danger of running into a military police patrol, wanting to know, What are you doing here so far away from your own camp, now the mountain truly came to the Prophet, not because the Prophet did not want to go to the mountain, we are all reliable witnesses of how hard he tried, but because above the Prophet as we know there is the sergeant-major, the second lieutenant, the captain, and, this being a time of war, there are even fewer passes for leave than opportunities, even when assisted by invention. This Ouroana who is arriving, if she does not spend all her time shut away in her tent waiting for knight Heinrich to interrupt his carpentry in order to relieve inside her the anxieties which can so easily pass from a soul that wants to be mystical with God to the flesh that only longs to be mystical with flesh, this Ouroana, taking into account the reduced space in this theatre of operations, will be much more often and more readily in sight, when strolling and daydreaming through the encampment or when standing on the river-bank to watch the porpoises leap, during those tranquil hours we associate with evening, when the troops go off to try and recover from their exertions during the fierce heat of the day and the even fiercer heat of battle, It is to be hoped, meanwhile, that all efforts will now be concentrated on building those towers, because given the shortage of able-bodied men it would be tantamount to suicide to disperse them in activities with little chance of success, except for the odd diversion intended to keep the enemy occupied, so that the carpenters can get on in peace with their risky task. In his annotations to Osbern's letter, Fray Rogeiro provided, though he would make no mention of it in the definitive version, a detailed description of knight Heinrich's arrival at the encampment at the Porta de Ferro, including a certain reference, clearly irresistible, to the woman accompanying him, Ouroana in name, as lovely as the dawn, as mysterious as moonrise, to cite the words of the friar, which his own chastening prudence, on the one hand, and the delicate modesty of the person to whom these words were being addressed, on the other, advised him to erase. Now it is quite possible that this and other repressed stirrings of the soul might have been the cause, by means of sublimation, of the care with which Fray Rogeiro began to follow the sayings and doings of the German knight until this point, but above all after his unfortunate, but in no sense ignominious death, as will become clear in time. Putting it more clearly, we would say that because he was unable to satisfy his lust for Ouroana, Fray Rogeiro could find no better excuse, beside one he kept to himself, than to praise to the skies the man who enjoyed her favours. When it comes to human nature, you can expect anything.

Senhora Maria came at the usual time after lunch, and no sooner had she arrived than she began muttering in a manner at once discreet and obvious, a difficult feat to achieve, because it has the dual aim of trying to disguise the fact that you know something, while showing at the same time that you are not prepared to allow the other person to play the innocent. It is a diplomatic art *par excellence*, yet guided by intuition, if not by instinct, and which, generally speaking, has achieved its main objective, namely to give the proof-reader a vague feeling of panic, as if his most intimate secrets were about to be revealed in public. Senhora Maria is a sadist without knowing it. She greeted him from the bedroom door, muttered twice to warn Raimundo Silva that she might only be a poor cleaner but she still had enough sense of smell to pick up any remaining traces of perfume in the air. Raimundo Silva returned her greeting and went on writing after giving a rapid glance in her direction, determined to pretend that he did not know what was going on, Senhora Maria, taken aback to begin with, and then with that peculiar expression on her face, as much as to say, Just as

I thought, eyeing the bed, which, instead of the quick tidying-up at which Raimundo Silva was adept lest it be mistaken for a migrant's bunk, was irreproachable and showed every sign of a woman's touch. She coughed to attract attention, but Raimundo Silva pretended to be distracted, although his heart was in a state of foolish turmoil, I don't have to account for my life, he thought, annoyed with himself for seeking cowardly excuses, he who had just embarked on such a serious love affair, so he raised his head and asked, Did you want something, in a dry, brusque tone of voice which disarmed the woman's impertinence, No, Sir, nothing, I was simply looking. Raimundo Silva could have satisfied himself with this embarrassed reply, but he preferred to taunt her, Looking at what, Nothing, the bed, What's wrong with the bed, Nothing, it's been made, So what, Nothing, nothing, Senhora Maria turned away, too intimidated to ask the question that was on the tip of her tongue, Who made it, and so would never know what answer Raimundo Silva might have given, not that he knew himself. From then on, Senhora Maria stayed away from the bedroom, as if letting Raimundo Silva know that she considered that part of the house outside her jurisdiction, however, she was either unable or unwilling to repress her ill-tempered frustration, and making no attempt to go silently about her chores, she did her utmost to make as much noise as possible. Raimundo Silva decided to shrug this off with a smile, but the din was so loud that he was obliged to step into the corridor and plead, Could you make less noise, please, I'm trying to work, Senhora Maria could have retorted that she, too, was trying to get on with her work and that she did not have the luck of certain people who can earn a living seated in peace and quiet, but necessity, even when as conflictive as this, is stronger than willpower, and she said nothing. What annoys Senhora Maria most of all is that these dramatic changes are taking place without her knowledge, were she not the astute person she is, and one of these days she will unexpectedly find the other woman in the apartment, without being able to ask him the itching question, Who is this woman, who asked her to come here, men are such insensitive fools, what would it have cost Raimundo Silva to have taken her into his confidence, for however much it might hurt it would always be something of a palliative for such bitter jealousy, for this is the evil afflicting Senhora Maria although she does not know it. Other considerations of a practical and prosaic nature also occupy her mind, uppermost amongst them being the danger that she might lose her job if this other woman, assuming it is not just some casual affair, should start to interfere with her work, Clean this again, while holding up a dirty finger that has collected dust from the moulding on the door, that hateful gesture to which no cleaner has ever been known to respond with a phrase worthy of being recorded for posterity, If you stick it up your arse, you'll collect even more dirt. God help those who only came into this world to take orders, Senhora Maria thinks to herself, and she polishes the door for a second time, while, for no apparent reason, tears spring to her eyes just as she happens to glance into the mirror in the bathroom, and at that moment, not even the sight of her lovely hair consoles her. In the middle of the afternoon the telephone rang, Raimundo Silva took the call, it was from the publishers, a routine conversation about work to Senhora Maria's disappointment, Yes, I'm available, he was saying, Send me the manuscript at your convenience, unless you'd prefer me to come and pick it up, and the rest of the conversation was in much the same vein, revisions, deadlines, Senhora Maria had heard these monologues so many times before, the only difference being that the person at the other end of the line was inaudible, before it had been a certain Costa, now it was some woman, perhaps this was why Raimundo Silva's tone of voice became all lovey-dovey, one of Senhora Maria's favourite expressions, Ah, these men, but for all her cunning it never occurred to her that Raimundo Silva was actually speaking to the woman with whom he had slept the previous night, relishing the ineffable pleasure of using neutral words which they alone could translate into another language, that of emotion and capable of evoking other meanings, to utter the word book and hear the word kiss, to say yes and understand it to mean always, to hear good afternoon and sense the person is really saying, I love you. Had Senhora Maria known anything about the art of cryptography then she would have gone from here with the mystery solved, laughing up her sleeve at anyone who thought they could laugh at her, a somewhat laboured way of thinking because of her resentment, for neither Raimundo Silva nor Maria Sara have any idea that they are making Senhora Maria suffer, and if they did they would not ridicule her, otherwise they would not be deserving of so much happiness. This said, it is not inconceivable that Senhora Maria might come to like Maria Sara, you can expect everything of the heart, even the harmony of its contradictions.

Raimundo Silva is once more alone, for several seconds he was left wondering what to make of the amiable tone with which Senhora Maria took her leave, a disconcerting woman who turns up in a bad mood one minute and is all solicitous the next, but *The History of the Siege of Lisbon* brought him back to another reality, to the building of the tower destined to break, once and for all, the resistance of the Moors, and knowing that the existence of a nation depends on this, we cannot interrupt our work, although Raimundo Silva would have preferred to have Maria Sara here than to have to cope with operations about which he knows nothing, the dressing of joists, the trimming of wooden planks, the moulding of pegs, the twining of ropes, all these materials contributing to the construction of a tower which is not that of Babel, this present one will rise no higher than the battlements on the wall, and as for tongues, Dom Afonso Henriques has no intention of repeating their multiplicity, but of uprooting this one, both in the figurative and allegorical sense as in the literal and physical sense. When Maria Sara returns tomorrow afternoon as she promised on departing, to stay the night and the night after that, as well as the day in between which is a Sunday, he hopes to have made some progress with his writing, because there are other matters demanding his attention, and time has changed its name and is now called urgency, Calm down, Maria Sara will tell him, you can't fit more things into a year than a minute just because the one is a minute and the other a year, it's not the size of the glass that counts, but rather what each of us manages to put into it, even if it should overflow and be lost. Just as this tower will also be lost.

The construction took more than a week. From morning until night, knight Heinrich only lived for his project, and, even when resting in his tent, he would wake up imagining that one of the supporting beams was not strong enough, and it got to the point where he would get up in the middle of the night to check the solidity of certain joints and the tension of the ropes. He was such an admirable and compassionate man that when the work was at its peak, he was not above lending a hand if one of the soldiers happened to be showing signs of fatigue. On one of these occasions he found Mogueime at his back, for Mogueime, too, was helping to build the tower, and it so happened that Ouroana had come by to see how the work was progressing and naturally to keep her eyes on her lord and master, the only man for whom she should have any eyes, but this did not prevent her from noticing how the tall soldier behind kept staring at her, she had noticed him from the very first day, staring at her wherever they met, there in the encampment of Monte de São Fransisco, then in the Royal encampment, and now in this narrow stretch of land, so narrow that it was something of a miracle that all the troops could gather there without tripping over each other's feet, for example, this man and woman, who have done nothing more than look at each other. Mogueime could see a handspan away the nape of the German's broad neck, covered by a mane of sandy-coloured hair matted with dust and sweat, to kill him amidst all the confusion would not be difficult thus giving Ouroana her freedom, but bringing her no closer than she is at present. The temptations of violent death, intensifying one's remorse for having indulged them, should be taken to one's confessor, but to discover into the bargain that the friar also coveted the victim's woman, even if only a concubine, was more than he could face. In fury and rage he made a brusque gesture and struck the German on the back causing him to turn round, but calm and showing no surprise, such incidents were common in gatherings involving so much effort, and his steadfast look was enough to quell Mogueime's wrath, he was incapable of hating a man who had never done him any harm, just because he coveted his woman.

The tower was finished at last. It as an extraordinary piece of military engineering that moved on massive wheels and consisted of a complicated system of internal and external bracings which held together the four platforms that defined the vertical structure, one at the bottom resting on the fixed axles of the wheels, another at the top stretching out threateningly towards the city, and two intermediate ones that served to reinforce the entire structure and would afford temporary protection to the soldiers as they prepared to climb up. A pulley manoeuvred from below would allow baskets filled with weapons to be hoisted up without delay even in the heat of battle. When the job was judged to be finished, the troops raised cheers and applause, eager to launch their attack and confident that conquest would now be easy. Even the Moors must have felt alarmed for a bewildered silence had suppressed the insults that were constantly raining down from on high. The excitement in the encampment at the Porta de Ferro became even greater when it was reported that the towers of the French and the Normans were still not ready, therefore glory was within their reach, all they had to do was to push the assault tower up against the wall and the moment had come for Mem Ramires as captain to give the order, Push, lads, let's go for them, and they strained with all their might. Unfortunately no one had noticed that the terrain ahead was sloping, and therefore, as they advanced, already under enemy fire, the tower started leaning backwards and upwards, making it clear that even if they managed to reach the wall, the uppermost platform would be too far away to serve any purpose. Then knight Heinrich, embarrassed at his lack of foresight, gave orders to stop and start all over again, now the carpenters would give way to the pioneers, it was a question of digging a straight path and to the right, a truly dangerous task, for the diggers would have to work without cover under an avalanche of missiles of all kinds falling from above, and all the more lethal the nearer they came. Even so, and despite the casualties suffered, some twenty metres were opened up along which the tower could advance, serving as protection from the next onslaught. This was the situation, each man struggling to do his best, Moors on one side, Christians on the other, when suddenly the ground gave way on one side, causing three of the wheels to sink in up to the hubs and the tower to lurch precariously. There was a general outcry of fear and concern in the Portuguese camp, of fiendish triumph on the battlements where those swarthy Moors watched from their vantage point. Balancing dangerously, the tower creaked from top to bottom, the wooden frame subjected to tensions no one had allowed for, some of the couplings having already been shattered. In despair, watching to his chagrin what was supposed to be a magnificent demonstration of his ingenuity end in failure, knight Heinrich tore his hair out, ranted and cursed in the German tongue in a manner scarcely befitting someone of his reputation and worth, but which the coarseness inherent in these primitive times more than justified. Finally regaining his composure, he went to assess the situation and examine the damage at first hand only to conclude that the only solution, if it worked, would be to secure the upper beams on the side opposite to the inclination with long ropes, and get all the men with one mighty heave to release the buried wheels and wedge them progressively with stones until the tower went back to being upright. The plan was perfect, however, in order to achieve the desired effect it was necessary, first, to undertake the highly risky operation of freeing the wheels and removing the soil which at, this juncture, was still supporting the heavy construction, for that was where the sloping lower platform was stuck. It was an obstacle, a tangled knot, a handicap, a terrifying equation of enormous uncertainty, but there was no other solution, although, strictly speaking, we ought to call it the merest probability. This was the moment the Moors chose to despatch from on high a shower of javelins with incendiary torches that droned through the air like swarms of bees dispersing before settling haphazardly here and there, fortunately the strong wind upset the aim of the javelin throwers, but when the pitcher goes too often to the well it is broken at last, it only needed one javelin to hit its target for the others to follow suit, ill fortune finally bringing the tower down, not so much because of the incline aggravated by the excavation of the earth, but because of all the frantic efforts to extinguish the fires that had started up in various parts. Its sudden collapse left the soldiers who were securing the ropes on top of the tower either dead or seriously injured, and the same fate befell others who were working with spades at the wheels, and finally, an irreparable loss, knight Heinrich himself, struck down by an ignited javelin which his generous blood was still able to extinguish. With him, but crushed by a falling beam that landed on his chest, died his faithful squire, thus leaving Ouroana alone in the world, something which, recalled on an earlier occasion, is mentioned here, bearing in mind the importance of the fact for the continuation of this history. Impossible to describe the wild rejoicing of the Moors, reassured as they were, if any such reassurance were necessary, of Allah's supremacy over God, as confirmed by the resounding destruction of that cursed tower. No less easy to describe is the grief, anger and humiliation of the Portuguese, although there were some amongst them who could not refrain from muttering that anyone with a grain of commonsense or experience of warfare would have known that battles are won with swords and not with foreign inventions that can be as much of a disadvantage as an advantage. Once destroyed, the tower burned like a bonfire of giants, and it was never discovered how many men were reduced to crackling and ashes after being trapped by falling debris. A catastrophe.

Knight Heinrich's corpse was carried to his tent, where Ouroana, already informed of the tragedy, wept as was expected of a concubine, and that was that. The knight was laid out on his bunk, his hands joined in prayer and bound to his chest, and death having come so quickly, the expression on his face was quite serene, so serene that he might have been asleep, and, looking more closely, even wearing a smile, as if he were before the gates of paradise, with no other tower or weapon than the worth of his deeds on earth, but as certain of enjoying eternal bliss as of being dead. The heat is so intense that within hours his features will become distorted, his happy smile will disappear, between this illustrious corpse and another devoid of any special merits there will be no difference, sooner or later we all end up as equals in the face of death. Ouroana had uncombed her hair, as fair as that of any fair Galician, and she was weeping, somewhat weary of feeling no sorrow other than quiet pity for this man against whom her only complaint was that he should have abducted her by force, otherwise he had always treated her well, if we can imagine what the relationship must have been like between a concubine and her lord and master eight centuries ago. Ouroana was anxious to know what had happened to the faithful squire, for he must either be dead or gravely wounded not to be here mourning for his master, and they told her his body had been carried off immediately to the cemetery on the other side of the estuary, using this opportunity to clear away the charred beams and trunks lest they should impede the manoeuvre, so that both debris and intact corpses were removed in a single operation, while any smaller remains encountered were rapidly buried in a depression on the slope on this side, where it will be difficult for them to rise when the trumpets are sounded on the Day of Judgment. So Ouroana was now free of any master, direct or indirect, as she was at pains to show at the first opportunity, when one of knight Heinrich's armed guards, disregarding any respect for the deceased, tried to grab her when he found her on her own. In a flash, Ouroana was brandishing a dagger which she had removed with providential foresight from the knight's belt when they brought him to his tent, a crime that fortunately went undiscovered, for a knight must go to his grave, if not with all his weapons, at least with the smaller ones. Now then, a dagger in the frail hands of a woman, even if accustomed to working the land and looking after livestock, was not the kind of threat to dissuade a Teutonic warrior, undoubtedly aware of the superiority of his Aryan race, but there are eyes worth all the armaments of this world, and if the latter were incapable of scrutinising the heart of this wicked man, they could intimidate him from three paces away and their message could not have been clearer, If you lay a finger on me, I either kill you or I kill myself, Ouroana told him, and he drew back, less from fear of dying than for being held responsible for her death, even though he could always allege that the wretched woman, beside herself with grief, had taken her own life before his very eyes. But the soldier preferred to withdraw, imploring God that if he should survive these adventures on foreign soil, he might one day meet here, if here he were to remain, or in distant Germany, a woman like this Ouroana, who even if not Aryan he would accept with the greatest pleasure.

Raimundo Silva laid down his biro, rubbed his tired eyes, then re-read the closing lines, his own. He was rather pleased with them. He got up, placed his hands on his hips and leaned backwards, sighing with relief. He had been working for hours on end, had even forgotten dinner, he was so absorbed by the subject matter and the words that sometimes escaped him, had not even thought of Maria Sara, an omission that would be quite unforgivable if her presence inside him, save for the exaggeration of the metaphor, were not like the blood in his veins, something we had not really thought about, but which, being there and circulating, is an absolute condition of life. We repeat, save for the exaggeration of the metaphor. The two roses in the vase are standing in water from which they draw nourishment, it is true that they do not last long, but relatively speaking, neither do we. He opened the window and gazed down at the city. The Moors are celebrating the tower's destruction. The Amoreiras, smiled Raimundo Silva. On that side yonder stands the tent of knight Heinrich who will be buried tomorrow in the cemetery of São Vicente. Ouroana, not a tear in her eyes, keeps vigil over the corpse which is starting to smell. One of the five armed guards who has been wounded is missing. The one who tried to grab Ouroana stares at her from time to time, and remains pensive. Here outside, keeping out of sight, Mogueime prowls round the tent like a moth attracted by the light of the torches coming from the opening in the canvas flaps. Raimundo Silva consults his watch, if Maria Sara does not ring within the half hour, he will telephone her, How are you, my love, and she will reply, Alive, and he will say, It's a miracle.

FRAY ROGEIRO STATES that it was about this time that signs of famine in the Moorish stronghold were becoming apparent. And no wonder, if we consider that imprisoned behind those walls as if held in a garrote, were over sixty thousand families, a number that at first sight seems alarming and when looked at a second time seems even more alarming, inasmuch as, in those backward times, families consisting of a father, mother and one child were dubious exceptions, and even if we were to estimate such a low number of people in each family we would arrive at a population of two hundred thousand inhabitants, a calculation in its turn called into question by another source of information, according to which the men alone in Lisbon numbered a hundred and fifty-four thousand. Now then, if we consider that the Koran allows each man to have as many as four wives, all of whom naturally bear him children, and taking into account the slaves who although scarcely treated like humans still have to eat, and therefore must have been the first to feel the want of food, then we end up with numbers that prudence tells us we should treat with extreme caution, some four or five hundred thousand persons, just imagine. In any case, if there were not quite as many, we at least know that the number was high, and from the point of view of those living there, too high by far.

Were it not for that constant thirst for glory that from time immemorial gives not a moment's peace to kings, presidents and military leaders, this conquest of Lisbon from the Moors could have been achieved with all the tranquillity in this world, after all, only a fool steps into the lion's cage to engage in combat instead of depriving it of food and sitting down to watch it die from starvation. It is true that with the passing of the centuries we learn something, and nowadays it is fairly common practice to use the privation of food and other necessities and such other reasons as a means of persuading those who out of stubbornness or a lack of understanding have refused to capitulate. However, these five hundred thousand are different just as their history would be different. What is important here is to observe the concurrence of two quite distinct episodes, such as the destruction and burning down of the tower at Porta de Ferro and the first signs of famine in the city, which, united and compared in the minds of the king's chiefs of staff, made it clear that while they should continue with the struggle, in the strict meaning of the word, for the honour of the Portuguese army, good strategy would dictate intensifying the siege, because in due course not only would the Moors have devoured everything down to the last crumb and rat, but they would end up devouring each other. If the French and the Normans were to carry on building their towers, if the Lusitanians for their part were to apply the lessons learned from knight Heinrich in order to erect their own war machine, if the artillery were to keep up regular bombardments, and the archers were to throw darts, arrows, spears and javelins, thus putting to good use the daily output of weapons workshops of Braço de Prata, these would be nothing more than symbolic gestures to inscribe in the epics, when compared with the last and conclusive solution, famine. And so the various captains gave strict orders to their armies that they should guard the outer walls day and night, not just the gates, but above all any secluded corners, certain hidden angles that might afford protection, and also any stretches facing the sea, not because any supplies could be brought into the city by that route, for there could never be enough of them to meet their needs, but to prevent any messengers from getting through the blockade and carrying pleas for help to the villages in the Alentejo, both for provisions and volunteers to attack the assailants along the coast, the one being as welcome as the other. Their caution soon proved to be well-founded, when at dead of night with no moonlight a tiny canoe was discovered trying to sneak out between the galleys of the fleet and when the oarsman was brought before the admiral, he confessed to carrying letters addressed to the mayors of Almada and Palmela, from which it became clear how desperately the wretched inhabitants of Lisbon were in need of food. Despite the vigilance, the odd messenger must have crossed the lines, for weeks later, floating at the bottom of the wall that looked on to the river, the corpse of a Moor was picked up and when hoisted up on to the nearest watch-tower was found to be carrying a letter from the King of Evora, that fortunately never reached its destination, so cruel, inhuman and hypocritical was its message, considering that these were brothers of the same race and religion, and this was what the letter said, the King of Evora wishes the inhabitants of Lisbon their freedom, for some time now I have held a truce with the King of the Portuguese, and I cannot go back on my word and trouble him and his subjects with war, ransom your lives with your money, so that what should be used for your salvation is not used for your downfall, farewell. This man was king, and in order not to break the truce he had drawn up with our Afonso Henriques, forgetting that this same Afonso had broken it to storm and capture Santarém, he allowed the doomed populace of Lisbon to die an ignominious death, while the courier who had left Lisbon with a plea for help did not take advantage of the opportunity to escape to safe territory, but returned with the evil tidings, only to die before delivering the message announcing abandonment and betrayal. How true that men are not always in their right place, this Moor would have rushed to Lisbon had he been the King of Evora, but the King of Evora would obviously have fled right on the first mission, were it not for the fact that they brought him under escort as far as Cacilhas with the reply and told him, Go throw yourself into the sea and make no attempt to come back.

To transport the body of knight Heinrich to the cemetery

of São Vicente along those tortuous paths at the foot of the sheer slope, two paces away from the water to avoid being stoned or something worse, was, as people were already beginning to tell themselves, a most hazardous task. But the nobility of the deceased man and the magnitude of his final achievement justified this difficult undertaking, which after all bears no comparison with the torments suffered by the troops who now find themselves outside the Porta de Ferro and who took this very same route, an episode described somewhat superficially at the time. Four armed guards were carrying the coffin, with an escort of Portuguese soldiers sent by Mem Ramires, and Ouroana walked behind, as is only to be expected of someone who has lost the master whose pride and vanity she served. In other words, since she was no more than a casual concubine, she was not obliged to accompany the cortège, but she felt in all conscience that it would scarcely be fitting as a Christian to deprive him of this last token of respect, death had not separated them any more than life had, master and concubine for several days. Another life, however, instant and pressing, is coming from behind, a soldier who follows at a distance, not the cortège but this woman who on noticing him, asks herself, What do you want from me, man, what do you want from me, and no reply comes, but she knows very well that he wants to take the place of knight Heinrich, not the place he now occupies under a shroud in this swaying coffin, but another place, any old place where the living can surrender their bodies to each other, a real bed, a grassy patch, a pile of hay, a comfortable spot on the sand. Mogueime was in no doubt that Ouroana would be snatched up by some lord who took a fancy to her, this did not worry him, perhaps because, deep down, he was not convinced that one day, even with the assistance of fate, he might lay a finger on her, and if she, because no one really cared for her, should find no other solution than to join up with the women on the other side, not even then would he push open the gate of the hut she occupied in order to satisfy his male lust with a body that, because it was at everyone's disposal, could never be his. This soldier Mogueime who can neither read nor write, who no longer remembers the country where he was born nor why he was given a name that frankly sounds more Moorish than Christian, this soldier Mogueime, a simple rung on that ladder used to enter Santarém and now in this siege of Lisbon a poorly armed foot-soldier, this soldier Mogueime trails behind Ouroana like someone who knows no other way of avoiding death, while knowing that he will confront it time and time again and refusing to believe that life is no more than a finite series of postponements. But nothing could be further from soldier Mogueime's thoughts, soldier Mogueime wants that woman, and Portuguese poetry has not yet been born.

It was written sometime earlier, thanks to one of those lucid insights into the future that have no rational explanation, that one day Mogueime washed his bloodstained hands in the waters of the estuary, and that the corpses of two soldiers from the royal encampment who had taken Ouroana by force were subsequently discovered, both of them having been stabbed to death. Knowing with what agility Ouroana wielded knight Heinrich's dagger against the first armed man who tried to grab her, then we can easily imagine that in order to avenge her offended honour, the said Ouroana, unseen by witnesses in the waning light of evening or dawn, at an opportune moment, when her aggressors got within reach, plunged her dagger into their stomachs just below their coats of mail. These soldiers were definitely murdered, but not by Ouroana. But the fertile imagination runs on and bearing in mind that Mogueime's infatuation might have driven him out of jealousy to commit these crimes, the earlier description of Mogueime washing his bloodstained hands would make sense were it the blood of those two wretches which the waters quickly dissolved and swept away just as life evaporates with time. This might have been what happened but, in fact, nothing of the kind, the deaths of these men were mere coincidence, coincidences existed even then although no one paid much attention. One day when they had finally spoken to each other and entered into other intimacies, Ouroana would ask Mogueime if he was responsible for the murder of those lecherous soldiers, No, he replied, thinking to himself that he should have killed them in order to be more deserving of this woman's love.

Every cloud has a silver lining, a delightful proverb, predating any of the philosophical relativisms that have been spawned, and which wisely teaches us that it is pointless trying to judge life's events as if we were separating the wheat from the chaff. Our Mogueime had feared losing all hope of ever winning Ouroana if some nobleman, out of whim or bravado, or, who knows, because of some more serious but inconstant sentiment, should claim her for himself, removing her from the valley of life at least for the duration of the war. Fortunately, this did not happen, but the reason why it did not happen was most unfortunate, for it had become a public scandal that this solitary woman, although not a prostitute, had sold her favours to common soldiers, two of whom were to die in mysterious circumstances, an episode of no real historical interest, but which, as we know, served to reinforce the reasons for her neglect by gentlemen who do not want other men's leftovers and who are sufficiently superstitious not to tempt the devil, even if he should appear in the guise of such a ravishingly beautiful woman. Therefore abandoned by all for such conflicting reasons, Ouroana was washing clothes in a stream that flowed into the estuary, an honest occupation that earned her a living, when out of the corner of her eye she saw that soldier approach who follows her wherever she goes. Even though beards can make men look alike, it would not be difficult to recognise this fellow, for he is at least half a head taller than all the others, and his general appearance is most favourable. He sat on a boulder nearby, and there he remained in silence, watching, now she is straightening up her body, raising and lowering her arm to beat the clothes, the noise travels over the water, the sound is unmistakable, one smack followed by another, and then there is silence, the woman rests her two hands on the white stone, an ancient Roman sarcophagus, Mogueime looks but does not stir, and just at that moment the wind brings the shrill cry of the muezzin. The woman quickly turns her head to the left as if to hear his summons more clearly, and, Mogueime being on this side, a little further back, it would have been impossible for their eyes not to meet. Barefoot on the thick, damp sand, Mogueime can feel the weight of his entire body, as if he had become part of the boulder on which he is sitting, if the royal trumpets were now to give the signal to attack, he would hear nothing, what is echoing in his head is the muezzin's cry and he goes on hearing it as he watches the woman, and when she finally averts her eyes the silence becomes absolute, true there are sounds all around but they belong to another world, the mules pant and drink from the stream, and perhaps because he could find no better way of beginning what has to be done, Mogueime asks the woman, What is your name, how often we must have asked each other that question since the world began, What is your name, sometimes going on to give our own name, I'm Mogueime, to make a start, to give before receiving, and then we wait, until we hear the reply, when it comes, when we are not answered with silence, but not in this instance, My name is Ouroana, she told him, he already knew, but this was the first time he was hearing it from those lips.

Mogueime got to his feet and went up to her, six paces, a man walks for leagues and leagues during his lifetime only to end up exhausted and with blisters on his feet not to mention his soul, and then there comes a day when he barely takes six paces and finds what he is looking for, here, during this siege of Lisbon, this woman who was on her knees and has now risen to her feet to greet me, her hands are wet, her skirt drenched, and I do not know how we came to find ourselves in the shallow water, I can feel the gentle caress of the current on my ankles, the grating of tiny pebbles below, one of the stable-lads watering the mules, said in jest, Hey, big fellow, as if saying, Hey, bull, before making himself scarce, Mogueime hears nothing, has eyes only for Ouroana, her face comes close, so close he could touch it like a flower in bloom, in silence, stroking it with only two fingers that pass slowly over her cheeks and mouth, over her eyebrows, first the one, then the other, following their outline, then her forehead and hair, before asking her as his hand comes to rest on her shoulder, Would you like to stay with me from now on, and she replies, Yes, I would, then Mogueime's ears pricked up, all the king's trumpets were ringing out in jubilation and in such deafening tones that the trumpets of heaven must have joined in. Ouroana finished the washing there and then that she had promised to deliver that day while Mogueime told her about his life, nothing about his kinsmen because he did not know them, and she, on the other hand, told him nothing of her life after her abduction, and as for that other life it was like that of any country dweller, even then it was so, and not by coincidence. Ouroana took the clothes to the encampment at Monte da Graça, where she was living at the time, they told her to come back for payment, in kind, of course, but she did not mind, nor should anyone mind waiting for payment when they serve the gentry, for she was leaving for another life with this man by her side, and anyone who wants to find me will have to look for me where the battle is at its fiercest, before the Porta de Ferro, but not tonight, for this is our first night together, husband and wife, as far away as possible from the encampment where no one will see us give ourselves to each other under the starry sky, listening to the lapping of the waves, and when the moon comes up our eyes will still be open, Mogueime will say, There is no other paradise, and I shall reply, It was not paradise for Adam and Eve because the Lord told them they had sinned.

Maria Sara arrived at the appointed hour. She brought some food, provisions might be the better word, for she came with enough supplies to see them through a war and deeply conscious of her responsibilities, Yes, one kiss, two, three, but don't get distracted, you were working, carry on, there's a time for everything, however brief, and we shall have two whole nights and an entire day, an eternity, just give me a kiss, and now sit down, simply tell me how the history is coming along, Mogueime and Ouroana have already met, In plain language, you mean they've slept together, Yes, after a fashion, Why after a fashion, Because they had no bed, they slept under the light of the stars, Such good fortune,

A warm night, they were together and the tide was rising, I hope you've written down those words, No, I haven't written them down, but there's still time. Maria Sara carried her parcels to the kitchen, while Raimundo Silva, standing, was examining the sheets of paper with the expression of someone whose thoughts are elsewhere, Couldn't you write some more, she asked coming back into the room, or has my arrival distracted you, It's not really a question of you being or not being here, we're not some elderly couple who have lost their feelings and even any memory of ever having had them, on the contrary, we are Ouroana and Mogueime at the outset, Then I am distracting you, Thank God, but it did occur to me that I won't carry on writing here, why not, Difficult to say, moving out of the study was one way of escaping routine, of breaking a habit in the hope that it might help me to penetrate another age, but now that I am on the point of returning, I feel like going back to the chair and desk where I do my proof-reading, after all, that is my profession, Why this insistence on describing yourself as a proof-reader, So that things will be clear between Mogueime and Ouroana, Explain yourself, Just as he will never be captain, I shall never be a writer, And you're afraid Ouroana will turn her back on Mogueime when she discovers that she will never be a captain's wife, It has happened before, Yet this Ouroana had a better life when she was with her knight, but now she has made love with Mogueime, I assume he didn't force her, I'm not talking about Ouroana, You're talking about me, I know, but I don't like what I'm hearing, I can imagine, However long our relationship may last, I want to live it honestly, I liked you for what you are, and I hope that what I am does not prevent you from liking me, and that's that, Forgive me, Don't keep asking to be forgiven, you men are to blame, all you machos, when it isn't a question of your profession, it's your age, when it's not your age it's your social class, when it's not social class, it's money, when will you men learn to be your natural selves, No human being is natural, You don't have to be a proof-reader to know that, anyone with a grain of intelligence is aware of the fact, We seem to be at war, Of course we're at war, and it's a war of siege, each of us besieges the other and is besieged in turn, we want to break down the other's walls while defending our own, love means getting rid of all barriers, love is the end of all sieges. Raimundo Silva smiled, You're the one who should be writing this history, Your idea would never have occurred to me, to negate an incontrovertible historical fact, I myself no longer know what made me do it, Frankly, I'm convinced that the great divide between people is between those who say yes and those who say no, I'm well aware before you remind me that there are rich and poor, weak and strong, but that isn't the point, blessed are those who say no, for theirs should be the kingdom on earth, Why did you say Should be, The conditional was intentional, the kingdom on earth belongs to those who have the wit to put a *no* at the service of a *yes*, having been the perpetrators of a *no*, they rapidly erase it to restore a *yes*, Well said, dear Ouroana, Thank you, dear Mogueime, but I am only a simple woman for all my education, And I a simple man, despite being a proof-reader. They both laughed, and then between them, they carried his papers through to the study, a dictionary, other reference works, Raimundo Silva insisted on carrying the vase with two roses himself, Leave this to me, for I'm the one who thought of it. He arranged everything on the desk, sat down, looked very seriously at Maria Sara as if appraising from her presence there, the effect of the change of ambience, I'm now going to write about the miraculous events attributed after his death and burial to the much celebrated Heinrich, a German knight from the city of Bonn, as narrated in Fray Rogeiro's letter to that Osbern who was to achieve fame as a chronicler, a letter of little trust but of the greatest conviction which is what counts, And I, replied Maria Sara, until it is time for dinner which will be prepared and eaten at home this evening, will settle here on the sofa and read this edifying book about the miracles of St Antony, my appetite having been whetted by your reading of that prodigious moment when the mule exchanged its barley for the Blessed Sacrament, a phenomenon that was never to be repeated, because the aforesaid mule, being as sterile as all the others, left no offspring, Let us begin, Let us begin.

No more than a week had passed since knight Heinrich had been buried in the cemetery of São Vicente, the plot for foreign martyrs, than Fray Rogeiro was in his tent compiling the notes he had taken while touring the camps astride his faithful mule, which truly had all the qualities of its species, but suffered from an incurable gluttony that left not a blade of grass or grain of corn safe from its yellow teeth, Fray Rogeiro was still working well into the night, when, tired after his journey, he dozed off gently three times before falling into a deep sleep that seemed almost supernatural. It says here, that missing choir on Christmas eve because he was in the infirmary ministering to a dying priest, St Antony was rewarded when the walls divided so that he might adore the Blessed Sacrament during holy mass. Fray Rogeiro was asleep when an armed knight entered his tent with all his smaller weapons apart from his dagger, and going up to him he shook him by the shoulder three times, the first time gently, the second time vigorously, the third time with force. It says here that when St Antony was preaching in the open air it began to rain but only in the immediate surroundings so that his audience remained dry. Fray Rogeiro opened his startled eyes and saw standing before him knight Heinrich who told him, Arise, and go to that spot where the Portuguese buried my squire, remote from me, and take his corpse and bring it here to be buried alongside my grave. It says here that the plea of a devout woman was heard by St Antony a league away and that he restored the tresses of another that had been shorn from her head. Fray Rogeiro looked, and no longer seeing either the knight or any sign of a tomb, he thought he was sleeping and dreaming and so as not to be undeceived, he went back to sleep. It says here that when St Antony encountered a penitent whom he judged deserving of pardon, he absolved him, at the same time erasing all the letters from a sheet of paper on which the sinner's transgressions were listed. Fray Rogeiro had fallen back into a deep sleep in which he dreamt that some rancid food had given him that bad dream, when the knight reappeared, once more roused him and said, Wake up, friar, for I ordered you to go and find the corpse of my squire in that grave remote from mine, and you heard me but ignored my command. It says here that on spilling wine in a cellar, St Antony restored it to the cask. Fray Rogeiro must have been very tired to have gone back to sleep at once, disdaining first the request, then the order, but he was now troubled in his sleep as if aware that it would soon be interrupted, and so it happened, the knight entered in a towering rage and with a fierce and intimidating expression, solemnly rebuked him, You'll be in serious trouble if I have to ask you once more to carry out my orders. It says here that with the sign of the cross, St Antony turned a toad into a capon, and then with the same sign of the cross transformed the capon into a fish. Now then, Fray Rogeiro would not be worthy of his sacred ministry if he had not learned from the example of St Peter, which tells us that you may deny or refuse twice, but to do so a third time, even without the cock crowing, will expose you to serious reprisals, especially where there is the intervention of ghosts, whose material strength probably exceeds that of the living a hundredfold. It says here that St Antony with the sign of the cross plucked out the eyes of a heretic as a punishment, but out of compassion then restored them. Rising quickly from his pallet and picking up a lamp, Fray Rogeiro went down to the estuary, giving a fright to many a sentinel who thought they were seeing a ghost, stepped into a boat and, straining at the oars, crossed to the other side. It says here that St Antony miraculously repaired two broken glasses and restored spilled wine to its cask for a woman who pleaded his intercession, thus showing that miracles can be repeated without their efficacy being diminished in the slightest. Where Fray Rogeiro found the necessary strength for the Herculean task assigned him, it is difficult to say, unless fear itself drove him on, but he lost no time in opening the grave and removing the squire's corpse, which he carried on his back to the boat, and breaking out into a cold and hot sweat, returned to the point of his departure, carried the heavy burden uphill as far as São Vicente, and alongside the knight's tomb he dug another grave and reburied the squire's corpse. It says here that when St Antony was in Sicily, he saw one of his devotees fall into a swamp and immediately fished her out unscathed and spotlessly clean. Fray Rogeiro entered his tent and slept like a log for the rest of the night, and when he woke up next morning and remembered what had happened, he was not only suspicious, for his hands and habit were soiled with mud and other disagreeable stains, but outraged at the ingratitude of the knight who had not even come to thank him after so rudely interrupting his precious sleep. It says here that when St Antony was in Rome, he preached in only one language yet people of various nationalities understood him perfectly. Now then, this feat was not the last of knight Heinrich's wondrous manifestations, for it came about that at the head of his tombstone there appeared a palm similar to those the pilgrims would carry in their hands from Jerusalem three centuries later. It says here that in Ferrara, St Antony rescued a woman from an unjust death being plotted by her husband, by making a new-born child speak and declare its mother's innocence. The palm grew, produced leaves and became increasingly tall, and the king came and all the soldiers and ordinary people from the encampments and together they offered heartfelt thanks to God. It says here that in Rimini where he was stoned by the heretics, St Antony walked along the seashore and calling upon the fish, he delivered an admirable sermon. The sick began arriving and took leaves from that palm, and placing them on their neck they were cured there and then of all their ailments. It says here, that passing from Rimini to Padua, St Antony converted twenty-seven thieves with a single sermon. Such wonder, such an edifying miracle. It says here that after firmly reprimanding a boy who had kicked his own mother, the youth was so upset and sorry about the wrong he had done, that he went off to fetch a cutlass and without any warning cut off the offending foot. Others who were sick gathered the palms and then scorched and crushed them, and mixing the dust with water or wine, they drank it, whereupon all their aches and pains disappeared at once. It says here that the penitent youth lost so much blood that he was in danger of losing his life, and his cries brought everyone running from nearby to find out what was happening, and weeping bitterly he explained that Fray Antony had told him this was the punishment he deserved, and at that moment his mother arrived and protested that the friar had murdered her son, attributing the latter's rashness to the saint's excessive zeal. News of the palm's healing powers soon spread, so much so that very shortly the earth was stripped bare of both leaves and stalks, and because there was no effective vigilance, some came at night and pulled up that which had remained underground and carried it off. It says here that St Antony rushed to the youth's assistance and picking up the foot severed from his leg, he fitted it back into position with his own hands, made a quick sign of the cross, and the leg and foot were joined up as firmly and securely as before. There would be no end to the blessed inventory of knight Heinrich's miraculous deeds if we were to list all of them in every detail, besides it would take us well beyond the scope of this narrative, which is not simply to trace out the destiny of Lisbon, something everyone knows, but to explain how we managed, without the help of the crusaders, to bring off the patriotic enterprise of our King Afonso, the first with this name and first in everything. It says here that when St Antony was preaching in Milan, he appeared in Lisbon and had his father acquitted from a debt he did not owe, and it also says that when he was preaching in Padua, he appeared at the same time in Lisbon, where he made a dead man speak and rescued his father from death. Now then, after having witnessed so many marvellous events, two deaf-mutes who had arrived with the fleet, however no one knows whether English, Aquitanian, Breton, Fleming or from Cologne, went one day to the knight's tomb and lay down beside it, pleading with the utmost devotion that he might show them mercy and compassion. It says here that these were the most significant of the miracles worked by St Antony during his lifetime, but that innumerable miracles were recorded after his death and of such repute that they have compared more than favourably with those instigated by his actual presence, and to give but one example, St Antony made a sterile woman fertile, and transformed the shapeless lump she conceived into a comely creature, thus converting half a miracle into a complete one. Now as the two deaf-mutes lay there, they both fell asleep and knight Heinrich, in the guise of a pilgrim, appeared to them in a dream, and in his hand he was carrying a staff fashioned from palm and he spoke to those two young men and told them, Arise and rejoice, go forth in the knowledge that because of my merits and those of the martyrs who lie here, you have gained the Lord's grace, and that grace goes with you, and that said, he disappeared, and on awakening they found they could hear and also speak, but with such a stutter that it was impossible to tell which language they were speaking, whether it was English, Aquitanian, Breton, Flemish, or the dialect of Cologne, or, as many claimed, the language of the Portuguese, And then, Then the two stutterers returned to the knight's grave with even greater devotion, if that is possible, but their prayers were to no avail, and stutterers they remained for the rest of their lives, and only to be expected, for when it comes to miracles knight Heinrich cannot be compared to St Antony.

Let's have some dinner, suggested Maria Sara, and Raimundo Silva asked her, What do we have for eating, Perhaps some fish, perhaps a capon, but if miracles can also work in reverse, don't be surprised if a toad jumps out of the frying-pan.

MORE THAN TWO MONTHS have passed since the siege began, three months beyond the last payment of the soldiers' wages. Dom Afonso Henriques had high expectations, as we were informed in due course, of the skills of military engineering of knight Heinrich, and also of those unnamed Frenchmen and Normans, but the holy man's calamitous death, even though the mother of further prodigies, and the destruction of the tower that would be used to attack the wall south of the Porta de Ferro, caused the warring zeal of all to pass from incandescent heat to a gentle flame, as may be seen from the delay in the work of those foreigners and from the endless arguments in which the Portuguese master-carpenters waste their time, unable to agree whether it is worth repeating such and such of the German's inventions, by respecting the patent or introducing structural modifications that, in a manner of speaking, might add a national touch to the future tower. The king's aforesaid expectations had been strengthened for two reasons, the one stemming directly from the other, the first reason being that the favourable outcome of the assault meant that the city had been captured, and therefore, the second reason, he could disband the soldiers and send them home until the next campaign, thus saving on wages. Dom Afonso had been honest enough not to conceal the dire straits in which he found himself, his treasury depleted, something that could be turned to his advantage, because simplicity and candour are not qualities commonly found amongst those who govern the world with the exception of our own rulers. But this method of playing politics is never duly rewarded, and here we now have a king with the desirable city of Lisbon before his eyes but out of reach, and obliged moreover to scrape the bottom of his coffers to pay an army that is already grumbling about the delay. Of course this is not the first time that the Crown is late in paying, especially in a state of war, we need only think of the vicissitudes during a time of conflict, the problem of collecting money, transport, the question of exchanges, all these factors combined means that the summons to be paid is usually late and at an inconvenient hour, causing such distress that the poor soldier often dies before receiving his wages, sometimes a matter of minutes beforehand.

If only Dom Afonso Henriques had obtained the money a few days earlier then the history of this siege would have been different, not in its known conclusion, but in its intermediate results. The fact is that with the passage of time, it was already mid-September, and no one knowing how and where this unprecedented idea had come from, the soldiers began to mutter amongst themselves that being as manly or unmanly as the crusaders, they should be considered just as deserving of recompense, and that being subjected to the same death, they should have exactly the same rights as the others when it came to being paid. Putting it bluntly, what they wanted to know was what papal bulls gave the crusaders the mandate to plunder, and it has to be said that most of them had lost any interest in the enterprise, while the wretched Portuguese soldiers had to be content with miserable wages as they watched the foreigners feasting and rejoicing. Rumours of these stirrings and encounters reached the captains, but their pretension was so absurd and opposed to all laws and customs, whether written or transmitted by custom, that their only reaction was to shrug their shoulders and say dismissively, They're being childish, by which they meant, They're being small-minded, in those days people had some regard for etymology, unlike today when you cannot call anyone childish, even though patently minor, without a summons being served immediately for slander. Undecided, the captains sent a missive to

Dom Afonso Henriques advising him to pay out the wages without further delay, inasmuch as discipline was breaking down and the troops were becoming more restive each time the sergeants ordered them to attack, muttering to themselves, Why doesn't he go, after all he's wearing the stripes, and the commentary was most unfair, for no sergeant ever stayed behind in the trenches to watch the outcome of an assault, when he should advance to gather the laurels or remain to censure the cowardly deserters. At the end of yet another week, when subversive opinions were no longer being expressed in whispers but proclaimed aloud in gatherings either spontaneous or concerted, word spread that the soldiers were finally about to be paid. The captains sighed with relief, but soon held their breath when the pay-masters reported that no one had come forward to be paid. In the king's own encampment the turn-out was very small, and even that had to be interpreted as the result of intimidation, for the soldiers were in danger of coming face to face with Dom Afonso Henriques at any minute who would ask them, So, you've been to receive your wages, and where would the timid private find the courage to reply, No, I have not, Your Majesty, unless they pay me the same rate as the crusaders I shall be doing no more fighting.

The captains' greatest fear was that the Moors might learn of the disaffections spreading throughout the Christian encampments, and should take advantage of the unrest and sally forth from the five gates simultaneously sweeping some out to sea and sending others down the slopes to their death. Therefore, before it was too late, they summoned, not the officers for there were none, but a group of soldiers who, because they were always making their voices heard, had gained a certain ascendancy over the others, and fate decreed that at the Porta de Ferro, one of those soldiers should happen to be Mogueime whose love for Ouroana did not distract him from his responsibilities to society and from pursuing personal and collective interests. So three delegates went to the captain and when questioned they presented their case. Mem Ramires's impassioned speech, no doubt like those delivered in the other encampments, was full of patriotic exhortations, yet for all their novelty, they failed to dissuade the soldiers, and even the loud threats that followed produced little effect, and finally turning to Mogueime, an emotional Mem Ramires exclaimed, How is it possible that you Mogueime of all people could be involved in this conspiracy, you, who were my comrade in arms at Santarém, where you generously loaned me your shoulders and height so that I might throw a rope-ladder up to the battlements that all of us later climbed, and now, forgetful of the vital role you played on that glorious day, having repudiated your captain and shown ingratitude towards your king, there you are scheming with a gang of ambitious scoundrels, how is it possible, whereupon Mogueime, unperturbed, simply replied, Captain, if you should need to climb on to my shoulders again in order to reach the tallest battlement in Lisbon with your sword, your hands or a ladder, you may count on me, let's go at once, if you want, but that is not the question, our concern is that we should be paid like the foreigners, and take note, Captain, just how reasonable our demands are, for we have not come to ask that the foreigners should be paid what we have been paid. The other two delegates assented in silence, for such eloquence needed no repeating, and the conference ended.

Mem Ramires sent his report to the king, which was essentially the same as that of the other captains, suggesting with all respect that His Royal Highness should summon the leaders of this movement in the armed forces, who, perhaps in the presence of Your Majesty, might be rather less audacious and unreasonable. Dom Afonso Henriques was hesitant about making any such concession, but the situation was serious, the Moors might suddenly come to realise that their enemies were vacillating, and as a last resort, but furious, he sent for the leaders. When the five men entered the tent, the king with a fierce expression, his powerful arms crossed over his chest, gave vent to his wrath, I cannot decide whether I should order the feet that have brought you here to be cut off or your heads from which, should you dare, you will spout defiant words, and he stared with blazing eyes at the tallest of the delegates, who was, as one might have suspected, Mogueime. Now then, it was nice to see, perhaps only possible in those innocent times, how Mogueime grew in stature and his voice rang out clearly as he replied, If Your Royal Highness orders our head and feet to be cut off, your entire army will be without head or feet. Dom Afonso Henriques could not believe his ears, that a hired common soldier from the infantry should presume to claim for his base fraternity privileges reserved for a cavalry of noblemen, for there is a real army, the foot-soldiers only serving to surround the enemy on the battlefield or to form a cordon during a siege such as this one. Even so, and because nature had endowed him with some sense of humour, in keeping with the circumstances at that time, he found the delegate's reply amusing, not so much for the substance of the argument, which he thought more than debatable, but because of the felicitous play on words. Turning to the other four leaders who had also been convened, he said in jovial mockery, This country would appear to be getting off to a bad start, and then, altering his expression and looking directly at Mogueime, he added, I've seen you before, who are you, I took part in the conquest of Santarém, Your Majesty, replied Mogueime, and it was I who lent my shoulders to captain Mem Ramires who is standing over there, And do you think that gives you the right to come here to complain and make impossible demands, Not at all, Your Majesty, but my comrades insisted that I should act as their spokesman, And what exactly do you want, Your Majesty knows what we want, that we should be given our fair share of the booty, for we have come here prepared to shed our blood which when spilled is the same colour as that of the foreign crusaders, just as we will stink like them if death should strike and our corpses rot, And if I should refuse you any share of the booty, Then, Sir, you will capture the city with the few crusaders who have stayed behind, This is an act of insurrection you are committing, Sir, I beseech you not to take this attitude, for while it is true that there is some desire for gain on our part, bear in mind that it is also an act of justice to pay the same wages for the same task, and this new country will get off to a bad start unless it is fair-minded from the outset, remember, Sir, the words of our forefathers, That which is born crooked rarely ever grows straight, do not let Portugal become crooked, Sir, I implore you, Who taught you to speak with more eloquence than a prelate, The words are there, Sir, in the air, anyone can learn them. Dom Afonso Henriques was no longer scowling and stroking his beard with his right hand began to think, and there was something sad about his expression as if questioning so many of the decisions he had taken, and those others, as yet unknown, that he would have to weigh up in future according to his state of mind when he came to confront them, and lost in thought for several minutes, with a silence no one there present dared to interrupt, he finally spoke, telling them, Begone, your captains will inform you anon of the outcome of our discussions.

There was rejoicing in the five encampments, and even on the Monte da Graça all fears were dispelled when, the troops having gathered on parade, the heralds arrived to announce that in his bounty the king had decided that all the soldiers, no matter their rank or seniority, would have the same right to plunder the city, in keeping with the customs of the day and excepting the booty reserved for the crown and that promised to the crusaders. There was so much cheering and at such length, that the Moors genuinely feared that the moment had come for the final assault, although there had been no earlier preparations to warn them. No such assault, in fact, took place, but from the walls above they could see that the encampments were in a ferment of activity, the men like ants excited at the sudden discovery of a table laden with food at the side of a road where hitherto they had carried off nothing except dry awns of wheat and the odd crumb. Within an hour the master-carpenters had reached an agreement, within two hours the joiners were hard at work on the rot that had slowly been corroding the towers under construction, a figurative expression, since hylotrupes and anobia are not endowed with cutting and perforating instruments capable of coping with green wood and devouring it, and within three hours someone had the idea that by digging a deep tunnel under the wall and then filling it up with wood and setting it alight, the heat of this furnace would expand the stones and cause the joints to crumble, whereby, with a little assistance from God as well, the entire wall would come tumbling down before you could say amen. Here the sceptics will murmur and those who are always denigrating human nature that these men, formerly insensitive to any love for the fatherland and indifferent to the future of generations to come, out of their love for filthy lucre were now revealing themselves, not only by their hard physical labour, but also in the invisible and superior operations of soul and mind, but it has to be said that they are much deceived, because what moved wills and generated happiness there stemmed infinitely more from the spiritual satisfaction of forging equal justice for everyone as an integral and unassailable right.

With this renewed morale amongst the Christians that even from a distance was much in evidence, the Moors began to feel disheartened, and if in the majority of cases it was in the necessary struggle itself against nascent weakness that they sought new strength, there were some who succumbed to fears real and imagined and who tried to save their body by seeking with a hasty Christian baptism the condemnation of their Islamic soul. At dead of night and using improvised ropes, they descended from the walls and, concealed amidst the surrounding ruins and amongst the bushes, they awaited dawn in order to come out by daylight. With raised arms, and the rope they had used to descend wound round their neck as a sign of surrender and obedience, they walked towards the encampment, shouting all the while, Baptism, baptism, confiding in the saving virtue of a word which hitherto, resolute in their faith, they had found abhorrent. From afar, on seeing those submissive Moors, the Portuguese thought they were coming to negotiate the surrender of the city itself, although they found it strange that the gates had not been opened for them to leave nor the military protocol prescribed on such occasions been observed, and above all, as the presumed emissaries drew closer, it became all too apparent from their filthy and tattered clothes that these were not men of any social standing. But when it finally became clear what they wanted, impossible to describe the fury and demented wrath of the soldiers, suffice it to say that there were enough severed tongues, noses and ears there to fill a butcher's shop, and, as if that were not enough, they chased them back to the walls with blows and insults, some, who knows, hoping in vain for an unlikely pardon from those whom they had betrayed, but it was a sad affair, and all of them ended up there, fatally wounded, stoned and riddled with arrows by their own brethren. After this tragic episode, a heavy silence fell over the city, as if they had to rid themselves of a deeper mourning, perhaps that of an offended religion, perhaps the unbearable remorse of acts of fratricide, and that was the moment when, breaking down the last barriers of dignity and circumspection, famine showed itself at its most obscene in the city, for there is less obscenity in the intimate manifestations of the body than in seeing that body expire from starvation under the indifferent and ironic gaze of the gods who, having stopped feuding with each other, and being immortal, distract themselves from eternal boredom by applauding those who win and those who lose, the former because they have killed, the latter because they have died. In reverse order of ages, lives were extinguished like spent oil-lamps, first the babes in arms who could not suck a single drop of milk from their mothers' withered breasts, their insides rotted by the unsuitable nourishment forced down their throat as a last resort, then the older children who needed more food to survive than that the adults took from their mouths, especially the women, for they deprived themselves so that the men might have enough energy left to defend the walls, nevertheless, the elderly were those who resisted best of all, perhaps because of the scant nourishment required by their bodies which had decided for themselves to enter death as light as possible rather than overload the boat that would transport them across the ultimate river. By then the cats and dogs had already disappeared, the rats were pursued into the fetid darkness where they sought refuge, and now that in patios and gardens plants were stripped to their roots, the memory of feasting on a dog or cat was tantamount to dreaming of an era of abundance when people could still afford the luxury of throwing away bones that had barely been stripped of meat. Scraps were salvaged from rubbish dumps either for immediate consumption or to transform by some means or other into food, and the scavenging became so frenetic that the few remaining rats emerging from the darkness of night, found almost nothing to satisfy their indiscriminate voraciousness. Lisbon groaned in its misery, and it was a grotesque and terrible irony that the Moors had to celebrate Ramadan when hunger had made fasting impossible.

And so the Night of Destiny arrived, as described in chapter ninety-seven of the Koran commemorating the prophet's first revelation, and where, according to tradition, all the events throughout the year are recorded. For these Moors of Lisbon, however, destiny will not wait so long, it will be fulfilled within the next few days, and it has come quite unexpectedly, for it was not revealed on the Night a year ago, nor did they know how to read its secrets, that accursed Ibn Arrinque and his army of Galicians deceived because the Christians were still so far north. It is far from clear why the Moors should have lit great bonfires all along the battlements, which, like an enormous crown of flames circling the city, burned all that night, instilling fear and remorse in the hearts of the Portuguese, whose hopes of victory might have been shaken by that terrifying spectacle had they not been reliably informed of the desperate situation to which their wretched enemies had been reduced. At daybreak, when the muezzins summoned the faithful to prayer, the last columns of black smoke rose into the limpid sky, and tinged with crimson by the rising sun, they were wafted by a gentle breeze over the river in the direction of Almada, like some ominous warning.

The time had actually come. The excavation of the mine was finished, the three towers, Norman, French, and also that of the Portuguese, which had been quickly built to the height of the other two, rose up near the walls like giants ready to raise a mighty fist that would reduce to rubble and ashes a barrier fast losing the cement of willpower and the bravery of those who have defended it so far. Somnambulant, the Moors see the towers approach, and feel that their arms can barely raise their sword and stretch the cord of their bow, that their bleary eyes can no longer measure distances, they are facing defeat, worse than any death. Below, the flames engulf the wall, smoke belches from the tunnel, as if from the nostrils of an expiring dragon. And that is when the Moors with one final effort, trying to muster whatever strength remains from their own desperation, erupt from the Porta de Ferro in order to set fire once more to that threatening tower which they failed to destroy from above where it was better protected. On all sides people are killing and dying. The tower catches fire but the blaze has not spread, the Portuguese defend it with a fury equal to that of the Moors, but there came a moment when in terror, some wounded, others pretending they were, throwing down their arms or still bearing them, some fled, jumping into the water, shameful, just as well there are no crusaders present to see their cowardice and report it abroad where reputations are made and lost. As for Fray Rogeiro, there is no danger, he was elsewhere at the time, if anyone had told him what happened here, we can always ask, How can he be so sure if he was not there. The Moors in their turn began to weaken, while the Portuguese with greater courage were now advancing, imploring the intercession of all the saints and of the Holy Virgin Mary, and, either because of this, or because all materials have a limit to their resistance, the wall well and truly came crashing down, so that, once the dust and smoke had settled, the city could be seen at last, its narrow streets, the congested houses, people everywhere in a panic. The Moors, embittered by this disaster, withdrew, the Porta de Ferro slammed shut, not that it mattered, for another gap had appeared nearby where there was no gate, its only defence being the stalwarts amongst the Moors who rushed to cover the opening with such desperate wrath that they caused the Portuguese to vacillate once more, this made it all the more urgent to raise the tower over here to the height of the wall, at the same time as cries of fear and anguish could be heard coming from the other part of the city where the other two towers pushed up against the wall formed bridges for the soldiers who called out, Courage, courage, as they invaded the battlements, Lisbon had been conquered, Lisbon had been lost. After the fortress's surrender, the bloodshed ceased. However when the sun began to go down in the direction of the sea and touched the clear horizon, the voice of the muezzin could be heard coming from the great mosque, calling out for the last time from on high where he had taken refuge, *Allahu akbar*. The Moors came out in goose pimples at the summons of Allah, but the plea did not reach its end because a Christian soldier, more zealous than most, or thinking one more casualty was needed to conclude the war, went racing up the steps of the minaret and with one blow from his sword beheaded the old man, in whose blind eyes a light flickered at the moment of death.

It is three o'clock in the morning. Raimundo Silva puts down his pen, slowly gets to his feet, supporting himself with both hands spread on the table, as if suddenly overcome by the burden of all his years on this earth. He goes into the bedroom that is barely illuminated by a dim light, and carefully undresses, trying not to make a noise, but hoping deep down that Maria Sara will wake up, for no particular reason, simply so that he can tell her that the history has come to an end, and she, who was not asleep, after all, asks him, Have you finished, and he replied, Yes, I've finished, Would you like to tell me how it ends, With the death of the muezzin, And what about Mogueime, and Ouroana, what happened to them, As I see it, Ouroana will return to Galicia, and Mogueime will go with her, and before they leave they will find in Lisbon a dog that has survived in hiding and will accompany them on their journey, What makes you think that they should go away, Difficult to say, the logical thing would be for them to stay, Forget it, we're staying. Maria Sara's head is resting on Raimundo's shoulder, with his left hand he strokes her hair and cheek. They did not fall asleep at once. Beneath the verandah roof a shadow sighed.

AFTERWORD

This novel, whose title suggests a book on Portuguese history, permits the author to speculate about the difference between historiography, historical novels and "stories inserted into history" which is the type of book José Saramago himself prefers to write.

By questioning the validity of a historical source and imagining an alternative version of recorded events, the proof-reader Raimundo Silva not only rewrites an important chapter of Portuguese history but in the process irrevocably transforms his own life. This *History of the Siege of Lisbon* is therefore neither conventional history nor historical novel, but demonstrates Saramago's contention that history and fiction are constantly overlapping.

The book operates on two planes of action: one set in the twelfth century, packed with key episodes of the alternative history of the siege of Lisbon the proof-reader Raimundo Silva feels compelled to write; the other in the twentieth century, dealing with the routine existence of the proof-reader's daily life and a significant encounter with a new editor who challenges him to justify his radical departure from established historiography. Raimundo Silva who dominates the novel could be the alter ego of Saramago who refuses to accept history as it is traditionally presented and speculates about the gaps left in historical records which historians frequently gloss over with questionable theories and hypotheses. By placing real people into such historical lacunae, Saramago attempts to fill these voids more plausibly and in keeping with the modern reader's expectation of historical verisimilitude. Thus when the proof-reader Raimundo Silva starts writing the alternative history of the reconquest of Lisbon, he emulates Saramago's technique of placing human experience against a historical background, in other words, he tries to write a hybrid narrative embodying past events and contemporary reactions to another age so remote yet tangibly present.

In the pursuit of this parallel plot, Saramago raises a number of issues which are also a central concern in many of his other books. How reliable are historical sources, and how trustworthy are historians in dealing with uncertainties, improbabilities and the gaps or lacunae? How are we to interpret speeches allegedly made by historical characters? What can we know about the private emotions of the people who make these speeches and those who record them with varying degrees of accuracy? All these questions are discussed in the form of a series of dialogues. The dialogue between the proof-reader and the author reveals once more Saramago's iconoclastic attitude to history. For Saramago, historiography itself is fiction for it results from a selection of facts coherently organised, leaving forgotten or committing to oblivion many other facts which, had they been taken into consideration, would have given a different shape to the same history. This attitude is further illustrated in the dialogues the proof-reader has with his alter ego, the witness of human adventures during the siege of Lisbon, and with his editor, Maria Sara, who provides the challenge that motivates him to try his hand at writing his own history. Placing the main action within present-day Lisbon, Saramago removes the novel from the genre of historical narrative while providing a platform for reflections on the art of reconstructing the past and the difference between writing history and fiction.

As in his other novels, Saramago's paragraph-long sentences, minimally interrupted by punctuation, challenge the reader to follow his continuous stream of thought, thus permitting a stronger sense of interaction and a more diverse interpretation of phrases and clauses. Keen that his reader should move easily back and forth between the present, the recorded and the imagined past, in this novel Saramago also freely shifts between past and present tenses, conveying the impression of the timelessness of the human imagination. This temporal fluidity is further emphasised by the strategic location of the proof-reader's flat within the precinct of the old Moorish fortress, a kind of watchtower from where the perception of past and present alternate according to the proof-reader's mood.

Beneath these speculations about the function and form of historical writing, we discover that the central concerns of Saramago's novel focus on our ability to distinguish truth from falsehood, to differentiate between reliable and suspect historical reporting, and the difficulty of drawing the frontier between the two, or in Saramago's own words: "The truth is that history could have been written in many different ways and this idea of infinitude and variation are the essence of my writing. The possibility of the impossible, dreams and illusions, are the subject of my novels."

Giovanni Pontiero
Manchester, December 1995